I0719748

MAPLECROFT

MAPLECROFT

A HEARTBREAKINGLY BEAUTIFUL HISTORICAL ROMANCE NOVEL OF LOVE AND BETRAYAL, BASED ON A TRUE STORY

MAPLECROFT
BOOK 1

MARY-CLARE TERRILL

This is a work of fiction. Unless otherwise indicated, all the names, characters, businesses, places, events and incidents in this book are either the product of the author's imagination or used in a fictitious manner. As the author's picture of the past is incomplete, creative licence has been taken.

First published in 2024

Copyright © 2024 by Mary-Clare Terrill

All rights reserved.

No part of this book may be reproduced in any form or by any electronic or mechanical means, including information storage and retrieval systems, without written permission from the author, except for the use of brief quotations in a book review.

The Write Read

maryclarewriter.com

A catalogue record for this book is available from the National Library of Australia

ISBN 978 1 7635596 0 8

MAPLECROFT

A HEARTBREAKINGLY BEAUTIFUL HISTORICAL
ROMANCE NOVEL OF LOVE AND BETRAYAL,
BASED ON A TRUE STORY

MAPLECROFT
BOOK 1

MARY-CLARE TERRILL

THE WRITE READ

This is a work of fiction. Unless otherwise indicated, all the names, characters, businesses, places, events and incidents in this book are either the product of the author's imagination or used in a fictitious manner. As the author's picture of the past is incomplete, creative licence has been taken.

First published in 2024

Copyright © 2024 by Mary-Clare Terrill

All rights reserved.

No part of this book may be reproduced in any form or by any electronic or mechanical means, including information storage and retrieval systems, without written permission from the author, except for the use of brief quotations in a book review.

The Write Read

maryclarewriter.com

A catalogue record for this book is available from the National Library of Australia

ISBN 978 1 7635596 0 8

For Austin & Errington, for sharing their story

A YEAR AFTER.

She died upon this very night last year,
Unless I think, I almost guess her near;
I loved her well in life, and oft forgot
How oft she might have deemed I loved
her not.

I have small hope, as some men, we shall
Find
Within some other world; this life behind,
Our human love perfected; that would be
Another love, another life to me.

So when I think of her, moreover now
I see no angel woman, spirit brow,
All halo ringed; but eyes, dark cloud of
hair,
And face she hardly thought I found so
fair.
Now, as I think, this seems the strangest
part,
Worse than my loneness and my empty
heart,
That I may ne'er believe she yet might
know

And be surprised and glad I miss her so.
Yet if she should know, 'neath her joy
would stir,
Pain at my pain, in always wanting her,
Hearing about the house her laugh and
call,
The rustle of her gown, her footsteps'
fall.
So it were best she sleep well, while I
sit
Here in her room, where only shadows
flit,
And comes the rending thought that,
being man
Some day e'en memory will outrun this
span.

– Edith Dart, in Harper's Weekly*

*Poem found on the reverse of a framed photograph of Ellen 'Errington' Moss

Austin & Errington
Preston, Ontario, Canada
1905

1

May

The train's rich interior – its velvet green upholstery and dark mahogany panelling – is designed for a man of a certain station. And, by all appearances, the man seated within the everyday luxury of this modern steam train is befitting of such luxury in his double-breasted suit – silver-grey, the colour of his eyes – brown polished boots, moustache waxed at the edges. Even his pocket watch has a distinct sheen to it.

This man, known to his intimates as 'Austin,' glances at the hour – bright strobes of light coming in, flickering spruce pierced by the sun. Despite catching a glimpse of red over the top of his newspaper – a rabbit darting out of the way of a shotgun – Austin resumes his perusal of the morning paper; black print inking his fingers. Smudges of ink, along with his warm complexion – thanks to the South African sun – almost giving him away as a mere player. A man – though born of gentry – quite accustomed to polishing his own boots.

Distracted, Austin turns to the social pages of *The Galt Daily Reporter*, discovering – though with little interest – 'Mrs Henderson's cousin' visiting from Toronto; 'Mr Blackwood's brother' visiting from Quebec; 'Mrs Marigold's' poor health requiring several weeks bed rest. Interestingly, Austin's own imminent arrival does not feature. He is still deciding whether this is a gross oversight on his brother's part – *how is he to make business connections if his arrival to Preston goes unnoticed?* – or a fact of which he should be glad when a small, keenly polished boot springs up beside him, connecting with the mahogany frame of his seat.

Glancing over the top of the newspaper, Austin spies a red-headed boy swiftly retracting his legs, tucking them back against the seat. The boy bites down on his lip, placing his hands beneath his bottom; relieved to find the cracking pace of his mother's knitting needles, uninterrupted.

'Sorry... Sir,' the boy mutters.

But the boy can't help but feed his curiosity, his restlessness; Austin knows this to be true – he was, after all, a boy once himself. And while other children only seem to see what's right in front of them, this boy – Austin appreciates – has the foresight to look up, to observe the less-observed.

'Excuse me, sir,' the boys asks, just as Austin settles back into his newspaper. 'Is that your Gladstone?' The boy motions toward a faded, brown leather bag stored along the metal arm above the seat, which is coated in russet dust. 'You'll excuse me for saying so, sir... but, it's covered in dust!'

'Freddy!' The boy's mother lays down her knitting needles, as though resting cutlery on a plate. 'I do apologise, sir.'

'Not at all.' Austin lowers his newspaper. 'The young lad's

right; it's the dust of the Veldt. I expect the stuff will stay with me for some time. Gets into everything, you see.'

The boy twitches his nose, still looking up at the luggage as if stargazing. 'But why is it *red*...? I've never seen red dust before.'

'No, I don't suppose you have,' Austin smiles. He hadn't expected to step into storytelling mode, not least before setting foot in Preston, where he anticipated meeting his niece and nephew, entertaining them with stories of South Africa. Perhaps, he'd tell them of the chained monkey, of marching long distances with little water, of the land itself, *'the great lure of the wild.'* Having been an adventurer, it was unlikely he'd ever run out of stories to tell.

Apologising for the boy's intrusion, the mother introduces herself as Mrs Vincent O'Hare. Pleasantly dressed in a simple white blouse with puffed sleeves and embroidered collar, a dark navy skirt falling toward the toe of her lace-up boots. A costume replicated throughout the carriages, modified only by a lavender shawl, a gold locket reaching toward the high waist of her skirt.

'I'm afraid our son is full of nervous energy,' Mrs O'Hare says, placing her hand at the boy's knee with the tenderness of a mother's touch. The boy's hands, temporarily cupped together at his lap.

'Quite unnatural for a boy to remain cooped up, stowed away from the outside air,' Austin agrees, sympathising with the boy's restless nature before introducing himself; not as 'Trooper 519' or simply 'Moss' but 'Austin Moss.'

'Delighted to make your acquaintance, Mr Moss,' Mrs O'Hare says – If she recognises the 'Moss' name in connection with his brother, Frank, she doesn't say. 'Freddy's come from boarding school. My husband was supposed to meet him but was detained. Far be it for us to obstruct the course of justice.'

'Your husband's a judge?'

'No, a policeman.'

'A Sergeant,' the boy declares.

'I've come from the S.A.C. myself,' Austin says of the paramilitary force.

'South Africa?' the woman notes, eagerly. 'Were you there for the war before your police work, Mr Moss...? My brother fought in the Boer War under the Canadian Mounted Rifles. Sinclair Stephens... I don't suppose you knew him?'

Mrs O'Hare leans forward in her seat, creases forming at the corners of her mouth, a sudden sheen misting her eyes. Despite having siblings back in England and across the globe, Austin is often surprised by the far-reaching effects of war. Austin hadn't known this woman's brother, but wishes he had. It is a strange business speaking with families of the deceased; the knowledge they crave, the detail, never likely to set their mind at ease.

'I'm afraid not,' Austin replies after allowing an adequate lapse of time, giving the impression of racking his brain. 'I was in the New Zealand Mounted Rifles – a hussar, like your brother, yes – but whether our paths crossed; I cannot say.'

'Oh,' the woman says, straightening up, pulling the edges of her shawl to overlap as if suddenly noticing a draft. 'I see.'

'The Mounted Rifles?' the boy repeats, thoughtfully. 'So, you fought on a horse then, like Uncle Sinclair?'

'That's right, 'The Missus' was my horse. A real beauty, too.' Austin reaches for his overhead luggage, grabbing it by the handles to pull out a small leather-bound book, opening it to reveal photographs pasted on the inside, scribblings in pencil denoting their subject. 'There you are, that's The Missus,' Austin says, flicking past a photograph of himself with his chum Eddie Barlowe to earlier photographs taken in New Zealand. This one, he said, was taken out the front of the livery stables. 'She looks white as snow here, but she was actually silver-grey.'

As Austin and the boy sift through the album, the mother wonders whether the man's clipped speech is of English origin or whether the New Zealand accent sounds the same; but considers that the two of them have probably detained Mr Moss from his newspaper long enough. And, after mentioning her brother, Mrs O'Hare is suddenly in no mood to talk.

'Thank you for indulging us, Mr Moss,' Mrs O'Hare concludes the conversation with an air of resolve, before taking up her knitting, resuming the looping of woollen thread at half-speed.

Left to his newspaper, Austin returns to his solitary thoughts until they hear the train's whistle, its hissing steam, as the passengers alight and Austin is reunited with the rest of his luggage. A steamer trunk coated in the same dust, red particles picked up by the South African wind, infiltrating the contents of his luggage, crumpled inside the trunk's drawers and hanging space.

'Hello again,' says Mrs O'Hare, joining Austin on the platform.

'Fancy meeting you here,' Austin says, surprised at how glad he is to see a friendly face; how this feeling outweighs the sudden need to smoke his pipe.

Freddy tugs on his mother's sleeve, resting on tiptoes to whisper in her ear. The open air – the boy's natural environment – somehow stripping him of his former confidence. The woman smiles encouragingly but the boy blushes and shakes his head.

'Indeed, you are quite the globe-trotter,' the woman says, glancing down at Austin's steamer trunk, covered in numerous pasted labels collecting dust along their edges. 'Well, it seems Freddy here has lost his voice, but he would very much like me to pass on his newly formed desire to become an explorer – *just* like the "well-travelled man on the train."'

'An "explorer?"' Austin considers, before replying in a serious tone, a twinkle in his eye. 'Well, I certainly can't lay claim to the discovery of any foreign lands. But an *"adventurer"*? Now that's a title I can hang my hat on.'

Perhaps, one day, this young lad might get his wish should another war come afoot, Austin muses, though he rather hopes not.

'Well I wish you well,' Austin says, to the young lad looking up at him in awe, 'but heed my warning; the life of a wanderer, a rolling stone – well, it's a difficult habit to shake.'

Having made his journey by vessel, steam train and, finally, electric railcar, Austin is in no mood to sit; nor can he help his own nervous energy in his forthcoming reunion with his brother, Frank.

As the old car glides towards King Street, the clanging of metal a departure from the hissing steam, the pungent smell of burning coal still felt on Austin's skin and hair; he is relieved to find the town of Preston much changed. Not the English countryside of home, nor the alluring foreign land that held Austin's interest past the war's end – South Africa's rugged landscape, its warm sweet sugar cane air – but a land unique unto itself. Preston is the fresh start Austin has been resisting, like a medicinal tonic, life-giving but potentially abhorrent.

Steadying himself with the dangling handle, Austin peers through the blinds lining the sleepy-eyed windows to admire dwellings springing up close to the dirt road. Electric lampposts at regular intervals line the two mile street that once represented the town in its entirety. A single motor car shares the path with horses, bicycles, pedestrians, the old and the new melding together, existing side by side, as Austin imagines how King Street might look by night; lit up while darkness falls around it.

The thought is interrupted by a dog's barking, announcing the presence of a phaeton pulled by sleek, muscular horses, two spotted dogs running in behind. Three ladies, wearing top-heavy picture hats, huddling together in front of a milliner's window, appear unsettled by the stray dog's excited barking. Stepping past the ladies, unperturbed by the dog, is a young man in a bowler hat, nursing a garden bouquet presumably meant for his own sweetheart.

Beyond the Business Section, lies Central Park. Horse and carts backed up against a boardwalk display fresh produce in a flurry of colour. Old, familiar buildings from before: the Town Hall, churches of various denominations, the General store – different from his last visit, given the painted sign offering a telephone service in a room built onto the back.

Just before the bridge is Frank's factory where Austin will work as a bookkeeper and shipper, for the sum of $500 a year – Austin's reluctance to accept the job offer, made evident by the months of unanswered correspondence, has resulted in a rather disgruntled Frank. As the car passes over the river, Austin remembers the land as it had been, inhabited only by the gentle, grazing cattle and the occasional farmhouse. It is the Preston he remembers. Nestled along the confluence of the Speed River and the Grand River, most of Preston's industry and dwellings are penned inside the two rivers, save some of its earliest industry, Cherry's Flour Mills for one.

As the old car hooks a corner, lunging to one side as though straining to hear a whisper, Austin feels a semi-rough material brush past him as if he were drawing back a thick, woollen drape with the back of his hand. The drape falls away to reveal a man in a navy-blue cape, leaning down to reach for the handles of his doctor's bag.

Springing up, the physician appears to be a man of considerable years, shown by the jowly line of his jaw, the slight stoop in his back. Yet he is engendered with the nervous energy of a child; as jittery as the young lad from the train, now sitting with his mother further down the railcar, face pressed against the glass, counting bicycles as if counting sheep. Indeed, this physician possesses the kind of nervous energy many seek to replenish. Folks too often depleted by the trappings of modern society, stepping outside traditional gender roles; women expending too much time outside the home, and men in it. Preston is endowed with several respectable taverns and the life-giving properties of the mineral springs: many a businessman is drawn there to take its waters and replenish their stores.

Pulling up in close proximity to the Hotel Del Monte mineral springs and the Hotel Kress – the North American as Austin once knew it – the driver announces the stop, his voice filling the railcar in an exaggeratedly cheerful fashion, as if calling out this morning's headlines. The physician makes for the door in a hurry – though Austin suspects this is merely his temperament, rather than a pressing need – while the other passengers move slowly and patiently toward the exit. Austin gives a nod in the direction of the boy and his mother, the boy no longer sitting with his face pressed against the glass, the mother's knitting packed away. The mother offers Austin a gentle wave, her hand suspended in mid-air as if caught in the wind before drifting back to her side like an autumnal leaf falling from the sky.

Alighting from the railcar, Austin finds his brother, Frank, taking great strides toward him with an outstretched hand. Very erect and neat as a pin. In typical English fashion, the brothers wash away the last sixteen years with a firm handshake and a knowing look. There is no fanfare – Frank's wife and children remain at home – but the way Frank claps his hand to his brother's back tells of his delight. After getting used to the greying at Frank's temples, the lines sprouting from the corners of his eyes as Frank breaks out into a grin, his thick brush moustache a reminder of the old Frank, Austin is glad now to be reunited with his brother. Though he cannot help wondering how long it will be before Frank is unable to resist a jibe at him for leaving his letters unanswered month after month.

'Having a sticky, are we?' Frank says, making a disapproving clicking sound with his tongue as he notes his brother's eyes straying towards the group of young women gathered at the base of Lover's Lane. Their parasols butt gently against one another as they lean towards each other, hushed conversation descending into laughter.

'Life of a bachelor, eh?' Frank says, looking between Austin and the ladies, although, had he known it, the fairer sex couldn't have been further from Austin's mind. 'Ah well,' Frank says, as if sighing over his own bygone era, 'this way, I've brought the old pony-trap.'

It isn't long before the wheels crunching over gravel slow on approaching Frank's home, an old stone house with shuttered windows much like the one Austin stayed in as a boarder, when, as a youth of nineteen, he first tried his hand at farming via the hospitality of a Mr and Mrs Cowan.

Ida and the children are here to greet them. A nursemaid holds the baby dressed in bonnet and nightgown, while the children stand beside their mother in newly laundered clothes, looking as if they have been standing so all morning. Ida holds out her hand to Austin. Though not conventionally beautiful – in fact, Austin thinks her rather plain, her nose, not bulbous but quite rounded, her eyes, dark; a natural shadow falling beneath them – her manner, warm and genteel, makes her instantly and infinitely more attractive.

'Dear Austin,' Ida says, resting her hand in Austin's,

giving it a squeeze, 'you must know how thrilled we are to have you here. Frank can be a very determined chap, I know, but he simply couldn't let the possibility pass by of having his younger brother settle in Preston.'

Frank acknowledges this with a nod. Dutifully, the children remain by their mother's side.

'Well, I'm glad,' Austin says, noticing Frank and Ida's daughter – *what was her name?* – tugging at her bow, pulled tight against her curls; her brother, fidgeting beside her. 'And what of these two? You must have been bored as punch waiting around for your old Uncle Austin to appear?'

'It's not so bad,' the girl says, looking to Austin's luggage. 'Have you brought us something?'

The boy stops fidgeting. A look darts between Ida and her daughter and Austin is glad of their sister, Ella, who had insisted that Austin find room in his steamer trunk for some small trinkets for the children.

'Indeed, I have,' Austin replies.

The boy, a couple years the girl's junior, smiles up at Austin. His smile, revealing almost all his teeth.

'A handsome chap, for sure. Well, certainly, he takes after his mother,' Austin says, offering a friendly jibe.

'Not at all, he's got the Moss forehead,' Frank says, stepping back to admire his children. 'They all do... Well now, let's have some brew, shall we?'

The house, though charming, with its chintz wallpaper and ceiling roses, is otherwise sparsely furnished – an oddity, given that Frank owns (according to himself, at least), Preston's 'most renowned' furniture company. But Frank, a man who prides himself on his practicality is, perhaps, unlikely to house anything within his private castle that does not serve an obvious purpose; so to that end, it is the philodendrons dotted around the living room that are out of place.

Taking tea – the children dismissed from their duties –

Frank sits in his armchair, as strait-laced as a pair of boots; a direct contrast to his animated wife. It is only when conversation turns to the topic of business – Austin comparing the once sleepy German settlement with the bustling town as it now presents itself – that Frank's passion is ignited, declaring the boundless opportunity in the land of *'Preston the Progressive.'*

Frank's lecture is remarkably familiar to Austin, presented in the same vein as his largely unanswered letters, that nonetheless served their purpose in bringing his brother home. Austin's gaze examines Frank for signs of change, as he speaks. Without his bowler hat, Frank's hair, greying at the temples, appears almost white.

While Austin makes appropriate sounds to indicate he is listening, he is in no mood to tend to Frank's ego. Not after crossing rough seas, the sickness that fell upon fellow passengers imbuing him with its own kind of nausea – and then enduring the bustle of the train, burning coal, and hissing steam, the journey by electric railcar, then trap and pony. But indulge his brother he must; at least until dinnertime.

'Dinner, you say?' Austin repeats, upon hearing of their engagement at the Pattinson residence later that evening.

'Yes.' Ida places down her cup and saucer. 'I do hope we haven't overwhelmed you with engagements.'

'Not at all,' Austin says, his mood lifting at the prospect of refuge from Frank's monologue.

Frank dots biscuit crumbs with his finger. 'Surely, making connections could only befit a man in *your* position,' he says. Austin taking this to mean, *Surely, younger brother, you can use all the help you can get.*

Before freshening up for dinner, Frank and Austin retire to the study, Frank producing some fine pipe tobacco, Austin, savouring the experience. The suck of his pipe, the swirling smoke, were as delicious as sinking into a warm bath.

Once Austin lays eyes on the Pattinson residence, Frank's words feel slightly less condescending. For, indeed, George Pattinson is a powerful force to reckon with, and his house reinforces this.

'As newly elected M.P.P. for South Waterloo, Mr Pattinson has power in the official sense,' Frank relays to Austin. 'The man controls every board known to man.' Frank goes on to explain further; the many kindnesses received at his hand that ensure Mr Pattinson is admired and respected in a variety of circles.

His residence, Maplecroft, sits high on the hill of Eagle Street, overlooking the Pattinson Woollen Mills, the sixth largest woollen mill in Ontario. Designed by the same architect who designed the Parliament Buildings in Ottawa, his residence is rather stately and gothic in style. The surrounding gardens are divided into sections, split between ornamental and more practical purposes – Mr Pattinson apparently favouring purpose over beauty after losing his wife to septicaemia, the result of pricking her finger on a rosebush.

'Though, in truth,' Frank suggests, 'Mr Pattinson – George – cannot help but be drawn to the rose garden his late wife once tended.'

As they descend from the carriage, a butler lurches forward to greet them. There is a stern expression on his face, a ridged scar above his left eye. He moves with a stoop as if from a lifetime of ducking below low ceilings; though the ceilings in this house are high, the rooms, evidently, grand.

From the drawing room entrance, Austin can see that Mr Pattinson is shorter than he'd expected, especially given the oversize portrait behind the fireplace depicting him is far more imposing. And yet, as Mr Pattinson begins to speak – his lips framed by a walrus-thick moustache – Austin is reminded of Major Craddock; of the man's composure, the respect he commands without being showy or verbose.

'Certainly, The Lodge has noted your arrival with interest, Mr Moss,' George says in a manner that makes Austin wonder what Frank has shared.

The eldest son, Lynn, Austin is told, is studying abroad, learning the textile trade at Leeds University, preparing to follow in his father's footsteps. But the others are here to greet them. The second son – another Frank – not yet of university age, stands a little awkwardly as though not suited to social settings. The two youngest, Ruth and Elizabeth, stand patiently, awaiting their introduction. Elizabeth, clearly the more outgoing, declaring an immediate affection for 'Uncle Austin.' Austin's connection to Aunt Ida – their deceased mother's sister – rendering Austin immediately welcome in the eyes of Elizabeth who seems to have more say than is usual for a girl, or indeed, woman.

There is no lady of the house, so Pattinson's eldest daughter seems to naturally gravitate towards the role. Not unlike her aunt, Errington, though not traditionally hand-some, seems to possess what Austin thinks of as a *sweet, womanly nature.* She is short in stature, with a small waist and child-like hands.

Austin is struck by the way Errington speaks; the dimple emerging at her cheek; the prosaic words she uses: not gushing like other young women. To him, it makes her infinitely more appealing. Austin is ashamed of his thoughts, but at twenty-four, this lack of gushing and the omission of any mention of a suitor point towards an impression of Errington as something of an old maid. *Curious,* he thinks, *for she appears to be a most intriguing woman.*

'You took the long way round, I see,' Errington says to Ida, gesturing for the guests to be seated.

Ida shifts her gaze as the children are ushered away to the playroom – the baby, left at home with the nursemaid. 'How the horses struggle up that hill!'

Sitting upright in his chair, Austin observes Errington's countenance, the dimple at her cheek; the way the eyes of everyone there seem to gravitate towards her.

'A struggle, indeed,' Errington agrees. 'Don't ask me how I intend to manage climbing the Alps.'

'The *Swiss* Alps?'

'With my brother, Lynn,' Errington confirms, seemingly amused by Austin's enquiry. 'My very own European Odyssey.'

Austin can feel Errington's enthusiasm as she speaks of her impending adventure. Warm, inviting; mesmerising. *Strange.* Austin always considered physical beauty to be the biggest draw card in a woman, and yet there is something undeniably intriguing about this woman, her unconventional appearance so different from any maiden upon which Austin has laid eyes.

'But I hear, you're quite the globe-trotter, Mr Moss?' Errington's eyes sparkle, ablaze with speculation. 'I'll bet the children are greatly curious to hear of your adventures. Alluring foreign lands, exotic animals... I can only imagine. If I'm being honest, this *'lure of the wild'* is something I know little of, excepting in books, of course. Kipling and the like.'

'You've read Kipling?' Austin asks, impressed by Errington's mention of his most beloved author. He is reminded – suddenly, almost overwhelmingly – of quoting Kipling with his chums at Klerksdorp.

'His work fascinates me,' Errington replies. 'Indeed, I am greatly curious to hear of your adventures, Mr Moss, to compare literature with life. You must show me –'

Errington rises to her feet, drawing Austin to the other side of the room.

'Sorry.' Errington says, standing on tiptoes to reach the highest shelf. 'That one, there. Would you mind...?'

Reaching for the leather-bound atlas, gold fraktur inscribed on its spine, Austin's hand brushes past Errington's as he lowers the book from the shelf. The feel of her soft, ungloved hand. The look in her eyes...

Somehow, he resists the urge to step towards her, but she leans into him, her lips parting. 'I'd love to become better acquainted... with your adventures. See where you've been.'

Held by the scent of orange blossom and those bright eyes, Austin looks upon Errington with an unexpected intensity. She is now a prize he must have; a drug he must take.

'These books are the overflow from our library,' Errington continues, as if oblivious of her effect on Austin. 'I have them here with the aim to make a habit of studying, but I'm afraid I don't grace their pages nearly enough...'

'*Errington,*' George addresses his daughter, returning with a package for Frank, wrapped in brown paper. 'Tell me, you aren't boring our guest with that overworked atlas?' He turns to his guests. 'The girl could practically draw the maps herself; she frequents their pages so often.'

Errington's cheeks colour, but she continues to reach for the atlas, as familiar to her as daily prayer.

'Please,' Austin adjusts the weighty book in his hands, 'I insist.'

Seated upon the conversation chair, a shared space to look upon a shared page, Errington's finger traces the map as if gliding over silk. Austin and Errington's eyes fix on the page; their breathing almost synchronised. They remain thus, Errington's fingertips traversing the same ground until, reluctantly, they return to the group.

After that, conversation evades Austin as he sits among the party, the memory of Errington's scent, her touch, lingering unreasonably strongly; an impassable ford now between them. His awareness returns to the rest of the party just as Frank urges: 'Don't you agree?' to which Austin gives an affirmative nod, without hearing the question.

Suddenly, plans are set in motion.

'Why that's a capital idea! Why not tomorrow?' Ida's hands leave her lap in celebration. 'We could take the railcar to Idylwild?'

'After Church then,' George says, approving the plans. 'The 'children' will be delighted.'

Errington agrees, a twinkle in her eye; 'How fond they are of the woods at Idylwild.'

2

The preceding chatter, the sharing of recipes or making plans by the women, the laughter of men rushing in the punchline of a joke they've been waiting all week to tell their chums. Upon stepping inside the House of God all of this dissipates, replaced by an immediate hush of reverence. It seems even the clock tower halts precisely on time in its sounding of the hour. The only ones yet to be affected by stepping into a sacred place of worship are the children whose feet thump against the steps up to the double doors, or the baby grimacing under its bonnet, fussing in the arms of its mother.

As Austin bows toward the altar, the candles, like the Eucharist, standing for something more – not just the embodiment of Christ but recognition of the Lord – the 'Light of the World.' Throughout his thirty-five years, Austin has understood light mostly for its use, rather than its symbolism: the light of a dwindling fire; candlelight painting a yellow glow on to writing paper; the advent of electricity.

It is only upon leaving South Africa, that Austin began to reflect on his past life, writing to his dear friend, Eddie

Barlowe, laying down his confession as though Eddie was ordained to receive it.

Eddie – whose connection to Austin became all the more powerful with the loss of his dear brother, Dickie, Austin's closest school chum – did not delay in sending a return to Austin. Laying down his messy scroll, ineffectually blotting, and thus leaving a blob of ink in its wake – Eddie would have apologised for his messy script but has learnt two important lessons. Number one, nobody expects a doctor's handwriting to be neat. And number two, never apologise. A patient – the general public – must have complete confidence in their physician. And so, Eddie's reply was simply this: '*I do not like your remark, old chap – you might have been a bit straighter. Each of us know our past lives have not been conducive to holiness.*'

Austin couldn't imagine how Eddie, of all people, could tarnish himself with the same brush as himself. Eddie, who took his budding expertise to the trenches, his hands, bloodier than any butcher's in the pursuit of saving lives.

Now, Austin is thankful for the gloom of the church's interior. For where there is darkness, there is light. Austin thinks of the South African sky stretching out across the veldt, stars like pinholes in a blanket, revealing themselves in infinitely greater number than the skies of Preston where the heart of the town is lit up by electric lamps.

Austin takes his seat beneath the underbelly of wooden arches, lining the church ceiling like the ribcage of a whale. Despite the stained-glass windows, the lanterns hanging throughout the church, Austin suspects that irrespective of the hour, it is the cross resting behind the altar that projects the most light. Kneeling down at the pew, Austin leans forward, his head bent in prayer. Though the service is performed in unison – finding today's page in the Book of Common Prayer, looking toward Reverend Herbert as he speaks the Word of God, standing for song, sitting for psalms

– it isn't until the Lord's Prayer that Austin has an awareness of others, all seeking God's love and guidance.

As the Lord's Prayer takes flight with the echo of 'Hallowed be thy Name,' Austin feels a transformative strength, a sense of belonging, of being part of something bigger than oneself. Like songs sung at war, whole contingents filling their lungs, the chorus of voices in church are a powerful, affecting force. For, in unison, these voices crack open the light.

IDYLWILD IS A WONDERLAND FOR FISHING AND boating, a hideaway accessed only by railcar, embraced by locals who recognise this new form of transport as the single greatest development connecting Preston with neighbouring towns – and thus, the rest of the world. The industrial mark on the landscape, factories' dark curling smoke, is exchanged for fields of green set beside the river.

Frank, despite his initial objection to the outing, has perked up some, illustrating with his hands the mammoth Largemouth he caught when last at Idylwild. Despite his own passion for fishing, Austin is distracted by the sight of Errington in his periphery, who seems to be engaging in a game of missed looks, of 'now you see me.'

George Pattinson, also a keen fisherman, isn't present, but as discussed, Errington has come along with the 'children.'

'Look, Frank,' Errington says, slowly lifting her gaze from Austin as the overhanging sign of Idylwild comes into view. 'We're here.'

Ruth looks up from her book with a start, nursing a copy of *Twenty Thousand Leagues Under the Sea* – the best adventure of the day so far is to be found in the pages of her book. Elizabeth leaps up from her seat, her braids – making her appear much younger than her years – whipping the air.

Before the rest of the party has alighted the railcar, she disappears beneath the overhanging sign in search of wildflowers.

'*Uncle Austin*,' Errington announces finally, unpacking a picnic spread prepared by the kitchen staff at Maplecroft. 'I've come to hear of your adventures, and yet I haven't heard a word. Won't you join me for a paddle?'

By the river, there are several boats lined up, ready for use. Errington stands by the one she thinks most suitable, a rowboat.

'I want to see the expression on your face as you tell of your adventures,' she says.

'Nell!' Elizabeth calls out to Errington, catching up to the pair just as they are about to board the boat. 'I'll come with you.'

'Nell?' Austin repeats.

Errington smiles, taking a moment to present a more considered tone. 'Well, Beth, we'd be delighted to have you... But, you see, *Uncle Austin* here is going to tell of his time in South Africa. And I'm afraid,' Errington winces. 'You may find his escapades rather alarming. Scary, in fact!'

'I shan't be scared.' Elizabeth's voice shows her irritation at forever being treated as a child.

Austin looks from Errington to her sister. 'Well, of course, I will keep my audience in mind, but there are some rather ferocious animals of which I shall speak; sharp teeth, claws that rip apart their prey in an instant... I would not to wish to impinge upon sensitive ears.'

Impatient with the conversation so far, Elizabeth changes the subject. 'Are there monkeys in South Africa, *Uncle Austin*?'

'Why, at the S.A.C. we had a pet monkey. A real little rascal; chained up, of course.'

Elizabeth's face alters in obvious horror. 'Chained up? Oh, how cruel. Oh, I think I might cry!'

Elizabeth's attention-seeking tears, usually an irritation to Errington, now provided a welcome distraction.

'Oh, you poor dear,' she says, putting an arm around Elizabeth's shoulder, her hand gently massaging her neck beneath long, loosened braids. 'Run back to Aunt Ida, she'll know how to soothe you.'

Though inclined to argue, Elizabeth turns on her heel in a huff.

A dimple emerges at Errington's cheek as she holds out her hand, Austin helping her into the boat. Austin pulls back the oars, finding the rhythm as they glide through water. Only Errington notices Elizabeth reappear by the water's wooded edge, as the chatter of picnic-goers dissipates, replaced by the water lapping against the boat; Austin resting the oars as they drift through the rushes.

As the boat drifts, becoming hidden from view, Errington takes out a silver case from her skirt pocket – sewn in by her own hand for the purpose – and flicks it open to reveal a row of cigarettes. Placing one between her moistened lips, Errington casually strikes a match on the gunwale, closing her eyes as she inhales and the wires of tobacco in the cigarette turn cinder-orange.

'So, tell me,' Errington says, looking up at Austin, his blue-grey eyes more lucid than the water on which they drift. 'You must have left a great many loves behind, many an 'old flame?''

Austin looks at Errington, her slight raise of the eyebrows looking as if she was simply enquiring about the way in which Austin takes his tea. Had this comment come from one of the lads, Austin would have responded with a wag of his finger, *Uh-uh-ah, a gentleman never tells.*

'I suppose,' Austin begins, 'I cannot claim to be innocent of this charge; though none of the ladies I knew would qualify as an *"old flame".*'

'And,' Errington continues, 'I suppose you're wondering why I've not married. Well, that's simple. I have never seen any reason to... up until now, that is...'

Up until now?

Austin remembers – too late – why he keeps all women at arm's length – except to engage in a little fun, of course – they are so damn hard to read. He breathes out slowly, deeply, looking back toward the shoreline.

'May I take this to mean you've had an offer of marriage, Miss Pattinson? My sincerest...'

'Not exactly,' Errington interjects. 'Well, not of late.' She playfully blows a curl of smoke in Austin's direction before leaning back in the boat, skimming the water with her fingertips. 'It's all very new, you see.'

'I see...' Austin says, slowly gathering his thoughts, 'and if I'm not stepping out of line, may I ask...'

'Do you know the man?' Errington beams. 'Why yes, I believe you know him quite well.'

Austin watches the water ripple in concentric circles with Errington's touch. 'You know a lot about the world, Miss Pattinson, don't you? Much more than you let on, I think...'

'Ah, well.' Errington lets water droplets fly as she lifts her hand from the water. 'My sex doesn't afford me the type of worldly experience of which you are acquainted, but I am very fond of reading and study. I assume, Mr Moss, you are referring to my knowledge of ... geography, perhaps?'

They both smile. Austin readies himself to take up the oars, realising how far they've drifted into this private hideaway. Errington raises a hand in protest.

'Please,' she says. 'It's so pleasant here.'

'Do you know,' Austin begins, resting his hands on his knees. 'You refer to me to as *Uncle Austin,* not, I think, because of our family connection, but with a certain cheek; to fabricate a fiction others will find more acceptable.'

'You've found me out, Mr Moss,' Errington smiles. 'In that case, what of my fiction; which character might I be?'

'Oh, I have a character in mind.'

Flicking the cigarette downstream, Errington takes the wildflower from her hair – the one Elizabeth had placed there earlier – twirling it between her finger and thumb. 'And what character might that be?'

'The Old Curiosity Shop is the text,' Austin says, '...I assume you know it?'

Errington flashes Austin a tell-tale look that reveals an unexpected understanding, before a smile returns her to her natural, genteel nature.

'My apologies,' Austin concedes, 'I understand you are quite well-read, perhaps, more than I?' Though to Austin, a graduate of *Whitgift*, founded by the last Archbishop of Canterbury to be appointed by Queen Elizabeth, this seems unlikely. After all, hadn't Major Craddock, in his recommendation letter upon Austin's discharge from the army declared Austin's education, 'very much above the ordinary?'

'Oh, I doubt that,' Errington's smile acknowledges the understanding that a woman's intellect should never openly exceed a man's. 'But might I wager a guess? Perhaps, you are aligning me with the character of Little Nell. You'll notice my family also refer to me thus; a coincidence, I assure you.'

She looks back to the water, fixing her gaze on the way it ripples at the reeds. 'Sometimes, I do feel as lonely as she.'

Austin catches a moment of sadness in her eyes.

'I'm sorry,' Austin begins, 'I only meant that you, like Little Nell, seem to possess a sweet, virtuous nature at odds with the cheeky exterior you may choose to project at times.'

'Little Nell, eh?' Errington muses, a dimple emerging at her cheek as she crosses her ankles, her legs stretched out across the boat. 'Without the tragic end, I hope?'

'Yes,' Austin agrees, pressing against his knees to resume the posture of a gentleman. 'Without the tragic end.'

When Austin takes up the oars, there is the brush of reeds against the boat, followed by the gentle hush of the river as they glide back through the water. The two existing in semi-silence, with only the rhythm of the oars and their own pleasant thoughts, as Austin brings them gently back to shore, Errington leaning back in the boat, enjoying the last of the fading sun.

Along the wooded water's edge, the pair step out of the boat, concealed from picnic-goers by the spruce trees on the shore. Errington's boot slips, anchoring her firmly in the mud.

'Austin! I believe, I'm stuck!'

Slowly, as if gaining the trust of a skittish mare, Austin reaches down to loosen her bootlaces from their metal clasps. Errington's hand rests on Austin's muscular shoulder as she feels a rush of cool air as her entrapped ankle comes free of her boot. Swept up into Austin's arms, Errington breathes in his scent, a blend of shaving cream, port infused tobacco and an unfamiliar man scent. The combined effect was alluring, seductive, as if catching the aroma of wafting steam from a freshly made fruit pie while famished and being made to wait for it to cool.

The scent lingers as Austin gently deposits Errington onto a nearby log, still hidden from the clearing by a dip in the ground near the shore. Errington watches as Austin scrapes mud off her boot, with the aid of water from the river.

'May I?' Austin says finally, Errington shivering at the touch of Austin's hand as he replaces the boot; the layer of stocking against her porcelain ankle, unimagined by his strong, gentle hands.

Lauren
Muskoka, Canada
2019

3

July

On approach, the cottage emerges just before as we come to it. A hidden gem, mostly roof from the driveway. Zoe, jumping out of the car and into the dappled sunlight before the engine is even turned off. Em, hurrying past her, down the concrete steps.

As I navigate the steps – partially coming away as the land drops toward the water's edge – I find Em, standing by the screen door, arms crossed, body language portraying her disapproval.

'Where's Zo?' I ask.

Em shrugs.

Following the veranda around – discovering Zoe with outstretched arms, doing her best *Titanic* impression – I lean against the railing too, smiling when Em reaches my side. Together, we take in the sight of an old steamer making its way around a distant bend, the sun glistening on the water.

'Well,' Em presses away from the railing. 'If we're just gonna stand here all day, I'm gonna check out the dock.'

Following the path – embedded rock framed by a blanket of pine needles – I step onto the uneven planks of wood forming the dock, their large spacings showcasing the tiny fish darting below. As I stand at the dock's edge, the breeze heightening the smell of pine, the gentle waves lapping against the dock, for a moment – because this is all it takes – I forget. And I can almost imagine him here.

Babe, come look at this.

Nick wraps his arms around me from behind, a warmth folding over my back and around my waist. I press into him, smiling into the sun.

I'm going in.

You're not.

The warmth drops away as Nick wrestles with his t-shirt. My arms springing to my face, anticipating his splash.

There *is* laughter. But it is not mine, or *his*.

My eyes lift to meet the sound. Echoing across the water is the laughter of older kids, sliding into the water off a pale blue slide; adults slouched back in Muskoka chairs, probably sipping wine.

The giggling returns, so close as if it's in my head. I turn back toward the boat house to see a fully dressed Zoe, spinning around, a donut ring around her middle.

Nick teases that he is going to throw her in. Zoe squeals, eyes lighting up, dimples digging in.

Mum. 'Mum!'

'Hmm?' I rouse from this dream, heart aching as I feel *his* presence fade.

Zoe wrestles with the donut ring, slipping it back over her legs, after trying the other way and getting her shoulders stuck. 'Mum, can we go swimming?'

Stepping between the rowboat and a canoe, the fishing

and boating paraphernalia strung up along the cedar walls, I stand at the base of the stairs.

'Let me get your sister.'

Tackling the old, narrow steps, ducking my head as I step up into the loft of the boat house, I find Em at the far end of this dusty, darkened room, sprawled out on a mattress resting on metal springs, the iron bedframe flaking white paint.

Em opens one eye, the springs beneath squeaking as she shifts about. 'Can I have this room?'

The water beckons. Without stepping out, I push out the screen doors, peering past the wire coming unstuck, the railing rotting through, to the glistening water and the rocky cliff-face opposite. My t-shirt billowing, my face catching the breeze.

'Not a chance.'

Back at the house, removing the key from the lock box as per Mr Martin's instructions – passed on from the realtor – the solid front door opens with a creak, a distinctive smell rushing to my nostrils. *That* smell – unforgettable. Cedar, blended with pine. An old book, if you like, its pages carrying the scent of passing years. Its walls, housing the memory of generations. The house itself, ancient, still standing – like the water, the surrounding forest – exuding life-giving properties, a renewing quality. I breathe in deeply just to feel its effect.

Slowly, respectfully, I move through the place, feeling the worn, wooden banister beneath my palm as I grip the railing. A groove worn smooth, carved out by another's hand, at another time: a fading scar. Ascending the staircase, my feet landing upon a central curve – a subtle reminder of the layering of footsteps, year upon year – I reach a room, distinctly different to the rest, sparsely furnished, divided by partitions that fail to meet the ceiling.

In this room, there are boxes upon boxes overflowing with yellowed documents inked with faded scrawl. Intrigued, I lift the lid of a single box, stopping short as I register the name printed on the side, *Austin.* The contents are surely too old to be my father's but just seeing his name is enough to deter me from examining these forgotten things. Em circles back, completing her self-guided tour of the upstairs rooms.

'Not that one, Ok?' I say, shutting the door behind me.

Em looks over her shoulder, back at me, then back at the room.

'Yeah, I know,' she says. 'It's full of junk.'

Downstairs, moving from room to room – the glorious front bedroom with French doors opening out onto the veranda; the old-style kitchen complete with maid's quarters off to the side a reminder of a different era; the screened-in porch housing a dining table and matching chairs, studded with worn, red leather ... Finally, I return to the car, remembering the food in the cooler bags and the few practical items purchased for our first days. Dropping the bags at my feet, I remove the stopper keeping the fridge door open and plug in the fridge, unloading the basic necessities.

'Aren't you having something?' Em asks when I serve up.

Intuitively, I take a deep breath in, letting this place guide me: the smell of pine, the whisper of voices, the wisdom of years. *The water beckons.* 'Think I'll go for a swim.'

'Now?'

'Can I come?' Zoe asks with an open mouth, tackling a too-hot mouthful as she begins scoffing down her grilled cheese, orange and oozing.

'Let your food settle, ZoZo – then come.'

Zoe's make a show of sinking her bottom lip, before collecting the crumbs with her finger, picking away the melted cheese hardening on her plate.

'O.K.'

The dock is warm underfoot. I dip my toe, the silky top layer mirroring the warmth of the wood. The quality of the water, a milk-bath for my skin. Sunlight dances across the bay.

Water laps the dock like a mother rocking her baby. A slow and gentle rhythm accompanied by little else. No voices echoing across the water, no distant laughter, no old steamer. It is as if the day is new and I, alone, have awoken with the natural world.

Without knowing the depth of the water, I lower myself down the ladder, pushing off, churning the water as the cold trapped beneath takes my breath away. Paddling about like a puppy dog with drenched and floating fur in search of a sopping tennis ball, suddenly, I slow. Floating to the top, the warmer water lightly laps against my side, pooling at my belly, I lie there, my face to the sky, drifting: dreaming. With shadowy sounds of water filling my ears, I shut my eyes, giving in to a stillness that brings me to tears.

Warm tears, running into warm water, as though we are one. As though I am shedding, *becoming*. I look up at the sun's glow through the pink shades of my eyelids, holding my eyes shut, letting the moment linger, *until...*

I open my eyes, discovering a figure in my periphery standing at the edge of the dock. Immediately, the shadowy sound of my half-clogged ears changes as the water drains, gushing, then trickling. I look up in surprise, moving with sculling arms, splashing then resting upon a slime-covered rock, my arms folding over the edge of the dock.

'Oh, hello there!' the woman crouches down, a wide grin forming over red painted lips, her almost-white, blonde bob falling forward. 'You look like you've settled in!'

'Uh... Yes?'

'Oh, I'm sorry.' The woman stands upright, allowing me to take in her smart, summery attire, the name badge pinned to her chest. 'I'm Marilyn – the realtor... I've just come from an 'Open."

Beads of water drip from my face, like visible perspiration.

'Your father...' The woman named Marilyn hesitates. 'Well, I managed the property here... Among other things...'

Marilyn seems to lose her train of thought as I lose my footing on the slime-covered rock, stirring up some gunge. *My father.* How to articulate feelings toward a man whose fleeting presence in my life lasted just long enough to sear the burn of his departure?

'Oh,' I say, realising I should have hopped out of the water. 'Let me just... I'm Lauren.'

'Nice to meet you, Lauren,' Marilyn says, filling the silence as I climb up the ladder. 'You probably didn't expect a visitor, eh? I'm sorry to intrude. But I understood you were taking possession and thought I'd come by, introduce myself, given... Well,' Marilyn shrugs. 'You might say I have a special... interest in meeting you...'

'Oh?' I wrap a towel around my middle. 'Yes... Well, we just came today, actually.'

'Today?!' Marilyn laughs. 'And here you are taking a dip – God love it! Well, I won't shake your hand,' Marilyn observes the pool of water forming at my feet, darkening the dock where I stand, before turning her wrist inwards to glance at the gold watch catching the glint of the sun on her well-tanned and freckled wrist. 'It's nice to meet you...' Marilyn embarks on a brief moment of small talk – strangely 'small', given her apparent 'special interest' in meeting me.

'Listen, I gotta shoot, but if you need anything, *anything* at all, please reach out. Even if you think it's not something I can help with; I'll put you in contact with someone who can. We realtors make a business out of knowing our town, and its people.' Marilyn sighs as though reflecting on something funny, something familiar. 'Austin – I mean, your father, he...'

Standing in a dampened towel and dripping bathers, exposed in more ways than one, I bristle at the implied familiarity in her tone as Marilyn lets her sentence drift across the water.

In the distance, comes the slamming of the screen door as the girls trail down to the dock. Zoe, making a game of dodging the pine needles cast across the stepping stones.

Marilyn runs her fingers along the strap of her handbag, looking back toward the girls, then speaking hurriedly, and yet, intentionally vague. 'Listen, I know it's complicated... But if you're looking for... information... *whatever*... Well, I might be able to help there too.'

As Marilyn makes her way back up to her car, greeting the girls as she passes, I offer a half-hearted wave, before dragging out a fold-out chair, sinking back, spreading a towel across my body to shield me from the world and the sun.

Splash. The moment of peace is again broken, replaced by Em and then Zoe pushing off from the dock, playing in the water. But this is a different kind of peace. A peace felt in a mother's breast, at seeing her children play happily – and without pain – at seeing her children to safety. I am so out-of-my-skin grateful, so simultaneously angry; that I begin to cry.

Silent tears, falling for the joy we've found; for the years we've lost.

Splash. Nick is fully submerged. Rising, the water beading at his stubble as he pinches his face between his hands. Excess water, replaced by 'that' look in his eyes.

Swim with me.

Can't.

Swim with me, he says again.

Together, we make a splash.

4

———

August

Our activity follows the general habits of holidaymakers: swimming, canoeing. To onlookers, we appear to be a happy family; not broken, missing its core. But despite the joy – laughter in splashing about, humour in the locals struggling to understand our Australian accent – there is mostly sadness.

We hear from Lorraine often – the girls, more than I. Sometimes, I will catch Em in her room, on the computer, talking. Her voice, sad and low – or sometimes, animated, seemingly happy.

'Hi Lorraine,' I try not to sigh, because our conversations are never short. A woman, a mother – once a mother, always a mother – a grandmother; Lorraine worries. She wants to hear, again, everything Em has already told her.

'Are you sure you're really alright?' she will say.

'I'm fine,' I lie.

Lorraine, pausing as though the connection is bad, twisting her lips in disbelief. 'And the girls?'

'Fine.'

Distracted, at a loss, Lorraine will break our gaze, studying her calendar just beyond the screen, booking in the next time she will call. With Lorraine, life is as before but without the mounds of washing neatly folded; the dinner, left waiting on the stove.

But if it weren't for Lorraine – my chats with Sarah, the occasional group chat with the girls from the salon back home – I would have little contact with the outside world beyond engaging with a supermarket cashier, waving back at a neighbouring dock, or the return of a cheerful 'good morning' while out on a walk. Interactions with the outside world, experienced in bursts and from a distance.

Mostly it is just the three of us. My energy is sapped by trying to show the girls the 'best time;' trying to distract them – and myself – from our ever-present loss.

'Mum,' Em says, one afternoon, licking a drip of boysenberry ice-cream from the side of her cone as we walk. 'This is great. *Really.* But you needn't try *so* hard.'

I look at my own melting scoops and back at Em. *Isn't this what fun looks like; aren't we having fun?*

'What I mean,' Em throws her arm over my shoulder – an action that has become rare and precious. 'At some point, you just gotta *be.*'

It feels strange, my fourteen-year-old possessing greater wisdom than her mother. Having a teenager is difficult; I never know when I'm going to receive sarcasm; emotion in its heightened, exaggerated state; or, the girl underneath it all with much to teach to her grieving mum – *though I'm not even sure I'm doing that right.*

Later, as the sun sinks down, slipping beneath the horizon, I head down to the boat house as I do every evening.

'Want to come?' I say, doubtfully.

Em looks up from the months-old edition of *Seventeen*, bought right before the new summer dresses and melting ice-cream.

'I'm not goin' down there at night!' Zoe says, eyes still fixed on her TV show. 'Em says there's bats down there and they might get stuck in my hair!'

'So, wear a cap,' Em shrugs, replacing her magazine on the coffee table.

Down at the dock, Em and I settle into some fold-out chairs, the water moving beneath us in gentle rhythm. The moon stays mostly hidden behind the dark-grey clouds masking the stars.

'Not a super clear night.' Em is unimpressed.

'Maybe not,' I say, tilting my head back, breathing deeply as I shut my eyes. 'But it sure is peaceful.'

There is a lull and I almost wonder whether Em feels it too; feels *him* here, beside us.

'Saw you boarded up the doors to the balcony,' Em drops her head back to look toward the upstairs of the boat house immediately above us.

'Didn't look safe.'

'Yeah, I know,' Em says, before falling silent, giving in, at least, to the sound of water lapping against the dock; the moment, short-lived. 'Holy shiii –'

Em skids her chair back, leaping up. The pair of us, looking up toward the shadowy light of the moon; a backdrop to the return trip of the something dark, flying low. 'Was that a –?'

'Bat?' I say, sliding my feet back into my thongs. 'Think so.'

'Gawd!' Em holds her hands to her chest. 'I thought I was making that up.'

I give Em a nudge that says *don't tease your sister.*

'You know,' I say, peering behind us, craning my neck, before we prepare to make our way back. 'I found a photograph of a man standing on the edge of the railing up there, in old-school swimmers, very muscular.'

'What?' Em asks, delighted. 'Do you think he dove off? Did people do that – *do* people do that? Now, that's not a bad i –'

'Don't even –.'

'Kidding. Kidding,' Em says, throwing her arm around me for the second time in one day, before looking up, semi-suspicious. 'What else did you find in that room of 'stuff?''

'Don't know,' I say. 'Letters, documents, photographs; just 'stuff.''

'And the boxes are labelled 'Austin'?

'Yes.'

'That was your dad's name?'

I give the slightest nod.

Together, we slowly tackle the stepping stones back toward the house.

'But it's not *his* stuff, is it?' Em stops at the top of the railing to look back at the sharp shadows of pine standing at the water's edge, a contrast to the flashes of colour behind us of Zoe's TV show. 'I mean, you never really talk about him... I know more about your mum, than your dad.'

'I know.'

'And,' Em tries again, 'I mean, he kept all that 'stuff.' Your great-grandfather's? Also named Austin?'

'Your great-*great* grandfather. Everything in those boxes – everything I've seen, which isn't all that much – dated early 1900's.'

'So, it's old.'

I nod.

'But, I mean all that 'stuff' was kept; it wasn't thrown out.

So, whoever kept it... I mean, they must have cared enough to keep it.'

I'm saved by the screen door behind us creaking as it swings open. 'Why aren't you coming in?' Zoe asks, a little whiny, though still caught by the lure of TV.

'Just getting some air, ZoZo.'

'We saw a bat,' Em smirks; this, enough to send Zoe back inside.

I give Em a look, before pressing against the railing, preparing to return inside.

'Well...' I say, with a shrug, bidding the night adieu.

'Mum,' Em continues; she's persistent, this daughter of mine. 'Maybe Austin didn't throw out all of those letters, documents, photographs – whatever – because he *wanted* them to be found...'

'Which Austin?'

Em shrugs. 'Both? ... Maybe, he – they – want his story told.'

I let the door swing shut as Em follows me inside.

'Maybe.'

Soon after the girls go to bed, I reach for my phone, the sounds of outside finding their way in, a moth darting in and out of the lamp shade as I wait for the voicemail to connect. There are a few messages left in recent months – none of which I've listened to – I skip forward until the dates align but the message is gone. My father's voice – like the man – *gone*. Reaching toward the light, I turn off the lamp, the sounds of the night sharpening in the dark as tears run along my cheek, dampening my pillow. My body, held tight, shuddering as I let myself *feel*. Angry tears, because they fall for *him*.

5
———

August

'And where is everything now?'

'Nick's stuff – our old life?' My fingers drum along the edge of the mint-green pleather couch. 'Packed away in boxes. All of it, shoved away in a storage unit to deal with at another time.'

Val listens and nods. *Typical.* I chose to meet with a counsellor, rather than a therapist, because counsellors are meant to be practical. They are supposed to look at a situation and assess, *how can we fix things?* But there is no fix. Val has already told me this, informed me that we must simply move through the grief; let ourselves *feel.*

'I suppose you're going to tell me that's not healthy, that I should have dealt with Nick's belongings before we left. That I should have said goodbye.'

I do not pause long enough for Val to reply. Val's hands

rise and fall in her lap to rest upon her army-green silk buttoned dress, her yoga-treated body.

'But I wasn't ready. I don't think I'll ever be ready. In fact... I'm only here for the girls...' I look toward the closed door out to the waiting room – where I'd sat minutes earlier staring at the softly-coloured water colours on the walls, the well-cared for indoor plant-life; staring at the door to outside. 'I'm worried that in not dealing with my grief...' I begin, searching, my eyes washing over the walls – the décor, in similar tones to the waiting room; the room infused with the scent of lemon myrtle clearing my nasal passages whilst reminding me of cleaning product – all of it meant to be calming. An enforced relaxation.

'You won't be able to help them through theirs?' Val nods from her seated position, her perfectly erect posture. 'And do you let yourself feel? Do you allow yourself a good cry?'

Even to my counsellor – this person I have chosen to place my trust – I want to lie; I want to pretend to be strong. 'Sometimes.'

'And does it help?' Val sits casually, cross-legged, hands clasped together in her lap, the line of her dress falling open just below the knee.

I shrug. Val is a good listener and I feel comfortable – enough. But I'm not sure I'll be back; I'm not sure the advice of 'letting it all out' is practical – or useful.

'I didn't sort through his belongings myself,' I begin again, trying to steer our conversation back on course.

'The stuff in storage back in Oz?'

I nod. 'Lorraine did it mostly, while I was at work. Some things she wanted to keep for herself, others she thought best to put aside into boxes. His clothes went off to the Op shop, the neighbours helped set up a yard sale for all the stuff in the shed – Most of it, tools, machinery, I hadn't a clue how they function, let alone how much they'd be worth. But I just needed them *gone*.'

'And how do you feel about shedding Nick's belongings now?'

This question grabs me by the throat, unexpectedly. Val hands over the tissue box, its pattern soft and swirly like the waiting room paintings; colours blending into one.

The process of clearing Nick's things, of shoving them aside, happened so quickly, with such trauma, as if they were being yanked away without my consent. But had I been the one packing the boxes – feeling the cloth of his work shirts and singlets that once rested upon *his* skin, breathing in their scent – the boxes never would have been packed.

Lorraine hadn't wanted us to go. She tried several times to dissuade me from going, soon switching to the overused phrase 'when you come home;' and yet, she helped in every way possible to ensure the girls and I were ready to depart.

Once the boxes were packed – the girls and I living out of a suitcase – the furniture cleared, stacked away in storage, Lorraine scrubbed and bleached the bathroom while I vacuumed throughout. Within the week some eager renters had snapped up the place.

'So, then, the past is only temporarily packed away,' Val assesses.

'Both literally and metaphorically,' I agree, embarrassed by the wad of scrunched-up tissues resting in my palm.

'So, until you 'unpack' these feelings –' A crease appears at Val's brow; the expression catching like a yawn.

'You're suggesting I return to Australia?'

'I'm suggesting, that being *here*, in this room,' Val looks around, over to her degrees on the wall alongside the softly coloured paintings, the sheer curtains of this light-filled room. 'This is the first step. That, as I said at the start of our session, you are choosing to take firm action to support yourself and your daughters. And that is a really positive and practical step. But' Val swaps over her crossed legs causing the light to fall in different shades over her silk dress. 'It's going to take some work.'

'Ok... What do you suggest?' I ask, unzipping my purse, fishing out a loose sheet of paper and a pen, preparing to jot down a practical plan on the back of an old shopping list of crossed-out items.

Val places her hand gently on the table between us. 'You'll remember this – and, if you don't; go with what feels natural, go with what feels right.'

I return the paper and pen and reposition my purse on my lap, my fingers curling over its ribbed lining, grasping a little too tight.

'Ok, so.' Val clasps her hands back together. 'I would recommend doing what you're doing. Spending time together, sharing the summer is a beautiful way to feel close and connected. Make space for conversation with the girls about their father, let them remember him alongside your own memories.'

I loosen my grasp of my purse.

'And, when the time feels right, try to connect with this new community. Waving to the neighbour or chatting to the local cashier is a great start, but you're here to build a foundation. Make some real friends. Take up hairdressing again, if that's of interest; it's a wonderful way to meet the people within your community.'

'Ok.' I feel myself smiling and nodding. *Ok. Maybe stepping out of my comfort zone is exactly what I need.*

'*And,*' Val continues, 'be open to exploring the past, in all its forms. Grief has a funny – or, not so funny – way of bringing old trauma to the surface.'

'You're talking about my father,' I say, with a distinct shift in tone.

'I am.' Val's smile thinly disguises sympathy. 'And you should be too. Perhaps, start with that room of 'stuff' you described for me earlier... You might find engaging with your grandfather's life –'

'*Great*-grandfather,' I interject.

'Ok, great-grandfather,' Val corrects. 'You know, it might give you some perspective – while at a distance. Often in reaching back – sometimes further than you might deem necessary – often, in coming to know and understand someone else's story; we open ourselves up to learning more about our own.'

Austin & Errington
Preston, Ontario, Canada
1905

6

———

July

Errington's European Odyssey had been planned for some time, but after another restless night on board the ocean liner, she is glad to see dry land. Originally, it was her father who had taken some coaxing to support the idea of a European adventure, but in recent months, it was Errington who'd become less enthusiastic.

She began to press the issue upon her father on evenings he'd return home from the woollen mills whistling a tune, rarely heard since Errington's mother died.

'Maybe I should stay here? Elizabeth is rather a handful, these days,' she said. But it was an argument lost on Father, who need only present the threat of boarding school for Elizabeth to fall in to line.

'Errington,' Father said, taking his daughter's hand, looking upon her with dark, kind eyes. 'I won't have you missing out for the sake of the 'children'. You are to live your own life.' A sentiment, Father had long upheld; Errington had been sent to England after her mother's death, remaining there for a year until ready to resume life in Preston, not as a makeshift mother but a woman in her own right.

And yet, Errington's life, while her own, was prescribed by George. Perhaps, one day, from his bedroom window, overlooking the Maplecroft gardens, he had witnessed a flash of hands – a fleeting touch – and determined a trip away would be just the thing for his eldest daughter. Or else, listening to whatever nonsense Elizabeth had fed him; evidently jealous of this new distraction in Errington's life.

Though Errington knew nothing of what her father had seen, suspected, or been told, she did not try to dissuade him further, understanding that if her father meant for her to go, she would go. George, a self-made man – arriving to Canada from England at the age of sixteen, quickly learning the ropes of the woollen mill, establishing himself within the business until his own name would be carved above the entrance – had always afforded Errington a certain level of freedom, especially when it came to her education. Dux of her school, Errington had proved herself too smart for any man. Seemingly from the womb, or at the very least, from her earliest gown and bonnet, Errington breathed literature – unlike food – which she often left untouched – Errington consumed as much literature as was readily available and never felt full. She enjoyed exercising her intellect, despite Doctor Vardon insisting this could be a dangerous thing and regularly discouraging such overexertion and prescribing bouts of bed rest. Through books, Errington could live vicariously through others. So, of course, Austin's stories tempted her, though she still hadn't heard nearly enough.

At the age of fourteen, Errington holidayed in the States with her best girlfriend, Margaret Elmslie. The two girls discussed at length the power of literature as they lay side by side under the cover of darkness: their desire to be someone else, a character of their own choosing. And so, both girls returned home from their chaperoned trip with new Christian names. From then on Errington was to be referred to as 'Nellie,' 'Nell' for short. Dismissive of the name, George continued to refer to his daughter by her birth name, but because Maisie had also indulged this whim, the name eventually caught on and even the 'children' often referred to Errington as 'Nell.'

How interesting then, that Austin should assign Errington the same name she had assigned herself as if he knew her already. A kind of kindred spirit. Errington hadn't managed to bid Austin farewell in the way she would have liked, and so she resolved, on board the ship over fish pie and vegetables cooked in duck fat – more food than she would eat in a week – that she would write to him. It would be a formal letter in which she would find some pressing question to ask, one that could be read by others; assuming Austin had not yet moved into his own lodgings, Aunt Ida would surely be looking over his shoulder, keen to hear of her dear niece's travels. Errington decided to write soon after docking.

From the harbour, Errington watches as several men pull the rope tight through their hands, the steam ship taking its place amidst the chaos of the shipping yard. Overhanging cranes, barrels strewn across a jetty before being loaded onto the back of a waiting horse and cart. Crowds of men in bowler hats, others in uniform, women in puffed sleeves, given extra height by their hats piled high with adorning flowers: all there to greet the alighting passengers. Though much to Errington's surprise, Lynn, with his crooked smile, is nowhere to be found. And so, upon disembarkation, Errington feels awkward. Standing, in waiting, as if in possession of an empty dance card, she begins to feel unsteady on her feet, caught in the whirlwind of the Southampton docks.

'Alright, Miss?' asks a young lad, whose too-short trousers and low-sitting socks suggest he is not normally the type to approach a lady. 'Forgive us for askin', but you look a little lost.'

Errington reaches for her purse, perhaps to check it's still there – or, possibly, to offer the boy a small token for his kindness. She looks down at him, noticing the grime on his face, the youthful cheekiness beneath his cap, reminding her of one of the children working at the Pattinson Woollen Mills.

'Alright then?' the boy asks, glancing back to the other children in a similar state of grubbiness, moving further away from the docks.

'Yes, thank you,' Errington says, leaning down toward him in the same way she would engage with a child factory worker – though she'd usually be offering up penny candy from her skirt pocket, before sending them on their way. 'Go on then, catch up with your chums. I'll find my way.'

Within an instant, the boy disappears between the shoulders of the passing crowd, leaving Errington's purse intact and instilling in her a new resolve. As if taking hold of the small, dangling pencil, entering another's initials on her own dance card, Errington decides she will do some exploring of her own, without Lynn. Thankfully, she was yet to be joined by Mrs Waters – a fussy, old woman sourced by Uncle Hedley, whom Errington met when last in England, charged with accompanying Errington for the portion of the trip Lynn cannot.

Strolling along the River Thames – her luggage, taken directly to the Northwestern – Errington approaches the crowd gathered on the street across from Westminster, its imposing structure emulating its significant purpose as the Houses of Parliament. At first, she suspects a demonstration of sorts, hearing snippets of grievances, of the delay in mail making it near-impossible to pay bills in a timely fashion. But as she moves through the edge of the crowd, Errington spots a penguin parade of men in bowler hats, orange sashes strung across their shoulders and the gathering appears to be one of celebration.

Then she remembers. It is the height of marching season for the Orange Order, July 12th marking William of Orange's victory over King James II in 1688 in: The 'Glorious Revolution', the crowd refers to it and even after two hundred years, there is still a sense of revolutionary fervour in the air. Errington often marvels at the way history lives on, not just in literature, or architecture, but through people; such thoughts being the impetus for her desire to travel. Now, as she walks along this stretch of the River Thames, Errington has the sense that this walk is simply a moment in time, a space once inhabited by the people before her and the many generations to come; a fluid movement, fixed only in location.

Continuing on in a pensive, dream-like state – and reminding herself that she really must record some of these thoughts in her travel journal, if only for herself – Errington re-emerges from the crowd to a lovely walk bordered with ash trees and lampposts, soon to be disturbed by the wheels of a phaeton kicking up dust and the many townspeople and new arrivals darting across the street. A hive of activity taking place on a busy London street as if Errington were seeing it all from heaven above – where her mother, Maisie, and older sister, Madge, now rest.

In this sombre reflection, Errington seeks a quiet space, a reprieve from the crowd, and she finds it, appearing before her in the form of a most glorious cathedral, its doors, despite its grandeur, its majesty, welcoming her into God's loving arms. Errington makes her way to take her place on the pew, to kneel before God but as she does the air becomes close, her breathing – made shallow by her corset – becomes shallower still until she is breathless and weak. With a sickness, a light-headed tingling, dark stars cloud her vision, melding into a vision of darkness, blocking out the light.

THE SURPRISE OF RECEIVING A LETTER FROM Errington is, indeed, a pleasant one.

More than once, Austin had thought of writing. Drawing up the ink, his fountain pen poised, unsure of where to begin, of the tone to take, of where to send his communications. Understanding now, from Errington's note that she is to be staying with her Uncle Hedley on the 15th, he will write to this fixed address, c/o H. Pattinson Esq. There at Whitley Bay Austin imagines Errington at the beach, emerging from a bathing machine deposited along the shore to the blue-green water, splashing about in a cute little costume, turning the water white.

Resting on his writing desk is the post card Austin intends to send – a novel idea, sending Errington a post card of a landmark in her own hometown – picturing Hotel Del Monte, resting at the base of Lover's Lane. A place visited when they were able to snatch a moment alone, before Errington would abruptly have to take her leave. Not to mention the weeks spent on bed rest – her delay in telling Austin of her poor health, *'just a little mean'*, insisting that Austin *'mustn't imagine anything more than a tired feeling.'*

'Do you remember this place, I wonder?' Austin writes at the base of the Hotel Del Monte post card, before turning it over, to be filled with tongue-and-cheek flirtations, unlike Errington's very formal letter, written as if the whole world might be watching – perhaps, not aware of Austin recently securing lodgings of his own.

Also on his writing desk is a letter from 'Mother' – a term

adopted through marriage but most earnestly deserved, Elizabeth loving Austin as her own. (Austin's birth mother had died shortly after he was born. The thought often crossed Austin's mind that, surely, Charles – given the choice – would have settled for four children, instead of five.)

Mother has become as dear to him as his own mother might have been. Over the years, travelling across the globe in search of adventure, of new, exciting beginnings, Austin carried his leather-bound Bible across oceans; Mother's inscription keeping her close, '*Dear Austin, God's Speed. From your ever-loving Mother.*' From the furthest ends of the earth, Austin could hear Mother's voice in his head, guiding him. And while this hadn't altered his course, much in the way a sailor may adjust his sails according to the wind, the knowledge of her love always made him steadfast in his resolve.

'*I should like to meet her,*' Mother writes, her intention to invite Errington to *The Waldrons* clearly one of the reasons for her letter, '*especially after meeting her charming father, Mr George Pattinson, the year before last when he came to Croydon*'. ('*Did I meet a Mr George Pattinson?*' Austin wrote to Frank years earlier when Mother had first mentioned his visit.)

Though Austin would like Errington's invitation to be something of a surprise, he can't help but hint to it in his correspondence, '*Mother is in the habit of inviting only the most upstanding guests to The Waldrons... do you know, you may soon receive an invitation?*'

Taking up his pen, dipping it in ink, Austin writes, too, of the books Errington requested, suggesting Lawson and Paterson as authors – beyond Kipling – who offer a sense of the '*lure of the wild.*' Something, he knows, Errington craves to understand. An exotic wildness that both intrigues and terrifies her because it is beyond her experience, beyond what she may offer here in Preston.

At present, Austin's mind is not on South Africa. Far

from it. Indeed, even the dust of the veldt that infiltrated his suitcase is all but gone. Traces of South Africa remain only in his heart, and the preservation of a crocus pressed against the pages of the Transvaal Masonic By-Laws – an invitation to visit the local Masonic Lodge still yet to be extended to Austin, a fraternity over which he suspects Mr George Pattinson has great influence.

'You did not say what return you want on the letter,' Austin writes to Errington, unsure of how to sign-off. The nib of his pen pausing, Austin considers that despite his 'above average' education, it is difficult to find the words; his sights for the future, *their* future, not yet articulated. *'So, I will simply sign off as A.'*

Concealing the post card of The Hotel Del Monte behind the veil of an envelope, away from prying eyes, Austin deposits the letter on a silver tray to be taken to the post office by one of the maids at Austin's new lodgings, *'Saint's Rest,'* as he refers to it. It's true, as one of Eddie's past letters suggests, Austin's life *'has not been conducive to holiness.'* But in Errington's *'bright eyes,'* her dimpled smile, is the promise of a bright and happy future. A broad grin spreads across Austin's face as he wears the happy, slightly imbecilic look of a man in love.

Austin reaches for Errington's coat – the one she left behind as she dashed off from Lover's Lane – long and fitted, buttons designed to fit snugly at the bust. Holding the coat up to his face, Austin breathes in its fibres, filling his nostrils with Errington's orange blossom scent, as if his moustache is planted there, at the base of her neck. It is intoxicating, exhilarating; as it is to be in her presence... and then, just at that moment, a small silver tin drops from a pocket concealed within the coat's lining and splays open. Thin cigarette soldiers still rest in place; Austin removes one and strikes a match. From their texture and taste, Austin recognises

Ogden's 'Guinea Gold' and inhales, though he is not normally one to stray from his pipe.

Remembering the prohibition of his lodgings on smoking – one he suspects most lodgers ignore given the yellowing of the drapes – Austin takes to the balcony to let the swirling smoke dissipate into the night air. The moon sits like an oversize pebble in the sky, the waxing gibbous, not yet a perfect circle. The great square of Pegasus, its nose and hooves diving down toward earth. The winged horse gives Austin the impression of The Missus, his own horse in battle, shining like the silver glow of the stars. The cool night air: the shuddering snort of The Missus threatens to take him back...

But time has leaden wings, and just as Austin can no longer feel his lips at the base of Errington's neck, The Missus clops her heels, stirring up the dust of the veldt, rising red particles stealing away her sleek, muscular form as she dissipates into star dust. Flicking ash, watching it fall like gentle snow, Austin extinguishes the orange glow of his cigarette as if snuffing out a candle.

7

Looking up at the night sky, as if studying her atlas, Errington draws a line between the stars with her finger. Tiny dots in the sky; landmarks on a map. Polaris, the north star, acts as her compass, remaining almost still while the northern sky moves around it. From there, to Cassiopeia, Errington need only double the distance to find the Great Square of Pegasus, the four stars shaping themselves into the body of the winged horse, each one shining almost as brightly as the next. Often admiring this constellation, Errington has always been captivated by stories of myths and legends; their magic, immortalised in the stars.

In the hours creeping past midnight, Cassiopeia moves around Polaris, soon to be hidden just below the horizon, transforming from the shape of a 'W' to that of an 'M;' its own transformative alphabet. Out on the balcony, Errington is watching this process unfold. Hardly noticing the drop in temperature, she takes a drag of her cigarette, long and slow. It is not uncommon for Errington to exist between periods of broken sleep.

Hours earlier, Errington had been here on this balcony,

thinking of Austin, wondering whether he might be looking up at this same sky – though, of course, it would be hours before Preston fell under the cover of darkness. It caused her to wonder further about the *notion* of time, as many had in her parents' generation – a time before time-zones, when each locale had their own measure of time, before the advent of trains and railcars caused chaos when trying to connect these out of sync locations. Weeks spent on bed rest, versus the fleeting encounters with Austin made the passing of time seem a strange, almost *elastic* notion, something to be stretched out or hurried over at will. Its passing, either a blessing, or one of life's great tragedies.

'Don't let Father catch you with those nasty little coffin nails,' an unmistakeable voice said from behind.

'Lynn!'

Errington stubbed out her cigarette and threw her arms around her brother. 'I was worried! Where have you been?'

'Never mind that,' Lynn said, with a boyish grin. 'Since when do you smoke? You know, experts in Germany are claiming tobacco will kill you?'

'Ah,' Errington held up one finger. 'There is much to catch up on, dear brother. Let's have a drink. Little fizz, maybe?'

'Fizz? Not for me,' Lynn said, distancing himself from his usual position. 'But yes, let's sit. I'll join you for a night-cap.'

Without explanation of Lynn's previous whereabouts – nor any mention of Errington's earlier fainting episode – the pair talked long into the evening. Away from home, and without recording her confessions in ink, Errington was much less guarded in describing her feelings for Austin. And while she didn't reveal a name, Errington told something of her latest escapades, most significantly, that she may have found a suitor.

'A suitor?' Lynn sat up in his chair. 'Son of a gun, and here

I was thinking you'd grow to be an old maid at Maplecroft. Heck, at twenty-four, you're half-way there, eh Nellie.'

Errington gave her brother a playful shove. 'Tosh!' And then, more seriously, 'Anyway, it's hardly a laughing matter; I rather thought the same.'

'Why *are* you still single?' Lynn crossed his arms, his cheeky grin no longer sitting below his long nose and dark eyes. 'You've had offers.'

Errington cringed. 'Yes, but none I'd entertain.'

Lynn appeared deep in thought, Errington wondered if it might be wise to alleviate his thoughts by bringing them out into the open air. 'Well, come on, which fair maiden has stolen your heart?'

'None as yet,' Lynn said, without displaying an inch of sadness. His adventurous spirit was always strengthened by time away from Maplecroft – even if it were only temporary. At the moment, Lynn is studying the textile industry at Leeds before he takes up his pre-ordained position as superintendent of the Pattinson Woollen Mills. '*My* heart is whole,' Lynn said.

In the wee hours of the morning, Errington retires to bed, her eyes heavy with the promise of sleep as she finds her way back to Austin, unencumbered by time and place.

Austin's strong arms work the oars as they move through the water with only the subtle sounds of their environment heard beyond their own breath, their own beating hearts... As Austin brings them gently back to shore, Errington leans back, enjoying the last of a fading sun, before they must leave the welcome confines of the boat.

Oh dear, *Errington says at the muddied suction fixing her to the spot, her boot stuck in mud.* I believe, I'm stuck.

Austin loosens Errington's laces before sweeping Errington up in his arms, carrying her to the shore. His scent – that blend of shaving cream, port infused tobacco – is no longer unfamiliar. It is alluring, seductive...

May I? Austin asks, and she shivers at the touch of his hand as he moves to replace her boot, moving up her leg ...

You may have it all, Errington breathes.

These words are all Austin needs, his hand moving along the line of Errington's stocking, slowly inching beneath layer upon layer of silk and cotton.

This is new, she thinks, but there is a feeling of anticipation, a tingling beyond the top of her thighs as Austin's fingers meet the opening of her drawers...

'WHAT PRICED HEAD HAVE YOU?' LYNN ASKS IN THE morning, devouring a fry-up of bacon and eggs, mushrooms, sausages and offal.

'None at all,' Errington says, suggesting it is merely a lack of sleep, not her consumption of alcohol, that has left her a little worse for wear.

'Right,' Lynn says, with a knowing smile. 'Well, we have rather a big day of sight-seeing and gorging ourselves, so...' He surveys the way Errington's fork dances around the blackberries on her plate without transferring any to her mouth. Her slice of toast is half-eaten. 'Well, one of us of will be gorging ourselves.'

For most of the morning, Errington and Lynn take a stroll through The Common – Lynn's theory, that exerting energy will, somehow, lead to its replenishment, perplexes his sister, although their meander is, indeed, a pleasant one, traipsing the acres of woods and grasslands. From there they walk beside the lake and up to the cemetery where moss-covered headstones mark the death of children younger than their sister, Madge, who died at age ten from pneumonia; each one destined to remain a child forever.

A sad tradition, occurring throughout history; Austin, telling Errington of his own great-grandparents, Thomas Latham Moss and Fanny Salmon, naming multiple children after themselves until their namesakes survived. There is a small sea of tombstones within a clearing set beside the stone church. The woods are adorned with ivy, sunlight streaming through the yew trees.

Speaking in hushed tones so as not to disturb the dead, it is only upon leaving The Common that Errington and Lynn resume their usual banter, though it is more solemn than before; the active experience of remembering those dearly departed, inevitably leading to thoughts of Mother. But this solemn mood is soon replaced by a joyous one as they return to town and their party of two becomes a party of three.

'Patt! Pattinson!' a voice cries along a bustling London street. Errington and Lynn are standing before a row of gothic-style buildings four storeys high. Errington, peering in the window of a particular boutique, is admiring an oversized hat that Lynn suggests looks rather like a bird's nest, with feathers and flowers and even a robin perched on top. Errington is about to deliver a quick remark about men's fashion but, instead, turns to find Lynn greeting a young man of a similar age as if they were brothers.

'Mr Matterson is a friend from Leeds.'

After witnessing a long chat in the street, Errington suggests they go for ice-cream. Errington, who has a fondness for ice-cream, consumes her entire portion, cone and all, and waits idly while Lynn and Mr Matterson continue to talk underwater. Before long, Errington is returned to the hotel by her brother, who, wearing a boyish, apologetic look, rushes off.

'We'll shop tomorrow,' Lynn calls out as he skips back down the street toward Mr Matterson.

FOR SEVERAL MONTHS, ERRINGTON TRAVELS through Europe, relaying her thoughts on art, history and culture in the private pages of her journal – the glorious cathedral structures, '*that ever-feminine delight of shopping,*' and the Swiss Alps, which she finds most affecting. She writes: '*Glacier after glacier, snow peak after snow peak came into view and each time, with a sharp in-drawing of breath, I exclaimed: "this is the Matterhorn."*'

In preparation for their much-anticipated climb to Riffelalp – 'Only a modest climb,' Lynn suggests – Errington and Lynn take a shortcut through the vineyards. They pass a tangled mass of vines and some local women of the '*chunky, stumpy, stolid variety with prematurely old faces,*' as Errington later writes. The women are tying ropes to mountain goats and layering hand-crafted rugs over their donkeys, loading their cargo of wool and knitting needles. Barely noticing them, Lynn powers ahead, while Errington lags behind, slowed by the rugged terrain and by observation of her surroundings, spotting a chameleon changing colour; its skittish curiosity overpowering its ability to remain unseen.

'Nell, isn't it glorious!' Lynn says, as Errington finally catches up.

Sipping water and dabbing her brow, as they stand at the picturesque platform, Errington agrees. The mountains pushing up towards the heavens, are, perhaps, the most beautiful sight she has ever seen – '*Why is not a special language invented, a language consisting only of superlatives, with which one might describe the beauties of the Alps – the temples of the earth?*' she writes, later that evening.

But as they progress up the mountain, the steep ascent, together with the rarefied atmosphere, prove too much and Errington is obliged to give up just twenty minutes from the top; Lynn carries on for both of them. Her mortification is intensified when, on the descent, they are met by the native women leading their donkeys and goats up the path whilst knitting as casually as if they were *'seated by the domestic hearth.' 'Despite lacking the genteel nature of womanhood'* Errington admires their incredible talent.

As the day closes in, Lynn and Errington reconvene over a bottle of Bordeaux, struck by the sight of the return of the cattle to the milking pasture at evening, and Errington's journal records *'A thousand rocks and valleys iterating and reiterating the musical clanking of the bells, as the gentle animals file slowly into the field to the accompaniment of their drowsy tinklings until their toll of foaming milk is paid.'*

ARRIVING AT UNCLE HEDLEY'S AT WHITLEY BAY – Errington flitting between there and other points of interest; often, with old Mrs Waters in tow while Lynn elects to rendezvous with Mr Matterson – Errington finds multiple letters waiting, 'c/o H. Pattinson Esq.' on the mantelpiece.

'Came for you several weeks ago, I'm afraid,' says Uncle Hedley, casually leaning against the mantel, in the familiar pose of a retired bachelor.

Stealing away as soon as is polite to do so, Errington snatches precious moments to devour the letters, reading and re-reading their contents. One is written in a hand Errington does not recognise – the return address, Croydon, England – but the other bears the same hand as the one that made its mark on her dance card, back in Preston – first as 'Austin' and then simply, 'A.M.'

Appearing more ravenous than she has ever been in her life, Errington hurries through dinner, consuming every morsel of the game (caught by Uncle Hedley himself) served up on her plate. Dishes of green beans and roast potatoes cooked in fat and various other accompaniments are spread out on the table. This vast amount of food leads Errington to wonder whether this is how Uncle Hedley eats full-time; irrespective of the company he keeps.

'I don't eat like this all the time, I assure you,' Uncle Hedley says, as if reading Errington's thoughts. These thoughts, fleeting before they return to Austin.

Later that evening, retiring to her room, Errington sets to work, dipping the nib of her pen in ink to accept Austin's mother's invitation to The Waldrons. A letter, given Errington's natural good grace and solid upbringing, that is quick to write; unlike the next. The one for which Errington lingers over her turn of phrase, smiling as she writes.

Ellen Errington Pattinson
Whitley Bay, England

1 September 1905

Mr Austin Moss,
PRESTON, Ontario.

Thanks for the postcard – rather a good scheme putting it in
an envelope... Do you realize that you are going to win the bet?
I expect to go to Croydon on the 20th; your mother gave me a
very kind invitation ...So, of course I did not say what return I
wanted on the p.c. – did you expect one? Why don't you guess?
Oh dear! I think you might!
Errington,
Whitley Bay

8

———

October

Austin Moss,
Preston, Ont.

21 October 1905

Miss Errington Pattinson,
    c/o H. Pattinson Esq.
    Whitley Bay,
    Northumberland, England

...So glad you enjoyed your visit 'home' – I hoped you would. They tell me they were delighted with 'Little Nell'. Of course they were! Can't think of what you want – am no good at guessing.
    A.M. PRESTON

. . .

With the last playful word to Errington, Austin seals the envelope, placing it on a silver tray. He is delighted - and relieved – Errington's visit to The Waldrons went off without a hitch; Mother's letter declaring she found Miss Pattinson, *'an absolute delight.'* This welcome letter only strengthens Austin's resolve that he must, one day – and may God let that day be near – take Errington to be his bride. Though Austin hasn't said as much in his letters – preferring to make this declaration in person – he is almost certain, this happy occasion would suit Errington's heart too.

Other than correspondence with Mother, Austin has been tight-lipped about the budding romance, especially around Frank, preferring to secure his future first. Perhaps, it is unfair to hold onto old habits – Frank still commenting on Austin's general tardiness in responding to letters, despite his response rate (at least to a certain recipient), being much-improved of late – but Austin can't help but hold onto this unshakeable notion that Frank might meddle in his affairs.

Shrugging into his coat, Austin reaches for his hat, before leaving *'Saint's Rest'* and stepping out into the cold, night air. Walking briskly, he approaches the solid double doors of the Masonic Lodge with bated breath and begins the knock. A series of long and short taps. A kind of Morse code Austin has not heard played out since he was at The Golden Light in Potchefstroom. The doors open in response to the knock, as if by magic.

As his eyes adjust to the light, it takes a moment to notice the two wardens standing guard at the double doors within the interior of the temple: doors leading to the inner sanctum. Austin notes, mildly intrigued, that the guards look strikingly similar; an egg with two yolks, he thinks. The only distinguishable feature, a birth mark resting upon a cheek. Their voices are solemn as they utter words of ceremony; words loaded with meaning: 'We are the Brotherhood of Man.' This is the great responsibility of members, within the fraternity and here on earth.

Catching himself staring at the birth mark – that single, entirely superficial point of difference – Austin observes the guards' gaze as they engage in the handshake of brothers united, their eyes a concentrated stare. Within their seeing is a 'knowing' as they look beyond Austin's grey-blue eyes and neatly tweaked moustache to the depths of his soul, and he is struck by a feeling of being simultaneously seen and unseen.

Nothing more is said as Austin is permitted to move beyond these protected walls, through the next set of doors where two more bearded guards stand in customary dress. Their silk, tasselled aprons are adorned with the insignia of the *Grand Lodge of Ancient Free and Accepted Masons* specific to their country and province. After a slight delay – as though waiting for an unseen telephone operator to allow access – the bearded guards share in a reciprocal nod. Together, they accompany Austin, and all three descend the cold, uneven staircase.

As the final door opens, Austin lays eyes on the group of men gathered before an open book, lit by the dim light of a candle.

'Welcome, Brother,' says a voice coming out of the darkness. 'In the spirit of brotherliness, charity and mutual aid; we welcome you.'

Austin bows his head, understanding the elevated status of the man addressing him. 'Thank you, most Worshipful Grand Master,' he says, as the man's moustache – reminiscent of a walrus – comes into view. He is short in stature; and, outside this fraternity, known simply as Mr George Pattinson.

Contrary to Frank's claims, Austin hadn't needed to wait

for an invitation to be extended from the fraternity. In fact, it was up to Austin to seek out the fraternity of his own free will – a fact he should have remembered from his membership at The Golden Light – though it is true that every Lodge, across the globe, and indeed between districts, is run a little differently. Permitted to attend as a visitor, Austin shall be eligible for membership after formally residing in Preston for a year.

'I know little of furniture,' says the Grand Master after the formal proceedings – George and Austin are still within earshot of other freemasons – 'but, in time, if you find you need support in setting up an empire of your own? Well, I can't see that one business is too different from the next.'

Though he can't imagine there is much of anything Mr Pattinson knows 'little of' – a disconcerting notion given Austin's association with his daughter – Austin has no intention of 'looking a gift horse in the mouth.'

'Thank you,' he says, 'perhaps, one day, I shall avail myself of your kind offer, should it still be on the table.'

'Of course,' the Grand Master replies. 'I am only too happy to help those who help themselves.'

Though this is, undoubtedly, the pursuit of every man present, to share in faith and deed, to help others and to help oneself, Austin can't help but wonder why the change of heart. George Pattinson has never before been as forthcoming with his support for Austin as he is in this moment. Perhaps, Austin considers, he has passed some unknown test to gain Mr Pattinson's favour. He is a man of great power and influence, blessed by every man in this room, unified by a common goal.

Austin watches on as the men stand, hands on hearts, blessing not only their leader, but their own Supreme Being, and blessing all grand officers across the globe. Men of good character, wishing to dedicate their life to good, or, perhaps, to atone for a past life in this one; to travel into life hereafter with the weight of the world no longer resting on their shoulders because they have the power to do a little good in this world. Beyond any useful connections that may be made, any potential assistance, that is why Austin is here; to become a better man, to be his best self.

'May they square their lives by the strictest regard to the rules of morality... of equity, so that when... consigned to the silent grave, it may be inscribed on his tomb 'here lies a good man.''

Angels couldn't ask for more, Austin thinks to himself as this solemn prayer concludes with the final utterance, *'So mote it be.'*

'Well, if you're seeking a life conducive to holiness...' says a voice, as if picking up where Austin's thoughts left off. Its clipped English speech, somehow not as youthful sounding as before, is familiar nonetheless, 'your presence here shall set you on your rightful path.'

'Eddie!' Austin declares, overcome by the happy accident of stumbling upon his dear friend. Eddie's blonde hair is neatly parted, his moustache pencil-thin. He appears just as he does in the photograph pasted in Austin's small leather-bound book documenting life in South Africa. With the erect posture of a gentleman, he is dapper in his tweed suit and Masonic apron; the latter, befitting of a man whose life work is, quite literally, to come to the aid of others. 'You're here?'

'Of course, old chap,' Eddie replies as they embrace with a firm heart-felt handshake. 'I wrote of my intent to join you here in Preston. Did you not receive my letters?'

Austin remembers the letters resting beneath Errington's post card – the one picturing a line of bathing machines plonked along the beach at Whitley Bay, a further trigger for imagining Errington in a snug, little swimsuit. 'Yes, indeed,' Austin says, wishing he'd had the foresight to write back sooner, 'but I hadn't expected you to arrive so soon.'

'Ah, well, that's the thing about time, dear friend, it waxes and it wanes. And so,' Eddie says with a shrug, 'here I am.'

He holds the Masonic goblet cupped in his hands, the fine markings etched on glass peering out from his fingers; the set square and compass – ever a reminder of a freemason's earthly and spiritual duties – the pillars of Solomon's Temple, the Bible resting below The Eye of Providence.

'Wonderful, just wonderful,' Austin replies. It feels good to have an ally, someone in Austin's corner.

'Frank, you remember Doctor Edward Barlowe?' Austin says, as Frank shoulders up to Austin, gesturing toward the far corner of the room, as if to suggest *a moment in private if you please.*

'Hmm?' Frank raises an eyebrow, then flicks his head to one side, replacing a loose strand of hair as if suddenly remembering his manners. 'Oh yes, indeed,' he says, much more animated than before. 'I remember you as a young chap, climbing trees and wreaking havoc. You're Dickie's brother?'

Behind Eddie's smile, his usual glow, lies a solemn look, reminding Austin of the lady he met on the train the day he arrived in Preston. Mrs O'Hare. A name he'd not uttered since, though the image of her – the creases forming at her mouth, the fresh sheen veiling her eyes – at the mention of her brother stayed with Austin; particularly as he struggled to quieten his mind in the hours indistinguishable between night and morning spent at *'Saint's Rest'*.

'Yes, that's right,' Eddie says, allowing a pause for the memory of his dear brother, Dickie, who'd always been the more robust Barlowe son though the brothers looked greatly alike. According to Richard Barlowe Senior, a retired army General, and stern father to the Barlowe boys, Dickie, had a body 'made for war, destined for greatness.'

'I assure you,' Austin begins, taking the role of Eddie's

mother, redistributing the limelight, even after Dickie's death. 'Eddie will be one of Preston's most upstanding citizens.'

'Oh, yes?' Frank says, demonstrating the correct amount of mild interest as he negotiates his way through small talk.

Emerging smile-lines reappear on Eddie's sun-kissed face as he shares a brief synopsis of working in a medical tent in Pretoria during the Boer War, of later completing his training at Cambridge Medical School, covering various forms of medicine, albeit rather fleetingly – the health of women in childbirth practically skipped over. When speaking of his own experience within the Boer War; a different mode of fighting to his brother, though, perhaps, with equal bloodshed, Eddie omits the gory details that would make the red wine resting in his goblet hard to swallow. Instead, like a true freemason, he refers to the fellow feeling that accompanies doing 'good.'

'Now then,' Frank says, clearly suggesting *now that's done*, 'if I may steal my brother away for just a moment?'

Brushing his fingers over his thick moustache as the two brothers step to one side, Frank resumes the conversation he is most intent on having. 'I want to thank you for your little loan,' he begins.

Little?

Austin tilts his head to one side, gives his brother a look. 'Well, nothing's finalised as yet...'

'Who can put a price on the bond of brothers, eh?' Frank muses, assured now of securing Austin's word to help fund his own, expanding empire – a topic that had come up not long after Austin's arrival to Preston. 'Anyhow, I've taken the liberty of drawing up a statement with terms I'm sure you'll deem agreeable.'

And placing the envelope in the palm of Austin's hands, he closes his fingers over it, as if gifting him a sacred stone.

'Well, I hope, you'll find it agreeable, anyway,' Frank

laughs, lines radiating from the corners of his eyes like tributaries from a river. 'The funds are as good as spent!'

Somehow, in this quiet corner, surrounded by cold, stone walls – diametrically opposed to the warm environment promoted by its patrons – Frank secures Austin's word that he will come good on the aforementioned loan, assuming he agrees to Frank's terms.

Living the life of a bachelor – abstaining from liquor, though always with women at his disposal – Austin had set aside a tidy sum over the years; a portion of which, he anticipates, will soon be returned to him from his brother, Bert, in New Zealand who also previously sought a loan from Austin. As the youngest of the Great Croydon Mosses of his generation – and with the least to his name in terms of property and other assets – Austin has proven to be a useful source of income to both brothers residing in former colonies. Long before Austin set off to start a new life in Canada – Mother wishing him 'Godspeed' yet again – he had been only too happy to help 'dear old Bert'. Not just because, Austin knew, Bert would repay the funds at the first possible moment but because Bert was kind and true. The exemplar of a freemason.

Had it not been for the pull of adventure, to fight for the great and expanding Empire in exotic, foreign lands, *the great lure of the wild;'* Austin might as easily have spent the rest of his days in New Zealand, alongside his brother, Bert. Austin, continuing to reside in a simple slab-hut, built with the help of a few willing lads, set amongst a backdrop of rolling green.

Back at his lodgings, sitting at the edge of the worn spring-mattress that slumps in toward the middle of the mahogany bed, Austin examines Frank's note. Written on plain paper are the terms of the loan as stipulated by Frank. Five per cent interest payable bi-annually, for the borrowed sum of $1,000. The full loan to be repaid *'on demand.'* Frank's philosophy of

'I'll scratch your back, now you scratch mine' seems a reasonable one; though Austin can't imagine a situation where he may *'demand'* immediate payment without Frank taking exception.

Resolving to visit the bank the following morning, Austin lies back on the narrow bed, only marginally bigger than a stretcher. Unperturbed by the limited comfort of the mattress, or the sounds just outside his door – the creaking of floorboards, the sound of a dripping tap; the close proximity of Austin's landlord – Austin reaches one arm behind his head, as if choosing a shaded spot beneath an elm tree, designated for a little day-dreaming. His mind happily wanders to thoughts of Errington, his thoughts dancing around her as if gliding around a ballroom. It occurs to Austin that, perhaps, this is his time for happiness. Perhaps, his newly-laid plans may come to fruition sooner than he dares to hope. Austin's last remembered thought, before drifting off to sleep: *'What a curious thing. I thought life was pretty full and I was pretty well occupied and then I found I knew, had and was nothing – but now all I want – I have in prospect – and am the richest of all.'*

Keeping his word, Austin attends the bank the very next morning – located one short block away from Frank's factory – and releases the funds. Austin doesn't consider he might need the funds for a proposition of marriage, to establish himself in business and present himself as a reasonable and viable option for the eldest living daughter of one of Preston's most successful businessmen. The owner of the Pattinson Woollen Mills, the sixth largest woollen mill in Ontario. Nor does he consider that Frank's boasting – *'If I were out of my business tomorrow, I would not have the slightest anxiety over being able to find a situation or to open up a business at least as lucrative as my present one'* – may simply be hyperbole.

After a morning of signing papers, followed by an afternoon of Frank at the office in particularly high spirits, encouraging his brother to smoke a celebratory cigar after Austin finalises the details of the next shipment; Austin returns to his lodgings. Resting on the silver tray is a letter, marked with a universal postage stamp in red ink, bearing the image of a lady with flowing hair and dress, a personification of a country as both progressive and beautiful. Just behind her, a mail boat steams past one of New Zealand's most imposing mountains, Mount Egmont.

Bert Moss,
Carterton, Wellington,
New Zealand

9th September 1905

Mr Austin Moss,
PRESTON, Ontario.

Dear Austin,

It is so long between letters and the oceans between us so vast, that I will simply say this; the wife is happy, and the children are growing. I hope that you are enjoying your new home... And, I know, your experience over the last decade being as varied as it has been, has left you well-equipped for any challenge life might deliver.

Though, I'd rather spend these pages catching up on times of yore, I'm afraid things here are not quite as I would like – and without a steady income – I must request, dear brother, an extension on my loan. I suspect things may change – indeed, that is my hope – but please do let me know if this is not agreeable to you and I shall make other arrangements.

Your affectionate brother,
Bert, Carterton, Wellington, New Zealand

Austin folds the letter back over, breathing out a sigh; understanding his own plans must now be put on hold. *'Time has leaden wings.'*

Lauren
Muskoka, Ontario, Canada
2019

9

____

September

'Well?' I ask, holding the mirror up to show the back. 'What do you think?'

Marilyn concentrates on the reflected image, her red painted lips twitching to one side. 'Uh... I think a little more off, doll, if you don't mind.'

I run my fingers through her white-blonde hair, stopping just shy of the ends. 'I can go another inch?'

Marilyn nods.

'We can always do a last-minute trim before the big day,' I say, taking up my scissors.

Spending most of our session sharing the details of her son's wedding, set to take place in Hawaii – the family holidaying there beforehand – Marilyn emphasises how crucial it is to have her hair done by a hairdresser she can trust.

'What happened to your last hairdresser?'

Marilyn waves her hand, signifying some distant place.

'Gone. That's the problem with living in a holiday destination,' she sighs, 'people don't tend to stay.'

'I would have thought it would be the opposite.'

Marilyn shrugs, saying she is always glad for newcomers; they keep her in business. She asks how I like hairdressing – a question I'm not usually asked.

'It's alright,' I say, 'there's definitely an art to it and it puts me in the way of people, which is maybe something I need... But I've always loved the idea of studying natural medicine. Natural therapies are so much gentler on the body. There is so much untapped knowledge, you know?' I begin, surprised by the ease with which these words flow. 'I spoke to an indigenous elder once – she came to the girls' school back home to hold a smoking ceremony – and she took my breath away. Sharing knowledge of the medicinal qualities of various native plants; she, they, were so intelligent, so resourceful. I often think how reliant we've become on modern medicine; on finding a quick fix –'

'So why don't you?' Marilyn asks, as if it were just that easy. 'You could study part time, or online.'

'Right now,' I hesitate, 'I'm really just trying to put one foot in front of the other.'

'Sorry.' Marilyn tilts her head forward, as I even up both sides; gently reminding her to be still. 'How are you going anyway – with that room of 'stuff'?' Marilyn looks up from the hair falling over her face. 'You know, there was always a lock on that door, I doubt anyone had been inside that room for years before the last time your father returned....' Marilyn lifts her head, her gaze meeting mine via the mirror. There is a slight hesitation, a seriousness setting in around the corners of her lips as if she has something significant to say, her breathing audible. 'You know, your father –'

'Let's *not*... talk about my father,' I say, surprised how close I come to being rude. 'Sorry, I'm just not ready to go there.

But' I study the new length of Marilyn's hair. 'It is interesting, I suppose.'

'Always intrigued me,' Marilyn continues, seemingly unperturbed. 'A room full of secrets. Aren't you curious?'

'Yeah... I think, but it's just photographs and letters and stuff. I haven't really had time to look through it. But it's as if nothing was ever thrown away... If I take any more off...'

'Nope. Perfect,' Marilyn says, as I bring the mirror up; Marilyn, pushing her bob up with the palm of her hand as if to test its buoyancy. 'Just perfect... You know, a museum would love to get their hands on all that history!'

I raise an eyebrow, surprised that anyone might be more than mildly interested in a simple family history all in a shambles.

'You think?' I dust off loose hair, releasing the Velcro of Marilyn's smock.

'Definitely.'

Marilyn takes another look in the mounted mirror, tilting her head one way, then the other, her red painted lips curving into a satisfied smile. 'You should at least visit the Cambridge Archives before you throw any of it out. Cambridge includes the old area of Preston, where the letters were written. The folks there would be thrilled to know this kind of history still exists.'

I push the broom to one side while Marilyn fishes around in her purse for her wallet.

'Thank you so much,' she says before returning to the subject of the local archives. 'Gregory,' she announces. 'That's who you want to see... You know, if I'm being honest,' Marilyn hands over the cash. 'I may have already given him a heads up.'

I attempt to hand over the change to which Marilyn raises a hand. 'No; you severely undercharge.'

'O.K.' I say, pocketing the change into the back pocket of my denim skirt. 'Well, thank you.'

'No, thank you, and I hope you don't think I'm being too presumptuous; assuming you'd want to share your findings with the world. But letters like that,' Marilyn insists, indicating the box of letters I'd brought out onto the bench – yellowed envelopes overflowing a repurposed cardboard box with faded bananas pictured on the side. 'Well, they deserve to be shared... Don't you think?'

I bid Marilyn goodbye – my last client for the day, though I have amassed several in the short time I've begun hairdressing here – and glance up at the clock. *Three o'clock.* About half an hour before the girls will be making their way home from school.

If only to distract myself from thoughts of the girls' first day – whether they made friends, whether they are happy, whether they'll talk to me – and from thoughts of Nick that sting, I flick on the kettle then peer into the box as though it presents a threat. A coiled cobra, swollen and ready to strike. The very act of reaching inside the box, fills me with dread.

And yet, a strange electricity runs through me as I lay my hands upon the envelope resting on top. Addressed to *'Mr Austin Moss'.* I hold the envelope up to my nose, breathing it in before I sample a taste. Struck by the scent – tobacco and a faint perfume which I must surely be imagining – I open the envelope and fold out the carefully preserved, discoloured letter.

No sooner do I start reading, than I become fidgety at the words I can't easily decipher. There is so much alluded to that I cannot understand, but still. I am inexplicably restless and impatient to leave my seat for all sorts of reasons that make me uncomfortable. As the kettle clicks off, I rise without delay, then become lost in the brightly lit space of the fridge.

When I return to the bench, my hands almost stinging as I

cup the too-hot mug against my palms, I look across to the wall of windows and the world outside. The sky is free of clouds, yet I abandon my tea, and the letters, because it feels imperative to bring in the towels strung across the veranda.

Leaning against the railing, the stiffened towels draped over my shoulder, I look out to the water, my mind drifting as I begin thinking about time and place. How at one point, it might have been Errington admiring such a view; *her* fingertips brushing the warm, silky surface of the water. My musings, broken by the sound of the screen door blowing open, then shut, the spirits dancing in the wind.

Almost knocking over my cooled mug of tea, I return to the letters, selecting one at random. Somehow, I move past the barrier of the unfamiliar handwriting and read the letter in its entirety. The people and places are unknown, yet the voice of the letter is compelling. I select another, and another, until something changes in me, and old worries surge. I become stuck on the words; on what they might reveal. The last letter I read leaves an uncomfortable feeling and instead of selecting another, I examine the dates of the letters I've just read.

The first letter is from 1905, the next 1908, then 1906. This sense of disorder, along with that uncomfortable feeling and my general resistance to unearth the past, propels me to return the letters to their box. Because my life is already such a mess. Because, really, what would be the point in digging up the past?

Sitting beside the box, once ripe with fruit, now stale with largely untouched letters, I hear the door go; the girls returning home with smiling faces and a whole lot of homework.

Greeting the girls, I push the box to one side: abandoning the past for the present.

10

We finish the school week with a quick dip, drying off in front of a movie at home but in the end, I am the only one watching. Em ditches the movie to hang out in her room and Zoe falls asleep on the couch. Hearing me put Zoe to bed – bleary-eyed and with popcorn down her front – Em resurfaces from her room, lingering in the hallway, animated and ready for a chat.

Following me in and out of the bathroom as I brush my teeth, and she hers, Em plants herself at the edge of my bed, crossed-legged and wide awake, sharing her experience of the new school and the kids she has met; some even living close by.

'Everything is so different, Mum,' Em says. 'Even the lockers feel unique.'

With my head sinking into the pillow, just so tired but loving the way my daughter is opening up like a flower reaching for the sun, dreamily, I listen. My body feels a little tingly; it's relief that she is happy. Joy, at my daughter's happiness and the beautiful woman she is becoming and that I am here to witness the transformation day by day; pain, that, Nick is not.

The next morning, I lie between the sheets, breathing slow, deep breaths, tracing the knots of the ceiling with my eyes, greeting the new day with a calmness and presence of mind. This sense of quiet, soon replaced by the sound of the television blaring as if it were right beside me. As I tie the sash of my dressing gown and move towards the stairs, my nostrils pick up the smell of bacon.

'You can take over,' Em says, stepping away from the spitting pan.

Urging Zoe to turn down the T.V., I turn down the burner and plant a kiss at Em's forehead. Em disappears back upstairs, and I make myself a cup of tea.

After breakfast, we throw on our bathers, wet from the day before, and head down to the dock. The leaves are turning, the temperature is falling, and every swim feels like it might be the last of the season.

The girls last in the water longer than I do and as I laze about on the dock, my body blanketed by a towel, I melt into the sun's warmth, shutting my eyes against the speckled sunlight housed within my straw hat; opening my eyes to the voices that call out across the water. I sit up in my chair, pushing my hat back.

'Who are they?' I ask Em, squinting into the sun, witnessing older kids jumping off a rocky ledge and plunging into the water. 'Well, they seem to know you.'

Em opens one eye, then pushes up from the dock in a small push-up to face away from the sun. 'Just kids from school, I guess.'

Despite the huge amount of fun being had across the water and Em's previous enthusiasm for the kids at school, she seems reluctant to engage. But when I return from the house with a tray of hotdogs generously topped with ketchup and grated cheese; I discover the kids from the rocky platform have rowed over to greet her.

'Oh, hello,' I say with a dopey grin and my arms full.

The kids smile back at me, a little awkwardly. A girl with short, dripping plaits and a sunburnt nose explains she lives just across from us.

Em looks mildly uncomfortable when I suggest the kids stay and hang out, but the girl who introduces herself as Aimee, appears delighted, hopping back in her boat to tell her parents of the plan.

'Right,' Em hops up when the girls from school are out of earshot. 'You go grab some grub; I'll get the fire started.'

'*I'll* get the fire started,' I say, wrapping my towel around my waist, glancing over to Zoe, wrapping her prune-like fingers around the soft, golden bun, tomato sauce creating dimples at her cheeks. '*You* watch your sister while I duck out. And stay out of the water while I'm gone, Ok?'

Pulling up to the cottage with a carload of groceries, I pop open the trunk and load myself up, taking the uneven concrete steps as disproportionate scales, realising my own carelessness – how easy it would be to slip, my vision restricted by an armful of groceries. Following the sound of music blaring, I carry the groceries around the side of the house to the veranda, dropping them at my feet.

Em and her new friends are gathered around the fire pit. The music is playing from a portable speaker. I peer through the screen door behind me. The house appears quiet, the T.V. switched off. I call out to Zoe but there is no answer.

Taking the stepping stones two at a time, I then call out to Em. Em turns down the speaker.

'Where's Zo?' I repeat.

Em shrugs.

'She's not by the water?'

Em's new friends slouch around the fire pit as if this is their regular hang. One prods the fire with a stick which bothers me, but I am consumed with finding Zoe.

Striding toward the dock, I pass between the walls of knotty wood. Laughter comes from behind as I step into the sunlight pressing through the trees. Much closer than the distant voices heard from the fire pit.

'You didn't see me,' the voice teases as I peer back inside the boathouse.

Zoe is laid back in an inflated red and yellow donut resting between boating equipment. She looks up at me, peering over the pages of her sister's magazine. I take up the magazine, scanning its content.

'You scared me.'

'Sorry.'

I hand back the magazine. 'Alright, well, I'd like you to come up, ok? I don't like you being so close to the water on your own.'

Zoe pulls a face, mocking a drooping bottom lip. Her mood changes rapidly when I mention I bought marshmallows.

As I walk back through the boathouse, I notice the girl with plaits and sunburnt nose fling something into the fire – 'That'll get her going!'

Em smiles until she catches my gaze. The other girls laugh. Another kid flings an empty can of soda into the flames. Instinctively, I move toward the intense orange glow. Then, suddenly, I see it. Faded bananas printed on the disintegrating form of a box disappearing into nothing. A coiled cobra thrashing about; consumed by the flames.

'Where did you get that box?'

'Mum. *Relax.*'

The girl with sunburn goes red. Em storms ahead, leading

back toward the house. Both of us, stepping over the groceries, charge into the kitchen.

'Oh my God, Mum. Oh my God.'

'Those were not your letters,' I say, coldly. 'I can't even...' I stop myself from saying something I know I'll regret. 'I think your friends should go.'

'Mum –' Em protests.

I sink down to the floor, my face buried in my hands. And though I do not look up, I feel Em there and sense when she is gone. I hear footsteps fall upon the stairs, Em projecting as she takes the last of the steps.

'What do you care, anyway?'

It is painful even to breathe.

Everything. Those letters meant everything.

I raise my head a few inches from my bent knees. Em shoves a folder in front of my face. The shiny plastic, too close to reveal its contents.

'Look at it,' Em commands.

Slowly, I turn the pages of plastic pockets. Filed there, are the letters. The first ones marked *1905*. They appear to be in date order.

'Wanted to surprise you...' Em says. 'Didn't think you'd need the box.'

Austin & Errington
Preston, Ontario, Canada
1905

11

December

The reunion between Austin and Errington isn't at all what Errington had imagined. Austin's letters, sent in the form of a post card discreetly enclosed in an envelope, had ceased several weeks before her return to Maplecroft and while Austin had assured Errington – more than once, but only ever in the briefest of moments – that he'd thrown himself into work for the very purpose of accelerating the happy moment of her return, Errington couldn't help but wonder whether his interest in her might be waning. Despite her recent European Odyssey – Errington's descriptions of the wonders of man and nature recorded within her leather-bound journal worthy of publication – Errington considers her own life rather dull in contrast to the life Austin has led as a wanderer and adventurer. The life of a *'rolling stone.'*

Austin too, is surprised by the feeling he derives from the limited interactions with Errington, who is proving true to her sex in that she is becoming increasingly difficult to read – her manner is not unlike her very first letter in which she maintained the strictest of formalities. Indeed, it feels as though the pair have barely caught a single moment alone. And as he feels it will be rather too bold to write to Errington at home, without first consulting Mr Pattinson, Austin must rely on fleeting looks and the very rare, but precious brush of hands to convey his affection for her. Nonetheless, she is the only woman that has ever truly taken him by surprise; her fire, her daring, so well concealed from others.

It is Christmas time at Maplecroft. Outside, the snow is gently falling. Inside, the house is resplendent with Christmas cheer; the tall pine, newly cut, is layered in drippings of thick red bows, paper chains and hanging ornaments. It is the only season for which Mr Pattinson allows such displays of opulence; every detail, down to the scent of pine, a reminder of his late wife, Maisie, follows the traditions paying homage to her German heritage. Her maiden name, Erb, is also the name of Preston's founding fathers – not only is Errington daughter to one of Preston's wealthiest businessmen, but also a descendant of Preston's founding fathers.

Passing the ever-winding staircase decorated with laurel – the smell of pine infused with hints of cinnamon, maple glazed ham wafting in from the kitchen – Austin enters the drawing room and is immediately drawn to Errington, though their greeting is brief.

Dressed in silk the colour of Christmas – an angel standing before the tree – Errington is engaged by Ida, who fervently takes her hands in her own to relive the memory of a dearly departed sister and mother; whose presence and absence is made more acute by the holiday season. Austin finds himself next to his brother, who, enjoying the luxury of having an audience, waffles on about furniture sales projections; about expanding his design to incorporate pieces inspired by simple church pews; about plans for the new year; about the many ways he continues to spend Austin's funds. Doing his best to fix his gaze on Frank's face, but can't help his eyes wandering to the far side of the room.

'You're finding this a bore,' Frank declares, the ice clinking against his whisky glass as he takes a sip. 'That's one thing about being a good businessman,' he adds, 'your mind is always on the job.'

From across the room, Ida and Errington raise their glasses. The patterned carpet is a vast ocean between the island of Frank's boasting and the waiting oasis of Errington. *'He must go – go – go away from here! On the other side of the world he's overdue,'* Austin thinks, remembering Kipling's poem, 'The Feet of the Young Men,' and the way it spoke to his restless nature some years ago, of how it speaks to him now.

'Perhaps, you'd like to admire the Christmas tree up close?' Eddie quietly suggests to Austin, after bonding with Lynn over university life, 'assuming, Moss, that is what's capturing your attention on the far side of the room?'

Eddie crosses the floor with such ease; Austin is almost dumbfounded – but deeply grateful for the rescue.

'Tell me,' Eddie says, addressing Ida. 'I wonder, as the lady of the house, how do you find the local dispensary? Are medicines readily available here?'

Ida, a twinkle in her eye, is only too happy to discuss the great many concoctions sold at the dispensary to local housewives. Laudanum, practically on tap. The use of alcohol, a remedy to a great many things, often acquired through self-diagnosis.

Austin holds his breath as his whole body unconsciously moves toward Errington, admiring the ornaments of the Christmas tree, placed there by her brothers and sisters, Errington does not turn around, but rather senses *him* there – the neighbouring conversation, concerning all kinds of reme-

dies Errington is wholly familiar with, fading into the background.

Blending with the smell of pine, cinnamon, the sweetness of maple syrup and the lingering memory of Ida's rosewater perfume, are notes of shaving cream, port infused tobacco. Breathing in this heady scent, Errington feels the boning of her corset tighten; a light-headedness as her breathing becomes more constricted. There is a warmth, a tingling. Her cheeks feel as though they are on fire. It is too pleasurable, and yet too painful to turn around.

Austin examines the loose tendrils that escape Errington's pompadour and fall along her slender neck – his own words failing him in the closeness of her orange blossom scent, the soft line of her bare shoulders – and, intentionally misquoting Sir Walter Bessant, he breathes, '*Nellie's blushing cheeks...*'

Slowly, Errington turns, a sensual undressing to reveal her cheeks full of colour, though her gaze suddenly reaches past Austin.

Indeed, the whole room turns inwards, simultaneously. It is only Austin who takes a moment to register the man suddenly featuring in Errington's gaze. Austin's eyes move up from black, fine leather boots to dark fitted trousers, along the gold buttons of the burgundy waistcoat and black velvet jacket, to the cravat, also burgundy, adorned with a gold pin in the shape of a rose, a black jewel at its centre. Austin's gaze focusses on that jewel, mysterious and exotic, like its wearer.

Errington takes a breath, filling her lungs with as much air as her corset will allow. Austin can hear the way her breathing alters.

'Why Tony!' Errington declares with an overly enthusiastic European greeting, pressing her cheek to his, an audible smooching. 'How long it's been!'

'Yes, your father sent me a very kind invitation. Did he not inform you?'

Errington looks to Father, offering a wry smile. *Clearly not.*

'Welcome son,' Mr Pattinson says to this much-anticipated guest. 'A year in Spain, not to mention your years studying abroad, appear to have served you well... I do hope you are not offended by the impromptu nature of my invitation. I'd only just read of your return in *The Daily*.'

'Not at all,' the handsome stranger says with boyish delight, his dark eyes twinkling, light bouncing off his black, slicked back hair. 'I assure you, I'm only too glad to be here.'

'Why,' Errington declares, 'we've barely seen one another since our days at Preston Public School – Austin, this is Antonio De la Rosa – Tony, this is Austin Moss.'

'Errington's *uncle*,' George interjects, defining Austin in this way.

'Pleased to make your acquaintance,' Antonio says, offering little acknowledgement of Austin beyond a brief handshake, before turning to Errington. 'Come now, we've seen each other since then, in fact... Oh, it's not for me to say, but, oh my, how you've grown.'

Errington bats the air with her hand as if batting away a mosquito, and Austin is suddenly reminded of a play on words she'd written in one of her letters, combining his name with a pesky insect. ('A Moss-quito') Now, in this moment, at least for Austin, the joke feels like a fitting amalgamation of terms.

Watching this scene unfold – Errington's affection for this stranger; Mr Pattinson practically falling over himself to ensure his new guest's comfort, insisting that this olive-skinned baby-faced businessman, evidently a lawyer, be seated next to Errington at dinner – seeing all of this, makes Austin feel something of an imposter. There as a guest and

Frank's brother, but with no official claim to Errington, Austin can't help but feel a little cheated. As his discomfort becomes intolerable, he escapes the room, 'to take some air' and try to hold on to his rising temper; a rather unfortunate, inherited trait.

A freezing whip of air sends Austin promptly back inside, but not before he downs the entire glass of whisky still in his hand – the glass he accepted earlier to calm his nerves despite his usual vow against liquor. Now it provides the kick he so sorely needs to go back inside and face this Spanish fiend.

'Do I know the family?' Antonio asks between courses.

Errington tilts her head in question. She's forgotten how forward her childhood chum can be. *Perhaps, this is the Spanish way, and I never noticed before.*

'Beg your pardon?' she says, buying some time, while considering how to answer. 'I'm not sure I take your meaning.'

Antonio leans in a little closer, pointing towards her plate as if to ask a question of the meal, perhaps, commenting on the sauce or referring to the surprising tenderness of the braised ox heart, the indulgent taste of potatoes roasted in duck fat. 'There is a glow to your cheeks,' he says. 'You cannot hide it from me.'

Errington lowers her gaze, taking in the largely untouched food on her plate; or, perhaps, lifting it to survey the elaborate table decorations, topped with the oranges left in the children's Christmas stockings by 'Saint Nick'.

'Come on then,' he says. 'Surely, time hasn't turned you into a lady like this?'

Errington wonders why being called a 'lady' seems faintly insulting. She looks at Antonio whose boyish charm reminds her of Lynn; but is dressed in a sophisticated style that Lynn tries hard to avoid.

'Oh,' Errington says, 'I rather think it has.'

Antonio's gaze remains fixed; he reminds her of a child waiting for penny candy to fall into his eager hand.

'If you must know,' Errington begins, knowing that Antonio is unlikely to drop the subject without some small morsel of information to carry away with him. 'I dare say, yes, you may know of the family... You always made it your business to know everything about everyone when you lived here – and you'll do the same from your law office in New York, I'm sure.'

'That is true,' Antonio hesitates, '...unless I have reason to stay.'

Antonio raises a glass to Mr Pattinson who presides over the meal from the head of the table, the overseer, the overlord, the Grand Master. 'So where's that smile gone then, eh?' Antonio asks, as his little finger makes its way to Errington's own delicate pinkie giving it a squeeze, like two rings falling together and then apart. 'I'll bet he's not as attentive as you would you like, am I right?'

Errington searches Antonio's face framed by his dark slicked-back hair and decides it's safer not to answer.

'See,' he continues, 'I know you better than you may think. Listen, Nell, I've never known you to hold your tongue before. Especially when there's an injustice at play. And if you are not receiving the attention you deserve; that is, indeed, a grave injustice.'

Errington gives Antonio a look. Antonio shrugs, turning out his open palms.

'I'm simply saying that if something is bothering you; you'd best say.'

Errington lets the advice settle as Antonio takes up his cutlery to carve through the ox heart.

'Thank you.'

'You're welcome. And –' Antonio lays down his fork, 'just, in case, things don't go as planned; you know where I'll be.'

Errington has to stop herself from rolling her eyes.

'But –' Antonio continues, unperturbed by Errington's challenging stare. 'A word of warning. One of these days, another fair maiden may steal my heart *and* agree to marry me.'

AFTER A SERVING OF STEAMING PLUM PUDDING swimming in rich custard, Austin – the recipient of a penny concealed within his portion – is glad now of Elizabeth's announcement that 'the hour for sherry and a great many songs is upon us.' Her declaration made with a flourish, as though removing cloth from a magician's magic box.

Eager to disengage from the current seating arrangement, Austin is in much better spirits, volunteering that 'Eddie is quite the pianist.'

Not needing any further encouragement, Eddie sets himself up at the piano, briefly examining the sheet music. Elizabeth stands at his shoulder, ready to engage in song as Eddie works his fingers along the black and white keys. Her sometimes unpolished exterior, reinforced by an often forthright manner, is dispelled with the opening up of her lungs, revealing a charming young woman, equipped with the voice of an angel.

At the song's conclusion, Elizabeth proposes, 'a tribute to Mother,' handing Eddie the sheet music to 'O Tannenbaum,' which, of course, he is familiar with. A song, Errington knows word for word, despite requiring a miniature book of German phrases while travelling across Europe.

In his emerald green armchair, George sits, his walrus-like

moustache curling into a broad grin. The vision of his daughters united in song – despite Ruth being much too shy to showcase her own voice, pure and sweet – gives George a feeling of warmth, a happy reminder of his late wife and her love of music, making her presence feel infinitely more real.

It is, indeed, a beautiful tribute, and leads to a great many songs; a perfect way to conclude the evening. That is, until Antonio pleads with a smug kind of charm, 'If you would be so kind, just one more song?'

He is speaking to the crowd as a whole, to the host, to the pianist; but really, he is speaking to Errington.

Errington appears reluctant to engage in this duet, but after a little coaxing from Mr Pattinson, she concedes. Antonio's voice – honeyed with charm, delivering the mechanics of an opera singer – gives Austin an ill feeling. The rest of the gathered assembly appear to be in awe. Even Eddie declares at the conclusion of Silent Night, 'This man can sing!' Yet another strike against Austin, who doesn't dare reveal his own mediocre singing voice.

DESPITE TAKING AUSTIN'S WHISPER TO MEAN SO much more than the poem's depiction of *'blushing cheeks'* – Errington experiences yet another restless night. It is in the wee hours of morning, looking out at the moon and stars, the ever-present Cassiopeia never dipping below the horizon in the North American sky, that Errington finally elects to follow Antonio's advice. *If something is bothering you; you best say.*

Perhaps, Antonio is right – perhaps, love isn't a game to be played; perhaps, sometimes it is best to speak plainly. Charming and – objectively – handsome, Antonio had always been misguided in his affection toward Errington. She could never concede to marry a man who cared more for wealth than for words (unless he thought those words could be used to increase his wealth). Perhaps now, Errington considers, Antonio is finally willing to be as she has always regarded him; a very dear friend.

As the sun rises in the sky, glistening on the snow, Errington steps out, enveloped in her long winter coat with gold buttons along the bust, mitts, snow shoes and a floppy winter hat, not unlike a gentleman's night cap. Avoiding passing her father's woollen mills, Errington crosses over to Potter Street, walks down to the Business Section and back along King Street towards the General Store where she will avail herself of the telephone.

Within the tiny room attached to the back of the store – an alteration made to the original building with the coming of new technology – Errington turns the crank on the telephone box and waits for the operator. Speaking slowly into the mouthpiece – not simply to avoid an unpleasant whistling sound, but to avoid having to repeat her request, Errington asks for a connection to be made with the Preston Furniture Co.

Contrary to Errington's expectation, there is little delay.

'Good morning, Preston Furniture Co., Moss speaking.'

It's him. She hadn't expected it to be him. At the very least, Errington thought she would have to go through a 'receptionist' – *a new and novel term! Isn't the English language a marvel with its ever-evolving acquisition of words?* Were it not for the $1.50 already gobbled up by the telephone – though Father would hardly miss it – and the journey she'd made specifically for this purpose, Errington would have gladly returned the earpiece and left Mr Wurster's General Store.

'Hello...? Preston Furniture Co. This is Austin Moss...'

Errington's heart begins to race, she is lost for words,

caught off guard. The small space dedicated for the use of the telephone begins to feel smaller still.

'It's me,' she says, clearing her throat. 'It's... Errington.'

'Oh.'

Errington can't tell whether he's glad, or not.

'Well, this is a surprise,' Austin says, eager delight creeping into his voice.

'Yes... I hope I've not caught you at a bad time?'

'No, no, I...'

There is a hissing sound travelling down the telephone line. Errington holds out the earpiece, replacing it to her ear.

'Are you quite well?' comes Austin's voice via the earpiece.

'Yes,' Errington replies. 'Yes, I'm quite...'

Errington looks back toward Mr Wurster at the counter, cutting off a portion of cheese to place on metal scales.

'In actual fact,' Errington begins, returning her attention back to the telephone call. 'I'm not well at all. Indeed, I am rather miserable.' There is an astounded silence at the other end of the line. 'If this is a bad time...?' Errington asks.

'No,' Austin exclaims with a croaky voice, 'please con –'

But Austin is cut off by a horrible whistling echoing through the telephone. Errington waits for it to pass.

'If I may speak plainly,' Errington says, finally. 'One moment you are cajoling me with poetry. The next, you're leaving my letters unanswered with not so much as a word.' Errington's heated breath crackles through the telephone line. 'And it is disheartening because... Well, I rather thought...' she took a deep breath. *Say it!* '... I thought there might be *something* there.'

'Yes,' Austin replies, urgently. 'Yes, I rather thought so –'

Further whistling and rustling through the telephone line delays any further response.

'I'm sorry –' Austin begins.

'No, I'm –'

'It's just that I really must go. My brother is due to burst through the door at any moment, but I wish to assure you...'

'Yes?' She almost blushed at the eager note in her voice.

There is a tapping on the glass. Gentle, but seemingly thunderous. Errington ignores the intruding sound, her gloved hands clenching the earpiece more tightly than before.

'Yes, I... I'm sorry, I really must g –'

Before Errington even has time to replace the earpiece, the tapping at the glass starts up again.

Something dark is brewing within. And without a moment's notice; quite out of character, a total departure from Errington's *sweet, womanly nature,*' her voice enquires, irritably: 'Can I help you?!'

Through the immediate welling of tears, Errington spies Mrs O'Hare, one hand clutching the top of her high-waisted skirt which has become noticeably tighter over the passing weeks – a happy circumstance to fill the void of her only son being at boarding school. Replacing the earpiece, Errington is reluctant to remove herself from the little room.

'I'm sorry,' Errington says as Mrs O'Hare draws near, handing Errington a handkerchief.

'I wouldn't worry,' Mrs O'Hare says, a gold locket resting over her belly. 'If he's true, he'll stick by you.'

'And if he's not?' Errington asks, strangely unperturbed by what Mrs O'Hare might have heard, gratefully wiping away tears with Mrs O'Hare's white, embroidered handkerchief.

Mrs O'Hare wrinkles up her nose as if catching a whiff of pollen in the air. 'Well then, if he's not – you're a strong, young woman. You mustn't let a gentleman dampen your usual zest.'

Walking past the other patrons – including Hobson, the Pattinson butler quickly disappearing behind a day-old copy of *The Galt Daily Reporter*; and Mr Wurster scooping sugar out of a barrel into a paper bag resting on scales – Errington prepares to replace her snow shoes and brace herself against the cold.

On the way home, she takes into account things she'd previously failed to consider. The leaning in at the dinner table, the close conversation between her and Antonio. Antonio's little finger finding its way to hers – a signal from childhood, demonstrating the strength of their friendship at times when Errington had found herself on the outer, generally preferring books to people. The duet. How things with Antonio must have seemed to an onlooker.

With a guilty conscience and a sore head, Errington returns home, wrestling with *'that tired feeling'* Doctor Vardon claims to be a product of her sex. Slipping out of her snowshoes and pinching off her gloves, Errington quietens her activity to hear the voices coming from inside. As it isn't the first Wednesday of the month – their designated day for guests – and Errington is unaware of any other engagements, it is a surprise to discover they have company at Maplecroft.

'Have a seat, my dear,' Father says, as Errington comes into the drawing room.

Errington remains standing, resisting the fate she knows is coming. A fate of doing little else but lazing around and growing fat; *'...being rubbed with alcohol and fed with calves foot jelly and sweet breads and all sorts of delicacies.'* A fate that comes around too often with the coming of her menses. But resisting is like trying to remain upright when the air feels close and black spots begin to fill her vision.

Wiping his red nose with a handkerchief, before replacing it in the opening of his sleeve, it is Doctor Vardon who speaks next, rising to his feet while keeping a steady hand on the arm of his chair. Not simply to counteract any doubts his patient might be having, but because he is a man incapable of sitting still. A man in a rush, irrespective of whether he has somewhere to be.

'My dear,' Doctor Vardon says, speaking to Errington in hushed tones as though she were his own sweet child, or more likely, his grandchild. 'We needn't speak of your emotionally-charged behaviour, except to say – and I think you must agree – it evidences your need to rest. My, how tired you look! Those dark circles have crept back, haven't they? And, not to mention, you are so very thin...'

Giving him stare for stare, she examines Doctor Vardon's own sunken cheeks, his slight physique, but presses her lips together, before letting herself fall into the peach velvet upholstered rocking chair perched at the edge of the room.

'Very good.' Doctor Vardon says, clapping his hands together. 'Now, this time, let's see if we can't give those books of yours a rest too, hmm? Quiet the mind.'

Doctor Vardon walks over to an open book on the side table. 'One of yours, I presume?'

Errington nods.

Doctor Vardon picks up the book, examining the page with mild interest before slamming it shut.

After nestling between the sheets – a place she will quickly tire of given that there are only so many times she may endure Mrs Roantree reading aloud in that squeaky voice of hers, and it's her one small distraction – Errington engages in one last act of defiance. By the dull light of a candle, she pushes open the window, which squeaks in complaint. The gush of cool air is an escape route for an intended cloud of smoke. Placing the cigarette between her lips, she strikes the match. Having set up a tray at the edge of her bed – a little wobbly but nonetheless a workable arrangement – Errington dips the nib in ink and starts to write.

Ellen Errington Pattinson
Maplecroft, Preston, Ont.

30 December 1905

Mr Austin Moss,
    PRESTON, Ontario.

Dear Austin,

I can only apologise for the way I behaved. I had been stewing over things since before Christmas. Please do forgive the icy – and incoherent – telephone call.

I write also to inform you of another matter.

Dr Vardon, a few minutes ago informed Father that 'this girl is passing from the sublime to the ridiculous!' The train of reasoning is quite beyond my powers, but he has decided – perhaps because it is a respectable institution and equidistant between the two extremes that bed is the most suitable place for me.

Yours,
Nell

Placing the cigarette down, Errington blows out smoke before reaching for her perfume bottle – much like the medicine bottles resting at her bedside. Lifting the stopper, she dabs this natural distillation of fragrance on her finger, pressing it against the letter to leave her mark.

12

September 1906

Opposite Preston Public School, there is music; coming not from the band shell in the centre of Central Park as is usual on a Friday night – the band marching half a block in song from the top floor of the Fire Hall, their place of practice, to entertain the townspeople gathered at Central Park. Instead, this music comes from across the park, past the three-tiered fountain and the street-lamp overhanging one of the many park benches dotted along Central Park, to the other side of the winding path. Inside the Opera House, young ladies stand in their finest, dance cards at the ready; young men, and those, not so young, but bachelors nonetheless, taking up a tiny dangling pencil to scribble down their initials beside the Two Step or the Waltz.

'Save a dance for me, Little Nell,' Austin whispered one morning as the congregants converged on house of God; Austin and Errington timing their entry to 'accidentally'

brush past one another. Errington responding to his request with a cheeky smile – knowing she shall reserve several dances just for him.

Austin looks at the dance program, the one gifted to him as he walked through the double doors of the dance hall. He turns it over in his hands. *'Assembly at Preston Opera House'* printed on the front. The names of the stewards, J. L. Pattinson among others, printed on the back; Lynn, ever the dutiful son and well-rounded citizen, here in an official capacity leaving little time to dance with the ladies. Austin opens up the program to consider how many spaces he may fill on Errington's dance card without drawing attention.

Slowly, as the months went by, Errington had returned to society; to church, ladies' auxiliary, Sunday dinners at Maplecroft – the latter, Austin and Errington's greatest opportunity to lay eyes upon one another. *'Sunday evenings are a great institution, aren't they?'* A thought that lifts Austin's spirits multiple times during the week as he works for Frank in the factory, balancing the books and scheduling shipments of finely made furniture.

Austin is looking down at his program, examining the sketch of a woman mid-step – skirts swept back against her ankles, satin sash flowing out behind, opposite a gentleman partner dressed in simple black suit and boater hat – when a voice rouses him from his dreaming.

'Beg your pardon?' Austin asks, stepping to one side, imagining he is blocking the line of dancers and the flow of rustling skirts moving around the room as the music encourages them to soar.

'Is that your name, I see?' asks a woman, whose breasts threaten to escape the seam of her bodice. 'There are so many names scribbled there and I cannot for the life of me make out those initials,' says the voluptuous woman, adding, as she looks into the grey-blue of Austin's eyes, 'though, I dare say, I would remember if it was *you* who signed my dance card.'

She brings her dance card closer for Austin to make out the name printed beside the next Two Step about to commence.

Examining the program, Austin is surprised to discover his initials 'A.M.' written in messy script. 'Indeed...'

The woman claps her hands together, pushing her breasts closer together, her whole body squeezing in response to her delight.

'What I mean to say is,' Austin says hastily, scrambling to find the words. 'Indeed, the initials are rather difficult to decipher, but I'm afraid, it is not I who is entitled to have this next dance.'

'Oh, but I've been watching you,' says the woman, touching her hand to her chest, motioning that she speaks from the heart – or her breast. 'You're yet to engage in a single dance. Now, that's just a little unfair, Mr...?'

'Moss,' Austin says, recognising the woman standing before him as the daughter of Chief Loy, one of the many important public figures Austin had met at The Lodge; sure too, that this woman knows who he is. 'And you're Miss Mary Loy, aren't you?'

'Indeed, I am!' Despite her father's position, Miss Loy seems almost unreasonably impressed that in a town of just over two thousand people, this 'handsome, worldly man' – her words – knows her name; taking it to mean he has surely noticed her before.

Seeing no way to avoid it without causing considerable offence, and after a degree of coaxing, Austin takes her hand and the pair circle the room amidst a sea of rustling skirts floating around ankles like fast moving clouds. Spinning his dance partner around, Austin steals a quick glance at the woman before him as they continue to progress around the room. As he looks, he sees what he imagines to be there. The *'bright eyes'* of his own sweetheart shining under the twinkling chandelier. The dimple at her cheek. Revelling in *her* company, everything is as it should be – until his dance partner speaks.

'Hmm?'

'I said,' Miss Loy leans into Austin. 'I'm not the one you came here for, am I?'

Austin bows his head; it's time for the truth. 'I'm afraid, you've found me out,' he says, as politely as possible, before thanking this voluptuous but largely forgettable young woman for the dance and leaving the dance hall.

Outside, Austin does not feel a chill, as, perhaps, he should, but rather a warmth at being back by Errington's side. Her imagined presence, '*...not the Rose, but near the Rose,*' as close as he may come on this night; nonetheless, the mere thought rendering this night enchanting. '*Like bloom of peach, so softly spread.*' Together, they stroll along King Street, past Frank's factory and up over the bridge, heading towards the mineral springs, but really, just ambling; togetherness, their only destination.

Austin is just about to offer up a cigarette from the silver case inside Errington's jacket – the case and jacket, both of which he'd been meaning to return – when he hears a commotion coming from the Kress Hotel.

Unperturbed, he walks on; it is not his fight. Though difficult to decipher, the voices grow louder.

'I wouldn't go in there,' says a young lad upon Austin's approach, straightening his cap. 'Two fellas got the hump over a lady and what started out as a barney –' The sound of broken glass cuts through the night air, breaking up his train of thought.

The shattering of glass operates as its own kind of stereoscope, recalling past memories in a series of photographic images. A tavern brawl onboard the *R.M.S. Caronia* as if Austin were there now, still making his way across the Atlantic. The vision of Austin's chum from Klerksdorp, fuelled with equal parts of liquor and anger, being thrown against a wall of shelves containing spirits. The crash of bottles like the bursting of shrapnel. The gushing waterfall, much too easy to set alight; should a person seek to 'play with fire.'

With every thud and crash on board the *R.M.S. Caronia* is the flash of war. The cry to *'Fix Bayonets!'* The Missus hitting the ground with a thud at the clean shot fired. The weight of a dead Boer's lifeless body rendering Austin immovable.

The young lad at the hotel's entrance lunges backwards as the tornado of wrestling erupts through the tavern door.

As men try to peel the opponents apart – both men reeking of alcohol – it is clear the brawl is not evenly matched. The one, visibly stronger – bulk and muscle tight beneath his shirt – manoeuvres the other into a headlock. As if watching a building go up in flames, a thing of beauty and destruction, Austin stands back, letting the fight unfold; distancing himself, dismissing it as a little 'rough play.' *Sometimes it is best to let a man rid himself of anger, rather than to throw yourself in the line of fire.*

But as the red face with bulging veins begins to turn purple, Austin notes a scar above the left eye, recognising the underdog as the young lad who works at the Pattinson Woollen Mills – introduced to Austin as a *'fine example of a worker'* during a tour led by Mr Pattinson who now insists upon being referred to as 'George'. *Please,* he'd said to Austin, *we're practically brothers.*

The lad cannot be more than seventeen, still growing; no match for Bobby Black whose brutish behaviour is typical of a Saturday night.

'Fire!' Austin yells, with manufactured alarm. 'By George, there's a fire!'

Nestled in a crowd, it is surprising how quickly Austin is able to raise the alarm. How quickly others take up his words, indeed, spreading like wildfire. 'Fire?' other men cry. 'Did someone say fire?!'

Of course, it is all smoke and mirrors. The enormous amount of liquor pooling on the tavern floor – perhaps, thankfully not being soaked up by sawdust; no longer the 'done' thing except at the butcher's – has not been set alight. There are no raging flames. No orange glow. But the diversion itself is enough to free the lad from the headlock cutting off his blood supply.

Scraping himself up off the floor, bloodied and doused in alcohol and whisky-covered shards, the kid scrambles to make his escape, lunging right into the arms of law enforcement.

Knowing not what the scrap was about, Austin makes for the Town Hall, where the police station is housed. Stepping past the tall, white columns of the building's entrance to make enquiries, Austin discovers the lad is to spend the night unless bail is made.

'May I speak with him?' Austin asks.

Austin's interaction takes place not with Chief Loy – Preston's Chief of Police, and Mary Loy's father – but with Sergeant O'Hare; a man with distinctly red hair, the same flash of colour Austin had seen onboard the train the day he arrived in Preston. A boy named Freddy.

The policeman's rank is denoted by the epaulettes on his shoulders.

'It's not standard practice to admit members of the public until bail is received,' says Sergeant O'Hare, whose calm manner is decidedly different to that of his son's.

Remembering the boy who sat on his hands to stop himself from fidgeting, Austin wonders whether the boy will mellow over time to resemble his father. A question Austin had often asked of himself. For, in the young boy, Austin recognised his own restlessness, a trait he's possessed since birth, if only to prove his worthiness of life; of surviving his birth, when his mother had not.

'I believe I met your wife and son on board the *Grand Trunk,* months ago,' Austin says. 'Your son is most curious about the world; a keen observer. He noted the dust of the veldt on my bag, and we got to talking about South Africa.'

'South Africa? Are you a veteran, sir?'

'Indeed, I am,' Austin replies. 'And I believe your brother-in-law also fought as a hussar.'

'Yes,' Sergeant O'Hare draws a thin smile. 'Yes, he did.'

Sergeant O'Hare leans forward over the counter and points toward the far cell. 'Tell you what,' he says, remembering now his wife's retelling of the kind man on the train who'd indulged their son – the boy's inquisitive nature is ever a problem in a world where children are to be 'seen and not heard.' 'I don't see that having a quick word could do much harm, do you?'

THE YOUNG LAD BEHIND BARS – WHO APPEARS TO have sobered up a great deal – looks up at Austin, a little stunned.

'Yes, sir.' says the lad at Austin's introduction. 'I remember, sir. But please, why have you come? Don't tell the boss I've been banged up here. I'll get the sack for sure!'

Austin lowers his hand as if to temper the lad's anxiety. 'You needn't worry about that, lad. I have no intention of doing anything of the sort, though I cannot speak for the papers. I dare say none of us has a hope of visiting the lavatory without it being noted.'

As time wore on, Austin had come to understand this of Preston – while, initially, it was Errington who had exercised caution in her interactions with Austin under the gaze of prying eyes; now, it is Austin who treads with care. He recognises that with his name comes the vulnerability of public recognition, and that, unlike before, Austin has something to lose. A treasure that shall keep him here.

'But tell me,' Austin asks the question as if merely thinking aloud. 'All this over a woman?'

'I was defending her honour, sir,' says the young lad. 'I won't have no-one say a single false word about her,' he continues, pressing his face against the metal bars to conceal his scar. 'I know she's above my station, sir, but love is love. No-one can deny that.'

'No,' Austin agrees. 'I don't suppose they can.'

'Which is why you mustn't say anything to Mr Pattinson,' the young lad says, gripping the bars. 'Please sir, it'll be the end of me if you do.'

Austin takes a moment to arrange his thoughts concerning a man he is yet to figure out.

'I'm sure Mr Pattinson is a forgiving man,' he suggests – despite believing there was something slightly odd about the way Mr Pattinson warmed to him practically overnight; Austin couldn't help but think of *Matthew 5:44; 'Love your enemies, bless them that curse you.'* 'We both heard him speak kindly of your work last time I visited the mills,' Austin continues. 'From all accounts, any whispers I've heard, Mr Pattinson acts with a kind and giving hand. God knows, he's on every board known to man.'

'That maybe so, sir, but when his daughter is involved... well, I'm just saying that I don't imagine he'd be so kind, so forgiving then.'

'His daughter?' Austin repeats, sternly. 'Explain yourself, lad.'

'Please, sir, I've already said too much. Will you help me?' asks the lad. 'Will you pay to set me free?'

Austin examines the young man behind bars, the pleading look upon his face.

'Alright,' Austin says, trying not to sound troubled. 'But first you need to tell me how you and Mr Pattinson's daughter came to be ... involved?'

The young man's explanation is a short one. Mr Pattinson's daughter had stolen his heart. It had happened all of a sudden, taken him by surprise. He knew falling for the boss's daughter was less than ideal, but there it was. He was in love. And there wasn't a damned thing he could do to change this hopeless state. He only had eyes for Elizabeth.

Elizabeth – not Errington. Austin's relief is palpable, but he can't help but express his surprise. 'Elizabeth...? But she's practically a child!'

The young lad looks up at Austin. 'You'll pardon me for saying so, sir, but I assure you, she is grown enough for me.'

Though Austin struggles to imagine such a thing – to him Elizabeth is like a much younger sister – this young man has his sympathy, because Austin knows, first-hand, love's hopeless state.

At the police counter, Austin returns to the flash of red hair, the epaulettes on Sergeant O'Hare's shoulder held in place with a gold button, a crown in gold stitching. Austin lays down the money.

'Must be some talker?' says Sergeant O'Hare.

'Indeed, he has my sympathy,' Austin says, adding, 'I fear, he is a man in love.'

Sergeant O'Hare smiles heartily – a practice, he declares, he has taken to of late given thoughts of his much-awaited child budding inside its mother's womb. Sergeant O'Hare reaches for the ring of brass keys. 'Poor sod,' he laughs.

13

November

Given Errington's continued absence from society and still unable to make any real inquiries, Austin does not anticipate the coming of Sunday with the same active enthusiasm he usually does. And yet, he can't help but arrive at church with hope in his heart, scanning God's children dressed in their Sunday best, in search of *her*.

Unable to find Errington's face among the seas of faces – most cheerful, others looking rather pained – Austin looks up to the Celtic cross rising above the pitch of the church roof. A symbol of eternity for those who accept Christ, a sun god, a halo; sometimes worn, too, on a silver chain around Errington's neck, the cross sitting atop her breast, adorned with a ruby centre. She is eternal in His love. She is light. She is good.

As Austin passes through the double doors, a threshold that should quieten his mind, he is unable to dislodge thoughts of Errington; of his disappointment in not finding her here, looking up at him with a dimpled smile. Though imagination is a wonderful thing – and it is something both Austin and Errington must heavily rely on – it is, indeed, '... *not the Rose, but near the Rose.*'

'Hello, Uncle Austin,' says a familiar voice, sliding in next to him.

Elizabeth's big, brown eyes look up at Austin beneath her church hat, adorned with a gorgeous green silk bow.

'I have some information for you,' she says.

Eyes ahead, seeking guidance, looking toward the cross behind the altar and the morning light passing through stained glass, Austin feigns disinterest.

'My sister sends her regards,' Elizabeth says, waiting for some kind of response before adding, 'Ruth, that is.'

Austin gives Elizabeth a look. A smile spreads across her face.

'We both know I'm not talking about Ruth, don't we?'

Austin leans forward to suggest his desire for solitude. Despite the brim of her hat, Elizabeth leans in, whispering in Austin's ear. 'She is to leave for St. John's in the morning.'

Austin looks up now, unable to hide signs of his aching heart, thoughts of his poor, sweet Nell being hospitalised.

'Don't fret,' Elizabeth says, meeting Austin's gaze. 'She'll be ok. She always is. Anyway, the message is... Oh, I'm not really sure this business is worth it to me. I'm much too old for penny candy and ice-cream...'

Austin looks back toward the altar.

'Alright, you've got me,' Elizabeth says, unable hold back the news any longer. 'She's going via the CPR, leaving at 10am. She'll be looking for you.'

. . .

THOUGH AUSTIN STANDS WAITING TO CATCH A glimpse of Errington on board the Canadian Pacific Rail service, the timing proves most problematic when he bumps into Chief Loy at the very moment Austin is desperate to keep both eyes fixed ahead in anticipation of the coming railcar.

Ushering him to one side, Loy takes Austin by the shoulder in a friendly, yet forceful way. 'I understand you're not really one for dancing, Mr, Moss?'

Austin keeps quiet for a moment until it is clear Loy is waiting for a response. 'No Chief,' he says.

Despite having been a member of the S.A.C., here, Austin is simply a citizen bound by the law. There is a certain unease that arises from being in the company of the Chief of Police, not to mention Austin's recent interaction with the Chief's daughter.

'Good, that's good,' Loy says. 'Listen, I understand Mary can be rather persuasive, but she is, in fact, already spoken for.'

A crease appears at Austin's brow, and he has to stop himself from tweaking his moustache in a nervous reflex.

'You'll pardon me for being so blunt,' Loy continues, 'but I've always thought it best to be direct.'

Austin straightens up, rests his hands neatly behind his back. 'Yes, of course, Chief. I never once...'

'Relax soldier, you needn't explain,' Loy declares, taking his hands to rest on his girth with interlocking fingers. 'I know you're relatively new here, and I just thought it best we be clear. No hard feelings, eh?'

Austin nods, trying not to look too relieved.

With a firm pat on the back, Loy dismisses Austin, walking away whistling a tune that is immediately drowned out by the sudden whoosh of the old car rushing by. Austin crumples his hat with his fist, tossing it aside in frustration as the railcar disappears into the distance. Alone on the platform, Austin chases after his hat, now picked up by the wind.

Maplecroft

Austin Moss,
Preston, Ont.

13 November 1906

Miss Pattinson,
     St. John's Hospital
     Major Street, Toronto

Sweetheart mine,

It was too bad I missed seeing you after all, I am so sorry. I was waiting and was away just for one moment when the old car rushed by. Please forgive me... I hope it will not be for long, and that neither the pain nor the treatment are very bad to bear. What a shame it is you have to go there so much, you poor little thing. Is the worst part over; may I come in and sit beside you for a while? If I am quiet, perhaps the nurses won't notice me. Dearest, are you comfortable and not making your-self unhappy about anything? And does it make things any easier, me sitting and talking there?

Sweetheart, I love you so. I want you back, safe and well out of that place. I hope the time won't seem so long to you and that you'll never, never be inside a hospital again. Cheer up, Brown Eyes and let me see you smile as only you can. What a brave smile and a sweet one! You <u>are</u> a dear... good-night, sweetheart good-night.

Yours now and always,
     A., PRESTON.

Ellen Errington Pattinson,
St. John's Hospital,
Major Street, Toronto

13 November 1906

Mr Austin Moss,
      PRESTON

Dearest,

If you could see St. Agatha's – my room – you would, instead of saying "poor little thing", be congratulating me on my good fortune. It is such a pretty room – and the hospital is so very quiet. Did I tell you that it is built adjoining the Church of England Convent, and is under the charge of the Sisters of St. John?

Dr Scadding was here just a little while ago and left all sorts of pleasant directions. I am to rest – and be fed every few hours – and be rubbed with salt and alcohol and all kinds of restful and invigorating things. And, best of all, do nothing but grow fat.

Sweetheart, I've tried so hard to tell you – (but some things are difficult subjects to tackle and I'm afraid I made an awful hash of it) – but what I meant to tell you, dearest love, was this: that even if it should be necessary to have a little operation, it will be a very little one. It will take only a very short time and will not be a scrap painful – there will be absolutely no danger in any way – and after it I will not be in any way different, except improved.

I had such a bitter disappointment yesterday afternoon. Every passing glimpse of you means so much, dear, and I had hoped to see you from the car – but Father insisted that I had better go Grand Trunk Railway – never mind! Are you happy still? If I could make you so darling, you should indeed be happy.

Yours forever and ever,
Little Nell,
St. John's Hospital,
Major Street, Toronto.

Austin Moss,
'Saint's Rest,'
Preston Ont.

22 November 1906

Miss Pattinson
St. John's Hospital
Major Street, Toronto

<u>My</u> dear "Little Nell,"

Many thanks for your most welcome letter, which apparently crossed mine. I was so pleased to hear that you were comfortable and not having to undergo all sorts of tortures. Though I do hope this will be the last of those "little operations". They are worse than England's "little wars."

Does time hang heavy?... One "blessed confounded" sparrow told me that you were looking real well, ever so much better already. Are you a little lonely, too? There is a Bachelor's Ball on Thursday at Galt. I shan't go. There is no enticement.

Although I am not so happy as I mean to be one of these days, I want you to know, that writing <u>to</u> you and getting letters <u>from</u> you is the next best thing to being with you. Can you see me just beside you, sweetheart?

Yours always,
A., 'Saint's Rest,' PRESTON.

Ellen Errington Pattinson
St. John's Hospital,
Major Street, Toronto

22 November 1906
Mr Austin Moss,
PRESTON.

Dearest,

Will you come sit by me a while?... Your letter was lovely (that's a vain repetition because if it is <u>yours</u>, it is <u>of course</u> lovely) but why do you not tell me more about yourself? You had a horrid cough the last time I saw you. You need someone to look after you – do, do take care of yourself – and <u>keep Mary Loy at a distance</u>. (I, too, have a little birdie!) Oh dear, do be careful – I should die thinking that you were ill, and I couldn't even nurse you. That sounds selfish, but it's true. I should die doubly; once for your pain and once for the pain of being separated from you...

O Austin, you aren't really sitting here at all! You haven't said a word – and I'm sure if you were here you wouldn't sit so... well, you know you <u>wouldn't</u>. Do you miss me just a little bit? As for me, I'm ashamed – I daren't tell you how hopelessly lonely I am, I shouldn't tell you, I know, but oh! You know anyway I cannot live out of your sight.

Cheer up – someday, perhaps, they'll invent long distance sites for telephones and then 63 miles will not matter <u>quite</u> so much. Good-night – good-night – good-night.

With all my love to guard your sleep. Good night ...
Little Nell,
St. John's Hospital,
Major Street, Toronto.

IT IS THIS LAST LETTER THAT DOES AUSTIN IN, offering him no choice but to see Errington in the flesh and not just in some imagined dream. And so, he stands there in one of his most presentable suits, clutching his Gladstone – empty, save a single book – and raps on the door. A sound that falls like thunder amidst the song of warblers echoing through the trees in sweet melody. Austin is looking over his shoulder toward the dappled sunlight, to a squirrel scurrying up a nearby maple, when the door to the convent opens.

'Dear Sister, you'll pardon the interruption to your quiet existence, but I have come in support of the church.'

'How so, kind sir? Are you one of our generous donors?'

'Not so,' Austin says, examining the youthful face appearing beneath the wimple, the soft glow of her cheeks. 'However, while I am not in a position, at present, to offer financial aid, I offer assistance of another kind.'

'Have you come to volunteer in support of the poor and needy?'

Austin notices the nun's hand folding around the edge of the door, sensing that despite her serenity, she is, perhaps, running out of patience.

'Representing the Preston Furniture Co., Mr Moss is the name, I have come to make recommendations in regard to your furniture.'

'A salesman? We live under a vow of poverty,' the nun shakes her head. 'We thank you, but we have no need for such luxuries here.'

Austin rushes to speak as the gap of the open door narrows. 'What of literature, Sister?'

Austin reaches for the book inside his Gladstone bag, holding it up. The sister nods.

'Yes, we do have a small library, and may be open to donations of that nature, assuming the reading material is deemed appropriate?'

'Oh, it is. It is... But, Sister, the truth of the matter is that I have a dear friend staying here under your care. She is a lover of great literature and I wonder whether I might leave this small token to aid in her quick recovery?'

'Leave it with me, sir, I shall ask the matron. If it is permitted, I will pass it on. The patient's name?'

'Pattinson, Sister. She's staying in the St. Agatha's room.'

The young nun clasps her hands together, smiles sweetly.

'If it offers you some comfort, Mr Moss, St. Agatha's is, I believe, our most beautiful room. North facing, it receives a good amount of sunshine and being at the far end of the building, it is, indeed, very quiet.'

'Yes, *pretty and quiet* that is how she described it. And it's just that room at the end?'

The nun nods. 'Now, I really must go, but I will be sure to ask the matron.'

'I wonder,' Austin says, before the nun starts to turn on her heel. 'I am not in a position to donate funds, but my brother, the head of the Preston Furniture Co. is quite well to do. He did ask if I might take a tour of the chapel. You see, he's interested in crafting some simple pieces inspired by church pews. He did say that should I be permitted access, he would happily open his cheque book...'

Though still in training, the young nun is aware of the hospital relying on donations to keep their doors open. As a surgical hospital, serving women with conditions 'peculiar to the female sex,' St. John's is open to all women, including the poor and destitute. And while it is expected that those who can pay, must; most patients coming to St. John's with 'nervous complaints' and 'women's troubles' are unable to pay for their treatment.

With the quiet echo of his footsteps in the empty hall, Austin follows the young nun through to the chapel. From the rood screen, with its carved archway adorned with multiple figures (most prominently, the crucifixion), Austin can see through to the chapel. Its red cedar ceiling, the arches rising to the heavens unaided by any reinforcing beams, sits above a semi-circle of stained glass resting behind the altar, depicting a haloed Mary and Saint John. The whole space, a marvel. Its architectural beauty, an open invitation to kneel before God.

'We call that the Mary Window,' says the nun, noticing Austin's gaze resting on the stained glass. 'Take your time. It is quite the experience to feel God's close presence. I will make the request about that book of yours.'

With the disappearance of the young nun down a long corridor, Austin excuses himself from God's close presence to make for the far end of the hospital, stopping only when he stumbles across the words, *St. Agatha's,* painted on a door in German Fraktur.

Austin pushes the door open, gently at first, its squeaky hinges calling him inside. Thinking Errington is asleep, Austin reaches for the solid, wooden chair positioned beside the bed, looking up as he hears her gasp in surprise. Austin places a finger to her lips, then places the chair against the door to prevent intrusion.

'I brought you this,' he says, slipping Errington's cigarette case just beneath her pillow. 'And a book... I still have your jacket, though I doubt you'll have need for it in here. And besides, it has your scent...'

Errington catches Austin by the arm, drawing him near. Her breasts, resting just beneath her nightgown, press against the fabric of his double-breasted suit. Her face nuzzles into his shoulder as she inhales deeply, as if igniting some other part of her deep within, an intensified yearning.

'I wish I could bottle your scent,' she breathes, letting herself indulge in the moment in a dream-like state.

As Austin rests back on the edge of her bed, Errington

does not question this new reality. If it is a dream, so be it. She does not ask him how he got past the nurses or whether her father knows he's here; her only concern is that Austin is here now. A reality she is gripping onto with all her might.

But – like a dream – this happy circumstance is not permitted to play out for long. There is the sound of approaching footsteps. The squeak of the brass doorknob turning slowly. The solid, wooden chair threatening to budge.

'I'm here now, my darling,' Austin urges. 'If only for the briefest of moments, I'm here. And when you think of me, as I think of you; I will be here again, right by your side.'

As Austin's words linger, no longer able to feel the indentation of his weight dipping towards the mattress's edge, Errington tries desperately to hold onto the vision of him resting at the edge of her bed; Austin's image slipping away nonetheless. There is no denying it. He is gone.

Having climbed out of the window – open to release the 'bad air' – Austin finds himself suspended from the second storey of the gothic-style building. Shuffling one foot after the other along the narrow ledge, Austin keeps his eye on the neighbouring window. Without glancing at the sheer drop beneath him, balancing on one foot, Austin brings his whole body around as he lunges toward the neighbouring window ledge. Fortunately, this window, too, is open to release the 'bad air'. In uneasy haste, Austin makes himself squeeze through the narrow opening, breathing a sigh of relief as his feet touch the floorboards. A silent gasp, coming from the body suddenly sitting up in bed, mirrors the shock in Austin's own countenance.

And then comes a moment in which mutual shock is replaced with a very much one-sided eagerness; the aging patient producing a devilish smile, patting the space beside her.

Austin shakes his head and looks toward the door in apology; hearing the woman let out a sigh as he exits the room.

Out in the hall, the matron and nurse have their backs to Austin; each trying their hand at opening the door to the next room which appears to be stuck.

Believing there is no longer any need to tiptoe around, Austin announces his presence. 'Thank you, for showing me the chapel, Sister,' he declares. 'As you say, it was... most affecting.'

Both sisters look up guiltily, as if they've been caught outside chapel during prayer. The matron is the first to regain her authority as she looks between Austin and the young nun, who is now facing some degree of difficulty from her superior.

'May I?' Austin asks, using a greater degree of force to push against the chair still butted up against Errington's door. 'Perhaps, if you jolly it a little...'

And just like that, the door to St. Agatha's opens, sweeping the chair back towards the wall in its wake.

The matron breathes out a sigh.

'Sister, please escort Mr Moss out.'

IT IS NOT UNUSUAL FOR ERRINGTON TO DRIFT between various states of being, not only in terms of her emotions – kept under wraps here with heavy sedation – but through varying degrees of awareness. Sometimes, the passing of time exists as though it were all a dream. This last dream has been a particularly pleasant one, and one that will sustain Errington until her time here is up.

It is only as Errington reaches beneath her pillow and finds something tangible in the palm of her hand, that she realises that *this* dream must have materialised. Clutching the smooth, hard-edged silver case, Errington finds her way back to the dream. The silver case, draws him near, and she recalls the shoulder she nuzzles into as she breathes in his scent, the memory of their lingering embrace.

14

December

The following Sunday, the sky is a cloudless blue, the sun glistening off the fresh powder of newly fallen snow. As promised – and then postponed – Elizabeth has managed to coax Austin to take her out for a sleigh ride, though the enticement is really all his.

'I'll tell you what you want to know,' Elizabeth says, taking Austin's hand to help her into the open sleigh packed with furs. 'But first, let's ride.'

Handing over the funds for the ride to the man adjusting the harness, Austin takes charge of the reins, urging the horse forward. To the sound of the clip-clop of the horse's hooves and the horse's shuddering snort registering in the crisp, morning air, Austin and Elizabeth turn into King Street. The livery stables, the blacksmith, Clare Bros. Foundry all disappearing into the distance as the metal runners, curling up to meet the sleigh, smooth over the snow like a knife over icing.

It seems they are not the only ones to 'make hay while the sun shines.' A crowd gathers, spilling out from the General Store, ladies rugged up in thick coats with fur collars and mink hats, have come in for first picking of Mr Wurster's shipment of fine china. Just beyond, blanketed in snow, is Central Park, where children in double-breasted coats with brass buttons cup their gloved hands around the snow, compacting it into snowballs to throw at their chums.

'I do have a question,' Austin says, finally, as they approach the Business Section. 'How is...?'

Elizabeth tilts her head in a look of curiosity, exposing the braids pinned to her head hiding beneath her fur hat.

'How is...?' she repeats with a smirk.

Austin lets out a sigh, momentarily blocking out the barking of a rogue dog demonstrating contempt for a neigh-bouring canine. His hands tightening over the reins, a sign of his frustration at not being able to speak plainly.

'Alright, alright, keep your hair on!' Elizabeth says as they reach the next street corner; the spotted dogs kicking up snow as they engage in a chase back through Central Park. 'No need to work yourself up like a restless pup. Errington is... quite well. That is to say, she is on the improve but Father says she will have to remain there a while longer.'

Austin's gaze remains fixed up ahead, a railcar coming into view. Its rickety clacking sound, combined with the pull of the wind, heralds its approach. 'And... is she happy?' Austin asks, suddenly impatient with the crumbs of information filtering through Elizabeth.

'Happy enough. Sleepy mostly. Though I did hear her say a small thing... I think, maybe in her sleep...' Elizabeth is watching Austin closely, delighting in the feeling of having him eating out of the palm of her hand. 'Sheee sa-id...' Eliza-beth draws out each syllable, '...that she is not as happy as she *intends to be*' – whatever that means.'

'*I am quite well, my darling, though not as happy as I intend to be,*' Austin wrote to Errington some weeks ago.

'There now,' Elizabeth says, noticing Austin's grasp of the reins loosen as he breaks out into a grin. 'You aren't really such a grump, are you, Uncle Austin?'

Reassured by Elizabeth's report, Austin can't help but bask in this knowledge, that, truly, he is the '*richest of all.*' His happiness branded on his face.

Passing over Lowther Street, Elizabeth looks away from Austin, back toward the sleigh's tracks carved out in the snow, toward a shop window displaying oversize picture hats adorned with feathers, flowers, birds; a habitat of flora and fauna waiting to be bestowed atop one's head.

'Did you manage to take the books?' Austin asks, encouraging Elizabeth to turn back around. 'I wonder, what did she think of the Paterson and Lawson texts? Not too much '*lure of the wild,*' I hope?'

Elizabeth slumps back against the fur lap rug, crossing over her arms.

'I carted them *all* the way there,' Elizabeth says, looking rather bored. 'I even pretended they were on the syllabus. Told Father I simply have to make a head-start on my studies if I am to succeed at that far away Grammar School – though I hardly forgive him for electing to send me there.'

'You should have a read, it would probably be quite rounding for your education – Unless, that is, you are easily frightened by a good read.'

'Ha, frightened? I certainly am! Books often hold such strange ideas. Consider 'The Ladies' Book of Etiquette and Manual of Politeness'. Is that really to become my canonical text? Words are dangerous. They may, in fact, do more harm than good.'

There is a prolonged silence, leaving Austin to consider that Elizabeth is not a ship easily steered.

'Speaking of words, now I understand why you and Errington never let me join for a paddle... Or a stroll in the woods.' Elizabeth says, visibly pouting, her gloved hand resting over her skirt pocket – sewn by her own hand – concealing a letter. The letter, written in pencil, because St. John's does not permit writing with ink.

'You may come any given Sunday,' Austin says, still smiling. 'Now, tell me about the books, if you will.'

Elizabeth lets out a sigh.

'Why, I lugged all those books for nothing! According to Errington, the nurse had already removed Dorothy Forster from beside her bed. And the matron certainly wasn't about to let me bring in another book. I'm sure if I had brought the Bible, she wouldn't have said a thing! I suppose, it won't be the first time I shall be denied... I shall have to become better acquainted with being 'told' what to do or think.'

'I suppose you shall,' Austin agrees, directing the horse up Potter Street, taking care given the ice on the track. 'And I'd wager a Bible is already within arm's reach.'

As they pass the gothic-style houses, none quite as grand as Maplecroft, Elizabeth expresses her dismay at the prospect of being sent to boarding school. Her tone, only reinforcing Austin's perception of her as a cheeky, yet charming younger sister. Austin couldn't help, struggling with the notion declared by the young lad whose bail Austin paid. The notion that Elizabeth is, in fact, 'grown.' And in love.

EARLIER THAT MORNING, WITHOUT THE RUSH OF THE river – sound itself seemed frozen over – Elizabeth ran her finger over the scar that resides just above Jimmy's left eye, planting a kiss there.

'You poor dear,' she said, though the scar isn't hurting him. It's apparently a mark from childhood; the split skin resisting the healing process before closing over in a pale, pink line.

'You poor sweet thing,' Elizabeth said, brushing aside the dark mop of hair covering his eyes.

Jimmy smiled nervously. His calloused fingers and thumbs – stained with dye from the dyeing room – loosely dangled from his suspenders.

'I just had to see you!' Elizabeth declared with a level of melodrama for even the most romantic. 'And, I know, I shall just *die* being away from you. *Will you think of me as I think of you?*'

Reading Errington's stash of letters in secret, Elizabeth had taken to trying out certain phrases – though she wondered whether they didn't sound unnatural coming from her lips, even as she spoke.

Jimmy looked up to the sky, as if concentrating on the clouds, watching them take shape.

'Can't you bear to look at me?' she demanded, indignantly, before smiling. 'Maybe it's the thought of my departure that's too much? You poor, sweet thing! *You are a dear!*'

Elizabeth ran her hand down Jimmy's shoulder, along his well-formed physique, narrowing in at his woollen trousers, her gloved hand settling at Jimmy's crotch – her level of daring rising as her impending departure became more imminent.

Jimmy winced, not out of pain, but desperation. A throbbing running right through him. An urgency rising from his swollen trousers to his temple.

'Yes,' he said, writhing under her hand. 'Yes, of course.'

'And you'll wait for me?' Elizabeth kept her hand where it was.

'*Yes,*' he groaned.

'Good,' Elizabeth said, abruptly, turning on her heel and trudging back toward the mill without glancing back.

Approaching the entrance, walking under the words 'Geo.

Pattinson' inscribed in stone, Elizabeth resolved to declare her support for Father's decision. She would go to boarding school; not happily, but she would go. Because from what she's read – in the most urgent, passionate of letters – it is the longing, the expectation of lovers uniting, that is most exciting. And while Jimmy is rather a bore to talk to – just a boy, really – from a distance Elizabeth may write and imagine all kinds of wondrous things. Although, now she comes to think of it, she wonders whether Jimmy may be capable of anything more than simply making his mark on paper.

'BOARDING SCHOOL WON'T BE SUCH A BORE, YOU know,' Austin says, breaking the prolonged silence. 'You'll make your own fun. God knows, we did at Whitgift... I say,' Austin says, responding to Elizabeth's unapologetic frown, 'is it boarding school that's bothering you? Because, I am told, it is quite natural for a girl of your age to be sent away. Particularly, with your mother dearly departed, and Errington unwell, you'll need someone to whip you into shape – teach you all the domestic skills you need, so to speak.'

Elizabeth's gloved hand lifts suddenly, no longer resting over her skirt pocket where Errington's letter remains concealed.

'No one shall whip *me*, thank you very much; I suppose I shall have to learn to hold my tongue.'

Doubting whether Elizabeth is capable of such restraint, Austin smiles. And then it fades, as he wonders what else might be bothering her.

'Is it Errington that's bothering you? Is there something you're not telling me? Something I should know?'

Elizabeth claps her hands together, enjoying the way Austin hangs off her every word. It is almost tantalising to have this control over another person, much in the same way she'd had with Jimmy, down by the mills that morning. All his urges forcibly frozen over like the river. Now, sitting beside Austin, she considers drawing this feeling out by reporting on Errington's most recent visitor – though, in truth, Antonio has not been permitted to see Errington, only to leave the most gorgeous posy of Sweet Peas, truly the most romantic soft pink blooms, the colour of blushing cheeks; *'Nellie's blushing cheeks, I swear.'*

Elizabeth smiles at Austin, a sparkle in her big, brown eyes resembling sunlight glistening in the snow.

'Nothing more to report,' she declares, keeping Errington's letter concealed within her skirt pocket. 'But have you correspondence for Errington? I could pass it on. If you like?'

15

M *ay I sit beside you for a while?* asks a voice, as welcome as the coming of any given Sunday.

Errington is not surprised to see Austin standing in her hospital room. The light of the bay window, the sunlight reflecting off his tweaked moustache, makes him looks dream-like, floating like dust particles suspended in a strobe of natural light – *'Moving freely about like the motes we see in the sunbeam,'* as articulated by William Wallace in his book, *Epicureanism.*

Errington watches as Austin's gaze follows the line of the bay window before settling upon her once more, lying there beneath the chintz bed spread.

I suppose, it is some small consolation that you are comfortable, Austin says, taking in the room's decor, the room's furnishings more akin to a hotel room. *But I do not enjoy your being here. In fact, I wish you were not here at all.*

Austin's face hardens, lines creasing his brow.

You are so tired, my dear, Errington says, though it is she who can barely draw breath. *Who shall take care of you?*

Austin chuckles at the absurdity of the question.

I imagine it shall be you. He leans against the frame of the window, basking in the sun; a pussycat stretched out by the hearth.

Though, evidently, it is I who should be looking after you – if only, you'd let me, Austin says, as though Errington's agreement is all that is necessary for the two to live as man and wife.

The sunlight. Austin standing there within its glow, his newly acquired impatience reflects Errington's own mind – and body. Her fever.

She is no longer satisfied with the notion that *'Love is patient, love is kind.'* In her experience, love is urgent, love is desperate. Errington can feel the warmth of the sun falling over Austin's lips and warming his face. Desiring to be nearer still, Errington pushes herself up in the bed, the mattress squeaking in complaint, her body aching in sympathy.

Immediately, as if transporting telepathically from one spot to the next, Austin appears at Errington's side, readjusting her pillow, bringing the covers back up to meet her chin.

Commanded by her mind and body, by Austin's swift movements, Errington lies back down.

There, will that do? Austin asks, planting a kiss on Errington's forehead, then one over each eye. His touch, lingering.

The springs of the mattress are unyielding, but Errington's small frame rests lightly as if deposited on a bed of flowers. Her mind transports her to woods lined with trilliums, where she can still feel Austin's hot breath at her neck, the colour at her cheeks. The rush of the river almost drowns out Austin's speech, as he whispers into her ear, *I love you.*

'Do you remember our paddle along Speed River?' Austin once wrote, sharing some of the recent exploration of his mind. *'...I have been trying to imagine you up there – And I also – We two just paddling about together. Why, dearest, it would be just heavenly – too good to be true...'*

Trying hard to imagine this, while absorbing the memory of freshly laid kisses, Errington wakes, her eye catching the array of medicine bottles by her bed, the rectangular bottle of laudanum; the empty glass of red claret – half a bottle consumed at any one time, prescribed as 'a wholesome restorative for nervous debility'. And she remembers the sudden touch of the nurse's cold hands as defence against bedsores; the returning memory of Doctor Scadding's directive that she must remain here 'a while yet;' and most upsetting of all, the absence of Austin.

'NOT A POP-WALLAH TODAY, I SEE.'

Eddie presses his smooth physician's hands against the sticky bar to slid up onto a stool beside Austin, his polished boots resting on the brass railing at the base of the counter.

'I'm drowning my sorrows,' Austin says, dramatically, though it is clear from the absence of liquor hovering about his breath that he has just sat down.

Eddie assesses the way Austin is hunched over his drink, noting the sullen expression on his face.

'You may be considering it, but you haven't started yet,' Eddie says looking down at the transparent, mahogany-coloured liquid resting in Austin's glass. 'I don't know why you bother, old chap; you're really not a drinker.'

Remembering the calamity of alcohol mixed with foolishness that kept Austin busy in his police work back in Klerksdorp – when taverns were still buzzing with brawling, noisy miners, submerged beneath the steady flow of beer on tap – Austin pushes his glass just out of reach. Back in South Africa, he had come to know what it was to look on everyone not as a possible customer – as he had done in N.Z. – but as a possible criminal; '*the usual deadbeats who spend their last half dollar on beer rather than on beef.*'

'I suppose I'm lucky to have escaped love's clutches until now.' Austin breathes out a sigh. 'No matter the obstacle, "*The heart wants what the heart wants.*"'

'"– *Or else it does not care,*" Eddie finishes Austin's sentence. 'Dickinson.'

'Yes.'

'Well, love is preferable – however painful – to anything else humans may be conditioned to feel.'

'Perhaps, but at least in war things are clear-cut.'

'I'm not so sure of that,' Eddie says, thinking of the logic-defying hours upon hours spent working on a patient that would likely die, of the burning of Boer farms, the rounding up of Boer women and children into camps.

'Yes, but orders are orders,' Austin continues. 'There is no room for temptation, no room for independent thought; especially if you wish to remain in the land of the living.'

'*Personally, I wish there was another war. I am not anxious for gore but the 'air' here would be all the clearer if a kaffir rising were to take place, there are rumours, but nothing at all definite,*' Austin had written to Frank prior to coming to Preston, resistant as ever to leave the alluring South African landscape. It was a life Austin knew, a life he understood. A very different perspective to Eddie, who was never more glad to see the end to such bloodshed and suffering, and his role in it, in the lives he had not been able to save; the baby-faced men, the Boer women and children that haunt him still.

Austin signals to the man behind the bar to order a soda. The bartender, sleeves rolled-up, waves a cloth of over a glass before plonking it down and turning the bar gun to release a bubbling liquid. Sliding a nickel across the counter, Austin glances past the glass laid down before him to the rows of liquor housed on the mahogany shelves, lining the walls up to the pressed metal ceiling. Its pattern, a kaleidoscope sky.

'It's those blasted rest cures,' Austin says, finally, still looking up at the ceiling as if expecting it to change in shape or colour. 'I can't believe they are all they're cracked up to be. If anything, I believe, they cause *un*rest.'

Eddie rests a kind hand on Austin's shoulder. There is a lot he cannot say. For Eddie knows what it is to look upon every man, woman and child as a possible patient.

'I'm told the doctors at St. John's are very good. That the care received at the hand of the sisters of St. John the Divine is second to none.'

'And as for those *"little operations?"'* Austin continues, ignoring Eddie's professional reassurances. 'Why, they're *'worse than England's "little wars!"'*

Eddie privately shares Austin's concerns, and he is not the only one with misgivings. The Government in Ottawa has concerns about opium; about the necessity for new legislation to regulate patent medicines; calls for products containing cocaine, such as teething powder for infants, to be banned. Just across the border, medicines have only recently been required to declare potentially 'dangerous' contents – and there are objections from companies not wishing to disclose key ingredients of their 'miracle cure.' Yet to receive adequate pressure from the American Medical Association are products like *'Mrs Winslow's Soothing Syrup'* which continue to promote the morphine-alcohol cocktail as *'perfectly harmless and pleasant,'* with the label depicting heart-warming scenes of mother and child.

Eddie looks down at the blonde hairs covering his knuckles, which he has now taken to gloving during surgery; though many physicians continue to tend to their patients, including the delivery of babies, simply by rolling up their sleeves as if preparing for a fight.

'What do you know of Doctor Vardon?' Eddie asks his friend, avoiding eye-contact.

Over the course of several months Eddie has been gathering a not-altogether favourable opinion of the Pattinson's family physician. Residing in nearby Galt, Doctor Vardon is seen as an institution in Preston. Like George Pattinson, Thomas Vardon is an active citizen, a public figure, much admired. And yet, Eddie is certain that he knows his kind; the sort of physician who clings to archaic practices; perceiving female bodies as existing in a 'disease-like state;' reliant on rest cures for 'nervous women who are thin and lack blood;' who treat a woman's menstrual cycle as an illness for which bedrest is a cure; who administer narcotics as though simply prescribing tea and toast.

Eddie does not know enough about Errington's medical history to know whether her frequent bouts of bedrest are, indeed, necessary; nor does he know the precise operation that Errington has undergone. But knowing the radical surgeries young women are still subjected to: hysterectomies, oophorectomies, presacral neurectomies; all linking a woman's reproductive function to her mental balance; Eddie has grave concerns that these *'little operations'* may be, as Austin suggests, *'worse than England's little wars'* and perhaps, executed as such. The exercise of power by a dominant personality over a more vulnerable party, could, in his opinion, result in more harm than good. And despite Errington declaring that *'there will be absolutely no danger in any way – and after it I will not be in any way different – except improved,'* Eddie wonders how accurate this statement, relayed to him by Austin, actually is. Because depending on the operation, patients might, indeed, be irrevocably changed.

Austin rolls his glass on its axis, watching the melting ice sliding around the inside edge, before looking up at Eddie, forming a question with his gaze. *Why do you ask?*

'Oh, just curious,' Eddie says, dismissing the thought of Doctor Vardon rather too quickly.

Removing his Oom Paul pipe from his coat pocket – one of two with Boer War carvings; the other remaining in Errington's possession as 'some small part' of himself – Austin seems to accept Eddie's termination of this discussion, shifting his attention, instead, to the tamping and lighting of his pipe. The practice of preparing his pipe is as natural to Austin as procuring paste from a tin to lay upon an ivory toothbrush; tasks he performs with the greatest of care, particularly on Sundays. Following one long continuous suck of his pipe, Austin releases a cloud of smoke, adding to the miniature campfires wafting from the pipes of fellow patrons.

'Well, you know,' Austin says, like a witchdoctor, witnessing truth projected in the smoke. 'Curiosity killed the cat.'

Lauren
Muskoka, Ontario, Canada,
2019

16

———

September

'We haven't tried this yet.' Em crouches down, examining the rowboat resting just inside the boat house; the one we've walked right past all summer.

I hesitate. The boat isn't as light-weight as the canoe; this would have been Nick's job. 'I wouldn't even know how to get this bad boy into the water.'

'Come on, Mum.' Em looks down at me in mock-disappointment. 'You can do better than that. What happened to girl power and all that cra –'

'Alright, alright,' I run my hand over the boat's glossy trim, positioning my hands at its base. 'Here,' I say, 'get underneath it... Maybe the two of us can lift it.'

Em manoeuvres into position and, for a second, we have it... until the weight bears down, digging into the palms of my hands, my knees threaten to buckle, my pelvic floor is about to give. I take a single step back.

'No!' Em cries, her face turning red. 'Drop it!'

Em's end drops with a thud, slipping from her hands, before I have a chance to lower mine.

'Argh!' she yelps. 'I *said* drop it – I didn't say drop it on my toe.'

I try not to laugh. 'Hun, you dropped it first... Look at my hands,' I say, still gripping the base of the boat. I take a step back, examining the minute distance between the boat and the water. 'You want to give up? We can take the car into town; get an ice-cream.'

But Em is stubborn in her resolve. 'They teach us in school that we can achieve anything – that we can 'have it all,'' she says, 'but we can't even shift a boat.'

'I'm not sure that is what is meant by 'have it all –''

'So, either that's a total crock,' Em continues, 'Or, *I am Woman.*' Em makes a show of flexing her underdeveloped muscles; the skin at her biceps is soft and supple. 'So, which one is it?' There is fire in her belly. I smile.

'Hear me roar,' I laugh, still trying to understand why this means so much to her, but letting this go, going with it. 'Alright, alright,' I say. 'Come around this end.'

Gripping the edge of the bow, the pair of us throw our bodyweight back, pulling, yanking, dragging the rowboat. I speak in bursts, as we move the rowboat inch, by inch. 'This. Better. Be. Worth –'

With a splash, clumsily scrapping the edge of the dock and... 'She's in!'

'Zo!' Em calls, with an unusual fondness. 'Jump in – we're going to town. And this *"bad boy"* is about to depart!' Em declares, hurrying along the moment of embarkation – all of us, writing our own rules; ignoring the convention that labels any sea-worthy vessel as 'she.'

Out on the water, the wind picking up, we are so pleased

with ourselves, so brimming with joy that it is only as my muscles start to ache – that I begin to think I cannot row a single pace more – that we register the water flooding in.

'My feet are wet,' Zoe complains again, except this time I listen.

'Oh Zo!' I say, cupping my hands to collect and redistribute the water at our feet. 'Oh God.'

'Oh, crap.'

We are only marginally closer to town than home, drifting toward the buoys where speedboats zip around the bend. Turning my oar to avoid drifting directly into the path of a high-speed waterway, I miss the opportunity to grab the attention of a speedboat rushing by; and another, and another. People waving politely, perceiving the girls waving their arms about as a sign of friendliness, while I divide my attention between shovelling out the water – with the aid of my cap, which only partially holds – and figuring out what the hell I'm going to do. With no time to deliberate, suddenly it occurs to me that if there is less weight in the boat, the leak should slow down.

I can hear the girls' screaming as I plunge downward, alongside the side of the boat, rising back to the surface, breathless. The sound shifting; the shadowy sound of the water, their water-logged cries, replaced by something else.

'Why'd you do that?!' Em yells, anger mixed with panic. 'Why the hell, did you do that?'

It is the yelling, I believe, that saves us; a small powerboat – the kind designed for dropping a line off the edge while sinking a couple of beers – pulls up alongside.

'Need a hand?'

First, I notice his outstretched hand, then the face. Sandy, blonde hair poking out from a faded Captain's hat; piercing blue-grey eyes, the colour of the ocean. Tanned, of course; the total package is almost laughably stereotypic; straight out of a

B-grade Rom-Com. *It's never a balding man, with a pot belly, that comes to the aid of a damsel in distress.*

'Brace,' our rescuer introduces himself, as I take his strong, muscular hand, pulling me onto his boat.

Standing, with a foot on each boat, Brace holds the rowboat in place as the girls transfer onto his boat, stumbling as they find their new 'sea-legs', their excitement matched by that of a half-wet Labrador skirting the base of the boat in search of its tail.

With everyone safely aboard, Brace crouches down, his Hawaiian shirt billowing in the wind, as he engages in some fancy knot-work, tethering our boat to his.

The wind cuts across my face as we gather speed, taking away my speech as I sit, overwhelmed by relief and regret. Drawing closer to town, the girls delight in the adventure.

'I've got a shop,' Brace says, this time, speaking to me directly – not to the party as a whole. 'I'm actually a carpenter, but I should be able to patch this up...' He single-handily lifts the rowboat up out of the water to rest on dry land. 'You'll be back out there in no time,' he says, with a grin, causing me to grimace.

'I'm not sure I want to.' I stare down at the upturned boat, my hand to my face, wishing I could quickly disappear. 'But thank you... Are you sure?' My voice is filled with doubt.

But Brace will not hear of any other plan, so we pile into his old Chevy Silverado, parked right by the jetty, the four of us squeezing onto a bench seat made for three; Brace, calling '*Pete!*' as the smell of dog rushes past, making a b-line for the passenger seat.

'In the back with you,' Brace says, calling the dog away from the empty *Tim Horton's* coffee cups and crumpled receipts.

Despite it being a squeeze, the drive home is a pleasant one; conversation conducted with ease.

'You're Austin's daughter, aren't you?' Brace stares at the road ahead, sunlight falling into our laps as we drive over the bridge, the trees dropping away to reveal an open expanse of water. The ride, bumpier than before.

I breathe in the smells of the car: dust, hewn timber collecting at the footwell, the smell of wet dog still present.

'How'd you know?'

Brace chuckles without lifting his gaze from the road ahead. 'This town is a small one; you'll discover that soon enough... especially once the warm weather fades.'

My hand rises to my lips, I bite down on my nail. It tastes of the water. Remembering myself, I fold my hands into my lap. But still, I do not speak.

'I should say, up front,' Brace continues, making me wonder whether he is, in fact, speaking off the cuff. 'Your father, Austin – Well, he was good to me – Known him for years, though his visits were only ever sporadic.' Brace sighs, as though there is a much longer story to tell; and I do not relieve him of its telling.

Simply, I listen.

'My mother was a single mother; men didn't tend to stick around.' Brace's face changes shape as he speaks, as though his mind has taken him to a darker place. 'She swapped husbands, like some women update their handbags, though this last one stuck around some twenty-five years – but never a 'father' to me. But' Brace shrugs, 'perhaps, it's time to move on...'

'I reckon!' Em declares, reminding me of the girls' presence, almost forgotten until now.

'Maybe,' I laugh, unwilling to shake off – or even disclose – my own firmly-held grudge toward my father.

We're back, and suddenly, I look about realising I hadn't needed to give the address.

Brace turns off the engine. 'Like I said, I've done a fair bit of work here, over the years.'

I look between the sloping roof of the house and Brace, his strong hands draped over the steering wheel.

'Look, do you want a cuppa... or something?' I say, surprised when Brace doesn't refuse my offer.

Brace leaps out of his truck, to check his dog in the back. 'That'd be nice... Ok, if I let Pete out? We could have a coffee on the dock or –'

'No,' I cut him off, hastily, confused by the way my actions are leaping ahead of my usually careful thinking. 'The dock sounds great. Meet you there in a sec.'

Navigating the stepping stones, I approach the dock with two steaming cups of coffee to be greeted by Pete wagging his tail, dripping lines of wetness as he circles the dock, stopping only to paw at a knot hole showcasing some darting fish.

'Hey, boy,' I say, lowering the mugs onto the ledge, dropping down to give Pete a rub behind the ears. 'Where's Brace, eh?'

'Up here,' Brace calls from upstairs.

Something sinks deep in my stomach and my legs refuse to shift, my mind filling in the blanks of why Brace would be calling me upstairs. The obvious thought struck me. *The single bed by the boarded-up doors.*

'Oh, no,' Brace calls out, his footsteps, heard overhead, rushing toward the top of the stairs. 'Nothing like that,' he says, connecting the dots, before crouching down to reveal his face and waving me over. 'Come and see.'

A slick wetness rushes past my knees; Pete dashing past, scrambling up the stairs. Slowly, I follow, my heart quickening as I take the steps, struck by the greater presence of light as I emerge from the stairs.

'I removed your handiwork,' Brace says, crossing the room, referring to the single board I'd clumsily hammered to close off the balcony, deeming it too dangerous for the girls. 'I can put it back... But I just wanted to show you.' Brace steps

out onto the balcony, making me catch my breath. 'It's safe –
see.'

'God,' I say, half-expecting Brace to fall, despite his words.
'I certainly wasn't game enough to do *that*.'

'The foundation is fine.' Brace's grin widens. He has the
type of smile that shows all of his teeth, all perfectly straight
and white against his skin. 'But see here,' Brace runs his hand
along the railing, letting it crumble; demonstrating its rot.
'Here lies the problem. Replace the railing, and you'll be right
to go.'

I LOOK DOWN AT THE BUTTERY, PLAIN BAGEL HOUSED
in a white paper bag, the carry holder of coffee. 'Hey,' I say to
the shop attendant, indicating the 'something else' I'm after;
'Could you recommend a decent carpenter around here?'

Despite the line forming behind me, the shop attendant
looks at me curiously. 'I'm guessing, you haven't met Brace?
He's the only one I'd recommend – just quietly, though; don't
want to give the man a big head.'

'Brace,' I pretend, as though the name is unfamiliar. 'And
where might I find...?'

'Oh, that part's easy,' the shop attendant says, reeling off a
set of instructions with a knowing smile.

As I approach Brace's shop, there is music blaring amidst a
thunder of power tools, so I ignore the sign turned to 'closed'
and walk around to the back. There, balancing the tray of
coffees and the bagel – the butter making a clear window in
the paper bag – I find Brace, shirtless, working a sander over an
old launch. She's a glorious vessel, a genuine vintage piece.

Brace lifts his earmuffs away from his ears, reaching to
switch off the music.

'Hello,' he says with great surprise, slipping his arms into a

Hawaiian shirt. 'Didn't expect to see you here… Sorry,' he says, as though, remembering. 'I haven't got to your rowboat – I promise I will – but this here is my own little project; the '47 Shepherd.'

I shake my head, disregarding his unnecessary apology.

'I've only seen these in movies,' I say, examining his boat in awe.

'Ain't she a beauty?'

I nod, as together, we stand, united in our admiration.

'Ah,' I say finally, raising one hand, and then the other. 'I brought coffee – and a bagel.'

Brace accepts a coffee and the bagel – offering me half, which I decline as this is a gesture simply to offer my thanks – and the pair of us stand, sipping coffee, staring at the old launch.

'Yeah,' Brace says, picking up the thread of conversation. 'I love the smell of mahogany. And, you know, working with wood, there's so much life in it.' I can hear the passion in his voice. 'Not like working with metal or other materials.'

Brace grabs my hand – as though this is familiar, *natural* – guiding my hand to feel the boat's smooth surface. I breath in deeply; a touch to ignite my senses: deepening the smell of hewn timber – rich, full-bodied, exotic – strengthening the sight of such beauty. I bring my coffee to my lips. The experience making it all the more difficult to undertake my next excursion; the one I'd been putting off for weeks.

17

'A full set,' Gregory declares, pushing back his glasses, his dark brown eyes widening in wonder, marvelling at the folder. '*And* in date order... So, what you have here is a complete correspondence over an entire five-year courtship?'

I'm at the Cambridge Archives watching Gregory – clean shaven with a mop of dark curls, John Lennon glasses, a loosely stitched pullover with shirt collar poking through; the shape of his shoulders suggesting a sculpted physique hidden beneath.

'I think so,' I reply, continuously blown away by the friendliness of Canadians. *People are just so* nice.

'Gee!' Gregory exclaims, overcome by the wonders of an untapped archive as I share with him details of the other documents, letters, photographs and journals contained within a single room. 'It's a marvel. It really is. So what do you plan to do with it all?'

'Don't know,' I say, looking toward the historic map of Preston mounted on the wall, the Hall of Fame located in the next room where Gregory first pointed out a photograph of

Errington's father, George Pattinson, past M.P.P. for South Waterloo. Gregory, introducing me to a fellow co-worker as 'Preston royalty.' 'What do you think I *should* do?'

'Well,' Gregory tilts his head, the artificial light catching his silver ring with Aztec design, as he pushes dark curls off his face. 'Obviously, we'd appreciate any donation... But you might also want to consider the Doon Pioneer Village. The Waterloo Museum there, I suspect, would be very interested to take a look.'

'I'll think about it,' I say, contemplating Gregory's features: the closeness of his shave, the freshness of his scent, his slightly untamed crop of curls.

'Sure, just let me know,' Gregory says, subtle lines showing as he smiles. 'But how can I help? You said on the phone you were after a wedding photo... And the date was...?' Gregory checks his notepad of almost indecipherable scribbles and I notice the initials tattooed on his left ring finger along a bar of whiteness. 'April 1910?'

'That's right, April 27th – I have the original wedding announcement,' I say, considering how everyone has their own story, their own past. 'There is a photograph of Errington on her wedding day, but not of the couple together. In fact, most of the photographs seem to be of the Pattinsons, very little of the Moss side – Austin's side, that is. Although there is a small leather-bound book of pasted photographs featuring images from South Africa – the place, his chums, his horse – dated around the turn of the century.'

'The Boer War?'

'Yes, there's another small leather-bound book with minute dates and phrases. A Boer War journal, I believe... There is a book picturing Austin's photograph as 'Trooper 519,' and a Queen's Medal. A whole other life before Errington.'

Gregory looks up from his computer search. There is a

brightness to his brown eyes. 'Now that *is* interesting...' he says, before stumbling upon something evidently wonderful. 'Ah-ha!'

'Have you found something?

'*Not* a photograph,' Gregory angles the computer screen toward me, welcoming me into his space, thriving in the joy of discovery. 'But a newspaper write-up. There we are, I believe, that's them,' he says, beaming.

'Yes!' I only have to skim over the first line. 'That's them alright!'

When we finish our session – Gregory spending far more time with me than is perhaps necessary – I offer up my phone number, email and address. '*Just,*' I hesitate, 'in case, you find anything else.'

Gregory laughs as he receives the bit of paper.

'Right, well... Gee.'

Austin & Errington
Preston, Ontario, Canada
1907

149

18

———

July

Despite her absence on and off for six months of the last year, Austin and Errington have found a mode of existence that serves their basic need to live within each other's sight; as essential as food and water. Though, perhaps, Preston's worst kept secret, for now, they must keep their romance under wraps to maximise their time together; *Uncle Austin* is permitted to attend Maplecroft more than any suitor ever would. In keeping with the charade, Errington even gives the appearance of considering Antonio's offer of marriage – already approved by Father – before, naturally, turning him down on account of her 'responsibilities at home', the 'children,' her bouts of poor health, and, most significantly, because Antonio does not hold her heart.

I cannot bear to live out of your sight, Errington wrote once to Austin and has thought a thousand times since. Sunday evenings are still their most cherished time. From opposing ends of the room, the lovers maintain a discreet eye; Errington often letting her gaze linger, daring others to notice. In the reflection of the oversize mirrors in the Maplecroft drawing room, Errington can feel the way Austin looks at her – something he later narrates to her in private, her small hands gesturing in storytelling as he imagines a ring small enough to fit her finger. He loves the way her *'bright eyes'* catch the light of the chandelier like midnight pools capturing the light of the moon. From a distance, he may feel the warmth she projects, absorb her ever-present glow despite there being *'a whole crowd.'* There, in the shadows, they wait like performers in the wings.

'[W]ho was it that wrote something about the different strata of thought,' Errington wrote to Austin during a period of enforced separation *'– and isn't it true? I talk polite rubbish to the people here (whenever I can't get away to be alone) and all the time I'm thinking – and remembering every precious word and look...'* Even at Maplecroft, with the people she dearly loves, the loudest chorus in her head, the sound drowning out all others, is the knowledge of Austin's love.

But for the most part, Austin and Errington must exist, together, only in their shared imagination. *'Whatever our souls are made of, his and mine are the same'* – Though not a haunting, Errington finds herself thinking often of Emily Bronte's *Wuthering Heights*, of the way Austin and Errington fill each other's dreams as if they are the *'same'* – *and* yet, Errington is only too aware of the differences between them, of Austin's nostalgia of a past life she knows *'little of.'*

It's true that most of their days and often late nights are filled with mere dreaming; but a *'glimpse of fairyland'* may soon present itself in the form of a ball to be held at the country summer home of wealthy British family, the Everetts. An event Errington is determined to attend – even it be necessary to hide soiled linens on account of her menses – because the thought of yet another bout of bed rest; of narcotics rendering her without function for two, if not, three days; of missing the ball – and thus an opportunity to steal away! – does not bear thinking about.

THE IMPOSING EDIFICE OF TALL, WHITE COLUMNS set within elaborate English gardens exists as though a memory newly acquired; such grandeur, experienced anew. Within the oval-shaped room, Errington scans the crowd that expands quickly under her gaze as guest after guest alights from their horse and carriage – or motor car – to cross the threshold. Despite the crowd of people filling the space reserved for dancing, champagne and canapes, Errington spots Austin almost instantly.

Standing against the backdrop of tall velvet drapes, falling either side of the floor-to-ceiling windows, Austin appears engrossed in the world outside. From a distance, Errington watches, absorbed in Austin's quiet contemplation. The reflection of his blue-grey eyes in the tall window before him, remind Errington of pristine waters, mirroring the surrounding beauty of dark woods and blue skies – the sight of Summer when Errington is invariably sent away from the hustle and bustle of industrial Preston; this year to Maine.

There is something so peaceful about a reflected image, undisturbed by wind or rain. But changed conditions are inevitable, it seems. While Errington politely returns the friendly greeting of the many guests arriving determined to make an impression upon the eldest daughter of one of Preston's wealthiest businessmen and M.P.P. for South Waterloo; her view is greatly disrupted.

Still looking upon the apple orchard, Austin feels a sudden tap on his shoulder by the slight fingers of a female hand. He turns, the expression on his face quickly changing from surprise and delight to barely-concealed horror as he realises the hand belongs not to sweet Nell but the ever-persistent – and inconvenient – Mary Loy.

The voluptuous beast! Errington wrinkles her nose, as she spies Mary Loy from afar. *Why are her breasts always on display like produce on market day?*

Shrinking away from Mary Loy's hot breath in his ear, Austin takes an involuntary step backwards, almost bumping into a waiter who has managed to weave through the crowd, dexterously emptying his tray of little eggy pastries or tall glasses of champagne.

Mary Loy tilts her head to one side like a dog seated before a waiting dish and places her hands together as if in prayer.

Errington prepares to rescue Austin before he is lured onto the dance floor.

Austin averts his eyes from Mary Loy, and in doing so, spots Errington.

Leaning into Austin, Mary Loy lets out a laugh, louder than is natural, attracting the attention of the neighbouring crowd. *That girl is the ultimate 'moss-quito,'* Errington thinks to herself. *Bothersome, a nuisance, there to sample Austin's blood.*

Austin takes a further step back, preparing to ward her off, the velvet drapes pulling taut against his shoulder. But Mary Loy saunters off as though pleased with herself.

Errington continues to walk towards Austin, her gaze lowered, as though deciding how to engage him. Finally, standing close, as though daring an embrace, she lifts her gaze to his; a smile stretching across her face as she meets the brilliance of his eyes.

'Apple blossom – white and red,' Austin says at the sight of Errington's flushed cheeks.

Errington breathes out a slightly dramatic sigh, before waving away the compliment.

'More like a good, old mahogany shade, I'm afraid – so ugly! – and that's *before* going off to Maine. I dare not think how they shall look by the trip's end.'

'When do you leave?'

There is a tinge of disappointment in Austin's voice at this reminder of Errington's impending trip.

'The morning of the 12th. I wouldn't feel obliged to go, were it not for 'the children'... Oh, I'm happy to, really. A change of scenery will do them good, Frank especially.'

Errington shifts her gaze to the apple orchard outside, to the trees abundantly laden with ripening fruit. There is a sadness in her voice, regret for dwelling on her impending absence so soon after being reunited.

'It isn't fair, you know; you, carrying the others...,' Austin says, placing his hands behind his back to keep them from wandering. 'As the youngest of the 'Great Croydon Mosses,' I was, always the one being 'carried.' Rather selfish of me really, only ever looking out for yours truly.'

'Ah, but,' Errington raises her index finger. 'That may have been true in boyhood but since I've known you, I'd say you've done rather a lot for your siblings.'

Austin is looking out the window now; Errington joining his gaze. The treed arbour adorned with crisp apples, like berries on a sprig of holly, almost seems to beckon the lovers outdoors.

'Cheer up, one of these days, we may be together,' Austin says, letting his hand brush against hers as though recognising the trajectory of her thoughts. *'Sometimes happy mortals [do] get glimpses of fairyland...'*

Errington gives a smile, half-hopeful.

'I have tried to imagine it,' Austin continues, *'and wonder what I have done to deserve the past, the present and the rosy future... Deserve,'* he ponders. *'If I got what I deserve, I'd not*

escape a whipping and yet – instead of whipping, I have – I know I have – you, little girl. You – just you.'

With that same *happy solemn triumphant chant* – '*he loves me!'* – Errington looks at Austin with an eagerness; urging them both outside.

Fleeing the room to exit via the cloak room, the pair pass Mary Loy at the edge of the dance floor, held, reluctantly, in the arms of her newest suitor. It seems her show of affection towards Austin hadn't discouraged other interested parties.

'She's all yours,' Austin says to the suitor, with a wink.

Mary Loy gasps, her eyes darting behind her, as though someone has just trodden on the hem of her dress, a look of betrayal. Austin is tempted to explain how Miss Loy trapped him into engaging in her charades when Errington places a finger to his lips.

'Come,' she says.

Out in the apple orchard, Austin and Errington step quickly and breathlessly, as if about to reach the pinnacle of a great alpine climb. Passing the threshold of the treed arbour, they slip back behind a row of apple trees, overflowing with ripening fruit. Almost immediately, Austin reaches for the curve of her waist. Errington takes one hand – so much stronger and larger than her own – guiding it to her breast. Her nipples hardening beneath her bodice. Obediently, Austin lets his hand linger, cupping her breast, before teasing the tips of his fingers along the seam of her dress.

Errington breathes in; waiting, then encouraging; tentative, then urgent. And exceedingly glad of not needing to hide her linens.

What follows is an intrusion of noise, laughter, voices, music; here and then gone like the opening and shutting of a music box. The crunch of gravel underfoot, ceasing after a few short steps. Errington bites down on her lip. Austin stifles his breath.

In this 'underwater' moment – in which Errington may do nothing but remain motionless beneath the surface – the words of Mary Shelley's *Frankenstein* enter her mind. '*There is something at work in my soul, which I do not understand.*' And also, '*It is true, we shall be monsters, cut off from all the world; but on that account we shall be more attached to one another.*' Could this bodily urgency be an 'evil within?'

As the footsteps cease, Errington takes Austin by the hand – the other, holding up the hem of her dress – urging him to take flight without a second thought. Whipping past row upon row of trees bursting with fruit, the pair cut through long grass with eager abandon, seed heads catching on the lace of her dress, as they make for the dark cavern of the barn.

Their eyes gradually adjust to the darkness, helped by cracks of moonlight seeping through gaps either side of the barn doors. To Austin, inhaling her perfumed orange blossom scent has the same effect as powerful smelling salts, awakening something deep within. Swelling with desire, he draws Errington close to him. Errington, face pressed to the fibres of his jacket, breathes in the scent of port-infused tobacco so often absorbed by the paper on which he writes. Intoxicated by each other's unique scent, intermingling with the smell of hay – a reminder they are quite alone – Austin and Errington's hands move in search of one another. Errington's legs pressing against the seams of her skirts, before a rush of cool air, as Austin's strong, but gentle hands ascend, teasing the moist landscape of her inner thigh.

19

August

Austin Moss,
Preston, Ont.

12 August 1907

Miss Pattinson,
   Atlantic House, Old Orchard.
   Maine, U.S.A.

Dearest,

   Well, little girl, did you have a comfortable journey down? And are you in good quarters now you have arrived? You won't be bothered with housekeeping troubles, at least I hope not. I hope you will be able to have a good spell of rest and quiet, which you need as much as anyone. I know you will get overtired if someone doesn't look after you. I wish I were with you, only then you wouldn't have quite so much rest. I guess I would be worrying you all the time. Have you read Dorothy Forster yet and what do you like best in Lawson or Paterson? I don't think they will appeal to you quite so much as to yours truly as the life they tell of you will not know.

Well, little girl, for this holiday I'll just have to imagine myself alongside you on the rocks and paddling on the beach and slacking on the veranda. I hope the colour is coming back again to those cheeks. "How sweet, how fair are Nellie's blushing cheeks." There certainly was a little colour in those cheeks in the woods.

Do take care of yourself, sweetheart and do not undertake any startling journeys either afloat or ashore. Don't get lonesome, just shut your eyes and imagine. I was trying that just now and I don't mind telling you, it's rather a fraud. Please excuse this scrap; I thought you would like to know I was thinking of you now as always. So first good-night not good-bye or even au revoir.

Yours always and lovingly,

A

Seated at the kidney-shaped cherrywood writing desk, Errington lays out her writing materials in vain. For she knows, any moment, Elizabeth will charge through her bedroom door, demanding to see the monkeys down by the pier or pleading for the group to set out for ice-cream – no matter what kind of mood Frank is in or whether Ruth is content with a book in hand. Errington resolves to scrawl only a brief note, just to set Austin's mind at ease.

Errington hasn't experienced the slightest regret following their shared moment of passion in the apple orchard the night of the ball. Nor did she feel remorse for a similar moment shared in the woods – all of it unbearably wonderful. Yet, sooner or later, their eager touch will become too much to obey any kind of limit; their nuptials – not yet broached with Father – seem an eternity away.

And so, perhaps, their affection has become rather too conspicuous, as even Elizabeth – something of a co-conspirator, delivering messages and letters between the pair – has been demonstrating her disgust whenever she sees them by making an exaggerated clicking sound with her tongue as if discovering a spoiled dessert.

Despite the somewhat ominous probability that '*Beth… will talk,*' Errington has her suspicions that it was Elizabeth's own indiscretions that led to her enrolment in boarding school. Previously, the possibility of being sent away had only ever been lorded over Elizabeth as an idle threat. *Funny,* Errington considers: Father had always been quick to send *her* away; whatever the circumstance.

Fountain pen in hand, Errington is considering her turn of phrase; how best to set Austin's mind at ease without scribbling a mere rambling, when Elizabeth, almost on cue, bursts through the bedroom door, hysterical as ever, followed in quick succession by Ruth and Frank, shrieking, 'Fire! Fire!'

Ellen Errington Pattinson,
Maine, U.S.A.

16 August 1907
Austin Moss Esq.
PRESTON.

Dearest of all,
Your letter has just come – it was so good of you to write at once. I wanted to write this morning to quiet any anxiety you may have about us (Oh! I've wanted to write thousands of

times, during the last few days, but I have never had one minute alone!).

You have probably seen particulars of the fire – it was fearful – but really the most gorgeously beautiful sight imaginable. The buildings were all frame – and hotels, stores, cottages, all along the beach, went up at once. But, at any rate we are isolated here – and the wind was in the other direction. Beth was frightened and Ruth awed – and Frank helped save a few cottages. I wish you were here – oh dearest I love you so – but still – as the greater part of me is with you in Preston it is not so bad.

I have not had much time for reading. You know Frank has a rather restless streak in his disposition and we have all been trying to keep him from feeling fearfully dull – I read "Black Swans" almost first and like it – and some of the others tremendously – but there is one thought that is echoed in all of them. I have often, often thought it before, and now – these verses are emphasizing it – that in that life there is such a strange and strong inviting. Your life must now be terribly monotonous and cramped in comparison – and my vision is so narrow – I cannot see – I cannot even sympathize fully – because I do not know.

Dearest, I'm sorry I wrote that but it has worried me for a long time – so now you can see how I manage to torment myself – but I do know you love me – you have shown me and told me a thousand precious times... Aren't you glad we had that picnic day together? The others were there, of course, but you know "all men besides and women too are to me as shadows" – there were <u>really</u> just you and I...

Yours lovingly always and forever,

Nell, MAINE, U.S.A.

Maplecroft

Austin Moss,
Preston, Ont.

28 August 1907 - Sunday

Miss Pattinson, Maine, U.S.A.

Dearest,

Your most welcome letter has been in my pocket a whole week. And as you are so quaint I believe you like having letters from me, even the scrappy things I write. There is not much to say, except what I have told you once or twice and what I feel all the time. (I am a wee bit scared you may feel tired of me repeating it – although so far, if you are, you disguise it pretty well.) This is just to tell you that I love you and always have done, because I cannot tell you in person, as I have done one or two Sunday evenings… How's the new bathing suit, that is one of the things I must see – I think it would certainly be cute. Do they allow mixed bathing in Maine?

Am sorry if the fire spoiled your holiday but was so glad to hear you are not in any danger. A big fire is gorgeous, but rather awesome – there's no stopping it. Perhaps you can find things to do that will keep you out of mischief, not that there is much danger of that.

Now, <u>don't</u> torment yourself that I want to go back to the Western land, "the life certainly has a strange inviting when once to the work you have put your hand". I may want to go back, alright, but I want you more, much more, I want you most – I want you all and always – now you know…

Why, Bright Eyes, I am always looking after myself, being naturally selfish as you know I want the best little girl and intend to have her too in spite of one or two others, eh? Well, One and Only, I am not going to scold you but I expect you need someone to look after you. What did you have for break-fast, eh? One piece of toast as usual?

I shall expect to see you quite sunburned when you come back and hope you will be quite strong again, which you have <u>not</u> been for some time, even if you won't own up to it. Ruth and Beth are behaving, I hope: no flirtations or falling in the water or getting lost – I'm sure Frank is having a good time too, in a quiet way, nothing strenuous. They will keep you busy, keeping them out of mischief... Please excuse scraps. I hope it will "give you a moment's delight, sweetheart of mine" – Good-night Little Nell –

Yours lovingly now and always,
Austin, PRESTON

UNLIKE THE MONTH'S END, WHEN ALL ORDERS AND shipping details must be finalised – or the start of the month when all outstanding accounts must be paid in full – in the middle of the month, Austin's workload is often at its least strenuous. Accompanied by a calmness which evades him the rest of the time – except in dreaming or in the physical presence of *her* – Errington's *'bright eyes'* staring up at him, her slender hand touching his face. Austin, breathing in her orange blossom scent, lets his mind explore the possibilities of their touch. Musings that have led him here, undertaking a rather difficult yet much anticipated, conversation with Frank.

'What's all this about then, eh?' Frank's hands clasp together, disturbing the sawdust recently settled upon his desk.

The door to Frank's office is closed, muffling sounds of workmen crafting furniture, the continuous sawing and plan-ing, a buzz of industry taking place in the background like the distant sound of warblers filling the Summer air.

'We'll need to make this quick, old chap,' Frank says, his fingers interlocking like the movement of the cog concealed beneath the face of their Grandfather's pocket watch, now in Frank's keeping. 'I've another furniture buyer coming at half eleven to see the factory in action. An assurance of quality. Entirely unnecessary, but there you are.'

'Right,' Austin uncrosses his legs, placing his sweaty palms over the crease of his pant legs. 'I'll get straight to it, then.' Clearing his throat, Austin chooses his words carefully. 'Within the terms of my loan to the Preston Furniture Co., written in your hand, is the explicit agreement that funds are to be repaid, in full, *'on demand'* at such time as I may request them.'

Frank shifts in his chair, transferring sawdust from his hands to his trousers, before brushing his hands together. 'The blasted stuff still finds its way into absolutely everything,' Frank comments, 'after how many years?'

Austin waits as Frank attempts to rid himself of the ever-present sawdust.

'Yes,' Frank says, finally. 'That is the premise of our little loan.'

Somewhat resentful of the way Frank downplays the amount, Austin gives a nod of approval. He hadn't expected Frank to be so obliging.

'However...'

'Ah.'

'No, no,' Frank smooths his hand over thin air as if straightening a tablecloth, ironing out a crease. 'I'll be frank, I hadn't expected the request to come so *soon*. But,' Frank presses his lips together, 'truly, I was able to coax you here and I hope you may see that my account written to you some time ago, is, of course, wholly accurate.'

'*There are <u>any amount</u> of openings here once a man has a knowledge of Canadian business methods,*' Frank had written to Austin in Klerksdorp. '*If I were out of my business tomorrow, I would not have the slightest anxiety as to being able to find a situation or to open up a business at least as lucrative as my present one.*'

'Then you'll release the funds?'

'I shall, of course, keep my word as I am bound by our agreement. But I would urge you, dear brother, to take the time to secure a new business in good faith first. It may save us some paperwork. Besides, I rather think you will benefit from any extra time spent here at Preston Furniture Co. as you continue to learn Canadian business methods. There is a great deal to learn; more than you may realise.'

Frank removes Grandfather's pocket watch from his vest, noting the passing of time.

'I assume you *are* preparing to purchase a business of your own? And, you have a business in mind...?'

'Crown Furniture Co.' Austin declares, naming the very business that regularly fills his thoughts outside his hours at Preston Furniture Co., considering this the key to his and Errington's future happiness.

Setting up discussions with other interested parties that may act as a largely silent partner, Austin is already imagining making his mark on paper emblazoned with the logo of a crown; of seeking out workers and establishing offices within the Grist Mill where the business is housed.

'It may take some months, but I will certainly require the funds in the not-too-distant future,' Austin says, adding, 'I'm looking at a joint venture.'

'Ah, that is always a danger,' Frank says, hurriedly cautioning his brother. 'Certainly, an area to exercise caution...'

Maplecroft

Ellen Errington Pattinson
Maine, U.S.A

2 September 1907 – Saturday morning

Mr Austin Moss,
     PRESTON

Dearest,

This is our last day at Old Orchard – we start for home tomorrow morning; so, you see I am again obliged to answer your dear letter promptly – I am rather sorry in one way because where my letters are concerned anticipation must be infinitely better than realization – but probably by now you know what to expect! ... I have read "Dorothy Forster," and enjoyed it immensely – there are so many places mentioned with which I am familiar – Grandmother used to never tire of telling me stories of the Erringtons of Beaufront.

The other books I should like to keep for a little while – may I? They still leave an uncomfortable feeling – there is too much of the "lure of the wild" – but still I <u>do</u> know better than to mind, now. And you know, dearest, if you want, you may still have <u>both</u> the west – and anything else you fancy... There is one happy chorus growing louder and louder in my heart till every other thought is subdued. It is only this, dear: I'm coming home. Will you be a little – a tiny *bit – glad too?*

Do you know in your absence I've been kissing a substitute – an awfully cold, unresponsive one, though! It's poor old Oom Paul – I don't suppose he was ever kissed so much in his life as during the last year – and especially the last month. He is becoming quite worn under the treatment. I wonder – would it affect you in that way?

...Yours lovingly, ever and always,
Nell, MAINE, U.S.A

20

November

It wasn't intentional that Eddie's walk across town coincided with the sitting of the Medical Board – the drizzling snow preventing his usual morning stroll, postponed until the completion of his house calls – but it wasn't entirely a coincidence either. All day he had been restless, and, indeed, the preceding evening, in anticipation of the upcoming decision surrounding his proposal submitted to the Board last month.

Before taking his case to the Board, Eddie has spent much time gathering evidence. Beyond hand-washing – a discovery that goes as far back as Florence Nightingale in the Crimean War and earlier – Eddie believes patients would benefit from their physician donning a gown and gloves prior to surgery.

But, as he awaits a decision, despite this argument gaining credence in certain circles elsewhere, Eddie anticipates resistance to the proposed measure. The case being made, for example, that should a physician have to rush off from conducting an autopsy to attend to a mother in the final throes of labour, there may be little time for a costume change. As always, Eddie anticipates the notion of change to be looked upon with scepticism by many and embraced by few.

Cutting across Central Park, past the three-tiered, almost-frozen, fountain – sounds of children giggling outside Preston Public School halting in an instant with the return of their teacher – Eddie makes for the tall, white columns of the Town Hall, slowing upon approach.

'You're too early,' a man declares, stepping out past the columns. A swirl of smoke ascending from his pipe. 'I expect the meeting won't be over for some time... Heck, I'm not even sure we'll get through all matters of business.'

Although Eddie doesn't know his name, the man, also cloaked in a navy-blue cape, is instantly recognisable as a fellow physician.

'Doctor Scadding,' the man says, holding out a firm hand to shake, 'St. John's, Toronto. And you're Doctor Barlowe, I believe? Your face is pictured among the submissions.'

'Submissions? Are there very many others?'

Doctor Scadding holds out his pipe as though it were a drink he might spill and lets out a chuckle. 'Oh, yes. How they do build up!' Doctor Scadding takes a long slow, draw of his pipe. 'By the way, that was a joke before; we *never* get through all matters of business.'

As the snow begins to fall again, Eddie considers how he hadn't planned on stopping; but he now feels incapable of moving on.

'Sorry,' Doctor Scadding says, earnestly. A smile emerging as he relights the bowl of his pipe. 'I mustn't jest. I was young once too. One thing, son, you'll soon learn – and not just in Preston – nothing happens quickly and most things are learnt too late.'

Despite referring to Eddie as 'son' – a term which might well have been used to undermine Eddie's professionalism and years of experience – Doctor Scadding looks at Eddie with kindness in his eyes. The way a teacher may look upon a student who shows exceptional promise.

'Listen,' he says, before Eddie may take his leave. 'Perhaps, there's hope for the medical profession yet. You've still got that buzz, haven't you? The sense that you're doing real good in the world? I remember that feeling. Be glad it hasn't left you yet. No doubt, it will.'

Eddie wonders whether Doctor Scadding's cynicism will eventually infiltrate his own mind, in much the same way young men of university age submit to certain liberal ideologies, only to trade them in for the harsher perspective of the preceding generation. Eddy offers a half-hearted wave and begins to walk away. When he looks back, Doctor Scadding has disappeared between the columns.

Against a backdrop of white, another figure emerges, looking dishevelled and seemingly in last night's attire, his grubbiness contrasting the polished cleanliness of Eddie's own clothes, his crisp, white collar peeking out from his cape.

Eddie recognises the man as Harry Blackwood. A man who must have newly made bail. His name featured in this morning's paper for stealing from a fellow poker player who'd boasted he 'couldn't care' if he was out of work for a whole season because he had fifty dollars safely hidden inside his motor car. That evening, Harry Blackwood had apparently broken into the man's motor car, liberating the poker player of his dough. Blackwood was soon on the peg after the police traced the theft back to the man's careless boasting.

Eddie turns back to walk on, but not before his gaze meets the other man's. Blackwood gives a smirk, raising one hand in a wave, his grime-covered fingers, nails bitten down to the quick, lingering in the cold air as the sun falls away from the day.

Eddie shakes off the unpleasant feeling accompanying this encounter along with the cold and presses on toward the top of King Street. Not only have these run-ins with Scadding and Blackwood left a bad taste in his mouth, so too has an earlier house call in which Eddie had sent a young patient to hospital. A child suffering a raw, sore throat, watering eyes and worsening chest pain; the mother insisting nothing had changed in the household or beyond. Except that is, the recent purchase of a refrigerator – more flash than a motor car – installed within the family-operated business where the child spent ample time. When pressed, the mother agreed there had been a distinct smell coming from the new contraption but that it had begun to dissipate into the natural air. What had that to do with her child's symptoms? the mother asked. But Eddie knew the signs of ammonia poisoning, the very gas used in refrigerators.

Eddie is still thinking about this child, about how, perhaps, not all technological advances are a marvel, when he spots Doctor Vardon lugging his Gladstone up the step to board an electric railcar.

'Doctor Vardon?'

Vardon turns around slowly, his navy-blue cape billowing behind him like a sail catching the wind. Poised at the step, he stands expectantly, blinking. 'Well?'

'I...' Eddie looks toward the railcar and back to Vardon. 'Are you heading for Galt?'

'Toronto.' Vardon greets the driver with a nod as he purchases a ticket. 'Medical conference,' he says over his shoulder.

Eddie pushes two fingers between the coat buttons at his chest, before unbuttoning to feel around in his vest pocket. He hadn't anticipated boarding a railcar but luckily has some small dosh set aside for the planned purchase of postcards to send back home – one of the Hotel Del Monte with a painted garland of maple leaves he'd previously admired; and the other, for his young cousin, picturing kittens perched on a plank, mesmerised by something beyond the camera lens, captioned, *'Wonder what it is!'* Instead, Eddie hands over the coins to the driver.

Seated, Vardon's small frame is largely hidden behind the latest edition of *The Galt Daily Reporter*, opened up to the page three news. With few passengers on board, Eddie sits directly opposite Vardon whose eyes move from left to right as he actively reads the newspaper. Eddie clears his throat. Abruptly, Vardon throws down the newspaper. Holding onto the frame of the chair, he stands up quickly; surprisingly nimble for a man of his years.

'Can't bear to sit any longer,' Vardon declares, his pale, sun-spotted hand reaching for the handle dangling from the car ceiling. 'Sitting all morning and afternoon in that blasted meeting and here I am setting off, soon to endure another bout. Quite frankly, I loathe the thought! We really should conduct these things standing, don't you think? That would be most time effective... and far less dull. It can't be very good, this lazing about. The greatest minds of Ontario may very well wind up falling asleep!'

Eddie offers a weak smile, wondering what he's let himself in for. Vardon is notorious for being a talker; difficult to stop and impossible to stay on topic.

'Are you going?' Vardon asks, not waiting for an answer. 'No, I don't suppose you are. Typically, they reserve spots for the most experienced of physicians. It's rather elite, you know. A ticket money can't buy. Oh, don't worry,' Vardon says, positioning his feet to keep his Gladstone bag in place as it threatens to slide across the floor. 'You're not missing anything.' Vardon looks at Eddie directly, an intent look in his eyes, a slight frown as if searching for a diagnosis. 'Wait on, I didn't know you lived in Galt?'

'I don't,' Eddie says, casually shrugging. 'Actually, I wanted to speak with you... about my proposal.'

'Oh, yes?' Vardon leans one ear toward Eddie.

'The one I submitted to the Board.'

Vardon makes a sound to indicate he is listening.

'Well, I wondered,' Eddie begins, steadying himself as the car lunges to a stop, the driver announcing the street name in an overly cheerful declaration. 'Whether I may have your support?'

'Ah,' Vardon waggles his finger. 'It is not a matter of support, but one of practicality. A physician's time is precious, Doctor Barlowe. We mustn't place barriers in the way of getting on with our important work. I expect, one day, you'll aim to have a family of your own. Am I right?'

Eddie offers nothing in the way of a reply, just listens.

'Well already, most nights, I arrive home to Marjorie at half seven. If I adhere to protocol after protocol, nonsense after nonsense, that would surely be pushed out. Why, my dinner'd be stone cold, or else, severely overcooked!'

Vardon presses on, oblivious to Eddie's rising anger.

'Young people are so anxious these days, so eager for the next new thing. But,' Vardon shrugs 'never mind, you'll learn. As you can imagine, it's been a long time since I was in medical school, but I tell you, there's a lot they don't teach you.'

Enough is enough. Eddie grips the handle more tightly now, not bothering to hide the anger in his stare.

'Doctor Vardon,' he declares, standing much taller than his counterpart. 'Though my career may, thus far, fall short of yours in years – and while I quite agree about the failings of medical school – let it be known that I am, indeed, an experienced practitioner. I have had my hands inside young dying men pulled straight off the battlefield; some of whom I was able to save.

After my stint at Cambridge Medical School and the guidance of my superiors thereafter, I have read countless journals, made it my business to know and understand best practice and am quite up to date. Let me assure you, the measures I am proposing – which I think you will find are gaining credence elsewhere – are not timewasters as you seem to suggest, but most probably life-saving measures. The thing we *mustn't* do is skip procedures and protocols crucial to maintaining our patients' good health.'

Instantly regretting the need to defend his position, Eddie runs his fingers through his hair and drops his shoulders, still standing tall. Perhaps because of his youthful appearance – his blonde pencil moustache is the only facial hair he may pull off without looking boyish or untidy – Eddie finds himself continually taken at face value. And it doesn't help that he is surrounded by physicians, some of whom *look* old enough to have witnessed Queen Victoria's coronation; their archaic practices are a relic of the mid-nineteenth century.

There is a distinct pause as the two men eye each other. Vardon appears to be still as he sits himself back down, not the flighty bird he embodied moments earlier. The driver interrupts the semi-silence – there is a young boy toward the back of the car whistling a tune under his breath and a middle-aged woman producing an intermittent chesty cough. With the upbeat announcement of the next stop, Eddie steadies himself with the swinging handle and moves up toward the exit.

'I shall consider your recommendation,' Vardon calls out.

Eddie looks back to see Vardon peering over the top of his reopened newspaper. 'But I can't say this outburst has done you, or your recommendation, any good.'

Eddie presses his lips together and gives a nod. He knows.

With the sun shifting behind the clouds, the day closes in and after walking several blocks, finds himself at the Hotel Kress. In a state of despair, Eddie enters the establishment.

Passing through the entrance, beneath the flow of patrons spilling out onto the balconies, Eddie steps across the patterned carpet, past the cloak room and into the bar. Over his shoulder, he can feel the tension of a poker game, in which there is little sound, save for the laboured breathing of its players and the light tapping of knuckles on the table. Eddie glances over to see Austin's brother, Frank, seated behind a spread of cards and dosh. Never one to let a bad mood interfere with polite behaviour, Eddie considers going over there but decides better of it after noting the way Frank's body lurches forward, the expression on his face suggesting the game is not going as planned. So instead, Eddie orders a drink at the bar.

'Whadda you 'ave?' the bartender appears almost out of nowhere. His familiar gaze making Eddie quiver.

Working a semi-damp tea-towel around the edge of a pint glass, the bartender holds his gaze as he leans against the edge of the bar. The bartender's eyes are so dark, they are almost black. Eddie has almost forgotten the feeling.

'Just a pint. Whatever's on tap,' Eddie replies quickly, watching the glass fill with amber liquid, white froth lapping over the side.

The bartender runs a long slender finger along the smooth surface of the glass to mop up the spillage and lifts it to his mouth; his tongue sweeps along his skin, tasting the overflowing beer. He looks up at Eddie intently, biting his lower lip, relishing in the taste of the lingering ale.

'That all ya after?'

Eddie slides the coins across the bar with two fingers, their flat, round surface mirroring that of his Masonic ring. His touch lingering as the bartender accepts payment, and simultaneously, inserts his fingers along the inside of Eddie's palm. Eddie's hand prickles with his touch.

'Gotta piss,' the bartender calls over his shoulder to a barmaid who rolls her eyes at this open vulgarity.

Eddie stares out into the space previously occupied by the bartender. Without touching his pint, Eddie swings his feet down from the brass footrest, pushes out from the bar and takes his leave outside.

The outhouse is set well apart from the main establishment. And while the noise and light diminish, the stench grows more pungent as Eddie draws near. Tentatively, he peers inside, giving himself the willies as he steps back on a fallen branch which snaps underfoot. This is followed by laughter coming from behind the outhouse.

The bartender steps out from the shadows. 'Wasn't sure ya'd show,' he says.

Half-concealed amongst the shrubbery, hidden from the moonlight, Eddie reaches for the bartender's face. His full lips seem in direct contrast to the rough stubble of his chin and cheeks.

'Not here,' the bartender says, guiding Eddie back to seek comfort within the warmth of the cloak room.

At the creak and click of the door, Eddie responds to his lover's touch; as malleable as dough in the turning and kneading of bread-making. Amidst a sea of coats, he shuts his eyes tight, amplifying the ecstasy, blocking out the shame. When it's over, Eddie is surprised to find he is still holding his breath.

21

———

Eddie wasn't expecting to be disturbed so early. Peeling his eyes open, rubbing away sleep, he takes a guess at the hour. There is no twittering of birds. Despite being in a basement apartment with an absence of natural light, sounds of the world outside typically travel down the stairs, sounding the beginning of each day. As the knocking continues, Eddie stumbles out of bed, scrambling for his trousers, tossed beside the nightstand.

Though the door is unlocked, Eddie opens it to find Mrs Merriweather waiting at the top of the stairs. She is wearing a nightcap and has clearly been dragged out of bed herself at this peculiar hour, the candle held to her face casting great shadows in the passageway.

'Doctor Barlowe, I'm sorry to disturb you but there has been a message sent requesting your presence at...' the parlour maid hesitates, as if the location holds great pain. '*Maplecroft.* I have the boy here who delivered word.'

A young man no older than twelve or thirteen hovers behind Mrs Merriweather. Pressing together his unpolished boots, bringing his hands to rest behind his back, the boy presents himself as best he can.

'Did you come here all on your own?' Eddie asks, noticing the boy's trousers torn at the knee, exposing fresh blood.

'Yes, sir,' the boys nods. 'Ran all the way. Not bad in the dark, though I stumbled more than once.'

'May I see the letter?' Eddie asks of Mrs Merriweather, who at once thrusts the note into his hand; Eddie scanning its contents for indications of panic. 'Hmm, I see,' Eddie folds the note back over. 'Well, I'm not sure where I may secure a carriage at this hour.'

'Excuse me, sir, by now the Pattinson carriage will be waiting just outside. I was told to make a head start. The horses don't always take kindly to going up and down them hills, you see.'

'I see.' Eddie laces up his boots before gathering up his Gladstone bag, cape and hat. 'Well, we'd best make haste. Do accompany me in the carriage,' he says to the boy.

Mrs Merriweather ushers the pair out the door. 'Mind the carpets,' she says under her breath, as she notices the blood at the boy's knee. 'Doctor Barlowe, I shall have breakfast waiting for you upon your return. The cook shall fix you chops, scrambled eggs and bacon, just as you like,' she says. Mrs Merriweather, as always, is eager to please.

Entering the cold, dark air, Eddie tilts his hat to her in thanks at this agreeable offering and steps up onto the waiting carriage.

Upon first attempt, the clopping of the horses' hooves comes to a halt as they struggle up the hill, the driver slowly easing the carriage back down the slope before taking an alternate street.

'I had thought we'd take the most direct route, Doctor Barlowe, but it's too much for the horses,' the driver calls over his shoulder, his bearded face lit up ever so slightly by the hanging lantern and the light of the moon. 'My apologies, sir.'

Eddie acknowledges the driver before turning his attention to the boy whose gaze rests on the carriage floor.

'Why do you look so nervous, boy?' Eddie asks. 'You needn't fear me... Are you treated quite well at your place of work?'

'Yes, sir,' the boy says, looking up at Eddie. 'Very well.'

'But you look like a scared little rabbit. Are you not normally permitted to ride in the carriage?'

The boy leans in, speaking in a whisper.

'It's the man with the scar, sir, the Pattinson's butler, Mr Hobson... he gives me the willies.'

'Young man, it's hardly fair to prejudice yourself against someone on account of their disfigurement,' Eddie says, though unconvinced this is the actual source of the boy's concern. 'Has Mr Hobson ever done anything to hurt you, or to suggest you may be put in harm's way?'

'No, sir, I can't say he has. It's just that...' The boy has to stop himself from taking his thumb to his mouth, his nails all bitten down to the quick. 'I see him everywhere, sir,' the boy says, conveying a kind of horror in his eyes, unmistakable even in low light. 'Not just at Maplecroft, but all over. Even just now as we hopped into the carriage; he just appeared from nowhere – it gives me the creeps. It's as if there is no place for me to hide – not even in my mind. Indeed, he has not done me any harm, sir, but should I get on the wrong side of him ... I shall be very frightened, indeed.'

Whether the boy is imagining things, or, perhaps, affected by the elements, Eddie does not press the matter further, preferring to believe only in the presence of dark shadows. It's a belief he can't quite shake from the previous evening; he'd been assailed by that same eerie feeling only moments before stealing away to the cloak room; a forgotten space of furs, intense pleasure and resulting shame.

Upon his arrival at Maplecroft, the house stands in darkness save a top bedroom that hosts a faint yellow glow. As the carriage comes to a halt, kicking up snow turned to slush, the strongest aspect of the glow makes its way downstairs, the door opening before Eddie has a chance to knock. Mr Pattinson is waiting just inside – the wait staff, all otherwise engaged as per his instruction or else sound asleep – but George is no stranger to getting his hands dirty. Only last fall, he had personally polished the boots of all his house guests, visiting dignitaries from abroad. George considered it unacceptable to expect his staff to labour beyond their regular duties, he'd told Eddie, by seeing their reflection in another master's boots.

It is unusual for Eddie to see George in this way. Appearing contrary to his image captured by town photographer, James Esson; an image, no doubt, destined to, one day, hang in a Hall of Fame. Absent is his usual neatly parted hair, the clean-shaven face framing a thick but neatly trimmed moustache, his stiff, white collar. The yellow light of the candle casts unfortunate shadows over George's face.

'Mr Pattinson,' Eddie declares as George hands him a candle at the door, before leading him up the never-ending staircase.

Quickly and quietly, Eddie follows, balancing his Gladstone bag in one hand, the brass candle holder in the other. Having never seen this part of the house unlit, it seems to Eddie that Maplecroft loses some of its splendour. The ornate carvings of the staircase, ceiling roses, patterned wallpaper and equally intricate carpets, paintings dotting the walls like postage stamps; all are masked by the cover of darkness. The bright, cheery feel of Christmas festivities Eddie had been privy to on his first Christmas here in Preston –

and, indeed, the one after that are now obscured in the shadows.

As they walk, George does his best to convey the current state of affairs.

The last stair creaks as first George, then Eddie, settle upon the landing. There, Eddie can see a soft, yellow light escaping a half-open door. George allows Eddie to walk on ahead. Upon approach, Eddie walks on delicate feet, careful not to disturb the patient, her face framed by loose, tousled hair.

When, at last, he is close enough to discover Errington's eyes open, Eddie smiles. 'Miss Pattinson, you're awake. How are you feeling?'

Though Errington's eyes remain open, her face does not change in expression.

George speaks from the doorway. 'I can never tell if she's awake or asleep. I have often tried to gently wake her in this state but usually to no avail.'

Eddie watches for a moment, as Errington's small, delicate hand reaches out, caressing the air. He takes her hand in his. It sits weightless, failing to register his touch. Eddie waves his fingers in front of Errington's vacant gaze.

'She is, indeed, oblivious to my presence, though, one must resist the urge to wake a person from this kind of slumber. Does she walk around in this state?'

Errington releases a long, slow groan, clutching at her lower abdomen, before sinking deeper into sleep.

'There are occasions,' George agrees, 'when Errington may be found by the window, under the gentle light of the stars. Eyes open, yet unseeing. But that, Doctor Barlowe,' George says, crossing his arms, 'is the least of our concerns. Allow me to fetch my notes. I have in the study, a compilation of observations; a record of instances of irrational behaviour, of a heightened emotional state – an account, far more thorough than the one, I know, my daughter keeps. Of course, not all observations are my own – that would be quite impossible – but they are, I believe, an accurate account of Errington's declining health.'

As George descends the staircase, in search of his notes, Errington rouses from her sleep.

'Doctor Barlowe?' she says, bleary-eyed. 'Has Father sent you? Oh, I hope we didn't disturb...' Errington begins to sit up, before letting her shoulders land back against the pillow. 'Oh, dear. It seems, I am rather nauseous.'

Eddie examines the empty bottles, the tins of pills piled on Errington's nightstand set up like the crowded window of a dispensary. 'Tell me,' he says, his eyes shifting from tin to tin; each one declaring itself the 'best and only' cure for 'women's troubles, headaches and liver complaints,' before taking in the bottles, and settling on the empty bottle of laudanum. 'Are these all for you?'

'Who else?' Errington breathes a sigh, before abruptly changing the subject. 'Thank you for coming, Doctor – though I'm not sure it was necessary – although I dare say, Doctor Vardon, would not take kindly to being summoned as you were.'

'Ah, yes, well, Doctor Vardon is at a conference in Toronto.'

Eddie examines Errington with care, gently lifting her small, dainty wrist to test the strength of her pulse, before examining the whites of her eyes, the clamminess at her forehead.

'You take a regular dose of laudanum?'

'For my insomnia,' Errington nods.

'And your diet?'

Eddie appears concerned as he examines Errington's small frame and slightly, gaunt cheeks.

'Not the best, I'm afraid,' Errington confesses – the thought of food makes her queasy. 'But, whenever I am laid up, I am regularly fed sweetmeats, calves' foot jelly, far more often than I would like.'

Eddie turns his attention to the draft coming from the bay window.

'Letting out the bad air, I suppose,' Eddie says, walking over to the window, pulling it shut. 'Miss Pattinson, how would you describe your relationship with laudanum?'

'My *relationship?*' Errington asks, puzzled, watching Eddie as he paces the room.

'Yes,' Eddie begins. 'How does it affect you? That is to say, do you feel particularly ill at times when you are prompted to engage its use?' Eddie examines Errington with a critical eye.

'Laudanum, admittedly, is a rather loathsome but loyal friend, accompanying me through all of life's highs and lows. But, Doctor Barlowe, do you wish for me to speak in candour?'

'Please.'

'Doctor Vardon and Father know better than I, I know, and, it's true, at present, I do feel worse without the laudanum... aching and nauseated,' Errington says, sitting up in bed, 'but oftentimes, I feel... nothing more than a tiredness, perhaps, hardly warranting its use...'

Eddie rests his physician hands – strong and lean – on the knob of the bed frame, as if comfortably propping himself up with a walking stick, settling in to listen to his patient reveal her feelings. Which she will do imminently, he thinks. He knows that expression on her face, like troubled clouds settling overhead. He's seen it before on other patients.

'Oh, Doctor Barlowe, I am miserable – and it hasn't a thing to do with my health. You're Austin's friend, so you must know of my affections for him – and his for me – and now that he is to be back and forth to Quebec on business, I cannot live like this. Tucked away in my room, out of his sight. Do you know, Doctor Barlowe, I have never sought a second opinion – or rather, Father has never sought one – but sometimes, I wonder if all these bouts of bedrest, rest cures, dare I mention hospitalisations? All of it; aren't just a means of… Oh, it's too horrid for words but sometimes I can't help but wonder…'

'Yes…?' Eddie urges, despite the sound of approaching footsteps. 'Go on.'

But the time between the creak of the top stair and the appearance of George clutching a fat leather-bound book, detailing Errington's decline, is too short.

'Here is the bulk of my notes,' George says, handling the book as though it were the Holy Bible. 'I'm afraid it spans several years… Ah, you're awake.'

'Yes,' Errington says, still with a look of concern.

'You were sleeping with your eyes open,' Eddie says. 'Very common.'

'Oh… was I?' Errington begins, sounding, ashamed to think how she may have behaved; what she might have said.

'Nothing to concern yourself with, dear,' George reassures her. 'We both know you think some strange things now and then, but no such nonsense was exhibited this evening. Doctor Barlowe, am I right? How do you find her?' He doesn't wait for a response but turns back to her. 'That's a girl, lay down quietly now, you mustn't exert yourself.'

'Well, Errington,' Eddie begins, turning to face his patient. 'I recommend you have some tea and toast or something else you fancy, as long as it is not air. And secondly, I urge you to get some sleep.'

'I quite agree,' George says, examining the ominous dark circles under Errington's eyes. 'Reading up until all hours is rather a problem for Errington – she, and especially Ruth, are particularly partial to the library, despite it being a rather masculine domain. And in regard to Errington's eating habits, your comment is not uncommon to my ears. But, Doctor

Barlowe, surely you can suggest something stronger than tea and toast?' George declares with a chuckle, as though he is bemused by the sudden emergence of 'modern medicine,' claims of the potential harm associated with widely available remedies that have been in use for longer than this young physician has been alive.

'Mr Pattinson, I'm afraid, I cannot condone the use of laudanum if that is, in fact, what you are alluding to. The effects on the liver alone, not to mention other vital organs, are still very much unknown. There are growing concerns that overuse may lead to a dependency; a state in which one must rely on its use to get through each and every day.'

'But you must see the girl is not herself?!' George talks as though Errington is no longer in the room. Eddie's irritation rises.

'Mr Pattinson.' His voice is rather abrupt now, very different from his normal even tone. 'If you are suggesting that our patient is more herself on laudanum, than without it; then that is, indeed, cause for concern.'

'Doctor Barlowe,' George's voice holds a similar tone to Eddie's – each addressing the other with a level of contempt. 'My daughter has relied on this drug for a number of years. I have no intention of changing course. I had thought you might benefit from perusing my notes, but I can see now that we have taken up quite enough of your time. We shall be sorry, on all accounts, to detain you a moment longer.'

Eddie has come to believe George Pattinson to be a reasonable man, with a compassionate and eager ear, known for many a philanthropic kindness. He would love nothing more than to plead his case with this man, not just because his daughter's life may well be at stake, but because Mr Pattinson is the very kind of upwardly mobile businessman Eddie needs to enlist for his emerging propositions to grow wings. He would surely love to inform Mr Pattinson that the face of medicine is changing – in the same way new modes of transport and emerging technologies are appearing before our very eyes. Surely, as a man of parliament, Mr Pattison must be aware of the talk in Ottawa surrounding legislation to support the regulation of patent medicines – not to mention the many concerns being raised about opium and the like.

'Doctor Barlowe, as a member of parliament, I am well aware of current debates. Do not confuse my insistence on maintaining past measures with an insistence upon ignorance. The legislation currently being devised is based on the notion of informed choice. In no way, is it about restricting one's access to much-needed medications. Now,' George says, rubbing his hands together as if confirming his own victory. 'Rather than delving any further into my management of household affairs, I think it best we call it a night. My sincerest apologies for calling you out at this quite unforgivable hour.'

Eddie gathers his things, before giving Errington a last, desperate look. 'Good evening, Miss Pattinson,' Eddie says, his voice almost breaking in defeat.

WITH THE SOUND OF THE CARRIAGE PULLING AWAY, George presses the heavy, solid door shut, heading for the study without delay, sinking down into his olive-green armchair.

'Well, Hobson,' George addresses the head butler, who like a coat on a hook, hangs in waiting. 'Did you find anything?'

Though Hobson remains stolidly upright, he appears pained to admit he did not find a single thing of significance upon rifling through Doctor Barlowe's things. With his arm propped up against the arm rest, George rests the weight of his head – made heavy by tonight's unsuccessful and troublesome ordeal – in his hands, his fingertips pressing into his temple.

'The audacity!' George declares in afterthought, lifting his head up. 'Questioning my running of the household! Why, he's practically a boy! And after the hospitality shown to him at Christmas year upon year...' George thrums his fingers against the armchair. 'Hobson, is Mrs Roantree up and at 'em? ... Have her bring Errington in some tea and toast. Then instruct her to ensure that Errington takes those pills by her bed. She may venture out at first light to secure some more laudanum from the dispensary. We shan't take any chances until Doctor Vardon's return.'

22

March 1908

'Good news,' Frank says, ushering Austin into his office. Frank is like the cat that swallowed the canary, incapable of wiping the smile off his face. 'Exciting for both of us, really.'

Austin lowers himself into the chair opposite Frank.

'Tell me.'

Frank reaches for his pipe and tin of tobacco. Pinching small clumps into his pipe, Austin accepts the second-rate tobacco and decides this can't be too much of a celebration.

'Now then,' Frank begins. 'I have taken the liberty of securing the Crown Furniture Co.; effectively reducing the competition.' Frank's forehead creases with surprise at the expression on Austin's face. 'You're not pleased, dear brother? Let me say I intend to make you a partner – at 20% profit of this new entity; enabling you to continue learning Canadian business methods without bearing the full burden of running a business. Of course,' Frank pauses, 'your financial outlay may be slightly more.'

Dumbfounded, Austin stares into the smoke.

'Now, we will be a little stretched at first. But I've run the numbers and given it is I who called you here to Preston – as Bert did when you set sail for New Zealand – I do feel a sense of responsibility to come to your aid... That said,' Frank runs his finger along the line of his mouth as if wiping away a crumb. 'One mustn't rely on the kindness of others. You must learn to stand on your own two feet.'

Austin can feel his face turning red; Frank's words are failing to act as the soothing balm he expects.

'I do hope you are not displeased. I know, we didn't exactly talk it over first, but you must understand; I only desire your success.'

Austin rises to his feet, no longer nursing his pipe. 'You need not have taken such liberties.'

'Well, then,' Frank shrugs. 'Perhaps, you need a little time; take the afternoon.'

HAVING WALKED NEARLY THE ENTIRE LENGTH OF King Street – swallowing quick gulps of air, while breathing in the pollen of wildflowers shooting up en masse in fields on the outskirts of town, mixed with nearby factory smoke – Austin is no more calm than when the news first broke. One thing is certain. Austin will not let Frank bully him out of pursuing his plans as he envisioned them. With Frank's proposal, it could take years before Austin is in a position to make Errington his bride. Years he does not have. He cannot wait. Though much too fired up to settle things just now, Austin finds himself only a few yards away from the Grist Mill where Crown Furniture is housed.

The stone building, with red painted trim, brings about a

rush of dashed hopes. Dreams of buying up the Crown Furniture Co.; of renting a house nearby – at least, until Austin is in a position to buy; of coming home to Errington waiting on the porch, a pussycat dancing around her feet; of reading the newspaper in his favourite chair beside his favourite person; of doing all the *'little jobs'* that make a house a home; of being the one take to care of *her*, always and forever.

Austin is still suspended in this dream-like state when he hears footsteps.

'Hello,' Eddie says in a jovial manner. 'Fancy meeting you here. You running errands for Frank?'

Austin looks over his shoulder, ensuring no one else is within earshot. 'Took the afternoon off; just to blow off steam.'

'That's not like you. Isn't it once a soldier, always a soldier? Thought your type was all about routine.' Eddie ponders for a moment, pressing his finger to his lips and pencil-thin moustache. 'You haven't got the blue devils, have you?'

'No, no,' Austin says, as the pair turn to walk away together – though neither states where they were originally heading. 'Nothing like that... Family matters, I'm afraid.'

'Oh.' Eddie's lips, forming the shape of the letter. 'Well, you know where I stand on that – after Dickie died, I was burdened with all the things I hadn't said. Frank may be a domineering type, but one never truly understands what they possess until it is gone.'

'You're right,' Austin declares. 'Of course, I know, you're right.'

Eddie shoots Austin a sympathetic look.

'But things aren't turning out quite as you planned?' Eddie lets his hands drop by his side as they walk along. 'Things rarely do. But consider your hesitation to leave South Africa. I'll bet you never imagined you'd love anything – or anyone – more than that alluring land. Now, look at you – you're a love-sick pup!'

Austin thinks of the sketches he drew in his old notebook, going back to when he set sail on the S.S. Arawa to make a life in New Zealand; well before his time in South Africa. He remembers the sketch of a rugged-looking man bent over a desk, holding writing paper in place as he writes with a quill pen, a pipe hanging from his mouth with swirling smoke. A self-portrait. In the nearby pages – along with the many sketches of other passengers he'd tried to capture candidly – Austin had sketched a scruffy-looking pup with big, pleading eyes; the caption, 'Poor Pup.' Perhaps, *this* was to be his self-portrait.

'It's true. Between The Missus,' Austin says, thinking of his beloved mare with great fondness, 'and the great lure of the wild, I hadn't thought life capable of offering any greater fulfilment.'

Eddie ceases walking.

'Listen, I am not in the habit of stating the obvious. But here, dear friend, I will make an exception. Other than being under the charge of your Commander, both in the army and in the force, as long as I have known you, you have never let anyone dictate your life, not even your father – God knows, had I adopted my father's dream for both his sons, I may have never left the battlefield; just as poor old Dickie. God rest his soul.'

Austin bows his head in memory of his fallen friend.

'My point is this,' Eddie continues, sticking to his course. 'Should you wish to marry his daughter, you'd best speak to Mr Pattinson – and soon. Though I cannot say I see eye-to-eye with the man in all matters, I do know that he has the respect, and admiration, of an entire town – nay, an entire district. The man has a great deal of sway as you well know. Perhaps, it's time he knew of your intentions.'

. . .

THAT VERY AFTERNOON, UNDERSTANDING THAT, sometimes, it takes those outside your situation to see what you cannot, Austin decides to pay a visit to Maplecroft, hiring a cab to ensure he arrives looking dapper. With the clip-clop of the horses trudging up the hill, Austin keeps watch as they approach Maplecroft gardens: verdant hedges, a cast iron water pump, lily-pond, vegetable patch and rose garden; the latter, of which Mr Pattinson tends to personally as a tribute to his dearly departed wife, Maisie.

It was upon taking a turn in that very garden, that Errington had shared with Austin, memories of her mother, but also, thoughts of how she believed her mother's death had changed Father into a more cautious man – though Errington could not speak for the initial months following the death on account of being sent away.

She spoke too, of a letter she'd come across in the top drawer of Father's walnut desk, written in her grandmother's hand, at the time of her parents' wedding. Her grandmother declaring with great snobbery – considering Errington's mother was an 'Erb' – that she would need advice on a wedding present because she *wouldn't know what size moccasin* the new bride would be. A snobbery often projected onto the colonies.

As the carriage slows to a stop, Austin looks up at the imposing gothic-style home, set behind the newly sprouting leaves of trees previously scaled back like fish bones. Austin is no stranger to grandeur, brought up in his parents' ivy-clad home back in Croydon, England, and, even more, his grandfather's estate at Ford Place, with its dormer windows peering above the roofline like multiplying emergent, prize-winning mushrooms. Yet, Austin begins to feel unsettled; his growing awareness of sweaty palms and quickened breath, cut short as

Elizabeth – home from boarding school – rushes up to the carriage.

'Uncle Austin!' Elizabeth declares, throwing her arms around Austin with a squeeze. 'To what do we owe the pleasure?'

Elizabeth stands back to meet Austin's gaze.

'I wasn't expecting to see you until Sunday,' she says, her big eyes full of anticipation. 'Have you come to take me out?'

'If only,' Austin says with a smile. 'Is your father home?'

'Father?' Elizabeth looks surprised. 'Yes, he's in the library. Shall I fetch him?'

'Perhaps, simply tell him of my arrival,' Austin says, considering Mr Pattinson is not a man to be 'fetched.'

'Of course,' Elizabeth says with a decisive nod. 'I mean, I would ask what it's about, but I'm sure you'd never tell. Or, would you, Uncle Austin? Would you, indeed? I am missing the comings and goings of this place, and my role as messenger between the two of you. Other than late-night shenanigans at the boarding house when we must make our own fun; life has become frightfully dull.'

'I see you are just as spirited as before,' Austin laughs just as Mr Pattinson appears at the door.

'Austin!' George declares, particularly chipper, 'to what do we owe the pleasure? We weren't expecting to see you until Sunday.'

'Yes,' Austin agrees. 'I am sorry to come somewhat unannounced. I did send word but I'm afraid I couldn't delay my visit any longer. You see, I have a matter of great importance to discuss... is now a convenient time?'

George looks at Austin for a moment, creating an unnaturally long pause.

'Do come in... Have a wet, won't you? I'll have Mrs Roantree put on some tea.'

From the outset, the visit seems to be going exceptionally

well; Mr Pattinson, only too happy to 'help those who help themselves;' agreeing to put in a 'good word' with the proprietor of the Crown Furniture Co. He is to see him this very night at the town meeting. Austin can hardly believe his luck!

'I'd only ask,' George says, his chin planted squarely between his thumb and forefinger, 'that you keep this between us. I don't want to create an upset with Frank... Moreover, I find business is best conducted, *quietly*.'

'I thank you,' Austin agrees, matching George's tone. 'You cannot know what this means.'

George sips his tea, resting the cup back on its saucer.

'Yes, well, I've known the proprietor for many years,' George says. 'In the main, he is a most agreeable fellow.'

Austin presses his hands against his thighs, signalling his imminent departure – considering he best make haste while things are swinging in his favour.

'As for that other matter,' George says with a clear shift in tone as if to suggest, *not so fast*. 'Perhaps, at the age of twenty-six, Errington is well past the usual marrying age – God knows, she's had more offers of marriage than some men have teeth. However, let me be clear.' George leans forward in his chair. 'I have no intention of consenting to a situation that is less than ideal.'

'Yes, sir,' Austin says, rising to his feet, trying not to sound too eager. With the possibility of marriage close at hand, he is determined not to put a foot wrong.

WITH THE SOUND OF THE CARRIAGE PULLING AWAY, Hobson appears, George sensing his presence.

'What can I tell you, Hobson?' George says, casually walking past the staircase leading to the room where Errington lies tucked up in bed yet again – Doctor Vardon's orders. 'The show's not over yet.'

'No, sir.'

'I mean the cheek of it,' George says with a sneer, turning to face Hobson who stands now at the edge of the library. 'Doesn't he realise he's only welcome at Maplecroft because of his connection to Frank?!'

'What do you intend to do, sir?' asks Hobson, resting his hands at the arch of his back, his belly protruding outward.

'Nothing,' George says, selecting from a row of cloth and leather-bound books. 'I'm not going to do a darn thing; certainly nothing to assist *that* man in his venture. If Maisie were here, I'm sure she'd tell me to put the 'poor man' out of his misery, but I simply cannot risk another upset; certainly not with Errington's nerves just as they are. If the man has any sense at all; surely, he will come to the appropriate conclusion and take himself off.'

George carries on the conversation as though Hobson has sought further clarification – though, of course, he would never be so overtly bold as to say so. Simply, Hobson exists as a useful shadow, providing an audience when a sounding board is needed, acting as his master's eyes and ears. This is how George remains in tune with people and their needs; addressing his workers' concerns just as matters come to light; proposing changes in parliament that reflect the will of the masses – or, at least, the loudest voices willing to show their cards. This is how George maintains the running of his affairs; how his suspicions are confirmed; how he knows when to send his daughters away – though he much prefers them to be close at hand.

'A mere Remittance Man,' George spits out, making a tut-tut sound. 'That's what he is! I dare say any funds in his possession may hardly be attributed to his military service or police work. Men on leave – and thereafter – routinely washing away their savings with intoxicating liquor and loose women. Can you imagine, Hobson?'

Hobson eyes remain fixed to the spot, a suitably stern expression on his face.

'No,' George continues. 'I cannot abide a man such as that. And what of the atrocities committed during war? I'm ashamed to say, Hobson, that our troops regularly engaged in the looting and pillaging of Boer farms before routinely setting them alight. Not to mention the camps – didn't they paint us in a bad light then?! The British army holding prisoners of war, women and children, without necessities (even soap!) and leaving them to starve. And this was to be a gentleman's war! Don't mistake my meaning, Hobson, I'm a staunch supporter of the Empire, but, as for Austin; he is no hero. Not in my book.'

23

———

Having hardly slept, Austin slips away from his lodgings before breakfast, just in time to see the sun come up over the river as he approaches Frank's factory gates. *Red sky in the morning sailors take warning,* Austin thinks to himself at the sight of the red glow reflecting off the water and mirrored in the sky. Though his mood is drastically altered since the previous morning, he is sure his brother will soon be seeing red when he hears what Austin has to say – irrespective of the hour.

By now the proprietor of Crown Furniture Co. will be half-way to Quebec, there to attend the annual trade fair; an event, Austin is due to attend as representative of the Preston Furniture Co. – Frank, only too glad to send his brother in his place.

Clinging to new hope – praying Mr Pattinson's 'word' has had the desired effect –Austin hopes to engage in talks with the proprietor of Crown Furniture Co. as soon as is humanly possible. But first, there are several accounts that need to be settled before Austin's departure; owing to Frank's insistence upon a delay in payment for reasons undisclosed – most likely, now, it seems, to gather the extra funds needed to close in on a business Austin had declared he, himself, was going to purchase. But despite this wrongdoing – which he shall soon make right – Austin continues to approach his work with pride; a quality, carried over from his time in South Africa. Lt. Col. H.W. Madre declared upon Austin's departure from the S.A.C.: *'Mr Moss is sober, honest and reliable and I can recommend him for any position of trust.'*

It is just as Austin is finalising the last of the accounts that Frank bursts into his office, rearranging the books on his desk and muttering under his breath.

'Well, aren't you going to wish me good morning?' Frank says, in a huff.

'Good morning.'

'Not it's not.'

'It's not?'

'No, because late last night I received a message that the deal is off. The bastard has rescinded the deal. *Our* deal,' Frank declares with an exaggerated hand gesture encircling the two brothers, before reaching inside his vest pocket for his pipe.

'Right, well –'

Austin shuffles the papers before him into a neat stack.

'Well? Aren't you positively livid?'

Seated at the edge of Austin's desk, legs crossed, Frank looks over at his brother before returning to his ineffectual striking of a match.

'I mean, I know it wasn't exactly how you pictured things, but it would have been a start. And a good one at that.'

Frank hands Austin the tin of matches. After the bowl is successfully lit, Frank appears pensive.

'Wait on,' he says, suspiciously, following a long, slow suck of his pipe. 'Why are you here so early? Making up for yesterday's early departure, are we?'

'Oh, just finalising some accounts. I'll drop these to the bank and then, uh –' Austin bundles the papers next to his coat. 'What else did Gruetzner say?'

'Only that, overnight, it seems, his situation had changed. Apparently, it was no longer necessary for him to sell. All of a sudden, he feels a 'civic duty' to ensure the place falls into the right hands.' Frank scoffs. '*The right hands*, can you imagine? Doesn't he realise the success of Preston Furniture Co.? I mean, it's "*everyone's first choice for school and office furniture*".'

'So, the advertisement reads.'

'Yes, well, it's true, isn't it?'

'Actually, I arrived early on account of the trade fair. Just wanted to see to the accounts before my departure.'

'Oh yes, the trade fair. What a big waste of time that is!' Frank says, relighting his bowl, this time with a steady hand. 'Of course, we must be seen to attend but God help me, it's a bore, isn't it?'

Austin says nothing more of the trade fair, nor of his intentions there. On the short walk to the bank, he crosses over Eagle Street, glancing up toward the Pattinson Woollen Mills and Maplecroft, half-expecting to see Errington coming down the hill with a rustle of her skirts as she walks, a spring in her step.

Given Errington's recent absence from society – of which Austin has obtained little word, inducing greater anxiety within him – Austin is working especially hard to remind himself of the near and happy future. For once Austin's business plans take hold, never again shall they live out of each other's sight. It is just as this thought comes – as so often in the form of a daily prayer – that the man Austin is most indebted to appears before him, like an apparition, or a sign from God.

'Ah, just the man,' Austin declares, a smile sweeping across his face.

'Oh?' Mr Pattinson frowns, fingertips pressing against his walrus-shaped moustache as if in retrieval of memory.

'Yes, I... I wanted to reiterate my thanks.' Austin prompts. 'For putting in a good word... with Mr Gruetzner.'

Mr Pattinson, giving a decisive nod, a tip of his bowler hat, before entering the bank; no doubt, to see to his own affairs.

Soon after arriving in Quebec, Austin changes out of his lounge suit, deciding he shall defer writing to Errington until he may include definite news. Instead, he immerses himself in the happenings of Quebec as he makes his way to the fair, watching the people around him. Small-waisted ladies perched on park benches, facing out toward the St. Lawrence. Men in bowler hats and dark suits striding as though ignorant of the riverscape and stunning turrets of the Chateau Frontenac, quite a part of the every-day to them.

Strolling beside the escarpment, Austin approaches the monument of Samuel de Champlain, the founder of Quebec City, set high on a pedestal of limestone. Though the view is spectacular – the St. Lawrence River, the Laurentian Mountain ranges, the stone buildings of the lower town – Champlain stands, facing the sight most pleasing to him; Quebec City.

As Austin moves through the crowd – fortune tellers and vagabonds hovering at the edge of the fair; much like the way they inhabit society – he spots a painted sign picturing a crown, Crown Furniture Co. There it is.

Despite the initially warm reception, Mr George Gruetzner, the proprietor, makes his position clear. He is not only unwilling to sell to Frank; he will not sell to *any* interested party. Providing no explanation, only apologising for taking up Austin's time with past discussions; Gruetzner reiterates that the Crown Furniture Co. is no longer for sale.

'But please, as a Masonic brother, allow me to appeal to your good character.' Austin struggles to conceal his desperation. 'What if I may still be of use...? You have political aspirations; am I correct?'

'Indeed,' Gruetzner pushes the metal frame of his glasses back against his nose. 'But I cannot see –'

'Then engage me as a contractor. With my help, you may be freer to engage in other pursuits... In New Zealand, I worked for a fruiterer, Laery & Co.; I know what it is to look upon every man as a potential customer.'

'I take your point, Mr Moss, but fruit – is not furniture.'

Austin presses a card detailing the address of his hotel into Gruetzner's hand.

'The hotel bar. This evening at six. Join me for a soda. If you do not accept what I have to say; I shan't press the matter further.'

Gruetzner slips the card into his vest pocket. 'It's never just a soda.' His voice carrying over the crowd as Austin bids him adieu. 'I'll see you at six, Mr Moss.'

Feb. 14, 1897

   Feb. 28, 1898

   June 27, 1898

   Sept. 26, 1900

   Dec. 25, 1900

   Mar. 3, 1901

   June 20, 1901

   Oct. 31, 1901

   Dec. 30, 1901

July 16, 1902
Oct. 5, 1902
Dec. 8, 1902 operation:
Mar. 22, 1903
June 28, 1903
Aug. 2, 1903
Jan. 20, 1904
Feb. 24, 1904
April 18, 1904
June 30, 1904
Aug. 3, 1904
Sept. 7, 1904
Nov. 16, 1904
Jan. 5, 1905 operation appendicitis
Jan. 22, 1905
April 7, 1905
–
–
–
June 18, 1906
July 28, 1906
Nov. 16, 1906 operation
March 26, 1907
May 15, 1907
June 20, 1907
Aug. ?, 1907
Nov. 27, 1907
Jan 20, 1908

TURNING TO THE BACK PAGE OF HER BLACK, leather-bound journal, through a veil of tears, Errington inscribes today's date, '*April 23, 1908.*'

Looking over the sequence of dates in her journal – listed there as one might record births and deaths in a family Bible –

Errington searches for a pattern, or rather a disruption to the pattern. Year upon year, Errington's record of 'poor health' has been all too consistent – with the exception of 1905; the year in which Errington left several dates unentered. The year of her European Odyssey, the year she first fell for Austin.

In fact, if anyone were to happen upon her journal – flicking through Errington's efforts to economise, the lists of past Christmas gifts, home visiting hours of other Prestonians transferred from their calling cards – to study these particular recorded dates; a person might wonder whether Errington wasn't simply recording her menses! *Though, isn't it true?* she wonders. *One often accompanies the other; emotions running high inevitably resulting in a bout of bedrest.*

Drying her eyes, Errington reaches for a bundle of Austin's letters, carefully stowed away in a box beneath her bed. Selecting one at random, she smiles to herself, savouring every word, experiencing the letter anew. A great many times, Errington has read and re-read the letters, enjoying the author's shift from flirtatious to daring – *'Can't think of what you want – am no good at guessing'* to *'There certainly was a little colour in those cheeks in the woods.'*

Errington feels her cheeks flush with colour. Austin's words, his imagined presence fill her with joy, but with that joy comes the pain of not always being by his side. This intensity of feeling causing her to question nothing – and everything. Furtively, Errington replaces Austin's letters, pushing the box out of sight, back behind the dust ruffle.

It is the damning – yet somehow, unsurprising – news that has worked Errington up into her present state. Doctor Vardon, here a short time ago – with navy cape, Gladstone bag, and perpetual nervous energy – is insisting Errington return to St. John's; arranging that Errington's younger brother, Frank, will accompany her. Distraught upon receipt of this news – forever a slave to the limitations of her sex –

Errington's unstoppable tears served only to support Doctor Vardon's case.

Yet after consulting the letters, Errington is firm in her resolve. She will not accept yet another prolonged absence. She will not. Austin is right, those *'little operations'* are *'worse than England's "little wars."'*

Lauren
Muskoka, Ontario, Canada
2019

24

September

Zoe pushes off from the edge of the dock, pointing us toward the township. Holding us there, I watch as Em steps into the second canoe; her eyes following the footsteps of the man entering the dock.

'Hey…?' I say with surprise, slowly placing this man outside his usual context; not sporting his John Lennon glasses or ill-fitting pullover. 'Gregory, isn't it? From the Archives?'

Gregory holds up a large envelope, his voice travelling across the water; his voice is unmistakable. 'Yes. And I found something…'

I begin to turn, drawing us back in.

Gregory waves his hands dismissively. 'Don't come back in on my account… I'll just drop this…' He looks about the boat house, settling for a spot just inside, placing a buoy on top to hold it in place. 'Hope you don't think it too forward… Coming to your house… But I was driving by and –.'

Gregory's awkwardness makes me smile.

'What is it?' I ask, shielding my face from the sun.

'Oh!' Gregory says, bursting; fired with the same passion I'd witnessed at the Archives. 'It's everything! I mean, *not* everything. But it's probably the greatest clue I think we'll find. It's thrilling what can be discovered… though, of course, impossible to know it all.'

'Tell me,' I say, straightening up the boat, signalling over my shoulder for Zoe to rest her paddle.

'I mean, maybe –'

'Why don't you tell us *after* the paddle?' Em interjects, arms crossed over the life jacket she'd reluctantly put on.

I give Em a look.

'Oh!' Gregory apologises. 'Of course… Sorry, I'll just –'

'Come on, then,' Em says, surprisingly, lunging herself to the front of her canoe, leaving room at the stern. 'There's room in my canoe if you want. *And,*' Em throws back a water-marked cushion, 'you can use this for your knees.'

'Gee!' Gregory looks between the canoe, me and the stepping stones leading back up to the drive. 'Gee, I'm not really dressed –'

'Come,' I hear myself echoing Em's sentiment, because I'm trying something new. 'It'll be… fun.'

Making our way around the island, amidst the roar of passing motorboats, the echo of voices bouncing off the water, the softer sounds of nature, I keep just close enough to hear Gregory fumbling apologies with multiple 'I certainly wasn't planning –' But as we drift closer into shore, manoeuvring around a rock distinguishable by the ripples moving around it, there is a shift in their conversation and I have to strain to hear.

'So why *Gregory*?' Em says with mild teenage disgust. 'Not Greg?'

'Oh! Bit formal, isn't it?' Gregory agrees, his clothing coping a spray as Em's paddle wobbles against the pull of the water.

'Watch, Em.'

Gregory shakes his head, though he seems to be concentrating. 'Uh, why Gregory...? Many of the locals here, I've known my whole life; my parents always called me 'Gregory' – thought it sounded more refined. So everyone else does, too.'

Em reaches forward, putting greater power into her J-stroke as they take the bend, her stroke still a little jagged. 'And aren't the archives located in Cambridge... I mean, why are you *here*?'

'Oh,' Gregory assesses. 'Well, that's easy; I live here – mostly. I work remotely.'

The water becomes choppy, forcing us to go single file to avoid pushing out into the bay. As we pass through the cut, silence descends, and their conversation becomes lost to me.

'Well,' I say, shifting my weight up onto the dock, holding the edge of the canoe as Zoe steps out. 'How was that?'

'That was wonderful,' Gregory says, wearing a grin despite his dampened attire. 'I've barely set foot in a boat for weeks and with summer officially over, I couldn't resist getting out on the water – thank you, for insisting I come.'

Em shrugs, then steps up onto the dock, leaving Gregory to tether the boat. '*Greg* here was telling me about his research – about *Austin.*'

'Errington really,' Gregory looks up from his knot, rising to stand, retrieving the envelope he'd brought. 'When you showed me the envelopes addressed to St. John's Hospital, Toronto, I couldn't help but take a closer look...'

I begin to thank Gregory for conducting research in his own time; for delivering it personally.

Gregory shakes his head, his tight curls catching the sun. 'I have a personal interest in conducting such research... You see, *my* great-grandmother died in childbirth. Sadly, it was common in those days. But, however devastating, it is fascinating to consider how far we've come.'

'Tell me about it,' Em says without sarcasm.

I look at Em, as if admiring an artwork – as something interesting; layered and complex.

'Before we left Australia,' Em continues, 'I was studying the Bubonic Plague and the things they used to do... bloodletting... I mean, all kinds of crazy shi –'

'Ah, yes,' Gregory reminisces, as if this were a positive part of history. 'The Black Death, though; of course, now we are going back hundreds of years; right back to the Middle Ages.'

'Seems there's lots to discuss,' I say, looking between Gregory the archivist and my own budding historian (who knew?). 'Think I'll put the kettle on.'

'Ah,' Gregory chuckles. 'I'm afraid, once I get started...'

I smile; surprising myself by the natural curve of my lips. There is something sweet in his nature. And it no longer feels strange seeing this human out of context. In fact, it feels... kind of nice.

25

'W*orse than England's little wars?*' Sarah repeats over the phone. 'God! What did they do to her?'

I take a breath, ready to expound on all the possible theories I have on Errington, the treatments, what ailed her – but saying nothing of the man assisting in my research, now known to me as 'Greg.'

'Actually,' Sarah stops me, bringing her mouth a little too close to the phone, her voice louder than before. 'I don't want to know. I've had enough experience of hospitals to last me a lifetime.'

There is a gurgling, followed by a gentle cooing.

'Hiii Baby Iz... Or is it Trey?'

'It's Iz.' Sarah's voice goes up several octaves as she addresses her tiny daughter. 'Say hiiiiii.' This is followed by a pause, then more gurgling. 'She says hi... Actually, I *do* want to know; I mean, what do you think was wrong with Errington? Doesn't it seem kind of cruel to keep the lovers apart for so long when, in the end –?'

'I think so.'

The gurgling turns to more of a whimper.

'Everything al –?'

'Fine,' Sarah interjects. 'We're fine. But I tell you what as soon as 'Daddy' arrives home, I'll be ready to offload this little lady so I can, you know, take a shower. Maybe go to the toilet in peace.'

I laugh in sympathy. 'Where's Trey?'

'On the mat. That little champion is happy doin' push-ups. And when he's had enough, I just roll him over. *Nothing* fazes that kid.'

'Well, I should probably let you –'

'Oh, please don't,' Sarah insists. 'This is, like, my one adult interaction for the day, I'm savouring it 'til Trav gets home, and I bombard him with 'how was your day?' No, please, tell me more.'

'Well…' I look out toward the glistening water, the rowers passing by with easy care, the couple diving off the rock across the bay to swim along the water's edge. 'I think maybe she suffered 'nervous complaints' – or, rather, that's what the people around her believed… I'm not so sure she suffered much of anything in the early days, besides the misery of being sent away.'

'Nervous complaints?'

'Originally known as hysteria. You might remember a highly sexualised, rather creepy film a few years back… I think you and I saw it together…'

'Vaguely.'

'I don't know, Sare, the more I read of their letters – their desperate need to be together – *and* the more I research; all these rest cures, hospitalisations, it just doesn't seem…'

'Necessary?'

'Exactly. And I have no way of knowing for sure, no access to medical records. I visited St. John's Hospital in Toronto; they had a general history but nothing specific to Errington.

Except this one thing I read before they updated their website recently; that the hospital dealt with issues *peculiar to the female sex.*'

'We are a peculiar bunch,' Sarah says, as if rethinking the whole decision to have children.

'And, I mean, they relied on some pretty hardcore drugs, Laudanum for one; given for all sorts of reasons: menstruation, childbirth, hysteria, depression, fainting fits. Anything, almost.'

'And...' Sarah begins. There is a pause, sounds of rummaging, then more cooing. 'Sorry, I never wanted to be one of *those* mums.'

'Don't worry about it.'

The screen door screeches as I head back inside to make some lunch, while holding the phone with my shoulder.

'Mmm, ok. So... what about that counsellor then? She helping?'

'I...' I say, selecting multiple slices of thick bakery bread, 'haven't been back.'

'Loz,' Sarah speaks sternly as if in practice for future disappointments – preparing for the day she'll utter the phrase, *I'm not angry; just disappointed.*

'I will. I will. Just haven't been back *yet*. But the advice was not...' I stand, staring at an open fridge, 'unhelpful.'

'Good. That's good,' Sarah says, as if checking another thing off her list. 'And Lorraine? How's she –'

'Lorraine,' I say, pausing from gathering the cheese and butter and dumping them on the counter beside the frying pan and slices of bread. 'I can't believe I didn't tell you. Get ready for this; *Lorraine is* coming *to Canada!*'

'Coming to Canada?' Sarah repeats. 'What, like on holiday...?'

'No,' I correct her. 'Like possibly *moving* to Canada.'

'Moving to Canada?'

'Possibly. Sare,' I begin slicing cheese and buttering bread. 'I have to say, why are you repeating everything I say?'

'Because you're dropping a lot of bombshells. And... Baby-brain. It's a thing.'

'Yeah.'

'And it doesn't disappear when the babies are out either.'

'Hun,' I adopt a soothing tone; it feels good to be the one offering support. 'They're only eight weeks old. You're getting very little sleep. Think you can cut yourself some slack.'

'Yeah, I know,' Sarah sighs. 'Gosh, I feel terrible complaining about my situation. I mean,' Sarah is scrambling now, my silence tells her it's too painful to openly speak of Nick. 'Look at Errington... She never really got to experience motherhood... The thought of –'

For a moment, I hang on the end of the line, waiting for Sarah to speak. 'Sare... Are you crying?'

Sarah sniffles, then laughs. 'It's been a rough morning... Ok, it's been a rough couple of months. Plus, I can't watch a single thing on TV relating to kids now without tearing up. And Errington's story is just so sad, you know, so tragic.'

'Yeah,' I say glancing toward the folder of letters, set beside Errington's journal of her European Odyssey; remnants of a past life spread across the kitchen bench, taking up residence further in my home and in my heart. 'I think that's why I'm having so much trouble connecting with her. She writes *beautifully* but, I mean, Austin was an adventurer, you know, he has this really interesting past. And he lives on. I mean, I guess, so does she.'

'*Plus* he was epically handsome. That picture you sent; I mean those eyes! It's like they could see right through you, deep down into the depths of your soul.'

'Exactly. But with Errington, I feel like I'm struggling to see past her tragic end; to understand the woman she was.

Because she was so such more, you know; *we* are so much more… I just hate how tragedy defines –'

But the words catch in my throat. I've strayed into the danger zone…

'Loz…? Honey? You know, it doesn't have to…'

'I know,' I say weakly, messily wiping my nose with the back of my hand. 'It's been a rough…'

'Yeah,' Sarah agrees. 'Yeah, it has.'

'Listen,' I say, sucking back the tears. 'I better go, Brace reckons he's almost done, and I told him I'd bring him a sandwich a good half hour ago.'

'Brace?' Sarah repeats, the name sounding unfamiliar and strange on her tongue. 'Who the hell is *Brace*?'

'Oh, and I gotta shoot Greg a text.'

'Greg? Who is –?'

'Gotta go.'

Navigating the stepping stones, strewn with pine needles, I balance the tray in both hands, careful not to spill the coffee, or let the plates slide off the shallow lip of the tray. Slowly, taking one step at a time, I begin apologising for taking so long before I emerge upstairs, stopping mid-sentence at the sight of Brace teetering on the edge of the railing, his body facing the water: the screen doors partially obscuring my view.

'What are you doing?!' I cry, the coffee spilling at my feet as I clumsily lower the tray to the ground, keeping my eyes on Brace.

Brace looks back at me over his shoulder, his blue-grey eyes filling with glee. Without saying a word, he leaps off the edge. My heart simultaneously plunging to the pit of my stomach as I rush to the balcony. His splash, followed by another; peering over the edge, I arrive in time to see Em hit the water. Brace rises from white water, his golden locks dripping, his grin wide.

'What do you think?' I hardly hear him call. 'Pretty great, eh?'

I lean over the railing, desperately trying to close the distance between us; watching to see Em resurface. 'Oh God! Em!'

Em's grin falls from her face.

'Out of the water!' I demand, rushing back down the stairs. 'Out!' I cry, arriving at the water's edge.

By the time I reach the ladder, Brace has already leapt out of the water and is standing, dripping, a dampness pooling at his feet.

'Uh...' Brace scruffs up his water-logged locks, as if scratching for the answer. 'Guess, I better shoot.'

My eyes widen.

'Sorry,' he says, though my gaze has already shifted to the stepping stones beckoning Brace back to his truck. 'Didn't mean to overstep.'

Without packing up his tools, Brace tackles the stepping stones, two at a time, until, finally, he is out of sight. Em, shadowing me from behind, head lowered, goosebumps forming on her arms and legs and newly budding breasts.

'Sorry, Mum,' she says. 'I know; that was dumb.'

Austin & Errington
Preston, Ontario, Canada
1908

215

26

———

April

Looking back toward the billowing red-brick smokestack – a key feature of Preston's skyline – Errington is adamant she shall soon be *'much improved'*. But as the domed towers of Union Station come into view, Errington experiences a pang of guilt at ditching Frank – a lesser feeling than the dread of returning to St. John's; forbidden from literature, life, and love.

As the train screeches to a stop, Errington disappears into the crowd as planned. Catching her breath, she boards the train bound for Quebec, soon to be reunited with Austin. Errington calls him into being; his waxed moustache and devilish smile overlays the blurred scenery rushing by as she sits against the buttoned chair-back, restless and impatient.

Hurrying along the escarpment, then looking upon the monument of Samuel de Champlain; Errington's gaze connects with Austin's. The moment is miraculous, impatient, urgent.

'We must leave today. Now, if possible,' Errington, hardly having time to detail the plan to steal away to a small room above her uncle's chemist shop in Hexham, England.

On board the ship, Errington is taken ill; spending most of the journey below deck, her appetite dwindling to minuscule proportions. And upon disembarkation, time holds no meaning. Errington is unable to retrieve a single memory of their journey from Liverpool to Hexham; not the hissing steam, nor the pungent smell of burning coal felt on her skin and hair.

Under the yellow light of the moon, the guiding light of Cassiopeia, they climb the open stairwell of the fire escape toward the small precious room above the chemist shop; Austin carrying his soon-to-be bride over the threshold.

But in the darkness – in this climactic bliss – Errington's eyes adjust, taking on a wakeful state; recognising the name plate on the open door, *St. Agatha's;* the unmistakable chintz of this familiar room; the sister's voice – a sister of St. John the Divine.

'My dear,' the sister says sweetly, heat radiating from her hand as though Saint John himself has placed healing in those hands. 'The little operation went well.'

27

May

Calling upon the Lodge's core members from 'refreshment to labour,' George Pattinson approaches the double doors of the Masonic Lodge with a sigh. He does not take pleasure in such unpleasantness – nor is he one to listen to idle gossip – but when there is a great deal of talk surrounding certain members and their personal conduct, such concerns must be addressed. The by-laws stipulate, very clearly, the ways in which members must be held accountable to themselves, their brothers, and society at large. Not to mention the law itself; criminalising such 'gross indecency', naturally inclusive of touching, dancing, kissing.

It is not through personal vendetta that George takes it upon himself, as Grand Master, to call in to question the membership of Doctor Edward Barlowe; but rather, to uphold the principles of what it is to be a freemason. Indeed, George does not believe the allegations of such criminality. Had he believed Doctor Barlowe guilty of homosexual relations, he most certainly would not have called him to his daughter's bedside (with the intention of allowing Hobson time to sift through Barlowe's personal effects in search of material damning long-term friend and ally, Doctor Vardon). Even so, George believes Doctor Barlowe's membership must be revoked until such charges are tried and dismissed; though whatever the outcome, the charges will remain on record. Not even the Grand Master himself, has the power to alter the official record.

Evidently, George's opinion in regard to Doctor Barlowe's membership is unanimous. A quick and seemingly unremarkable decision is made; permitting ample time to discuss preparations for the upcoming visit from the Grand Master of the entire Waterloo district. With responsibilities delegated, ceremonial rituals and hymns selected and refined, the party conclude the gathering by drinking to the good health of *'brothers united.'* Thus, setting forth a wave of toasting and good cheer.

In the toast that follows, mention is made of the recent article printed in the 'Special Souvenir Number of Industrial Preston,' showcasing the local Grand Master himself, George Pattinson, and his thriving woollen mills; praised for withstanding *'competition from abroad'* that has seen *'native industry...[suffer] most severely.'*

'We are well-pleased,' Mayor Clare says, holding the article up with both hands. 'Aren't we brothers?'

A resounding cheer follows in response as every man raises his glass, etched with Masonic symbols. Then several more acknowledgements are made; the accomplishments of the members, correspondence from past members now residing in other parts of the world: New Zealand, India, South Africa. The meeting adjourns.

Placing down an empty goblet, George takes Frank Moss aside; sensing he still seems to have his nose out of joint.

'I hope you understand why the sale of the Crown Furniture Co. could not go ahead?'

Lowering his chin onto intertwined fingers, Frank looks up from his half-full goblet.

'Your brother,' George continues, 'would have been considered a partner – albeit a silent one – and, I'm afraid, that would have placed me in a rather difficult position.'

Frank gawks at him, 'You don't mean to give your consent?'

'Certainly not,' George says, extinguishing this possibility, 'but,' he concedes, 'given Errington's fragile state, I simply cannot risk another upset by declaring it openly. She must believe there is a chance.'

Frank nods silently, as though the action assists in his thinking.

'What ever happened to that young lawyer chap?' Frank asks, steering the conversation away from Austin.

'De la Rosa?' George suggests. 'Yes, that would have been a fine match. But –' George offers a shrug, 'one may only lead a horse to water.'

'Errington, in this case, being the horse?'

'Yes.'

'And you say you don't want me to have a quiet word with my brother?'

George, having already placed down his sceptre, abruptly ceases the removal of his robe.

'I implore you, sir, do not!'

But before Frank can apologise – for he dares not meddle in George's affairs – George adds, 'My daughter – your niece – though perpetually weak, is exceptionally strong-willed. A stubbornness I dare not tempt – bred from her mother's side, of course.'

'Of course.' Frank agrees, resolving to let the matter rest. *'So, mote it be.'*

Upon leaving the Lodge, George has Errington on his mind. Space now to think of her, having made it through another week, heavy with engagements. Public School Board meetings, Parliament in session, business at the Lodge, consultations with Mr Adam Beck – a man, at the heart of many a philanthropic kindness (much like George himself), dedicated to supporting Waterloo County activists in bringing electricity to the county. The latter, taking up a great deal of George's time and thinking in the form of an evolving Hydro-Electric Scheme.

Despite Beck's rather dramatic presentations – something of a circus act – illustrating the advantages of electricity in the barn and in the home, the pair are indeed more alike than one might first suppose as both men have suffered the recent anxiety of nursing a daughter back to health. Beck, becoming increasingly vocal on the matter of access to medical care, after his daughter suffered terribly with Tuberculosis, but mercifully recovering after he sought the finest specialists across America and Europe.

Indeed, it is this sentiment – this renewed urgency to do a little good in the world, especially following so much hurt in his home and in his heart – that lingers in George's mind as he steps up into the waiting carriage. Upon entering his own castle high on the hill, trudging upstairs with a worn and worried look on his face, George sits down at his writing desk, pulls out a cheque from beneath a pile of neatly stacked papers and makes out the name, 'St. John's Hospital.' On the short carriage ride home, George, a man of conviction, has resolved to double his normal gifted amount to St. John's.

This increased generosity, being two-fold. Firstly, on

account of the fine care afforded to his daughter, Errington. And, secondly, in support of St. John the Divine, embodied in the sisters who daily live out this greater purpose – St. John's Hospital, a hospital for women, particularly for those without means, committed to addressing issues 'peculiar to the female sex,' and to decreasing the high maternal and infant mortality rates that continue to plague society of all classes.

EARLY IN THE MORNING, JUST AS AN ORANGE GLOW escapes the trappings of his thick, velvet curtains, George readies himself for the day, dressing in the clothes laid out for him by Hobson, who, usually composed, is semi-horrified to find Mr Pattinson mostly dressed with little need for his services, save swapping over a tie and assistance in shrugging into his lounge suit jacket. In donning his attire without his normal routine, it seems George is attempting to prepare his mental state; knowing not how he shall find his daughter.

Upon arrival, the matron opens the door to the convent before George even raises his hand to knock. For a sister – traditionally embodying natural serenity – the matron is unusually animated in her greeting. Most grateful, it seems, for the envelope handed her – to be opened the instant Mr Pattinson is delivered to his daughter – sandwiching Mr Pattinson's hand in both of hers, blessing him, and his cheque.

'Please Sister, there is no need for your profusion of thanks. I simply wish to express my gratitude for the fine care you provide my daughter; and to those less fortunate. Indeed, I am indebted to all the sisters who humbly exhibit such generosity of spirit. Now, if you'd be so kind, I would like to see my daughter.'

Bowing her head, the matron steps aside, permitting George to enter.

'Of course, Mr Pattinson,' she says, before turning on her heel.

In silence, George follows the matron past the chapel with its rood screen depicting the crucifixion, red cedar ceiling and stained-glass Mary Window catching the corner of his eye. They walk on – George, following the matron's determined steps up the hall – until, at last, they reach St. Agatha's.

The matron pauses at the door. 'Mr Pattinson, I pray that you are not alarmed. While it's true she hasn't the strength to return home to Maplecroft just yet; be assured, Errington is much improved.'

George can scarcely believe a whole week has passed since the day of Errington's arrival here – he having shifted his morning engagements for the purpose of accompanying her to hospital. How small, how frail she had been. George looks toward the door, eager to see her countenance, colour in her cheeks.

'May I?'

'Ah,' the matron says in acknowledgment. 'I must not delay your reunion a moment longer. Time is precious, I know.'

The matron presses open the door, revealing Errington, small beneath the layer of bed covers. Errington looks up with a weak smile.

'I shall leave you now,' the matron says, pressing her hands together as if in prayer. 'Please do not hesitate to ring the bell. We are never far away.'

'My dear,' George says, upon the matron taking her leave. George rests the back of Errington's hand against his cheek. 'But you are so cold! Let me have them bring you another blanket.'

'Thank you, but no. I do not wish to deprive the other patients. The room itself is already far too grand. Though the chintz…' Errington considers, 'I do believe Mother would have approved of the chintz.'

Despite finding herself *here*, Errington is not angry or upset. She understands the strength of her father's love, revealing itself every time Doctor Vardon is ordered to her side; every time she is made to endure bed rest or sent away on rest cures. Even in her deepest despair, there is always light. Not just in the glory of God – for that is true. Not only in the knowledge of Austin's unwavering love – for that is undoubtedly true. But in the depth of her father's love. The exercising of caution; a resulting scar of heartbreak, left in the wake of Errington's dearly departed mother – wounds first opened by the loss of Errington's ten-year-old sister, Madge.

George smiles briefly at Maisie's memory. 'But never mind the other patients. Are *you* quite well?'

'Yes, I…'

'What is it?' George takes Errington's hand, enclosing it within his own. 'It pains me terribly to see you this way.'

Kept close to Errington's heart is a locket. Though, at present, it rests in the hospital drawer; Errington rarely parts with it. Inscribed with her mother's initials, M. E. P., the locket features a flower etched into a smooth, golden surface, an emerald at its centre. Inside, to the left is an oval shaped photograph of Errington's father, George, as a young man, much in love; to the right is a photograph of Austin wearing a flat cap and pipe, pulling an oar through the water. The two loves of Errington's life.

Errington places her hand to her chest, the place where her locket would normally reside.

'There is something,' Errington begins. 'Though I had not wished to divulge it from a hospital bed…' Errington takes a breath, her whole body shaking as she speaks. 'Father, there is but one man who holds my affection. Indeed, he has done so since his arrival to Preston.'

'Shhh. Come now.'

'Father, I dreamt a dream that you forbade the match,' Errington continues, determined in her resolve, 'but, you have never denied me before and I cannot go on –'

George presses a finger to Errington's lips. 'Hush now, child,' he says, tenderly brushing his fingertips over Errington's forehead. 'You are not well.'

Errington lowers her father's hand to rest upon the covers.

'Indeed, sir, it is not a case of being unwell.' This time – unlike so many times before – she will *not* leave her feelings left unsaid. '*Love…*' It is so freeing to speak its name. 'As I'm sure you may remember, does strange things to us all.'

'Yes,' George concedes, seemingly unsurprised by Errington's declaration. 'Most mornings, I wake to the painful realisation of finding myself alone. It's true, I feel the loss of your mother every day.'

'Then you know,' Errington urges, tears welling in her eyes. 'You know, it cannot be undone. *Love* cannot be undone.'

'Yes…' George utters with a faraway look. 'Yes, I do know *that.*'

It starts in much the same way; their arms entangled, the scent of violets filling his nostrils as he breathes in, as if inhaling powerful smelling salts, his lips tracing the line of her neck, trailing their way to her lips. The tenderness of her lips touching his. It is perfection and it is real. As real as when their lips met tentatively all those years ago; then urgently; then with a teasing kind of patience – believing they had time – her body moulding into his.

But it never lasts. Even in dreams George must watch his violet fade from life. Her quickened breath, the quickened beating of her heart; sending him into shock. Dizzy and confused, as if it were he who suffers this fate; his heart that might soon stop. Kissing her, his lips dampened with the clamminess of her forehead, from the tears that fall, his lips lingering, held that they might leave a lasting impression upon her skin. But she is fading. The dream, his darling Maisie, *fading*.

With a sharp in-drawing of breath, George rubs his eyes, greeted by the morning glow escaping the trappings of his thick, velvet curtains; light falling across the vacant space beside him. With a shaky hand, he reaches for the family Bible at his bedside; his fingertips caressing the name of his late wife written on the page there, as if to bring her into being – or, else scrub out the name. For in this marking, half of him is gone. His own dear love, lost to him except in dreams and waking memory; in the embodiment of their children of which he must protect.

28

July

It has been some weeks since Errington's most recent bout in hospital and still Father is not satisfied with her state of health – Errington is permitted to venture no further than Maplecroft gardens. It's true, she *is* exhausted; but only through her continued insistence that she is, indeed, 'quite well.' So it is by no small feat that Errington is able to persuade Father to allow her to visit the dispensary with the 'essential task' of procuring more laudanum – though, indeed, this might as easily be fetched by a servant.

Grateful for being allowed to leave the grounds, it is only upon stumbling across Mrs O'Hare that Errington begins to regret the decision to venture out – such a detainment only fuelling her anxiety at being kept apart from the outside world.

'Miss Pattinson!' Mrs O'Hare declares. 'Do you know, just now, I saw the happiest of sights! Why it was your dear *Uncle*

Austin coming out of the Hotel Del Monte; paired up with a *most* attractive woman.'

Errington's eyes widen. Could Mrs O'Hare be ignorant of the object of Errington's affection; as she was, some years earlier, happening upon a distraught Errington at the back of Mr Wurster's General Store?

'You know, when your uncle first arrived, he willingly indulged our Freddy with photographs of South Africa,' Mrs O'Hare says, as if sharing this anew. 'Ever since then, I have thought well of him... But oh!' Her look of delight, fading. 'I have neglected to inquire after your health... Are you quite well?'

'I am quite recovered, I thank you.'

'I am glad to hear it.' Mrs O'Hare smiles, warmly. 'You'll pardon my forthright manner just now; I must confess I was quite overcome with delight. I dare say, Mr Moss – the *nicest* man, isn't he? – shan't remain a bachelor for long!'

'Yes,' Errington stifles laughter – for whoever this mysterious woman is, whatever the mix up; it is, indeed, Errington's hope that Austin 'shan't remain a bachelor.' 'I will be sure to convey your goodwill,' Errington manages, but can't help but make further inquiries. 'And the woman by my... *uncle's* side; pray, what was she like?'

Mrs O'Hare's enthusiasm returns at full capacity. 'Oh! Truly the most handsome of women! Several years his senior to be sure but with such striking, feminine features – pretty tendrils of hair about her face, a slender neck – one could hardly blame a man...'

AUSTIN ISN'T ONE FOR CROWDS, PREFERRING solitude, or the company – when he can get it – of his own sweetheart. But being tasked with showing Ella a good time, and understanding the benefits of placating Frank, Austin is here, nonetheless. Sitting much too far from Errington, much too close to Frank, and quite apart from Ella who declared she hadn't much interest in observing a 'sparring' match before leaving on the arm of Eddie – a self-appointed guide to take the 'Moss sister' through the fair.

'Go on then,' Frank says, giving Austin a nudge as the call comes, coaxing some brave, willing, and, perhaps, not very bright man to the ring. 'Up and at 'em.'

'What?'

Austin sits uncomfortably in his chair, wishing he'd never declared his recognition of the black fighter standing in the ring. Men in bowler hats are jeering in the crowd, waiting impatiently for another would-be bruiser to enter the ring. The man officiating the match scans the crowd eagerly, determined not to lose his audience, a line of sweat forming along the band of his boater hat.

'You there,' he says to Frank. 'You look like a man who knows how to fight.'

Frank touches his chest in mime, then places a firm hand on Austin's shoulder.

'Not I,' Frank says. 'But my brother, here... Now, he would be a fine match.'

The crowd's cheering rises in volume, lifts up toward the tent ceiling, making it near-impossible for Austin's objections to be heard. Besides, the crowd has worked itself up to such fervour that any attempt to deny the fight would not only prove difficult, but insult Austin's very manhood.

Austin does, however, hold one advantage.

Back in Klerksdorp, Austin had seen this boxer in the ring – folks called him 'Smiley' because of his two white chompers missing at the front, but Austin knew him as 'Sonny Jones.' Austin hadn't undergone any great exchange with the man at the time, but as a matter of principle, he always makes a point of knowing and employing the use of a man's name. Black, stockily built, skin glistening like freshly washed fruit; he had reminded Austin of heavyweight champion, Jack Johnson; a ball of muscle with kind eyes that turned fierce in the ring. Austin knew Jones to be an accomplished fighter, witnessing his defeat only once; caught off guard by a powerful, straight left, sending Jones flying, face to the floor. A move of 'check mate.'

All of a sudden, money is being waved about. Even Frank is clenching several little flags of paper notes, urging them forward before Austin has even left his seat.

The bell rings. The two men dance about. Austin, down to his undershirt, sack pants, and ill-fitting gloves handed to him by the officiator. To the sound of heavy breathing, the shuffling of anxious feet and heckling from the crowd; Austin homes in on Jones's shifting form, creeping closer with every non-connecting jab, his head rolling along his shoulders in the absence of a neck. Despite the dizziness of this dance, it feels as though the fight is yet to begin, the pair engaging in mere theatrics for the benefit of the crowd, agitating their impatience for blood.

Looking up at Jones, for a moment, Austin thinks he sees recognition in the black man's eyes, as though Jones might have some memory of this particular face in the crowd, now matched against him. Caught up in this moment, Austin, slow to react, misses his cue that the fight has truly begun, not catching the changes in his opponent; the furrow at his brow, his kind eyes turning hungry, desperate for blood, a wild animal in need of a kill.

With a gush of air pushing past Austin's face, Austin dances about before retaliating with a straight left. Not connecting but altering Jones's positioning. Jones becoming immediately more guarded – a boy sighting a teacher's bamboo cane – more calculating in the way he releases quick jabs; the last of the sequence, a decent right, connecting with Austin's left eye. Wincing at the sting filling his vision, Austin looks up at Jones. A mottled, waving boulder before him. Austin can see the way Jones is filled up by the crowd, his face, momentarily restored as more man, less beast. His arms, less well-placed, as he relaxes into taking another swing. Austin, taking hold of his opponent's openness with the timing of a straight left. And the punch is perfect; Austin's fist, a clock hand falling exactly on the hour; a shot fired, connects with his opponent right between the eyes.

The bell rings, both men return to their corner. Frank petting Austin, roughing him up like he would a canine, rubbing his fingers together in front of Austin's clouded vision; reminding him of the little flags riding on this fight. Sound itself almost overwhelms Austin; Frank's insistent tone, the roar of the crowd, chimes with the sound from within him; the ringing in his ears, the labour of his breathing, the beating of his heart.

The bell rings and the action is immediate. Jones no longer bothering to 'work' the crowd, though Austin continues to dance about. There is a rising nausea Austin manages to keep down, but the burning ache of his muscles, the throbbing at his left eye, remind him he is no longer a young man.

The fight lasts more rounds than Austin had bargained for. The bell rings. And rings. Austin is reliant on tiring out his opponent. This shiny mass of muscle growing more dangerous, more awesome with every exhaustive round. Without Jones's build, his strength, Austin cannot outrun fate for long. He looks across to the crowd. *She* is still there. The expression on her face concealed beneath her large hat, her small hands covering her half-open mouth.

A gust of air flies past his face, bringing him back into the immediate present. Austin is surprised to find Jones less on guard, showing signs of exhaustion, throwing punches with little regard for his defence. Seeing his chance, Austin takes a gamble, veering from his straight left, he sends forth a series of quick jabs, following this up with a powerful right cross, connecting right between the eyes. Jones is down, his hand trying to stem the streaming flow of red, his nose, cracked and off-centre.

Even as the officiator slams his hand down at the count's end, Austin is still bracing himself in disbelief. Propped up in place by the strength of another man, Austin's fist lifts up toward the heavens and he is declared 'the victor.' A voluptuous young woman approaches the ring, trophy in hand, as the only woman Austin cares to see disappears.

OUTSIDE THE TENT – THE CHEERING NOT YET subsided – Errington fumbles with her silver case, bringing a cigarette to her lips. The S-bend of her dress is accentuated as she leans forward, striking the match with a shaky hand. The flame bites at her fingertips.

'Blast!' she exclaims, throwing down both the cigarette and silver case.

Austin is still out of breath as he catches up to her. Wiping blood and sweat from his brow, before resuming the pose of a gentleman despite his semi-classical attire. 'Errington... You left...?'

For the duration of the fight Errington could not look away but neither could she condone such behaviour. Despite any past sniggers she may have heard undermining the conduct of soldiers in the Boer War – their brutality, the inhumane conditions of the camps – Errington has always held Austin, as both man, and soldier, in high regard. She looked upon Austin's Queen's medal resting upon blue velvet in admiration, a pin for every battle he fought: Belfast, Driefontein, Diamond Hill, Johannesburg, Orange Free State,

Cape Colony. In coaxing Austin to share artefacts of a life she could not know, Errington took to her atlas, running her finger along the smooth surface of the pages representing the place where Austin had trekked 52 miles in 22 hours; camped without water; engaged in a *'small scrap'* as he stormed yet another kopje. In her eyes, Austin was brave, adventurous; *good*. Never before had Errington considered Austin might be capable of such thuggery, so wholly apart from the battlefield; of engaging in a 'sport,' historically of the lower classes.

'Yes, I...' Errington is glad not to have to explain herself with the approach of Miss Ella Moss on the arm of Doctor Barlowe.

'Errington, my dear!' Ella declares. 'Please thank your father, again, for his kind invitation to Honey Harbour...' Ella's face takes on a knowing expression as she notices Austin's injuries. 'Ah, yes, Frank had a wager he might draw you into the ring.'

'Good God man,' Eddie examines Austin's wounds. 'It looks as though you put yourself in the way of a team of horses!'

This exchange diverts attention from Austin and Errington's own encounter, but only briefly. Alone again, held within Austin's gaze, Errington tugs at her glove, freeing her hand to meet Austin's cheek. Austin winces at her touch.

'Oh, has it been so long?' Errington smiles sweetly. 'I hope this recoiling in response to my touch will not become a permanent occurrence?'

'Sweet Nell,' Austin says, his face leaning into her palm like an *'old pussy fing.'* 'Your touch, wherever it may linger, shall induce anything but a recoiling.'

Errington's cheeks colour with memories of moments up the Speed River and in the woods; her body aching, hungry for Austin's touch, last experienced much too long ago. Her lips part. Looking into his blue-grey eyes, Errington considers how cruel it is; even together, they must engage their imag-ination.

The crowds are recalled and, suddenly, despite Ella and Eddie walking away, they are not quite so alone.

'Oh, I still feel excessively silly...' Errington says – choosing this to say, above everything else waiting to escape her lips. 'You know; for mistaking your sister.'

'For what? A lady having secured my good opinion?' Austin teases. 'Oh, I'm afraid, *that* position is already taken. No, I... I should have told you of her impending arrival. That is regrettable... And as for my part in the fight just now... Indeed, I am not a man without fault.'

'And yet...' Errington accepts Austin's arm as they walk, understanding their love is unwavering; knowing, there can be no obstacle, no seemingly insurmountable barrier, that may prevent a life shared. 'I am no less consumed; by you. Just *you*.'

As the lovers amble along the fair, a gloved-hand scoops up the small silver case lying on the ground where Errington has heedlessly dropped it; a thumb lingers over the embossed initials pertaining to its owner. Carefully, the hand deposits the case within a vest pocket to be reclaimed as evidence.

Maplecroft

Ellen Errington Pattinson
Honey Harbour

13 July 1908

Austin Moss Esqr.,
PRESTON.

My own dear love,

Are you thinking to-night of us?

The cottage is too cute for anything – but it is awfully small – <u>and</u> the <u>moss</u>-quitoes, as you English people call them, are absolutely awful. Today I swept the entire house – all the shelves and cupboards have been washed out – and the cooking utensils <u>thoroughly</u> cleaned. The furry coat in the coffee-pot would have delighted your heart, I'm sure – but diligent use of boiling water and bath-brick has at last had its reward – and the coffee tomorrow will not taste woolly... Now, how can I tempt you into looking forward to your visit? The fishing is really very good. Frank got two good bass off the wharf this evening – and Beth and Cousin Jean caught seven nice perch (in between picking huckleberries) – the Bay is lovelier than ever – and the boating and canoeing are perfect. Please, <u>please</u> stay as long as you can and <u>do</u> try to get a little extra time – demand it of "the Boss." If only we were not on an island I'd phone you, for I think I could make it more emphatic over a phone.

Do you know there's a full moon on the eleventh? Do you miss me, sweetheart? Aren't you glad we have the memory of that happy night up the Hespeler River – it makes the distance seem so much less.

Frank is waiting to row over with the mail, so good-night dear, good-night and God bless you –
Ever Errington, HONEY HARBOUR.

Austin Moss,
Preston, Ont.

23 July 1908

Miss Pattinson,
   Honey Harbour.

Sweetheart mine,
   Thank you so much for your letter. I was so pleased to hear such a good account of the island and its inhabitants. As regards to cleaning and scrubbing, I guess the scolding on that topic will keep (but you <u>will</u> get it later). Beloved, you do not offer any suggestions as to what to bring so I am just fetching a toothbrush and razor for myself. Ella has a trunk or so, I believe.
   I spent yesterday very busy as usual. After dropping Ella at Frank's, I did not get "home" till late, and so spent the time which should have been occupied in writing, reading certain letters received during the last 3 years, being carried to all sorts of places and finally arriving at a certain island... Only 16 days more.
   Au Revoir Dearest, Yours as ever,
   A., PRESTON.

P.S. I am told Lynn is coming on the 7th. Will there be room? Please let me know how long Ella and I may stay.

Lauren
Muskoka, Ontario, Canada
2019

29

———

September

'Gee,' Greg looks upon the room 'full of stuff' with wonder. 'Feels like I've been let into a secret gateway; a private portal back in time.'

'I know, right?' I agree, heaving a box out of the way, in search of the Boer War journal. 'But, I mean, you're around this kind of stuff every day.'

'Sure, but it's still thrilling, and I have a photographic memory as well so –' Greg leaps forward into the centre of the room, steadying his glasses. 'Oh!' His whole body leans in, marvelling at the small leather-bound book, its pages threatening to escape their binding. 'Is *this* what you're looking for? Austin's Boer War journal?'

Carefully, Greg turns the pages as delicate as butterfly wings, reading the daily activity, the mix of action and inaction, accompanying the minute dates and phrases.

Wed 7 Reveille 2:30 through Oliphant's nek & small scrap,

stormed kopje, few bullets, less breath, observation all afternoon, two troops in reserve for flanking... 9 prisoners.

– Austin Moss, Trooper 519, second contingent, New Zealand Mounted Rifles, November 7, 1900

'Fascinating,' Greg says, resting the journal on a box of letters, 'just fascinating.'

'I think it tells something of the soldier's experience,' I agree, 'however succinct the writing.' Seeing the brightness in Greg's brown eyes, letting his passion become my own, I reach for a letter of Austin's, written to his brother, Frank, marked April 15th 1904, nearly two years post-war; a letter, I believe Greg will find most interesting. How often I've put aside things I believe Greg might like.

> *Personally, I wish there was another war. I am not anxious for gore but the 'air' here would be all the clearer if a kaffir rising were to take place, there are rumours, but nothing at all definite.*

'Well now,' a deep crease forms in Greg's brow. 'Here's the unfortunate thing about delving into the past – this term here,' Greg's hand displays a white band where a wedding ring was once worn, 'is, perhaps, the most offensive term in South African English; now associated with the apartheid regime.'

'So...' I look between Greg and the yellowed letter with its romantic-looking scrawl, 'my ancestor was a racist?'

Greg looks up from the letter, his look softening. 'If we're being honest... And I think we owe it to ourselves, and others – *ours* probably were. We only have to look at history, at the treatment of various ethnicities and racial groups –'

'Well, that's an uncomfortable truth,' I interject, straightening the boxes against the wall; somehow unable to meet Greg's gaze.

'Isn't it though?' Greg chuckles uncomfortably, shifting

focus to study a photograph of Austin in uniform, alongside his chum – the appearance of the man standing next to Austin 'in keeping with the age of this house,' Greg suggests, 'see his blonde pencil-thin moustache, hair neatly parted; the erect posture of an Edwardian gentleman.' Turning over the photograph in his hands, Greg reads aloud the handwritten scrawl on the back – '*Doctor Barlowe & Trooper 519.*'

Our eyes meet as Greg takes delight in Austin's playful notation. Our gaze held as I wonder about delving into the past; about having a man in my home.

'Uh,' feeling unsettled, I recommence engaging in busy work, rearranging boxes, straightening the books on the book-shelf. 'I think I may have read this all wrong...'

'Not at all,' Greg declares, casually crossing his arms, shifting his weight to one side as if settling in for a chat. 'This is why we study the past; to learn from it. To understand who we were, who we are; who we wish to become.' Greg's love of history overrides all other awareness as he speaks. 'And, I mean, every decision that is made, every action, every love story; they all have a ripple effect. *You* would not be here if it weren't for Austin and Errington's love. *Your children* would not be here if it weren't for –'

'My love for my husband.'

Greg nods in a way that incorporates his shoulders, new awareness registering my changed position in the room, as I stand by the door. 'I... was going to say if it weren't for Austin and Errington... But, yes, quite right. If it weren't for...'

'Greg,' I say, still breathing in the freshness of his scent. 'I think you should probably go.'

'Oh.' Greg looks about the room, as though looking for something lost. 'Oh right... yes.'

'Only,' I say, because I knew my words had come out harshly. I had invited Greg to explore these archives and now sounded like I was arbitrarily rescinding that invitation 'We're picking up my Mother-In-Law in the morning and I –'

'We?... You and...?'

'The girls and I,' I say, closing the topic, ignoring Greg's comment about how positive it is that I still have a solid relationship with my mother-in-law. 'Sorry, I guess I'm just tired. Maybe it wasn't such a good idea to unpack the past. Maybe –' I continue apologising as Greg rushes out the door.

'Oh, I forgot.' Greg turns back to face me, caught part-way between the front steps and his car. I consider offering an explanation. I consider, maybe, now is the time to say the words out aloud. But then Greg speaks. 'I've got... Here.'

I take the notepaper from his hands and open it up back along the folds. 'What is this?'

There are a series of websites scribbled on the notepaper; I can just make them out.

'Just some sites I thought Emily might like to check out. You know,' he chuckles awkwardly, 'on the Black Death.'

I hold the notepaper up in thanks before closing it over in my palm. When the door is shut – the sound of Greg's car pulling away – I lean against the door and cry. *I want Nick* I cry. *I want my Nicky.* And I know I'm not ready to say it aloud.

Like Errington, I close my eyes, imagining *him* beside me, his head resting on my shoulder, or mine on his. I utter her words as if they are my own.

Best Beloved...are you sitting here beside me, looking out over the water – with your head resting on my shoulder...?

But he doesn't come. *He doesn't come.*

Instead, what comes is a memory of my father. There is something about the lined paper still resting in the palm of my hand that serves as a bridge between memories. Pale blue lines, pink border, shiny plastic edge along the binder holes. Even the way it's folded into tiny squares sparks something within.

Perhaps, it is the paper combined with my hot tears, the way they dampen and render it almost see-through like fish and chips in butchers' paper ... the way the ink starts to smudge; that sends me back to early high school, my back slumped against the toilet door.

The assignment had been to write my earliest memory. And though I'd usually say to anyone who asked – out of rudeness or curiosity or just plain naivety – 'It's just been Mum and I for as long as I can remember;' that wasn't true.

There's a photograph of me, naked, with pigtails peering out of a white laundry bucket, my father in the chair behind in faded shorts and a tight-fitting t-shirt, wearing a wide grin upon his face. Actual photographic evidence of happiness; a man who *couldn't* have been happy. There are several like these. If photographs told the whole picture, it would appear, for my youngest years, that it had just been Dad and me. But photographs lie. What they represent is not always how things *are*.

After a while, the photo albums of my childhood change from featuring *him* – blue-grey eyes looking at me with love and wonder – to simply photos of me, documenting all the 'firsts' thereafter. Within my mother's modest home, the photo albums became relegated to a forgotten space within the television cabinet, gathering dust beneath the rubble of old videos. Sometimes, I'd lay the albums out. Write with my finger in the dust. Then, I'd open them up.

And there, my father would be. Then, not there at all. My father was like a central character poorly written out of a TV drama with next to no explanation for his departure. Except, deep inside, I understood it was all *my* fault.

Sometimes, I think those photographs of my father and me *are* my earliest memories. They come before the trauma, the change, the guilt. So, choosing to reach further back to a point of happiness – as the assignment demanded – I wrote about me in the bucket; about the man grinning behind me with love in his eyes. About the disparity between photographs and real life.

My body took on a sickly feeling as the teacher inched towards me like a shark coming for its prey, circling in, collecting student work in a dishevelled pile – other students, folding their work in interesting ways; the student beside me, doodling in place of actual writing, then ripping the edges. Paper, by paper, the teacher drew near.

Folding the lined paper into tiny squares, thrusting it into the zippered pocket of my tartan skirt, my hand shot up. 'I've got bad cramps' I declared, making my male teacher uncomfortable before bolting to the bathroom; my assignment safely tucked away.

For the rest of the double lesson, I stayed there, on the toilet floor, amidst old green chewy and smudged graffitied messages, my back against the door of the cubicle. As I read over my assignment, the offensively bright bathroom lights bounced off the glossy plastic. And my tears dampened the paper, smudging its ink. As I wept, for the things *I* had done.

Austin & Errington
Preston, Ontario, Canada
1908

245

30

—————

November

From his bedroom window, George studies the Maplecroft grounds, split between beauty and purpose, stripped bare by the coming of winter. Rose bushes cut back to thorny stems; vegetable patches laying in waiting. Nature – as in life – *waiting* for the coming season, for the bringing of new life. Indeed – in life – it is of that which George is most afraid.

And yet, despite his position within society, the numerous boards on which he belongs, his political influence and voice as one of Preston's most successful businessmen; George cannot hold back this coming season.

Even as he sees it unfold before his eyes – the pair coming into view as they amble back through the woods, emerging from the spruce – as he witnesses the glint of a ring resting on Errington's hand before pocketing it upon approach, George is a man without power. Knowing his daughter's will, her strong determined nature – despite her weak constitution – George is no more able to intercept the union than he is to change the will of God. His fate – and the fate of those he loves so fiercely – decided long ago.

A fate, he remembers, first told to him by a gypsy peering into a teacup. What a laugh it had been; how young they were. Maisie and George stealing away, entering the tent of a gypsy, Maisie insisting upon the reading as if there were any doubt he would ask for her hand. Her reading, one of hope and happiness because of her focus on the present moment. His, set between two worlds of joy and pain.

'Ah, in your life,' the gypsy said, indicating the tea leaves that landed near the rim of the cup, and those that lay at its base, 'you will know great happiness and great *misery*.'

Hobson makes his presence known with a decisive knock and an apology; as always, never far behind the news.

George steps away from the window, memories of the past intermingling with the threat of an ominous future. 'I know it, Hobson, for I saw it for myself.' George's face hardens. 'And I know too, that I am powerless against it. And yet; I must try.'

31

December

Ella Moss,
12 The Waldrons,
Croydon, England

5 December 1908

Austin Moss,
Preston, Ont.

My dearest old A.,

By the 12 o'clock post I received a very welcome letter from you: the contents of which I immediately passed on to Mother & Father... who were all most keenly interested in your news. I __am__ glad to hear it & I do hope it means ultimate success & settling: though I gather from what you say you are not sure of this. Well old boy you know what I feel, & how "truly thank-

ful" I should be if your efforts are smiled upon! It must mean heaps of work & responsibility & I hope you will feel well fit & equal to it. I shall look out most keenly for further news and progress. Father was – & Mother too – awfully interested... Just now I suppose you are head over ears in work, thought & worry. I hope you & Frank are not rivals!!?Preston seems quite like a dream now, <u>not</u> a nightmare. Work & people & acquaintances seem to accumulate: & time flies. I have just become a member of the Allied Artists Association, which holds a Salon at the Albert Hall in July... So, I hope to increase interest & profit & possible £. S. D. See how mercenary I am getting... With ever so much love & congratulations.

    From your loving sister Ella.

E. Mary Moss,
12 The Waldrons,
Croydon, England

30 December 1908

Austin Moss,
    Preston, Ont.

My dearest Austin,

    I cannot attempt to tell you with what real pleasure I read your letter the other evening and have thought over its contents ever since. I have long felt how you needed and would value a true love and if I had dared to wish for you, I think Errington would have come tumbling foremost into my mind. Three years ago, when she came to stay a short time with us, I felt at once she was a sweet surprise and I liked her from the first hour and the feeling has never changed. And now I hope to love her, if I may, as belonging to you, and I have a deep-down hope that both you and she will never regret the step you have taken but find in each other a want supplied who makes life worth living.

I am not going to say much, old boy, but I am very, very glad for you, and wish you all good wishes that you would wish yourselves, and the best of wishes would I leave unwritten but which you may imagine would be in my heart; for I have loved you, as I think you know, ever since you were a very little boy.

You must be very busy with all this new business; the next few months will be a time of anxiety and will need wisdom in the handling!

I have not written to Errington yet, but I will send my love to her by you.

Your very affectionate mother,

E. Mary Moss

With Gruetzner finally relenting, Austin had managed to secure the Crown Furniture Co. Almost immediately, Austin had gone to Maplecroft to seek Mr Pattinson's blessing to marry Errington. Here, he falls short of this task; George congratulating Austin on his purchase, before declaring, 'But, I'm sure, you understand, a man could not befit himself as a suitor before having paid his dues. One must be successful in business for no less than one year, or else, how may he – or the family, for that matter – be sure the proposal is a solid one?'

While such a sleight of hand would likely stop another man in his tracks, Austin was undeterred. For three and a half years, he has been captivated by Errington, from their first meeting at Maplecroft when he discovered her unconventional beauty, the way she unashamedly 'made eyes' at him without the bashfulness that usually accompanied a woman's gaze.

Austin had been immediately drawn in by Errington's *'sweet, womanly nature,'* her evident intelligence, her playful streak; the flash of a porcelain ankle, the arching of her back within the rowboat, the blowing of smoke in Austin's direction, the parting of her lips. Lips, suggestive of man's greatest urges, of an aching in his loins and at his chest, and stranger still, igniting something deep within his mind. Austin remained in awe of Errington's daring; daring to hold her own opinion, to unashamedly prove that she knew more than some men, to strive for knowledge in areas of geography, history, astronomy. All of this, setting her apart from society's dictation of what a woman ought to be, and yet, remaining most attractively female.

Austin could not delay their engagement any more than he could survive without food or water – a concept, not entirely foreign to him, at least as a solider; *'Camped, wonderful, no water,'* Austin had penned with mild sarcasm in his pocket-sized journal as Trooper 519. But, as a soldier – and, indeed, a man, a Masonic brother – Austin understands he shall always be beholden to another man; just as a salesman is bound to his customer. And so, the only possible solution had been to propose to Errington in secret until he could prove his worth in work; words that escaped so freely, taken up with such delight.

The family, back home, were, of course, thrilled; though Austin had made it clear they must guard the news until the engagement became official. Austin had hoped to resolve the matter within a few trying months.

Five months on, Austin is no further ahead, regularly travelling back and forth to Quebec and Montreal, in pursuit of making yet another sale. Throwing all of his energies into work, with little time to sleep, much less eat, Austin exists but on few sips from his 'canteen' – mere glimpses of time spent with Errington – to sustain himself through this particular 'war.'

Upon their last meeting – having effectively timed their individual outings – Austin gifted Errington a fine-looking brooch, of which Errington held little reserve in showing her approval. The pair were spotted at the station looking rather 'cosy' by one of Austin's buyers, Mr Valiquette, down from Montreal. Oddly enough, there seemed to be no consequences, except that subsequently Errington announced that, yet again, she shall soon be sent away.

Ellen Errington Pattinson,
Maplecroft,
Preston, Ont.

11 May 1909 – Tuesday morning

Austin Moss Esq.,
   Queen's Hotel,
   Montreal, Quebec

Austin dearest,
   My voice has not come back sufficiently to thank you, even in writing, for the lovely brooch – I have been getting it out to admire it on average twelve times through the morning – and wearing it all afternoon and evening – but I really did thank you all the way up from Galt and again shortly after leaving Toronto. You are such a dear! Always thinking of things for me; I wonder, do you <u>never</u> think of yourself? I shall have to do that for you.
   I am wondering how you are getting on and hoping the

buyers are sensible enough to see the immense superiority of the Crown Furniture Co.'s goods... It is so lonely with you away – oh darling, it gets harder every time. Do take care of yourself. Remember not to have those dear eyes of yours looking so weary when you come home. Close them now just for a minute and imagine that this is a real kiss.

Yours so lovingly,
Little Nell, Maplecroft.
P.S. This is only just to let you know how full my whole heart is with you and with your love for me. Yours, Nell.

Austin Moss,
The Queen's Hotel,
Montreal

12 May 1909 – Wednesday

Miss Pattinson,
PRESTON.

Sweetheart mine,

Just a line to thank you oh, so much for your dear, encouraging letter; I had it this afternoon. You do write such sweet letters; they are just like you. I took your advice about the eyes and closed them for some time, much to the amazement of the man next to me. I am writing at the public room at The Queens as you may see. Mr Valiquette asked kindly after "my good lady" so I explained, and he hopes to see you sometime... The streets are fairly crowded now that it is fine, but none are in the same street with my little girl. So long sweetheart. So long my love.

Yrs as ever,
A.

Looking upon the freshwater lake, the rocky terrain leading down to the water's edge, Errington sits on a cool and shady veranda, thinking of Austin. Judd's cottage, reminding her of the *'too-cute'* cottage they stayed at last summer. Juddhaven itself, with its freshwater and its majestic forest; the smell of pine in the air, a happy reminder of Honey Harbour and the time Austin and Errington shared, unencumbered. Sure, the others were there – Ella, proving to be no less a trial than Elizabeth (despite being so much her senior) – but really, it was just the two of them; *a happy thought, indeed!*

Just now, as she hears the idle chatter of the other ladies holidaying here – all members of the Ladies Auxiliary – Errington imagines herself quite alone, save one other. A gentle head resting on her shoulder. Those precious blue-grey eyes closed off to the world as she feels him breathing in her floral scent, worn for his pleasure. Or, perhaps, it is her head nestled on his shoulder, her face pressing against the roughness of his coat, tickling her cheek as his moustache does when they are truly alone.

'But at the laste, as everything hath ende...' And Errington's happy musings are interrupted by the other ladies, just as Austin and Errington's time alone last summer was punctuated by the presence of their own siblings. Every interruption, exacerbating Errington's desperate need to become Austin's wife.

Maplecroft

Ellen Errington Pattinson,
Judd's Cottage,
Juddhaven, Lake Rousseau

26 July 1909

Austin Moss Esq.,
    PRESTON, Ont.

Best Beloved,

Are you up in your room this afternoon, I wonder? Or are you sitting here beside me, looking out over the water – with your head resting on my shoulder and your eyes closed? Oh! I forgot – there is no pleasure in smoking if one cannot see the smoke, so perhaps your eyes would be open!

O sweetheart I do hope you'll get rested. You do look so tired and worried sometimes, it is that horrid old business, I know! You <u>shouldn't</u> look so weary and worried for it is getting on wonderfully and I <u>was</u> so proud of you when you told me what the auditor said. You dear, dear love, it would be too terribly lonely if you hadn't said you were 'coming up too.' And as it is you are really here I can see you and hear you and feel your arms supporting me and the dear roughness of your coat against my face... Some day you will have all the petting you can stand – You're just a wee bit fond of petting, aren't you?

This is only to tell you over and over again how much I love you.

So long – So long – Yours forever and ever,
Little Nell,
Judd's Cottage,
Juddhaven, Lake Rousseau.

P.S. I can't get away from these girls for one minute to write – as they all write at the same time, and worse still, sit

near enough to dip in to my ink – so it is hard to say all I want
– but you <u>know</u>, don't you dearest.
   L.N.

Austin Moss,
The Crown Furniture CO.,
Preston, Ont.

29 July 1909

Miss Pattinson,
   Judd's Cottage,
   Judd's Landing,
   Lake Rousseau, Muskoka.

Well sweetheart, how's it going now? You dear!
   You must excuse this scrawl; I am writing under great difficulty. Please take care of yrself, I do hope this is a real holiday as you have not been charged this time with the care of any "infant" – who are known to be a trial, even if they are as interesting as Beth or Ella. How I wish I was up there with you. Next time we are going together, aren't we?
   What sweet letters you do write. They are not my strong point having only a limited command of expression, but this will let you know I love you more than ever and I haven't forgotten you, even if you did think so, and you do think weird things sometimes.
   I am coming along with this letter and if you don't know what happens right here X I will show you when we are next up the Speed River. This is just to tell you that you must look after yourself and not do any desperate stunts. So long little girl, so long. X did you get that?
   Yrs lovingly,
   A.

P.S. Please let me know what you think of the Crown Furniture Co. letterhead.

32

January 1910

Ellen Errington Pattinson,
Maplecroft,
Preston, Ont.

21 January 1910

Mr Austin Moss,
    PRESTON, Ont.

Austin dearest,

    I read and enjoyed most of the letters very much, but next time dear, don't give me any of Ella's letters where she is describing an "old flame" – odious phrase! I'm surprised at Ella's using it; she has in most things exquisite taste – she showed me a photo of another girl, to whom she applied the same description, when I was staying in Croydon – Most *mistaken of her, wasn't it, as you've always <u>said</u> you hadn't any – O sweetheart if I've ever made you one half or one sixtieth as miserable, I'm sorry. <u>Why</u> did you give it to me?*

...this will perhaps let you know again that I worship you now, that I have worshipped you for four years and that as long as I live – and afterwards – the whole of life will be just worship of you.

Yours always,
Little Nell

'I t is a fine thing, having luck on one's side,' Austin says to Mr Gruetzner one afternoon as they depart from the Lodge, Gruetzner, taking the opportunity to inquire after the Crown Furniture Co. 'Of course, it is much too soon to declare myself a success,' Austin laughs nervously, 'but rest assured, Crown Furniture is in capable hands.'

'Good, very good,' Gruetzner says, with a nod. 'Oh, I'm glad to be rid of it, really, I am. Let someone else do the work, I say. But it did take some time to come to this. Well,' Gruetzner continues, lifting his top hat, waving his hand over his small crop of hair. 'Perhaps, I had some help in coming to the decision to sell.'

'Yes,' Austin agrees. 'I was under the impression that Mr Pattinson had a friendly word. Perhaps, more than once?'

Gruetzner turns an ear toward Austin. 'I'm sorry?'

Austin repeats his meaning.

'George?' Gruetzner declares, with a smirk. 'Not at all! If anything, George Pattinson was instrumental in making me keep the thing. He was forever in my ear –'

All of a sudden, Austin is very quiet.

'You know, your brother once made me an offer too,' Gruetzner continues. 'Said he came in place of you. I could never work out why you elected your brother to handle your affairs; you know, I would have sold it direct. But then a tidy sum appeared at my door, a creditor claiming that *they* owed *me* money. Well, when someone is throwing dollars my way, I have more sense than to question it. After that, I no longer had a need to sell and considered I might keep it running a while longer. And I knew, as soon I'd had enough, exactly who my buyer would be; knowing how badly you wanted Crown Furniture Co. Really, you didn't know about this? I can scarcely believe it hasn't come up before!'

Gruetzner lets out a snort, a laugh that turns into a cough, causing him to reach for his handkerchief.

'Nor I,' Austin says, before bidding Gruetzner 'good day,' and heading out of the Lodge before the Grand Master is due to exit.

Striding along King Street, Austin cuts through the park, playing over in his mind everything he has ever done to offend George Pattinson.

Despite the pub brawl and the short stint in jail, it had taken some time before the young lad whose bail Austin had paid – the lad who claimed, rather boldly, that Elizabeth was 'quite grown' – had got the chuck from Pattinson Woollen Mills. Austin remembered the kid to be a good sort of lad – and he knew how tricky Elizabeth could be – and, feeling sorry for the poor kid, offered him a job. Though his terms of employment could not be very competitive – employing only a hand full of workers, not nearly the sizeable operation of the Pattinson Woollen Mills – Austin made the offer nonetheless; understanding the many lessons learnt through the passage of time. Not the least of which, he thought, were the perils of pursuing the boss's daughter or, *daughters* as had been the case back in New Zealand. Perhaps, *this* had been a strike against Austin's name?

Restless and unsettled, Austin moves about the park like a

monkey on a chain being teased and taunted. In fact, Austin's concentration is so focussed that he almost bumps into a woman dressed in a rich, fur coat and picture hat.

Startled, Austin looks up.

'Surely, this intrusion is not an unwelcome one?' Errington teases, peering up from her oversize picture hat.

Austin's expression softens at the sight of Errington's features. *How sweet, how dear.*

'Not in the least,' Austin says. 'But I'm afraid, I'm not the best of company; something Gruetzner said just now has shocked me.'

'Well, what can Gruetzner say to upset you so?' Errington tries desperately to understand, taking Austin's hand. 'My love, you have the business already. Crown Furniture Co. is yours – as I shall soon be too. Oh, if you only knew and understood; I am already so much yours!'

Austin's gaze is lowered in searching for something.

'My love,' Errington urges. 'Why should Gruetzner matter now?'

'I cannot fathom...' Austin is thinking aloud. 'Why on earth your father would claim to put in a good word for me, *if* that was never his intention... If, in fact, he was intent on doing quite the opposite...'

Errington's face hardens, her big brown eyes holding an emotion Austin has never witnessed there before.

'Because' Errington says – an anger rising from within. 'He means *never to* give his consent.'

THOUGH ERRINGTON'S DECLINE HAS COME ON gradually – over the course of several years – this is the moment, George fears that she will be lost to him forever. Although he has done everything within his power to ensure

Errington receives the very best care, that she does not overexert herself when the colour goes from her cheeks and her eyes hang dark shadows; here, in this moment, George must acknowledge his own failings.

He signs the last cheque in the pile on his desk, replacing the fountain pen in its holder.

'Are you quite well?' George asks, feeling Errington's presence at his study door.

'No, sir,' Errington's lips form a thin line. 'I am not.'

George gestures for Errington to have a seat, which she declines.

'My dear...' George begins, knowing what the fierce look in her eyes means; though his objections are much too late, he tries a calm approach, hoping she might 'see reason'. *Austin Moss does not have the means... He may not afford you a grand house, magnificent grounds, nor the proper care you need... And should you wish to have children...?*

'Errington,' George continues, because he must; he would never forgive himself if he didn't try to steer her away from catastrophe. 'I'm afraid, you do not know the extent of your illness... Perhaps, it was unfair, conducting things in this way...'

George observes the way Errington's small hands – child-like – press into the soft leather covering of his desk, leaving the slight indent of her knuckles.

'Loved and admired by the whole of Preston...' Errington shakes her head. 'But they do not *know* you. They do not *know* who you are. And they do not *know* what you are capable of...'

Raising her hand, Errington's gaze shifts as she reaches across the desk. George hasn't bothered to conceal the silver case, left faithfully by Hobson – a cigarette case typical of an actress – Errington holds up the case in outrage.

'What else?' There is a hollowness to her voice. A madness in her eyes. 'What else of mine do you keep?'

George's throat constricts as Errington professes her 'love' for a man inferior to this family – a mere 'remittance man' – and knows defeat: George *knows* his daughter's determination; her unbreakable spirit.

Holding George's gaze, Errington presses open the case, placing a thin soldier, a single 'coffin nail' between her lips; striking a match against George's desk – all of it theatre; in which Errington will pay the ultimate price for her actions. A final act of defiance as Errington brings the flame to the cigarette between her lips.

As if breathing in powerful smelling salts, Errington's eyes drift back as she inhales. George's knuckles turn white. The igniting of a flame, the thick plume of smoke, the blackening of George's heart.

And, just like that; Errington is gone. *So mote it be,* George sighs as his daughter disappears. *So mote it be.*

Mr George Pattinson
Announces the marriage of his daughter
Ellen Errington
To
Mr Austin Moss
Son of Mr Charles J. Moss, Croydon, Surrey, Eng.
On Wednesday, April the twenty seventh
St. John's Church, Preston

33

February

Charles Moss,
12 The Waldrons,
Croydon, England

26 January 1910

Austin Moss Esq.,
*   PRESTON, Ontario,*
Canada

My dear Austin,
*   You are naturally expecting a letter from me to express my pleasure as well as that of others at the news conveyed to Mother in your and Errington's letters – You both have my warmest wishes for your real welfare and happiness. You have no idea how the secret which you entrusted to us more than a*

year ago has burnt our breach bones. It is such a relief to let it escape and that we are now allowed to publish the news everywhere...

With kindest love and best wishes to Errington and yourself,

Your affectionate Father,
Charles Moss,

Austin Moss,
The Queen's Hotel,
Montreal

12 February 1910

Miss Pattinson,
*   PRESTON, Ont.*

Sweetheart,

"We" arrived safely 7:30 this morning – rather chilly atmosphere in Montreal. You were a dear to come down last night. Sorry I couldn't get out of the car, but "Father" introduced me to the two who you saw in the railcar, members of the "House" – see what a lot of aristocrats I'm meeting.

I write this to tell you "I love you" as I couldn't tell you yesterday and so I got mad today and bullied the buyers in to taking $901.30 worth of Crown stuff – what do you think of that?! Mr Anthes, our traveller has a sample room (of other firms' goods) and so a lot of our clients call on him there and it saves "us" a lot of running round. I have some fairly good orders – with promises of more to follow.

Father's and Mother's letters were very nice. They both wrote <u>after</u> they heard, and I think that Mother was tickled *all over and so was my father too. Fancy them being tickled but it is a fact, nevertheless. Saw Jack re house before I left, seventeen per month – too much as house is not up to date by any means but we'll go and see it first chance, shall we? As for the "cosy rooms" a la Ella, we can have them too. You can make them cosy, and I'll enjoy them – equal division of labour isn't it.*

I hope to be in Preston Monday evening – till then; now and always I love you – You know it, don't you? And am yours always,

A.

THE CROWN FURNITURE CO.
of Preston
FURNITURE MANUFACTURERS
PRESTON, ONT.
Canada

I HEREBY AGREE TO LEASE for the term of one year from April 1ˢᵗ. 1910 the house and premises approximately 100 feet on William St., corner of Lowther and William streets, for the sum of $15.00 per month, payable monthly.
Moss

'Come now, let's have a toast,' Eddie insists, raising his glass. 'To married life.'

'To married life,' Austin agrees.

Eddie examines Austin's countenance. His twinkling blue-grey eyes, the glow of his skin, his waxed moustache stretched across a broad grin. In all the years Eddie has known Austin –

even in boyhood, back in Croydon, as an adventurous young lad always in cahoots with Dickie – never has Eddie seen Austin look so well.

'Does my impending nuptials induce you to rope in a fair maiden of your own?' Austin says, cheekily.

'Me?' Eddie tilts his glass on its axis. 'No, not I, old chap. I'm afraid, my heart remains whole. But' Eddie says, shrugging this off, 'we can't all be destined for the kind of happiness designed for you and Errington.'

Eddie thinks of Jane Austen's Pride and Prejudice, of happiness in marriage, of Elizabeth's declaration of Jane's good character above her own; '*...I never could be so happy as you. Till I have your disposition, your goodness, I never can have your happiness.*'

If it were up to Austin, he might suggest it is Eddie who has the purity and goodness of Jane – Eddie, remembering a past letter in which Austin confessed, '*Perhaps, I might have been a bit straighter.*' And Eddie taking exception to the remark.

Yet Eddie knows Austin to be a man of principle and faith, a man diligent, law-abiding, true to his Masonic pledge. Endeavouring each and every day to be a 'better man.' To be the *best* kind of man. Though Eddie does not believe himself worthy of such happiness – *how oft he'd returned to the Hotel Kress; amplifying the ecstasy, blocking out the shame* – his emotions are welling up with pride and joy for Austin.

'Oh, but I would like to see you settled, old man,' Austin coaxes, unwittingly adding to the 'happiness' of his dear friend. 'I'm sure your father would quite agree...'

Eddie gives Austin a playful jab to the ribs. 'You and I both know my father is the last man on earth I aim to please.'

'Nevertheless,' Austin looks upon the mahogany shelving of liquor, arranged not unlike a library, shelving rising to the pressed metal ceiling. 'Whatever your marital status, I do hope you'll be our family physician. Errington is not a young woman – nor, I, a young man – and we should like to try for children right away.' Austin's eyes appear almost translucent – sparkling like shallow water over sand – his thoughts and desires, close to the surface. 'I need someone I can trust.'

Austin holds Eddie's gaze; perhaps considering the delicate nature of childbirth, the ill-fate of his own dear mother after Austin was born.

Eddie nods in agreement.

Though Eddie has long thought ill of Doctor Vardon, and the archaic practices he represents, this opinion is not something he may very easily air. Indeed, it is much neater for Austin to come to this decision himself, requesting for Eddie to be their family physician.

As if placing a hand to the Bible, Eddie makes a solemn vow to his dearest friend, 'I shall do everything within my power to keep your wife and future infant safe. You may have my word on that.'

Austin pats Eddie on the back, his hand lingering in mateship.

'Errington is determined we shall have big, strong sons that take after me – God help them,' Austin beams, as though the seed were already planted.

Eddie smiles. 'Moss miniatures; how wonderful.'

Maplecroft

Ella Moss,
12 The Waldrons,
Croydon, England

14 April 1910 – Sunday 5.30

Austin Moss Esq.,
    PRESTON, Ontario,
    Canada

My dearest A.,

Just a few lines to reach you, I hope, while still a bachelor! To give you, once more, the very best wishes & hopes for the double-harness life just about to begin. I wish I could be present at the ceremony but shall think of you instead... I can safely say, we shall drink your health.

I am going to imagine the Loy house as quite a model miniature. I hope Errington will like it as well as you and will not feel too cramped in it after Maplecroft. After all, she is not going far away from her old home. Leaving her father to live without her will be harder than going to a smaller house, but if he finds he has gained a good son, he won't regret having given up his daughter's constant companionship. May it be a real home to both of you as I feel sure it will.

Goodbye, dear old boy, God bless you. My hopes for you so far have been fulfilled, that it encourages me still to hope –
With ever so much love,

I am always.

Yr loving sister, Ella

As THE ORGANIST STRIKES THE FIRST CHORD OF Mendelssohn's wedding march, the church doors open like the breaking of new light. Austin does not register the influx of fresh, spring air; the crowd outside, there to gush over the bride; the bridesmaids dressed in pale yellow crepe de chine. His mind is occupied, gaze fixed. Until, at last, there in the archway, on the arm of her father, stands an angel surrounded by light.

Austin takes in this vision of *her*. Her high lace collar flowing into a most faithfully tailored French ivory satin – the material, a detail Errington had let slip, teasing, after numerous dress fittings, that Austin might appreciate the feel of it too. The satin adhering to her curves and small waist, feels like the way his hands are made to cup her breast, reminds her of the way their lips touch. From the gathering at the base of her train; to the smooth, satin gloves slipping beneath her embroidered sleeve; to the detail at her bust – *so much a tease!* – Austin's eyes explore the landscape of her body, sheathed in satin. Finally, they rest upon her *'apple-blossom cheeks,'* her *'bright eyes' holding* his gaze.

As Errington approaches, Austin breathes in the scent of orange blossom – the wreath surmounting Errington's veil – and the lilies of the valley held within her bouquet. A blending of floral perfumes, recalling Errington's own intoxicating scent.

As Tolstoy puts it, *'We are asleep until we fall in love!'* Errington takes her place beside Austin and, already, life is full of promise.

*'The prettiest wedding to take place in Preston in a long time
was that solemnized this afternoon at St. John's Church, when
Miss Ellen Errington, eldest daughter of George Pattinson, Esq.,
M. P. P., became the wife of Mr Austin Moss, of Preston.'
– Galt Daily Reporter, 27 April 1910*

Lauren
Muskoka, Ontario, Canada
2019

34

September

We are all in a rush; though the girls and I leave early in the morning to embark on the several hour long drive, rocky cliffs and woods either side of the road, drawing ever-near to the insane number of lanes funnelling toward the airport. The morning sun bounces off the windscreen as I squint into the rear-view mirror; no one is permitted to talk as I merge lanes.

'Should have taken a taxi,' Em grumbles.

'Shhhhush,' I say, through gritted teeth as though a single comment might derail the whole trip.

'Sor-ree,' Em says, muttering under her breath, 'touchy.'

'We *are* going to stop at Tim Hortons – aren't we?' Zoe begins again, unable to pick up on cues to zip it.

'Yessss, Zoe,' Em sighs. 'We're goin' to Timmies.'

I raise an eyebrow, torn between insisting the girls keep

quiet and concentrating on the road ahead. The car parking situation, no less tense as we circle the multi-storey car park, watching the digital clock tick over as the last foreseeable park slips out of grasp.

'Eight 'o' five,' Em narrates. 'Eight 'o' six.'

'*Not* helping.'

'Found one!' Zoe yells, causing me to jolt to a stop, almost reversing into the car behind.

Ok. I breathe again when we are finally parked.

On the walk to the terminal, we are all buzzing, Zoe talking at a frenetic pace, mostly about honey-glazed Timbits; Em racing ahead. At the airport, everyone is in a rush, loading luggage, printing tickets, checking the arrivals board for updates. As we wait behind the metal railing, watching the doors for signs of life, I feel nervous; jittery. Finally, there is the tease of a single passenger, then another, and another, until we are greeted by a chorus of suitcase wheels gliding in unison; Lorraine, striding right past us as we rush to meet her.

'Oh! Oh, there you are!' she draws Em's cheek to her lips; Em throwing both arms around her Nan; Zoe cuddling her side; me, throwing a kiss over the top. Lorraine, then coming in for the hug, long and tight.

'Ah,' I say, blinking through a haze of tears. 'I need sleep.'

'What you need is a hug!' Lorraine throws her arms around me once more as I think of the old fridge magnet Nick once bought as a joke, it's a sentiment never more true than right now; *Loz needs a hug.* Thinking too, how he'd approach me from behind – my hands busy in the kitchen sink – just holding me, feeling me; like I feel him now.

'I *have* missed you,' I say, surprised by my own emotion.

Helping Lorraine with her bags – Zoe leading the way – we sit down to a breakfast of coffee and donuts, ordering a box of Timbits for the road.

'Huh,' Lorraine comments, sipping her coffee-pot coffee with cream. 'Guess I'll have to get used to *that*... Guess, there's a lot I'll have to get used to, huh.'

Greeted by the warm, trapped, polluted air, we navigate the car park; re-joining the mammoth headache of entering the busiest highway in Ontario; if not the world.

As I merge into the next lane, and then the next – like Tarzan swinging from tree to tree rather than controlled driving – Lorraine continues talking full-speed. She is determined to share details of the 'nice young man' serving drinks on the flight; the 'large women' seated next to her – either side; the in-flight movie with its two-dimensional characters and predictable end.

'Lorraine,' I say, checking the surrounding traffic, the distance of the car in front. 'I just need a min –'

'Yellow car!' Zoe squeals from the back. 'Found one!'

'Zo.'

Em leans forward, arm hanging over the edge of my seat. 'It's this game we play, Nan, where we –'

'Em,' I warn, a tightness at my chest. 'Would you just –'

'They're alright,' Lorraine says, her mood opposite to my own until she steals a glance, noticing the way her words land, and suggests to her granddaughter: 'Maybe sit back, love, there's a girl.'

Hemmed in by cars swarming all around, anxiety grips me like a noxious weed, infiltrating every part of my being; altering my ability to see clearly.

Lorraine pulls the visor down to steal another glance of the girls in the back, momentarily blocking my view. 'And...' she begins, again, as if in search of conversation; searching, then failing, to find something to keep things light. 'What about your dad?'

'Do you mean *their* dad? Nick?' My brow folds into a crease, surprised by Lorraine bringing Nick up when I'd already forewarned her that the girls are struggling right now; the very mention of his name bringing them to tears.

'No, love,' Lorraine places a gentle hand at my shoulder, allowing a small respectful silence. 'I mean *your* father. Have you looked any further into –'

I shrug off Lorraine's hand, my eyes boring into the car in front. '*My* father?' If I wasn't hemmed in, I'd stop the car out of protest. 'Why would you even...?'

From the corner of my eye, I see the way Lorraine gathers her hands toward her lips, as if to prevent the words spilling out. But the floodgates don't hold. 'I only meant... All this research into family history, going to the local archives and what-not, isn't that all tied to finding out about your own father. I mean, you say how blessed you've been to have inherited this beautiful place – which I'm just *dying* to see. A place, only yours because of your father. I mean, don't you owe it to him to, at least –'

I can feel my temperature rising, the heat rushing to my head, making me stressed and uncomfortable. 'I. Owe. Him. *Nothing.*'

'Mum doesn't take well to talking while driving,' Em says, leaning forward once more. 'Or talking about her old daddy-O... Oh.'

Em's face changes as I deliver my tirade.

'What *I* don't take well to; is being railroaded in *my* car, on the way to *my* house. Being tricked into whatever *this* is.'

'Trick?' Lorraine's voice grows cold. 'Darling, there's no trick.'

An SUV pulls in front, causing me to slam on the brakes, giving Lorraine the final word as the cars either side sail past.

'I got this,' I yell. '*Alright,* I've got this.'

For the remainder of the journey we travel in silence, recovering from the near miss, and Lorraine turns towards her window. 'It's beautiful,' she says finally, as we draw near.

Pulling up to the cottage, Lorraine exits the car and I watch as she walks away, Em taking her by the hand, showing her to her room. In the cool and shaded hallway, I stand at the bottom of the stairs, my finger running over the old groove cut into the banister. I call out to Lorraine but receive no answer. Ignoring me, I'd say. And why not?

Stewing at the kitchen bench, alongside the sound of the boiling kettle, I reach for the folder of letters and traverse the stepping stones down to the dock to pour over *their* words; willing the past to carry me away from the present.

Once there, I drag out a chair and sit by the water's edge; alerted to the presence of Brace, upstairs, by the sound of rustling overhead as he shifts about to reach the underside of the railing with his paintbrush – in my heightened state of emotion, I hadn't noticed his truck pulled off to the side.

'Well, hello down there,' his voice echoes over the water as I crane my neck, partially looking into the sun.

Immediately, I rise, uncomfortable in believing myself alone.

'Oh.' The heat, drained from my cheeks, rising again. 'This is a surprise.'

Brace nods, continuing to work his paintbrush along the underside of the railing, commenting on how the paint is half-absorbed in the first coat.

'Uh...' I say, feeling awkward that he is here; now. 'Think we should probably talk.'

Brace lowers his paintbrush to rest upon the edge of the paint tin. 'I agree.'

'I'll...' I hesitate. 'I'll come up.'

As I cross the floor, I practise the speech I'd prepared in my head; the one where I assert my authority as parent to my daughters, where I place some distance between myself and this man who has seemingly come out of nowhere, and looks so at home in my house.

'Listen,' we say, in exactly the same moment, causing the pair of us to laugh awkwardly until I insist Brace go first.

'Listen,' he says again, scratching the back of his head, a slick of paint transferring onto his golden locks. 'I didn't mean to overstep... I should have sought your permission; I didn't know it would cause such a stir...'

I can feel my expression hardening with annoyance at this poorly constructed apology.

'Uh,' Brace breathes a sigh. 'This isn't going so well... What I mean to say...' There is a smile on Brace's lips, flashing all his teeth; a grin that has probably got him out of a lot of strife over the years.

Unaffected by his smile, I listen as Brace explains that he has seen others jump off this same railing many times before; that he tested it himself first; that my '...father –'

'Let's *not,*' I interject, 'talk about my father.'

And before I can make up for my tone – my apparent rudeness – the sound of footsteps thunder below; here and then, gone.

'I should...' I say, looking back towards the stairs.

'Right,' Brace agrees, looking upon his paint stuff.

'Thank you,' I add. 'I mean it; it's just... now is not really a great –'

'Time,' Brace agrees, saving me from offering excuses. 'I should have let you know I was coming... I'll come back another time.'

He makes a joke about tradespeople never appearing when you want them, and both of us let out stilted laughter. The sound of footsteps reappears – accompanying my own as I descend the staircase – Lorraine appearing at the dock.

'Who's there?' Her voice is cold, expressionless.

But before I can explain, Brace comes down the stairs, revealing first his paint-speckled boots, then the rest of him, carrying his shirt in his hands.

Hurriedly, awkwardly, I introduce Brace as 'the carpenter.'

'Uh, do you mind if I wash the paint out of my hair?' Brace nods towards the water, laying his shirt over a chair back. The water turns white as he dives in from the edge of the dock, resurfacing with a sheen on his tanned skin.

Lorraine's gaze sets upon Brace as he climbs the ladder, emerging from the water, his golden locks dripping. Carefully, taking in his blue-grey eyes – assessing – watching as he throws on his shirt over muscular arms.

'Uh, I'll go,' Brace announces, as though he is aware of Lorraine's examination. 'Won't make it back for a while though... I'm off to *Hawaii.*' His voice, distinctly lacking excitement.

'Oh,' I say, not really wanting to engage in small-talk, 'that's where Mar –'

'Marilyn,' Brace says. 'I know; it's my half-brother's wedding.'

'Marilyn is your mother?'

Brace raises an eyebrow, before confirming with a nod.

'Well,' I say, 'I would not have picked *that.*'

Upon Brace leaving, recent memory returns to the surface; Lorraine and I left with the awkwardness of our unresolved conflict. Dragging a second fold-out chair, together, we sit, watching the water; watching and waiting.

When Lorraine finally speaks, my eyes are shut, laced with tears. I open them as she speaks, watching the sunlight glistening on the water.

'Lauren, I understand this is hard. Perhaps, you forget – I lost a son too.' Lorraine's voice turns shaky as I turn to face her. 'But the pain isn't just going to disappear; and you shouldn't expect it to. Grief knows no boundaries.'

'Lorraine, I am so... so, sorry for the way I spoke to you.' I look back toward the water. 'Sometimes I think I'm ok. And

other times,' I shake my head. 'I don't know what happened…
But I'm truly –'

'Save it,' Lorraine says, her square fake nails wrapping
around the arm rests of her fold-out chair. 'We both know
that's been building for a while now, hasn't it?'

I let out a deep sigh and sink further into my chair,
mouthing the word 'sorry.'

Lorraine, follows my lead, sinking into her chair too, as if
melted by the sun. 'You know,' she says, examining the sun on
the water, the surrounding woods, the view to the township
across the bay. 'About what I said earlier…'

'We don't need to go over –'

'No, no,' Lorraine insists. 'I mean about there being a lot
to get used to; I could easily get used to this.'

The sun on my face and shoulders, the sound of the water
lapping the dock in gentle rhythm; I shut my eyes, breathing in
the pine-air. 'I know *exactly* what you mean.'

Behind us, I hear the sound of the girls approaching,
shifting about in the boat house, followed by a splash as Zoe
leaps over the edge of the dock, a donut ring around her
middle.

'Careful!' I hold the folder of letters close to my heart,
though the spray of water doesn't come close.

Lorraine smiles, glad at the girls splashing about; happy.
She nods toward the folder. 'Read me one of those letters.'

I look at Lorraine semi-suspiciously. 'You sure? You've had
an epic flight… And a hell of a time with that daughter-in-law
of yours… You must be wrecked.'

'Absolutely, knackered,' Lorraine agrees. 'But' she says,
reaching forward to roll up her pantlegs, allowing her legs a
little sun. 'I'm determined not to sleep until the sun goes
down.' Lorraine looks across at the folder once more. 'Read
me one… if you like.'

'Ok.'

As I pull the folder away from my chest, preparing to sink into the familiar words of a love whose very existence – several generations later – led to my own; I consider that there is so much I still do not know. That, in fact, there is so much I wish to find out.

Within that precious room, an archival goldmine of a past life, I have only touched the surface. It would take years to read and transcribe every letter, journal, document, to truly appreciate every photograph. But the past has a way of clarifying the present. And, from what I've read of Austin and Errington, I believe, words have the power to heal.

I take up my favourite letter.

'*Best beloved,*' I begin.

SITTING OUT THE FRONT OF TIMMIES, ENJOYING THE morning rays, Pete is drinking from the dish Taylah put out at the start of her shift. 'For *all* the dogs 'round here,' she said. 'Don't want him to get a big head.' It was then that Brace and Taylah shared a joke, as they often did – Brace, not likely to ask Taylah out despite her good looks; and Taylah only wishing to be asked – Brace believes – for the simple pleasure of denying him. *Mean, really.*

But Brace is more than ok with his own company, and that of Pete's. Before the newcomers, he wasn't even sure he cared much for family either.

Just as Pete is having a good old drink, a woman with bare, sagging arms, her nails matching the colour of her dress, bends down to give Pete a scratch behind the ears.

'He likes that,' Brace smiles.

'Sorry,' she says, standing. 'Probably should have asked first. But I just love animals – and children – a natural born nurturer, you see... You're 'the carpenter,' aren't you?'

'I am,' Brace says, because he has been wondering if this woman, met briefly on Lauren's dock, would remember him. 'You're the mother-in-law.'

'I am,' she agrees, standing back, nodding – her eyes casting over him as they did upon their first meeting, as if still making her assessment. 'Not sure about the coffee here, what do you think?'

'I think it's a matter of perspective,' Brace says, turning the half-empty cup in his hand, inspecting its contents.

A gust of wind gathers, causing Brace to avert his eyes from this friendly stranger, to look back toward the shop. The summery dress, the white-blonde bob; unmistakable.

'Hello, Henry,' she says, as she comes back out, a pre-ordered coffee and bagel in hand. Her voice, formal as if dealing with her real estate competitor.

Brace nods in acknowledgement, watching her walk away.

'Brace ... a nickname then?' The mother-in-law asks, having gone back to giving Pete a good old rub. 'That Mum?' she adds.

'In the flesh,' Brace says, confirming all her assertions.

'Right well,' the mother-in-law stands, shooting a look back, as the car behind them pulls away. 'Wouldn't kill you to smile.'

Brace offers an unnatural grin, baring all his teeth.

'Better,' the mother-in-law says, lowering herself to sit, when he thought she was just about to leave. 'There's some cupboards at the house... in the kitchen; that need repairing...'

'Ok...' Brace says, surprised to find this woman doesn't find him a threat; most mothers do.

'Yeah, I was wondering if you wouldn't mind fixing them up for us...? It's a bugger, you know, every time I reach into the medicine cabinet, the whole thing comes unhinged.'

'Sure,' Brace says, because it is none of his business to enquire after the 'man of the house,' to ask after the whereabouts of this woman's son. 'I'll take a look when I can make it back to finish painting the railing.'

The mother-in-law stands, deciding not to grab a coffee, after all.

'Thanks,' she says, calling over her shoulder, 'Oh, and – enjoy the wedding.'

35

———————

October

Amidst the pastels of the waiting room, I fill my mind with excuses, the toxic reasoning that kept me away. It's strange, how a fully grown adult can feel like a child under the gaze of a health professional. How we tick the box 'never smoked' on a medical form, or relay average alcohol intake based on our best day, not our worst. *We want honest help, but are we really honest with ourselves?*

When I enter the light-filled room – almost exactly as I found it – Val doesn't ask why I've not been back, doesn't comment on the time elapsed, except to say with a twinkle in her eye behind new glasses: 'It's nice to see you again.'

It is surprising how little prompting I require, all the major topics just waiting to flow out: guilt over Lorraine; guilt over the girls; guilt, anger, sadness – *all* the emotions – over Nick; confusion over Brace, over Greg.

285

'Unfortunately,' Val crosses over her legs, her posture perfectly erect, 'I do not have the answers, only the *tools.*'

I forge a smile, reminded now why it took some time to get back here. Then, something surprising happens.

The memory, flooding back like tears finally permitted to fall. In this light-filled room, I return to the darkened hallway of my childhood home. Dusty photographs sitting atop the dresser: my parents' wedding photo, obscured by baby pictures, me in the bucket. A vase of plastic stems and papery petals, a faux version of those pictured as my mother's bouquet. The distant sound of abandoned cartoons.

From the living room window, I'd seen a car pull up. Though out of sight, I heard my father step outside to meet it, I heard the crunch of gravel, a car door slam. I could see the reflection of the red car in the window closest to the T.V. but not the people. Voices from outside came as an indecipherable murmur. I turned up the volume on the T.V.

With my eyes fixed to the colourful cartoons, I heard my father return to the house, a delay between him entering and shutting the door. I grew conscious of footsteps behind me, stepping lightly, as if not to disturb a sleeping baby. After a while, I began to feel ignored, marooned on the soft leather couch.

Finding myself in the darkened hallway of my parents' home, seeking a different form of entertainment, I yank open the bottom drawer to fetch some printer paper, abandoning the drawer at the sound of laughter. Feminine, unusual to our home. Perhaps it is my mother, journeyed here in someone else's car. Whoever it is, she sounds happy. Moving toward the sound, I place my small hand upon my parents' bedroom door. And push.

In the changed light, I see the half-open curtains, the unmade bed. A woman – not my mother – lunging forward, grabbing at the sheets, covering up her semi-flat, drooping breasts. My father, dressed, buttons mismatched with button-holes, catches my eye.

As he moves toward the door, I wait for him to crouch down and explain as he normally does about things I don't quite understand. In waiting, I shift all my weight on to one foot, unbalanced by the presence of this woman who must be sick, too, because she is in my mother's bed.

But my father does not crouch down. Instead, looking angered by the disruption, he pushes the door shut.

Staring at the white, glossy paint inches from my nose, I hear the metallic clang of the door locking, and the laughter of my father and his guest begins again. Tears streaming down my cheeks, I withdraw to my room, in great sobs, seeking out the comfort of Teddy.

Eventually, after nuzzling into Teddy's matted brown fur for some time, I feel a hand upon my shoulder, the tickle of whiskers at my ear as my father kisses me, pulling me up to his chest, telling me not to worry. But even as I hug into my father's chest; even as I nod so convincingly in the name of secrecy; I know I will tell my mother.

'At the time,' I say, 'I did not understand what I had seen.'

Val holds her glasses by the arm, her eyes appearing half-dressed without them. 'How could you?' she says in sympathy. 'You were only a child... And to discover your father's infidelity in such a way.'

For a while, Val simply listens as I try to remember the sight of the 'other woman'. It seems important to put a face to the woman who came between my family – though, I suspect, she was not the first. I could tell from the softness at her arms, the tightness around her face, that she was older than my mother. The woman's hair pulled tight into a ponytail. She was not particularly pretty or thin.

'My mother went very quiet,' I say. 'At the time, I didn't understand her reaction... My father was never welcome in our home again. And after a while, he stopped trying to visit me altogether.'

Val emphasises that my parents' separation was not my fault. That this burden is not mine to carry. I'm surprised that just hearing these words has such a big effect – they make me feel *seen*. I hadn't realised how much I needed to hear this. My eyes flicker shut at the renewed memory of my parents' bedroom door; white, glossy paint inches from my nose.

After a time, the room gets quiet, and my thoughts get loud. I look at Val who seems to notice the shift; it is as though she now has access to my mood, the workings of my mind. She looks at me, holding my gaze, my trust; willing me to delve deeper, to go where I have been resisting.

'Let's talk about Nick.'

Val waits for her words to settle.

Slowly, I nod. 'Ok.'

'First, I should ask if you've shared this detail of your life with others?' Val's face forms an apology, her hands neatly clasped in her lap, her body still. 'Sometimes in moving to a new place we try to leave the pain behind, try to outrun our grief.'

I nod in recognition. *I hadn't known I was running away.*

Val leans forward with a box of tissues, its swirling pattern like the waking blur of a dream. 'Maybe,' she nods encouragingly. 'Perhaps, it's time to let people *here* know what you are going through.'

'But...' My voice breaks with the weight of my thoughts. 'How... How can I possibly say it aloud?'

As if given my first test, there in the waiting room, sitting among the pastels, is Marilyn, free of make-up, her white-blonde bob swept back into a shell clip. Instead of making for the receptionist, settling my account, then rocketing out of there, I drop down in the chair beside Marilyn.

'Hello,' she squeaks. 'I look like hell, I know.'

'You don't seem surprised to see me?'

Marilyn touches her face. 'Oh. Just embarrassed... would have put my face on if I *knew* I was going to run into someone I know.'

I shake my head, touching Marilyn's freckled wrist, before making to leave. 'Don't worry about it.'

Marilyn touches my arm, gesturing for me to stay.

'How was... the wedding?' I ask, lowering myself back into the chair.

Marilyn heaves a sigh. 'I'm just glad it's over... It's never easy getting all the family together... We are a complicated bunch.'

I nod, wondering if all families find it more complicated to be together, or apart.

'Listen...' Marilyn begins, and as she speaks, I begin to understand that *this* is her test. 'Look, I understand you might not be ready to hear this... You are sometimes rather guarded, like your father, I suppose –'

'My father –'

'Please,' Marilyn insists. 'I want you to know. I *need* you to know,' she corrects. 'Your father was... *something* to me... I mean, he was a fairly private man, and our time together was always fleeting, but I just thought...' Marilyn breaths out, expelling all the discomfort of this loosely held secret. 'I thought you should know.'

I look toward the door to outside, imagining how different the air quality will feel without these surrounding four walls. 'Of course he was,' I say, trying to understand, trying to be kind. 'I'm sorry for not letting you get that out sooner... And I'm sorry...' I hesitate, because my father's death is, for me, still so complicated. 'I'm sorry for *your* loss.'

I rise to stand, determining now is not the moment to heap grief upon grief. 'I'll see you, Marilyn,' I say, surprised how easy it is to overlook another's pain.

'When you're ready...' the receptionist meets my gaze as I turn to walk away. But something catches me, like the words so often caught in my throat, the emotions I still am not ready for.

'Marilyn,' I say, with surprising ease. '*My husband died. Only this year,*' the words come flowing; a flood where I'd expected a drought. 'He died in a workplace accident... I'm not sure you knew that... I'm not sure anyone here knows.'

Marilyn's face crinkles, the lines around her soft pink lips like a fault line in a windscreen. 'Oh. *Lauren.*'

'I'm ok,' I say, quickly. 'I'm... ok.'

Marilyn's arms reach for me. 'Oh. Lauren.' The words are muffled into my shoulder until Marilyn holds me at arm's length, studies my face. 'What an idiot I've been...' Marilyn shakes her head, plants her face in her hands. '...Trying to set you up with dear sweet, Gregory...' She shakes her head again, chastising herself for assuming I was divorced or separated, for not reading the signs of a grieving widow. '*Idiot.*'

I touch Marilyn's shoulder; and a smile emerges.

'Well, no wonder you sent him packing.' Marilyn takes hold of both my hands. 'I am, so, *so* sorry.'

We laugh through our tears even as I follow's Marilyn's line of vision to the receptionist slinking her body to one side of the glass screen.

'Hey!' Marilyn declares in mock-anger. 'We're having a breakthrough here!' This alone ignites within us an eruption of laughter; even the receptionist is laughing, possibly out of relief. *How strange is this feeling,* I find myself thinking. *I hadn't expected to laugh.*

I fan my face with my hands, open my eyes wide to try to reabsorb the tears. On the periphery, I see Val standing at the door, hands clasped.

'Oh,' I say, now feeling the urge to move things along. 'Think you're next.'

'Oh no!' Marilyn bats her hand away. 'I'm not here for an appointment,' she jests, following Val directly into her room; the door closing behind them.

Half-listening to the cheery small-talk of the receptionist, I settle my account, then step out onto the street, the light-filled space following me outside. Despite the increasingly cooler weather, today the sun burns a little brighter than before and I do not try to outrun this feeling. Instead, I soak it in, walking slowly, with a warmth at my shoulders, a tear gliding down my cheek.

'Didn't expect to find you here,' I say, approaching the boat house balcony; Brace is there, running his paintbrush along the railing.

'Yeah...' Brace looks up from his crouched position 'I... needed something to occupy the mind; the '47 Shepherd just wasn't cutting it.'

'Uh-oh,' I say, washing away any tension from before. 'It's never good when even the old passion project just won't do... You want to talk about it?'

Brace shrugs. 'Not really... Let's just say Hawaii was about as good as I thought it would be... Marilyn and I...' Brace shakes his head, his golden locks falling in front of his eyes. 'Well... I made some pretty wild accusations, and they did *not* go down well.'

'Wild accusations never do,' I say, making Brace smile; a smile disappearing as quickly as it comes. Brace rubs his palms against the golden stubble at his cheek, stifling a yawn.

'Couldn't you have got a haircut for the wedding?' I say in mock disappointment, noticing the way Brace's hair keeps falling into his eyes; paint smears clumping his locks where he's been pushing them off his face. 'Come on then,' I say, when Brace doesn't dismiss the idea out of hand. 'I'll give you one now.'

'Now?'

Before Brace can argue, pine needles collect underfoot as I hurry back to the house, grabbing my scissors, comb, spray bottle, mirror. Brace examines the paraphernalia with mild suspicion on my return, as I urge him to take a seat on one of the deck chairs.

'Uh, not too short, eh?' Brace says, tentatively. 'Just a trim.'

'Just the dead ends,' I agree, 'relax!' He sets his gaze upon the glistening water, the knotted wood of the boat house framing his outlook.

'Not a bad view,' he says.

'I reckon.'

As my scissors do the work, silence drifts between us; the sound of gentle waves lapping against the dock punctuated by the soft slice of scissors cutting hair, a golden shedding falling at my feet. When I am done – tidying up here and there – I hand Brace the mirror, our hands touching as he takes it slowly from my hand.

'What do you think?' I ask, our eyes meeting in the mirror as I crouch down, peering over his shoulder, surprisingly nervous as I wait for his reaction.

'I...' Brace contemplates himself. 'Yeah,' he nods, his lips forming a smile. 'Yeah, I like it.'

Brace's eyes shift in the mirror, from his reflection, back to *mine.* Suddenly, I avert my eyes, retreating into a joke, because there *is* something between us – something I cannot name. 'Just wait 'til you see the back.' I laugh, teasing, implying an imperfect job.

'What have you done to me, eh?' Brace's face lights up, then changes, like passing clouds or shifting shadow, his usual lightness of expression replaced by a darkness, rarely seen. 'Lauren...' he begins, 'I haven't been entirely honest with you.'

A smile falls away from my lips. *And I'd thought men and women could be friends.*

It is not in the telling – Brace is definitely not a diplomat – but in the news itself, that I am left gobsmacked; Brace revealing his belief that Austin – *my* Austin – is his natural father. It seems I have a half-brother.

'But have you any proof?' I ask, 'I mean, what are you expecting to come from this? The house, this place...?'

I scramble for words to understand the extent of this betrayal. Brace reaches out to touch my shoulder just as I take a step back, almost tripping on the tip of a canoe.

'No,' Brace insists, offering me a hand up – which I disregard. 'Nothing like that. Austin is not listed on my birth certificate. I have no claim; nor would I wish –'

'So, what are you after then...? Why are you doing this, Brace? Why have you come into our lives?'

Brace fumbles with his words, confessing how his blue with Marilyn in Hawaii had everything to do with his refusal to let 'sleeping dogs lie.'

Brace reaches to touch my arm, and again I pull away. Yet something holds me here as I let Brace speak; describing his interactions with Austin over the years – my father choosing to spend time, year after year, with his illegitimate love child over his daughter born in wedlock.

'Well,' I shrug, because there is so much left unsaid; and yet, nothing left to say. 'He quit being a father to me the day he left my mum.'

Brace reaches for my arm and this time I do not pull away.

'I'm sorry life happened like that.'

'So am I,' I say, understanding that when it counts, when it matters most; Brace somehow finds the words.

Eventually, we amble back along the stepping stones; but

instead of Brace returning to his truck we sit on the top step of the veranda.

'So, you're really not looking for anything?' I say, dropping my chin to my palm, my elbow resting on my knee. 'The house...? This place? You're sure?'

'I wouldn't want it,' Brace says, staring out to the water; so much beauty held within his gaze. 'I've found my family; that's enough for me.'

It's hard to imagine anyone not wanting *this* and yet, there is something truthful in Brace's gaze. His expression, like the stillness of the water; drifting, dreaming.

'Then I'm glad,' I say.

Brace, throwing his arm around me, somehow knowing. *Loz needs a hug*.

Austin & Errington
Preston, Ontario, Canada
1910

37

———————

April

Army Form B.243
Form of Will, No. 1.
*To be used by a soldier desirous of leaving the whole of his Effects
to one Person.*
I *Austin Moss*
of *Preston Ontario*
*do hereby revoke all former Wills by me made and declare this
to be my last Will. After payment of my just Debts and Funeral
Expenses, I give to my*
(b) *Wife*
(c) *Ellen Errington Moss*
(d) *Preston*
absolutely (e) *for her sole & separate use, her receipt alone being
a sufficient discharge.*
*None of my brothers or sister or blood relatives of theirs are to
have any part of my property or management thereof.*

In witness whereof, I have hereunto set my hand
this 27 day of April A.D. 1910
(f) Austin Moss

Resting back in the boat, Errington observes the muscle of Austin's strong arms working the oars – arms that held her so tenderly last night; this morning; moments ago. Gliding past the tree-lined shore, Errington inhales the pine-scented air blending with the sweet smell of pipe tobacco, lingering on her skin. Dreamily, her fingers skim the water's smooth surface as Austin rests the oars, reaching for the Kodak Brownie at her feet.

'Not another,' Errington says, droplets of water flying as she brings her hands up to hide her face; the dimple at her cheek peering out between splayed fingers.

Undeterred, Austin holds up the camera. Winding the handle, adjusting the aperture and shutter speed.

Looking through the viewfinder, Austin muses over Errington, held within the frame; over a life – a future – wholly apart from the one captured years earlier and pasted in his pocket-sized leather-bound book: the S.A.C; 'The Missus'; the South African plains and kopjes.

Understanding himself *'the richest of all,'* destined by God to live forever in *her* glow; considering how dear Errington is, how deeply he feels the beauty of her soul, the warmth of her spirit; Austin is dissatisfied with the image held within the frame. As though this mere apparatus is incapable of capturing a person, not simply as they appear from one moment to the next, but as they truly are; the twinkle in her eye, yes, the dimple at her cheek, but also, the feeling that comes with simply being in her presence.

Austin examines the box-shaped camera. 'The lens does not do you justice, my dear.'

'Then *please*,' Errington says, no longer hiding her face, 'take a picture of the boat house; *our boat house* as it shall be forever known in our hearts.' She twists around to peer over her shoulder. A slight breeze billowing through her blouse. 'I should like to remember it. Not just for the comfort of its walls, or the sound of the water lapping the dock, or the memory of being positively famished,' she laughs, 'I can scarcely believe my appetite! I dare say, no-one else would believe it...'

'In all things has my appetite been satisfied.' Austin lowers the camera. A look is shared between them.

Errington smiles a suspicious-looking smile. 'I'm not sure I trust you on that, Mr Moss.'

'And why might that be, *Mrs* Moss...?'

Raising the camera with one hand, Austin leans against the side of the boat, pretending to tip them overboard.

Errington squeals. 'You wouldn't dare!'

The ripples of water disseminate as Austin repositions himself in the centre of the boat.

'No,' Errington confirms, 'you wouldn't; not without protecting your precious Brownie from becoming water-logged – and thus quite unusable. How that would ruin your fun! Though, I dare say *I* should not miss it quite so much.'

'Ah,' Austin concedes. 'You know your husband too well, *Mrs* Moss.'

'Indeed, I do, Mr Moss.'

'Very well.' Austin looks into the viewfinder; *their* boat house filling the frame, the lodgings of their honeymoon in the cosy room upstairs, the balcony Austin dived off in a burst of playfulness. Errington remembers capturing the moment with Austin's Brownie. 'But one of these days I *will* capture your likeness.'

Errington smiles into the sun, bursting into laughter as Austin takes the photograph; shifting it ever so slightly to capture his own sweetheart, exuding the kind of inner warmth he'd been waiting to capture.

38

September

Sitting back in his favourite armchair of their marital home, _The Galt Daily Reporter_ draped over his lap, Austin thinks of a particular poem; one he had transcribed into his journal as a young lad bound for New Zealand. A poem reflecting the absence of a good woman.

Returning home at close of day,
Who gently chides my long delay?
And at <u>my side delights</u> to stay? Nobody.
Who sets for me the easy chair?
Spreads out the paper with such care?
And lays <u>my slippers ready </u>there? Nobody.
When plunged in deep and dire distress
When anxious cares my heart oppress.
Who whispers <u>hopes of happiness?</u> Nobody.
– Author unknown

Mostly, Austin had penned nonsense in that leather-bound book: quotes, jokes, proverbs – '*Why is a colt like an egg; no use till he's broken.*' '*Why is a lady's bustle like a historical novel; it's fiction founded on fact.*' Mere silliness, set beside a few rough sketches. Passengers of the *S.S. Arawa*; an old chap hunched over, mid-story; a man in uniform; a woman, peering beneath a large, plumed hat; a woman who'd shared Austin's bed, a subtle curve for her cleavage; a dog with sad eyes. Amidst the sketches and silliness, the poetry reminiscing of 'home,' as a young man, Austin had tried – most heartily – to convince himself of one thing; that being a bachelor was the life to lead.

> In a garden, fair
> Tis' a sweet spot there,
> The Batchelor's Bungalow.
> – Author unknown

Yet, in marriage, Austin is more happily situated in life than he ever thought possible. So many hundred times more wonderful – though it seems an impossibility. And yet, it is in this happy state of bliss – Austin, privy to '*all the petting [he] can stand*' – that Errington places the envelope before him.

Austin, freely reaching for Errington's hand, plants a kiss along the slender line of her arm. Errington smiles, a dimple emerging at her cheek, their gaze lingering; before she dashes away, with a swishing of skirts, remembering 'the muffins!'

Her orange blossom scent still lingers.

Sitting among their shared belongings – the piano adorned with freshly picked snapdragons; the miniature elephant with ivory tusks; the pair of paintings depicting peasant girls carrying baskets by the sea; the kitten swishing its tail at his feet – Austin takes up the letter opener. The act of slicing open the envelope, bringing him out of this glorious newly-wed bubble and into the world of the letter.

Stumbling over the contents describing his father's failing health, Austin is immediately burdened with knowledge. How cruel that Austin must leave a newly happy life, so recently begun – Errington will stay behind, for, to be sure, they can only afford one ticket and third class at that. But thinking of his father – the pain he must be in – Austin cannot deny his imminent departure.

'*How safe and how happy are they, who on the good Shepherd rely. He gives them out strength for their day, their wants he will surely supply*' Austin considers the words lovingly transcribed by Mother in the opening pages of his Bible, so many years ago.

He shall leave for England to see his dying father; on the '*good Shepherd*' he must rely.

Mrs Austin Moss,
Preston, Ont.

22 September 1910

Austin Moss Esq.,
  2nd Cabin Passenger,
  Room 517,
  Empress of Britain,
  Rimouski, Quebec

Dearest sweetheart,

There is only time for a little scribble to tell you that I love you, I love you, I <u>love</u> you – Be careful of yourself, old pussy fing – and don't forget all the admonition of your wife. You are so dear and so thoughtful – so many hundred times dearer than before we were married (though it seems an impossibility) and I'll miss you fearfully every hour of the day and night. But it is only for a little while, and I'm <u>so</u> glad you're going – and so glad you'll be home for this little time with your father so he'll see how happy you look – I hope they'll think so.

I'll miss you, pussy – but we won't think of that – we'll only remember how glad we are that it was possible for you to go – and how glad we are we have each other. I love you – old fing – Here's a kiss for each eye, and one big one for your mouth. So long –
  Your wife,
  L.N. XXXX, PRESTON.

Austin Moss Esq.,
R.M.S. Empress of Britain
en route to Quebec

September 1910

Mrs Austin Moss
     PRESTON, Ont.

Sweetheart mine,

Oh, sweetheart, how are you? Are you taking care of yourself? What a dear sweet little girl, your letter was certainly more than worth waiting for and just exactly what was needed. Just a breath of you, really you, and I know I looked awfully pleased with myself. I miss the little jobs, I think. No refrigerator, no clock, no 'little cat.' No dear wee thing to say halloo – no beautiful old lady to tidy things up, no wide-awake old fing at sleepy time. No muffins – but little fing I'll be back right after you feel this. Soon those dear eyes will be shining eyes, and little dimples will be there too...

Hope Ruth is with you and tell her from me to see that you both have a slack time. Hope you can dust the elephant (I never heard of dusting an elephant before) or play with that blamed kitten but no work of the scrub kind, but I know you won't for you 'promised.'

My love. Oh, you dear old lonely sweetheart. The wee house will soon be 'Home' as much as love can make it. So long for a wee while.

Ever so lovingly your husband,
"Austin"
"Pooosie," R.M.S., Empress of Britain
P.S. Chase the kitten with the broom for me and do you feel this – and this? Bestest love.

IDA REPLACES THE DECANTER, HANDING ERRINGTON a crystal glass, clinking with ice.

'To married life,' she says, looking back toward a cosy corner of her niece's marital home, occupied by Errington, and nephew Frank.

Standing within the sunlight streaming in through the window, Errington raises her glass to the warmth in Aunt Ida's voice before twirling, as though wearing a spectacular gown, layer upon layer of tulle and satin falling around her.

Frank appears unmoved. Balancing her glass in one hand, Errington plants herself by him, perching herself on the arm of the sofa. With his back to the sun, Frank sits with a worn look on his face.

'Let's dance,' Errington says, tilting her head back, trying to coax her brother.

But Frank is resistant.

Setting down her glass on the small, round table, Errington kicks off her shoes, each fur-lined slipper dropping to the floor as she places a thin soldier between her lips. A puff of smoke fills the air as Errington draws back, resting her forearm at Frank's shoulder.

Ida looks over lovingly at her niece and nephew. The vision of her dear, blossoming niece in the sunlight, thinly veiled beneath a trail of slowly dissipating, curling smoke makes Errington appear dream-like.

'Aunt Ida,' Errington catches Ida's widening grin. 'How about a tune?'

Willingly, Ida takes to the piano, her feet just reaching the pedals as her fingers thunder along the keys; a sound calling Errington to her feet.

'Come,' Errington rests her cigarette at the edge of the

ashtray bordered with crowns, before sipping from her glass; ice pressing coolly against her lips as she takes Frank's hand.

'Brahms,' Frank smiles, successfully urged to his feet; because there is something so freeing about the Liebeslieder Waltzes, op. 52.

As the pair begin dancing – Ida's piano playing transporting them to a grand hall, an imagined kaleidoscope of swishing skirts – a scent wafting from the kitchen begins to assault their nostrils.

Errington twirls, then kicks out one foot. And again; before registering the smell.

'The muffins!' Errington breaks free of Frank, mid-twirl.

But the music keeps on. A thunderous, glorious sound, filling Errington's marital home with music as a church organ fills every arch, reaches every beam.

'Frank!' Errington calls. 'Come on!'

With the tray safely retrieved and sitting above the coal range, oven mitts cast aside; Frank willingly takes the lead and the pair glide. Every twirl, every dizzying turn recalling the dancing of their childhood – Maplecroft carpets underfoot, the room more spacious than this.

Perhaps, because of the way this experience brings them back to a different time and place, while making memories anew – or, perhaps, because of Ida's willingness to go on playing – the dancing continues. Until Errington is breathless; until the heat of the coal range is too affecting; until dark spots cloud Errington's vision, blotting out the light. The tessellated tiles rise to meet her, cold against her face.

Within the hour, Doctor Vardon is by Errington's side.

Maplecroft

Mrs Austin Moss,
Preston, Ont.

27 September 1910

Mr Austin Moss Esq.
  12 The Waldrons,
  Croydon, Sussex,
  England

Dearest Pussy,

This is our fifth 'monthaversary' – I wonder if you are thinking of it – you dear old thing. Your letter from Rimouski came and now I cannot have any more for such a long, long time – but it was just like you, and I read it over and over, and try to think you are here. I hope your cabin mates prove passable...and that you will have <u>such</u> lovely weather and such a happy visit. Frank... was in last night and he and I danced until a quarter to twelve to Aunt Ida's accompaniment. The kitchen is near enough for the sound to carry and the floor is better for dancing than the Maplecroft carpets.

Tomorrow it will be a week since you left and oh! Poosie, it has been a long week. Even the dear little home has lost its cheeriness with you away – but it will only be two weeks more and I'm trying not to be lonely.

Be careful of yourself, old thing. Do you feel this? There are dozens in the letter for you, sweetheart, all such loving ones.

So long, darling.

Your loving, loving wife.

L.N.

Austin Moss Esq.,
24 Eversley Place, St Leonards, Sussex

1 October 1910

Mrs Austin Moss
  Preston, Ont.

Sweetheart mine,

How are you? Quite well thank you? Taking care of your-self? You Old Thing – I know you've been toiling away – do have a rest and let me see you looking well and happy. Do it to please me – Well – we landed 1ˢᵗ thing Friday morn; I was pleased all over to see Ella – very well and pleased with herself. We had a Hansom cab to Charing X and a mild lunch and came on here. The house is on the 'borders' of St Leonard's and Hastings, right on the seafront with a pretty plot of Geraniums on the other side of the road and then the sea wall.

Through the open windows (large ones onto a balcony) one can hear the sea (and the motor buses). Father was at the Station to meet us and while at first sight I thought him thin, to walk with him and <u>talk</u> one does not think of him as thin at all, but as a hale hearty old man – <u>very</u> fond of a joke and in good spirits. Mother was at the house waiting for us and she looks only fairly well – but they all agree that the three weeks here have done wonders. We all go back on Thursday, they to stop at Croydon and me to catch the Friday boat. Ella looks well but is certainly 'nervy.' Mother shows great signs of a weary and anxious time but the cheerfulness of all three is wonderful and most 'inspiriting.' They were tickled absolutely all over to see me and both said and acted so. The weather here is warm, bright and sunny and although the end of the season, the place seems full. We're staying here right on the sea front in very comfortable rooms – and Father eats 'slops' only but has a *good healthy appetite and sleeps like a top nine hours to ten hours per night. There is only a small difficulty in understanding him. So far, I have not had to ask him twice what he meant, and he talks very freely... I'll be home in such a little while after you get this. Both Mother and Father chuckled when I asked them if I looked happy and did your ears burn – for they talked of you. Oh, sweetheart you sweet old Thing – What a love you are. I'll soon be seeing you again, till then and always.*

Your loving husband,
'P.'

39

April 1911

Though Austin was away, Eddie still wonders why he was not sent for. Austin's insistence for Eddie to assume the role of their family physician had been a small win amidst a series of disappointments. Like change itself, much feared, many of Eddie's attempts to address the flaws of the medical profession – its archaic practices and dangerous medicines – have been thwarted. And while, Eddie understands the state of medicine relies on much more than the actions of one man, he can't help but feel contempt for Doctor Vardon. Forever harbouring suspicions that Doctor Vardon is, in some way, disrupting the course of modern medicine; and Eddie's part in it.

Even upon this morning's house call, Eddie is critical of Doctor Vardon. Soon after Eddie's arrival, he discovers the patient, a child, has become floppy and unresponsive. Breathing, but with a weakened pulse, pupils contracted.

'What did you give him?' Eddie demands of the nursemaid; her shaky hands rising to her face.

Like Lady Macbeth, the nursemaid's eyes stare out in horror; '...*who would have thought the old man to have had so much blood in him?*' Though the victim in this case is a child; the weapon, Eddies suspects, a syrup, its label claiming it to be '*perfectly harmless and pleasant to taste.*'

Gently, Eddie places his hand at the nurse's shoulder, encouraging her to meet his gaze. 'If I am to save him, I must know what I am dealing with.'

The nurse steps back toward a bottle set down by an open window, the curtains billowing in the breeze, helping to conceal a small bottle containing '*Mrs Winslow's Soothing Syrup.*'

Eddie holds the nursemaid's frightened gaze, before examining again the half-full bottle containing a lethal morphine-alcohol cocktail.

'Upon whose instruction did you administer this syrup?'

THOUGH THE NURSEMAID WAS UNWILLING TO ADMIT Doctor Vardon was at fault, Eddie is unrelenting in his determination to build a case against him; although it's an almost impossible task, with few willing to speak poorly of a man so well-established. Now formerly mayor of neighbouring Galt, and medical officer of health; Vardon practically *is* the institution.

Eddie understands too well that it will likely be some years before those playing Russian roulette with the lives of others may be held accountable – much like soldiers committing atrocities in the name of the Empire; perhaps, doing what they believed was right.

Eddie understands that Vardon does only as he has always

done; what his experience tells him is right; what he has been trained to do – or *not* trained to do given the definite gaps in a physician's training. That, if he must be held accountable, so too, must the whole of the profession be brought into question, with its practices that make the medieval barber-surgeon seem up to date.

It's true, Eddie's goal, his vision, is seemingly insurmountable. And yet, try he must; transcribing any small detail he has managed to unearth into his leather-bound book, kept wedged beneath his mattress in an envelope, already addressed to *The Medical Board*, as a promise to himself. The leather-bound book contains a damning collation of little scraps, written in Eddie's hand. Scraps that have spent the week – often longer – swimming about in his Gladstone: conversations recorded verbatim, clinical notes, recordings of patient symptoms and worsened conditions. A compilation of findings. A patchwork of patients unjustly served by the person – the profession – they most trust.

After an evening of pouring over old notes, and new findings, making connections and marking his own frustrations, Eddie rises from his bed. The smell of bacon and the less pleasant tang of offal leading him up the stairs to the breakfast room, he sits down to a pot of tea, brewing at the table. Eddie no sooner reaches for the bell than Mrs Merriweather bursts through the door. A steaming breakfast balancing on her arm.

'Doctor Barlowe!' Mrs Merriweather declares, her cheeks full of colour from the stove. 'Excellent timing.'

'Thank you, it looks and smells...' Eddie searches for the most appropriate adjective; takes up his cutlery.

Mrs Merriweather stands back, arms folded, waiting for Eddie to take his first mouthful.

'Not your usual chops, I know – though I did ask the cook. How is the offal?'

Rubbery, the flavour quite potent, Eddie continues to chew. 'Most pleasant,' he considers, swallowing a lump.

Mrs Merriweather is forever engaged in a task – her cheeks, often flushed, the frizz of her hair, regularly escaping the frill of her cap makes her somewhat removed from the traditional tall and slender parlour maid most folks prefer – but she is warm and kind and exceptionally thorough. It is only as Eddie takes his first bite, that Mrs Merriweather remains still; not bothering to fuss about the sideboard, or flap about the kitchen, but simply observing that Eddie is well-pleased. Reminding Eddie of his own nursemaid, who cared for Eddie from his infancy, he finds he quite enjoys Mrs Merriweather's attentions – indeed, there are times when she has reminded him of things forgotten: the watering of his philodendrons, the addition of a coat on a cold night, a town hall meeting or special church service; things small or large but always of use. Therefore, it is only the smallest of impositions for Eddie to convey his appreciation of each and every meal; that he gives some account of his comings and goings in which Mrs Merriweather shows great interest.

With a full stomach, his Gladstone in tow, Eddie bids Mrs Merriweather 'adieu,' catching an electric railcar rattling down the line within minutes of leaving his lodgings. Thinking of the convenience of the electric car, Eddie hops aboard with a quickened step followed by immediate regret; barely managing a smile as Doctor Vardon waves him over.

Eddie looks over his shoulder – quickly thinking that someone else might benefit from the seat beside Vardon; not least, Vardon, himself. Standing behind Eddie is a nanny in apron and bonnet accompanying an immaculately dressed child, the image of an Esson family photograph, excepting the plain background. The little boy is dressed in a white pinafore, high socks and polished shoes, his soft golden hair falling forward, disrupting his immaculate presentation, as he reaches deep into a bag of hard-boiled lollies. The pair are offered a seat near the front of the car before Eddie has the opportunity to offer them the seat he is trying most heartily to avoid.

'Oh, you know me,' Vardon says, as Eddie is forced to move further down the car with a sudden influx of passengers, 'I prefer to stand.'

Grabbing onto a handle suspended from a metal bar, Eddie has no choice but to stand opposite the other man.

'I'm glad you decided to join me,' Vardon says. 'I didn't think you'd appreciate such business being shouted down the car.'

Vardon holds an unreadable expression.

'What business might that be?'

'Oh, I'm not sure you'd be interested... I mean, I wouldn't wish to be a bore...'

'Doctor Vardon,' Eddie says in a tone he hopes is calm, 'you have my attention.'

Vardon's small frame sways gently back and forth as the car rattles down King Street. 'Well, in some ways,' Doctor Vardon teases the words out, perhaps waiting for a fire of language to slowly take hold, 'it pertains to The Lodge...'

Eddie presses his lips together.

'For reasons beyond my comprehension,' Eddie begins, feeling the space where his Masonic ring once sat along his finger. 'You and I both know The Lodge is no longer my concern.'

Vardon tilts his head in question.

'Doctor Vardon, please continue,' Eddie says, leaning over to see beyond Vardon and out the window. 'And do be concise.'

Vardon looks upon Eddie with a long, slow blink.

'Very well. For some time,' Vardon begins, making no effort to speed up his train of thought. 'I have had my suspicions that *someone* is building a malpractice case... against me.'

Vardon laughs out aloud. 'Can you imagine?! *I*, who have dedicated my whole life and training to the service of others? *I*, who have worked tirelessly to rise in the good opinion of my fellow man. Mayor of Galt. Medical officer. Oh, I needn't go on about my credentials.' Vardon waives his hand in the air, dismissively. 'You know.'

Amidst the various sounds in and outside of the railcar – the car rattling down the line, the crumpling of a newspaper, the rustling of a lolly bag – Eddie searches for the words to answer him.

'Which is why –' Vardon continues, interrupted only by the nanny at the front of the car speaking firmly to the little, blonde boy while trying hard not to draw attention, ('Slow down, Charlie; you'll spoil your appetite.')

Doctor Vardon looks up along the aisle of the car, returning his gaze to Eddie. 'Which is why,' he continues, 'I must caution you.'

'Me?'

'You,' Vardon confirms, before clearing his throat. 'Doctor Barlowe, people fear change. It makes them feel... out of control. As though their lives may spiral into something unrecognisable. Now, you, yourself, may feel different, may wish to embrace certain technologies, certain 'revolutionary' ways of being. But Doctor Barlowe... the question, is not, whether the new is better than the old –'

'It's not?'

Doctor Vardon shakes his head. 'It's about what we can live with. Need I remind you, Doctor Barlowe, that as a physician, your job is to gain the trust of the patient, to make them feel comfortable, respected, to act only within their consent and the wishes of their family.'

'Yes,' Eddie says with mild confusion. 'Yes, I agree...'

It is impossible to tell whether Vardon means to threaten or encourage. The car pulls to a sudden stop, catching Eddie unawares. He lunges forward, his Gladstone thrown to the floor; little scraps of paper escaping from his bag. Part way through shoving as many of these incriminating scribblings back into his Gladstone, a sound makes Eddie look up. The child at the front of the car is choking, reaching for his throat, expelling a sticky, candied mess, while sucking for air.

Abandoning his still-open Gladstone bag, Eddie leaps toward the front of the car, almost stumbling over a man's legs jutting out into the aisle, a woman whose knitting becomes entangled with Eddie's cape. By the time Eddie reaches him, the child begins to change colour.

With a firm thwack, Eddie delivers a few solid thumps with the flat of his hand to the child's back, dislodging the hard-boiled lolly; landing it among the sticky pool as it shatters into pieces. There is an outpouring of gratitude – a celebration – as the child weeps into his nanny's apron, that Eddie tries to ignore as he makes his way back down the car.

'Excellent work, Doctor Barlowe,' Vardon says, holding out the handles of Eddie's Gladstone; the incriminating pieces of paper neatly tucked away.

40

Casting out his line, in the last fading light, Eddie positions himself at the water's edge, wedging the mahogany and brass handled rod between two rocks. Austin takes his place beside Eddie.

Though the pair keep quiet – coaxing fish to the surface – there is a sense of togetherness between the chums that has been absent for months; given Austin's time away, his hours kept at work and at home; Eddie's influx of patients, their unexplained illnesses, and their reckless reliance on medicines dangerously marketed as *'harmless.'*

In a spirit of excitement, Austin confirmed the 'happy' news – so soon after the wedding day! – delivered upon his joyous return. And though Errington took to bed, Austin spoke of his wife's strong will, of her fighting spirit; but mostly, of her daily gratitude in being blessed with this impending joy.

Though not being standard practice to monitor expectant mothers; Eddie, nevertheless paid the odd visit, while postponing a most difficult conversation.

After the day on board the railcar – Doctor Vardon,

witnessing Eddie's scrappy notes recording the missteps of the senior physician – Eddie felt an increasing sense of doom. His world seemed to become smaller, despite Doctor Vardon behaving in much the same way towards him as he always had. In fact, Eddie could almost believe he'd imagined Doctor Vardon acknowledging his reconnaissance work after Eddie dislodged that hard-boiled lolly from the child's pharynx; *If only your detective work were as effective*, Eddie was sure Vardon had muttered.

Within that same week, a member of the Medical Board approached Eddie, declaring it regrettable that it had taken so long for his 'very astute' recommendations to be given the consideration they deserved. Eddie, puzzled, was beginning to think he had misjudged Doctor Vardon's character entirely; Vardon claiming responsibility for the renewed interest in Doctor Barlowe's work.

'Doctor Barlowe,' Doctor Vardon had said with an unnatural-looking smile, upon witnessing the discussion between Eddie and the board member. 'Now you see how I support you... How I encourage others to offer their support.'

'Yes,' Eddie stammered. 'Yes, I thank –'

'Very well, very well,' Doctor Vardon was impatient. 'You have seen this, and yet what you haven't seen – what remains to be seen – is how wholly capable I am of doing the opposite; should I discover that *someone* I am actively supporting, does not, in fact, support me; support the important work I do.'

Doctor Vardon's smile widened, and then ceased abruptly. 'I've been meaning to share with you,' he began, his voice sombre. 'Reports of... *a man... who takes pleasure in the company of* –'

Sure that Doctor Vardon had uttered the words *other men*, Eddie remained fixed to the spot, his insides pummelled with a dolly stick; the world around him closing in, his ears ringing, his pulse quickening. How easily his career would end; how swiftly he would face imprisonment. But it seemed he was to be spared – for now.

'When it comes to my patients, Doctor Barlowe,' Doctor Vardon's beady eyes, pegging him there like wet washing, 'keep your distance.'

From then on, Eddie made himself unavailable to patients under Doctor Vardon's care and avoided the Hotel Kress – as much as he could bear living out of *his* sight. He stopped making notes of Vardon's 'wrongdoings,' discarding the little scraps from his Gladstone straight into the fire, watching them curl, orange into ash.

'I worry, old man,' Austin says, bringing Eddie back to the present moment; the deep sigh of his words blending with the gentle hush of the river. 'Childbirth is a worrying business.'

Unable to meet Austin's gaze, Eddie nods to the river. Though Eddie suspects Errington downplays her discomfort; he believes in her fighting spirit. 'Your lady is strong.'

'Determined, yes,' Austin agrees. 'But I know she is not as strong – not quite so well – as she claims to be.' Austin's words carry across the water. 'I see it in her eyes and cheeks; in the absence of that apple-blossom glow; in her delicate frame growing, and yet, reducing.'

Eddie exhibits a fellow feeling of concern, understanding Errington's suffering is Austin's, seen in the lines etched upon his face, heard in the absence of laughter in his voice. 'Childbirth is not without its hurdles.'

There is a lull, as a couple stroll by; each party waiting to resume conversation once out of earshot of the other.

'Tell me it'll all work out, old man,' Austin breathes, staring out to the water. 'I need to hear it.'

'It will,' Eddie says, too quickly, bringing the difficult conversation to the fore. 'But I'm afraid; I cannot be your physician... Doctor Vardon has a great deal more experience than I and –'

'Doctor Vardon?!' Austin sits up, erect. 'What gives, my friend? You are not a supporter of Doctor Vardon's; that much I know.'

A look flashes between Austin and Eddie; one puzzled, the other inscrutable.

'I know, you've never said a word against him,' Austin says, thinking aloud. 'You are too much a gentleman... But you do not find him agreeable; of that, I am sure. And not because of his manner – or the way he undermines your experience; that would be reason enough for me – but there is something else, something that leaves you in utter distaste of the man. Tell me, if you are to abandon me now – if you are to place the only woman I have ever loved into the hands of a man you clearly despise, at least, I beg of you; state your reason.'

Eddie looks out toward the river, his gaze set beyond the immediate tug of his fishing rod, rippling the water, the rod threatening to dislodge itself.

'I'm sorry, old man,' Eddie breaths, his words laced with regret. 'I cannot.'

41

May

Standing at the top of the staircase, Errington positions herself by the railing, the pussycat at her feet. As she drops her hands by her side, momentarily disguising the shape of her protruding belly, Austin looks through the viewfinder of his Brownie.

Angling the camera toward the object of his affection – her hat adorned with flowers, as full as the Silver Lace creeping up over the railing – Austin tries hard not to draw out the taking of the photograph; given the concentration in her less-bright eyes. The thin and fading smile.

It was so encouraging when Errington declared she would like to step outside. 'Perhaps, take a turn,' she'd said in jest. Austin couldn't help but entertain the idea. And when Errington reappeared – after a long duration, making Austin wonder whether she hadn't returned to bed – Austin was glad to see Errington dressed, upright, with a smile on her face. It occurred to him then – save his rather stealthy drop-in at St. John's hospital – that in all the years he had longed for Errington, Austin had rarely seen evidence of her looking so poorly. Perhaps, that's why Austin had grown cynical of Errington's treatments and operations. Perhaps, if Austin had known the half of it. Perhaps, if he hadn't been kept in the dark; perhaps, *'that was just a little mean.'*

Austin thinks of his birth mother more than ever. How little they had shared beyond the womb. How little he had of her in the way of something tangible; a woman, a life, whittled down to a single keepsake. A piece of his mother's hair, tight braids unified into rope, bound together by a small, gold clip. A small, yet deeply affecting, token sent from 'home', following his father's death, accompanied by a note, written in Ella's hand: *'This was specifically left you by Father. It is made from our mother's hair.'*

As Austin readies himself to take the photograph, turning and pulling levers, he sees that Errington is not quite so well as she was minutes ago. Visibly shrinking under the weight of the hat Austin had purchased – bringing it home after several trips to the milliner's in which further muslin roses and silk violets were added.

'Beautiful,' he says, mustering a smile as Errington grips the railing; her body a thin sail without wind.

'And the hat...?' Errington's words a little slurred. 'Does it suit?'

Austin gives a decisive nod before climbing the few steps up to the veranda and offering his arm.

'No.' Errington hesitates, refusing Austin's arm and the nearby wicker chair. 'There's a chill in the air... Think I'll return inside.'

Austin's heart aches. 'Yes,' he utters. 'Yes, I think it best.'

Later, Austin peers in at Errington, a single yellowed hand resting upon her belly; Errington guarding their child as she drifts through sleep. Inching the door open, Austin breathes out a sigh, taking in the room's incomplete story: hat pins discarded on the dresser; a stack of books left unread; half-empty laudanum bottles and metal pill boxes; needlework cluttering her bedside, the embroidery of her initials, left unfinished, needle poised.

In the past, Austin had been a stronger man. As a soldier, he had trekked 52 miles in 22 hours. Felt the sun beating down on him, as unforgiving as the British flame engulfing Boer farms. Sweat, lining the khaki serge of his pantaloons. A rasping at the back of his throat that came with the knowledge of an empty flask. His body had endured a beating, and yet he remained strong. Undertaking all of this with a youthful arrogance.

Now, Austin is terrified of leaving their story 'incomplete.' Incapable of marching on with the weight of his thoughts – more debilitating than any pack he ever strapped onto his horse – he cannot trek on as he did before, defying the limitations of his own exhaustion. For it is Errington, her *bright eyes,*' the glow of her cheeks, that dimpled smile, *her* love; that is what fills his empty flask. To take from her waters, her life-giving mineral springs, is to know and understand himself, to recognise his own strength, first made known to him by God. And he shall deny her nothing.

'Go on, get outta here,' Wildman says to Austin, as they stand at the edge of the finishing room.

Light streaming in through the partially open blinds augments the industrial light hanging from overhead beams set beside a row of pipes running the length of the ceiling. The shelving is open and exposed: tools hanging in open cabinets, rolled up cloth stored along the overhead shelving, little dust, save the fine hewn timber collecting at the base of the work benches. Seemingly unperturbed by the natural unease of being observed, the men work away at pieces in their final stages.

Wildman examines the way his business partner admires the workmanship in practice. His arms crossed with satisfaction as he leans against a post, taking in the beautiful sight of *their* workers; shining up a podium with groves like a Corinthian column; applying polish to a music stand; perfecting the finish on a mahogany table with a generous coating of lacquer.

'Yes, the workmanship is excellent,' Wildman agrees, with an exaggerated nod. 'Now, I have everything in hand. Please, go and check on your lady, Moss, before you get us both in trouble.'

'Thank you, Wildman, but I'd best stay. I'm sure –'

'Sure she'll send word? Yes, I know,' Wildman interjects, turning his attention to young Jimmy, the ex-Pattinson Woollen Mills worker, approaching rather sheepishly. 'Go on, what is it, lad?'

Jimmy stammers, seemingly put off by Wildman's direct manner. Though, in truth, it's not Wildman's tone that makes Jimmy's shoulders slump, his head hang low; Wildman, is, unfortunately, the spitting image of Jimmy's stepfather, a cruel and violent man, who left his mark. Touching the scar above his eye – a wound made fresh by memory – Jimmy recalls burrowing into his mother's skirts; screaming, sliding, crumpling, his stepfather's whip springing open his flesh as if cutting into an orange, full of juice.

'If you please, sir,' Jimmy directs this to Austin, 'I believe you are required... at home, sir.'

For several days now, Austin has left the factory early and to no avail and thus sees no sense in rushing. Passing houses made of stone – old farmhouses no longer surrounded by milking cows – the odd, red brick building with arched windows, commonly like the one Austin and Errington are renting; Austin ambles along, happy in love and in life. He is glad, too, of their little place. It does not have the grandeur of Maplecroft, The Waldrons, or indeed Ford Place – the latter, Austin's grandfather's estate with ample woods to roam and hunt, its own church organ and place of worship within the home – but *theirs,* though modest, is a house full of love. *'The wee house' a "Home' as much as love can make it.'*

Dreaming of an Errington unencumbered by illness, Austin is strangely calm upon approach, only hurrying up the stairs to the veranda as he notices the pussycat – the most doted on creature that ever did live – scratching at the door, meowing loudly. A sound heightened with Austin's arrival; the cat pushing past with the opening of the screen door. Austin discovering freshly laundered linens strangely abandoned, a basket at his feet. Stepping lightly into the kitchen – not his normal domain except in changing over the ice – Austin listens for sounds of the house.

Returning home at close of day,
Who gently chides my long delay?
And at <u>my side delights</u> to stay...?

Rubbing itself against Austin's shins, the kitten moves between its master and the icebox. Obediently, Austin retrieves the glass bottle from the icebox, pooling milk in the china dish. The meowing changing to a motoring, accompanied by the creaking of floorboards overhead; a whimpering and moaning; a rush of footsteps.
'Mr Moss!' Miss Keyes stumbles upon Austin, threads of

honeyed hair escaping from her cap. 'It's happening,' she conveys, breathlessly. 'The baby. It's happening now.'

'Now?! Should I... What should I –?'

'Doctor Vardon is on his way. I've just come to fetch some water.' Miss Keyes grasps the handle of a tall china jug, directing Austin to the waiting newspaper by his favourite chair. 'You best settle in.'

Austin drops down into his chair; the audible cries rendering him helpless and utterly in God's hands. *The righteous cry, & the Lord heareth them, & delivereth them out of all their troubles.'*

42

Sitting against the cherry wood bedhead, Eddie pours over past letters from his mother – and some from Austin – words that always made him feel *seen* when, society; his father; the Medical Board, had rendered him invisible. Though these words do little to soothe him now.

Since the fishing trip, Eddie has not had the pleasure of Austin's company, his friend having withdrawn from most of his usual engagements. Once or twice, Eddie spied Austin kneeling before God but did not think it right to interrupt a man in prayer. Unable – or unwilling – to bear the shame of being turned away, Eddie keeps his distance.

It isn't that Eddie is a coward – his mind tries to convince him otherwise – but rather considers the passing of time his best chance of restoring his bond with Austin; letting fury turn to cinder. *'As tyme hem hurt, a tyme doth hem cure.'*

Being in Austin's company always made Eddie feel closer to Dickie, Austin understanding the complex relationship between brothers; Eddie's own relationship with his brother thwarted by Dickie's competitive spirit, by Eddie's shame at being the less robust Barlowe son.

Thinking now of Dickie – of their father's continued disappointment – Eddie leans back against the cherry wood bedhead, pushing the letters aside, his eyes exploring the poorly-lit ceiling as if navigating a night sky of disappearing stars. Eddie can hear the sounds of night-time, of nature over-taking man; a tiny scratching and scampering in the hope of a forgotten crumb. He can smell the wood of the fire falling away to an orange glow.

Eddie rubs his eyes, bundling the now jumbled letters back together, sliding them back under his mattress to rest beside the lately neglected leather-bound book. Beneath his lumpy mattress is a place of sacred things, a nesting place.

Snuffing the candle, the curling smoke filling his nostrils, Eddie lies back, the dark becoming lighter as his eyes adjust; sleep is negated by the hollow, aching of his heart. An aching not because of the deal he'd struck with God – somehow, he'd managed to keep his distance from the Hotel Kress, exchanging his own happiness for another's – but in the agony of resisting logic, of disregarding the evidence, recorded in the leather-bound book beneath his bed, semi-forgotten; of struggling to ignore all the ways in which medicine might fail us, fail *her*.

CUTTING THROUGH CENTRAL PARK – THE RISING sun giving the fountain a pinkish glow – Eddie takes the back streets. It has been raining, and the ground is wet underfoot; the crunch of loose stones beneath Eddie's boots grows louder as he hurries toward Lowther Street. Sunshine is breaking through maples in a kind of patterned lace, showing itself in full as Austin and Errington's red brick home comes into view – the building, common by way of appearance: veranda, white columns, arched windows. Yet none, Eddie imagines, so much a *home*.

Droplets cling to Eddie's cape as he brushes past the rain-drenched frothy, white vine trailing the lattice by the stairs. Passing the empty wicker chairs – a pipe, abandoned there – Eddie finds the front door open, the house unnervingly quiet.

Fuelled with an increasing sense of urgency – intensified by the strangeness of no maid or master to greet him – Eddie steps into the front hall, past the corner cabinet, the piano, the armchair; failing to notice Austin slumped down in his favourite chair, mouth slightly parted, head back in sleep's surrender.

From the bottom of the staircase, Eddie hears the creak of floorboards. The door at the top of the landing opens in a yawn, revealing the sight of polished boots, the crease of pant-legs, the edge of a navy-blue cape, falling like a curtain.

Doctor Vardon closes the door behind him and descends the staircase, stopping part-way. 'Doctor Barlowe... I was under the impression your presence here is no longer...'

Climbing the steps to meet him, Eddie looks past Vardon. 'How is she?'

Vardon presses his lips together. 'I'm afraid... it's a case of 'wait and see," he says, peering past Eddie. 'Now if you'll excuse –'

Eddie tightens his grasp of his Gladstone; somehow, he'd expected more of a fight. In broken sleep, Eddie had pictured a scene much like this one; Vardon leaning in close, speaking not above a whisper.

Perhaps, it's best we don't speak of your little trips to the Hotel Kress, hmm? Eddie had heard Vardon say. *Hotel cloak-rooms – filthy places as they are – I'm not sure the board would take too kindly –*

The scene resulting in a tussle on the narrow stairwell; Eddie lunging himself toward the old man, his Gladstone flying: stethoscope landing with a thud, scissors embedding themselves in the floor below like the sword in the stone – *so real, it had felt so real.*

But here, in this moment, Doctor Vardon steadies himself against the railing, impatient to pass; not privy to Eddie's musings. At the same moment, Austin appears, dark shadows beneath his eyes.

There is a moment of silence. Vardon's forehead wrinkles, imitating surprise. Eddie descends the stairwell, letting Vardon pass.

'Eddie?' Austin has never looked so poorly. 'Why…? You said you are no longer our physician.'

'That is why I have come,' Eddie presses upon Austin, as though there is still time. 'It was wrong of me to abandon you in your time of need. I made a promise, and I –'

'In all my dealings,' Austin's blue-grey eyes appear murky, like water after a storm. 'I have only ever known a man to be as good as his word…' Austin's gaze shifts to the closed door at the top of the stairs; to the groaning escaping the thin walls. 'One day, we shall address things left unsaid, but this is not that day. Because I refuse anything – not least a quarrel between old chums – to cloud the birth of our first child. I beg of you; don't make today less of a day.'

Eddie searches Austin's gaze, unwavering in its resolve.

'I'm sorry,' Eddie lowers his head. 'It was wrong of me to come.'

Outside, Vardon leans against the railing, speaking as Eddie trails past the Silver Lace, descending the stairs from the veranda.

'Inevitably,' Vardon says, 'people will always return to what they know.'

43

———

Everything took place in flashes; Doctor Vardon dismissing the midwife; Eddie, here and then gone; the rush of footsteps, the clanging of instruments, sounds unnatural to a woman's delicate nature; the rhythmic siren of newborn cries; Doctor Vardon permitting a 'five-minute interview' – talking prohibited.

Austin smiled and Errington smiled back, the whites of her eyes, somehow less yellow. Miss Keyes, a stand-in midwife – her credentials seeming to mainly be recognising the total authority of the doctor – presenting the tightly-wrapped bundle; adjusting Austin's hold, supporting the baby's head in the crook of Austin's arm. Then something shifted. Austin was ushered out of the room, the baby still in his arms.

Though fearful, Austin now stares down in wonder, mesmerised by tiny features peering out from a bonnet edged with lace: a rosebud mouth, tongue swirling, eyes still shut. The door bursting open, breaking Austin's gaze. Austin stands motionless, remembering the bundle in his arms.

'Please,' Austin urges. 'Take him. Take baby George.'

Austin looks away from the tray of bloodied instruments

as he enters the room; though the sight of blood means something different here. Doctor Vardon adjusts the sleeves of his street clothes. Austin gravitates toward Errington.

Despite her yellowed face, mottled by exertion and the heaviness of her eyelids; for a moment, Austin recognises a brightness in Errington's eyes. *'Bright eyes.'* But as his hand gently touches her face, caresses her forehead, Errington's eyes shut; the brightness veiled.

'You are strong,' Austin insists, examining Errington's small child-like fingers gripping the bundle placed at her chest. This one – smaller than the first – weak with life. 'You are so strong.'

Errington musters a half-smile. 'Call him Richard Austin... There is strength in the name... And because...' Her eyes flicker open, then shut. 'He needs your fire.'

Lauren
Muskoka, Ontario, Canada
2022

44

———

July

‘So, how has COVID been for you?’ Greg asks, draping his towel over the edge of the railing, droplets of water seeping through his shirt. ‘I mean the early days... We haven’t really talked about that.’

I lean back in my Muskoka chair, staring out to the water, thinking of the all the things left unsaid.

My recent journey back to Australia to sell the house and sort through Nick’s untouched belongings had sharpened the daily reminder of our loss with tangible pieces of the past, adding to the great, gaping hole left by Nick’s death a fresh sting. A feeling, I’ve come to realise, that may only ever soften with time. The dynamic of welcoming ‘Uncle Brace’ – as the girls now refer to him – into the fold is blended with feelings of abandonment and jealousy and everything my father’s name still holds – but sometimes, joy.

‘There’s a lot we haven’t talked about,’ I say.

'That's true,' Greg says, swiftly. 'Like the time you threw me out.'

I plant my face in my hands, peeking through the cracks. 'Oh God! ... That was such a long time ago.'

'And a world away,' Greg agrees, his smile sending a tingle right through me in a way it never has before.

'Does it feel cold to you?' I ask, despite it being the middle of summer. 'In the shade, I mean.'

Greg considers before shaking his head, his tight curls holding water, sticking in place. 'No,' he says. 'No, I think it's nice.'

I stretch my legs out in front of me, dropping my thongs to the floor, pointing my toes to the water. 'Hmmm... How has COVID been?' I consider. 'Umm... pretty awful – there's no denying that.'

Greg nods in agreement, probably thinking of his grandmother who died of COVID. 'No arguments here.'

'Yeah,' I offer Greg a look of sympathy. 'But also, I think I needed the time, you know... I've taken a step back from hairdressing to move towards the things I'm passionate about. I've started a course,' I say, 'in natural medicine.'

'That's great,' Greg says with genuine enthusiasm.

'Yeah, it is,' I agree. 'It's something I'm really excited about and... Obviously, I mean, there was a lot I needed to work through and still am. You know, I'm not sure that kind of pain ever goes away.'

Greg's gaze lifts out to the glistening water, the distant township barely visible across the bay. His gentle nodding, like the bobbing of the water, felt strangely affirming.

'But...' I say, placing my hand at the edge of Greg's arm rest. 'I'm definitely trying.'

Without meeting my gaze, Greg studies the proximity of our hands, shifting an inch closer to mine.

I smile, running my finger along the band of skin where

his wedding ring once sat – where the tattooed initials of his ex-wife still rest – before looping my pinkie finger over his.

'I've been doing a lot of soul searching,' I say, our pinkies held in place like the clasp of a necklace, 'about my dad. Brace and Marilyn have been really generous is sharing their memories – so different to my own. And while I don't think I will ever *forgive* him for leaving us; I think maybe, I'm starting to *understand*. Everything is so 'black and white' when you're a kid, you know?'

For a moment we sit in silence. The breeze carries the smell of pine; the veranda is cool and shady. The sun glistens on the water.

Greg shuffles his feet back inside his thongs. 'Thanks for inviting me for a swim,' he says.

Everything about this day has been wonderful; Greg preparing a picnic to eat at the dock; home-made cupcakes, three different cheeses, cantaloupe cut open with yogurt and blueberries in the centre. *You're a sweetie*, I thought as my gaze lingered between the berries and yoghurt swept up on my spoon and the hopeful look in Greg's eyes. He wanted to please, and yet, he was so self-assured. There'd been a change in him, the way his shoulder sat, relaxed and comfortable, the way he wore his shirt; no longer afraid to show what lay beneath. Dropping a line in the water – Greg confessing he'd watched several You-Tube videos on fishing like a 'pro' – we sat, indulging in the warmth of the sun, the gentle lapping of waves against the dock.

'Thanks for coming.' I look up at him, my body yearning to stay like this; silently delighting in each other's presence. 'Where are you off to now?'

Greg shrugs playfully, his shirt tightening over his shoulders and chest. 'Guess I didn't want to jinx it...'

I give Greg a gentle shove, surprised by the warmth of his skin.

Greg smiles.

I bite my lip. 'Stay.'

'Stay?' Greg contemplates for a moment, then takes my hand. 'Come on, then.'

I search his eyes.

'Come for a paddle.'

Out on the water, I let my fingertips skim the water. Drifting and dreaming. 'What is it we are doing?' I ask, finally, as Greg circles back the boat, getting us into position, the boat house directly behind.

'Making history.'

I think of the photograph of Errington, captured on her honeymoon. The twinkle in her eye, the dimple at her cheek. How full her heart seemed; how much life she had yet to live. *How much life I have yet to live.*

Smiling into the sun, I burst into laughter as Greg raises his phone to take my photograph, my heart clinging to joy.

When we leave the water, there is still a smile on my face. Navigating the stepping stones, Greg reaches for my hand, drawing me back. On his lips is the sweetness of icing. Breathing in the freshness of after shave infused with the smell of pine, I look into his dark brown eyes, placing my trust there. Our interlocking fingers slipping then tightening as we playfully delight in each other's touch. And I know, I need not do this alone.

Laughing, playing, we return to the house; my mood changing with a start as I catch sight of a figure on the far side of the veranda. It is not unusual to have visitors drop by, but something changes in me the second I see *his* face.

A man, strange, yet familiar. A face I've seen before; buried within an archival goldmine. *Blonde pencil-thin moustache, hair neatly parted, the erect posture of an Edwardian gentleman.*

As the man begins to speak – his manner of speech almost

archaic; *I'm terribly sorry* he begins – I examine him as though studying a photographic still.

Sunlight bounces off the water, creating a glow behind this man, as if entering a dream. Yet, with such clarity, somewhere in the bright, reflective light – as the man continues to speak – I see and remember, Greg studying the photograph as if it were happening now. I see him turning it over in his hands. I see Austin in uniform as 'Trooper 519'. His grey-blue eyes, startling, even in black and white. I see the man standing next to him, a smaller frame with finer features; identical to the man standing before us now. It is startling. Unfathomable. As if history has come to life.

Then, an act of magnetism, I feel my hand move toward this man. I feel the touch of his lips upon my skin as he draws my hand near, and I feel the tickle of his moustache upon my hand. Imprinting on my mind is the faded scrawl from the back of the photograph as the man introduces himself.

'Doctor Barlowe,' he says, as if reading my mind.

Austin & Errington
Preston, Ontario, Canada
1911

45

May

How quickly arrangements are made, Eddie considers as he packs the last of his things. Hanging his tweed suits within the crammed hanging space of his steamer trunk – almost certainly to resurface crumpled – Eddie is surprised at how easy it is to uproot himself.

Within this small, industrial town, Eddie had believed he could breathe new life, working to elevate medicine to other marks of advancement: the motor car, telephone, railcar, streetlight. Even as Eddie experienced resistance as he knew he would, even as the Masonic Lodge cast him aside; Eddie reached for the promise of *Preston the Progressive.* A place, evidently, 'progressive' only in the way society deems appropriate: machinery, electricity.

And after all that has passed between him and Doctor Vardon, between him and Austin, Eddie is determined to leave Preston at once. And yet, he cannot return 'home' a failure.

Instead, he is to be bound for London, Ontario. Mrs Merriweather had spoken of a cousin there – Eddie understanding it to be a place open to advancement; a place registering the concerns raised in Ottawa: the use of opioids, of dangerous medicines, of regulating patent medicines.

Craving anonymity, when Mrs Merriweather made the assumption that Eddie was returning to London, *England;* Eddie did not correct her.

'So soon?' Mrs Merriweather asked, with genuine sorrow.

'I'm afraid, I must,' Eddie said, still nursing his mother's letter – a letter, acting as supporting evidence, though containing nothing alarming in nature.

'Aye, Doctor Barlowe, you needn't explain,' Mrs Merriweather said kindly, 'I know what it is to be homesick.' Wishing him 'Godspeed,' Mrs Merriweather gifted Eddie a small Bible, a maple leaf pressed in its middle pages. 'A piece of Preston,' she said, distracted from her duties for a moment, before returning to wave a cloth in places already free of dust.

Packing the last of his things – struck by how little he has in the way of personal effects – Eddie deposits his luggage at the door.

'Sarah?' Eddie asks of the young maid, as the time of his departure closes in. 'Is Mrs Merriweather about?'

'No, Doctor Barlowe, I'm sorry; she is not.'

The maid leans against the carpet sweeper, pausing her work. Eddie remains fixed between the threshold of his lodgings and the main house.

'Oh.' Eddie sighs, unable to conceal his disappointment; he hadn't realised how much he'd warmed to the woman. 'Well, we said are goodbyes, really.'

'Doctor Barlowe,' the maid calls out, an afterthought after resuming her work. 'Mightn't mean much coming from the likes of me; but you are a fine doctor. My own aunt never looked so well as she did after seeing you; my uncle, too.'

Eddie offers a self-deprecating nod.

UPON APPROACH, EDDIE CAN HEAR THE EARLY morning chatter of farmers, the clip-clop of horse's hooves positioning their carts to line the boardwalk; the town, slowly waking. Central Park soon to become buzzing with maids sent to fetch only the freshest of produce, delighting in the excursion on this mild morning, despite the threatening rain. Their hands – reddened and cracked – showed why they were glad to be relieved of the previous day's work: soaking, scrubbing, boiling an entire household's linens.

'Doctor Barlowe,' calls a voice, too refined to be of the servant class.

Eddie peers past the three-tiered fountain, to see a fresh-faced woman in simple dress, white blouse, navy skirt, lavender shawl. A gold locket at her bust swings like a pendulum as she walks to meet him.

'Mrs O'Hare.'

'Are you off somewhere?'

Eddie looks down at his Gladstone, then his brolly; Mrs Merriweather – kind as she is useful – has made prior arrangements for his baggage to be taken to Preston Junction.

Mrs O'Hare conveys a look; difficult to read.

'Oh, my dear, I suppose you must have heard...' Mrs O'Hare brings her hand to her lips as Eddie fails to comprehend her meaning. 'Oh, Doctor Barlowe... I'm afraid... I'm so sorry to inform you... one of the Moss twins is with God now.'

Clutching her gold locket, her thumb subconsciously running over its smooth, golden surface, Mrs O'Hare shares every detail she has at hand; the whole town on tenterhooks, awaiting news of Mrs Moss – and the surviving twin.

Amidst the sorrow – sinking deeper with regret – Eddie fails to notice the gentle falling rain thicken into a pitter-patter at their feet; farmers pulling oil cloth back over their wagons like swiftly drawn curtains.

'Oh.' Mrs O'Hare holds her hand out to the sky, raindrops running off her gloved hand. 'Do you mind...?'

Eddie bursts open the brolly. 'Actually,' Eddie repositions his grasp of the ivory handle. 'I am going somewhere. *London.*'

'Returning home...? Oh... Oh, I see.' Mrs O'Hare draws herself further under the cover of the brolly. 'When do you leave, perhaps, we could arrange a proper farewell... The Ladies Auxiliary could –'

'No,' Eddie interjects. 'Thank you, but I leave today.'

'Today?'

'Yes, I'm afraid, I leave on the 12 o'clock train.'

'Oh, my. Oh, that is soon... We shall be sad to lose you, Doctor Barlowe. Indeed, this town shall feel smaller without you... Well then,' Mrs O'Hare declares, determined not to dwell on the news. 'I'd be delighted to bake you something. My own farewell and thank you.'

There is no refusing this kindness. It is a repayment of sorts, Eddie having saved the youngest O'Hare son from an almost certain death; yet another weak and feeble child, floppy and unresponsive at the hand of a morphine-alcohol cocktail. Eddie smiles in thanks.

'12 o'clock then. And, please,' Mrs O'Hare steps out into the rain. 'Pass on my condolences and thoughts and prayers... That is where you are headed?'

46
____

The journey between the farmer's market and Eddie's rushed arrival at Lowther Street represents a lapse in Eddie's memory – his mind, clouded by other things – the short trek, evidenced only in the smell of Eddie's wet woollens (given the ineffectual use of his brolly); sweat at his brow; his quickened heartbeat.

As he climbs the stairs, past the frothy white vine – spilling over the veranda like excess foam on lager – past the empty wicker chairs, Eddie leans his brolly against the window; noticing the curtains pulled shut.

Even as Eddie clenches his fist, resolved to make his presence known with a rapping at the door, there is a voice urging him away. Eddie almost imagining this voice to be his own – somehow older, somehow wiser – plagued by guilt and fear, by lives expiring on his watch – here and at war.

Turn on your heel, the voice says, embodied in the ghostly appearance of Doctor Vardon. His pale skin, almost translucent. *Turn on your heel – and quickly!*

Eddie takes a step back, observing Vardon through the

mesh of the screen door. Vardon's small frame shrinking within the door frame, his eyes scanning the distance.

'Nothing,' Vardon shakes his head. '*Nothing* to be done...'

Despite Eddie's presence, Vardon does not step out from the doorway, nor does he resume his usual state. There is none of his usual bubbling energy. Vardon is unnervingly still.

The door groans as Eddie opens it and walks through, placing a hand at Vardon's shoulder. Vardon, flinching at Eddie's touch; retrieves a handkerchief from his sleeve, rubbing it against his reddened nose.

'You...' Eddie searches for the words. Perhaps, he had been wrong. Perhaps Vardon is not the man Eddie had presumed him to be. Eddie tries again. 'You did your –'

'Best?' Vardon shakes his head. 'No. I failed her. *We* failed her.'

Steadying himself against the door frame, his shoulders slumped in defeat, Vardon steps past Eddie, descending the stairs.

In a lingering ghost-like presence, Eddie can feel the weight of Vardon's heartache; a once-nimble, energetic man, deteriorated overnight – not by age, but by the job itself; his inability to do more.

As the sun reveals itself this dreary May morning, Eddie rubs his hands against the grain of his stubble, his thin moustache brushing against his fingers. As though splashing water upon his face, bringing him back to this present moment, he registers a voice, gentle and kind.

'Doctor Barlowe,' says the maid with a gentle expression, soft wisps of hair escaping from beneath her cap. 'She is –'

'Saved by the Lord,' Eddie bows his head, relieving the maid of articulating Errington's fate.

The maid opens the door out wide. There is a baby cradled in the crook of her arm, flashing a frown at the cool rush of air.

'*No*,' the maid declares. 'Mrs Moss is still of this world.'

'Alive?'

The maid nods, eagerly. 'You've come to relieve Doctor Vardon, have you not? He's barely left her bedside. Never have I seen a doctor so invested in their patient.'

'Alive!' Eddie says, with renewed vigour, strengthening his hold of his Gladstone. 'And Mr Moss?'

'Church, sir.' The maid looks down at the babe in her arms. 'Mr Moss prays regularly. I see him often engaged thus. But you know what it is to kneel before God in a sacred place, to feel infinitely closer to the Lord,' the maid says, pensively. 'He attends before mass... in order to avoid their questions.'

Eddie peers down at the baby's face. He is not more than a few weeks old. Such small, sweet features peering out from a swell of blankets.

'He looks... strong.'

'Oh, he is,' the maid smiles, turning the baby out for Eddie's close inspection. 'Has a fierce set of lungs on him, mind.'

THE ROOM IS DARK AND QUIET. CRACKS OF LIGHT escaping the overlap of the curtains. Though Errington's eyes are shut, there remains the rise and fall of her chest. Her small frame; a wilting flower.

'I'm here now,' Eddie reaches for Errington's clammy hand.

Errington's smile is fleeting, as though dreaming.

'I'm sorry, it took so long.'

Errington squeezes Eddie's two fingers, gripping them as a newborn might.

You're here now, she breathes; her hand rises to her chest as she coughs.

Her cheeks appear yellow, her hair lacks sheen – its dull

quality, contrasting with the cool sweat at her brow. Eddie considers cracking open the curtains. Perhaps, a little sunlight might paint a healthier glow.

'I am here now,' Eddie agrees, giving her hand a squeeze.

Eddie articulates himself slowly, in a manner befitting the scene. But as he begins speaking, voicing the things left unsaid – his insistence that Errington was never quite so ill; never in need of the rest cures, operations, laudanum – Eddie's words spill out.

'I'm so sorry,' Eddie says, finally giving the explanation Errington so richly deserves. Tears gliding down his cheek. Eddie looks upon Errington as he imagines she once was; the colour – painted from memory – returning to her cheeks. She whispers to him.

Keep an eye on Austin – He will need a friend.

Eddie shakes his head, tears in his eyes.

As for little George, I know he will be cared for. But I want him to grow up feeling loved. Errington's words come – as though not simply inside Eddie's head – but all around. *To love and be loved; that is why we are here.*

Compelled to record truth, Eddie releases Errington's hand, knocking over the laudanum – its label soaking in the pooling liquid – as he moves towards the writing desk. Eddie shifting a mountain of books and needlework – the needle still held within the fabric. Lifting the brass lid of the inkwell, Eddie dips the nib of the pen and begins.

Dear Austin,

In most things you were right. Those 'little operations' are 'worse than England's little wars.' And, a man is 'only as good as his word' which is why, I mean to make good on mine...

Eddie is so invested in spilling out truth that he does not notice the way Errington settles deeper, drifts further.

...Cease all medications; particularly the laudanum. It may induce euphoria, but depression will likely follow. It must not be

relied upon. Instead... Eddie writes, detailing his instructions. His thumb and forefinger press against the Crown Furniture Co. emblem as he handles the paper with care, willing it to dry before turning it over; scribing the location of his leather-bound book – its pages, attesting to the archaic state of medicine practised in this town.

Caught in the fervour of speaking truth, Eddie holds up the writing paper, as he turns to face Errington; the sheet of paper, dropping to the floor to become swept beneath the dust ruffle as Eddie feels for a pulse.

Slipping, fading; her soul, caught between.

Eddie often wonders about the young men he could not save; about the women and children who needlessly died in the camps. Thinking of their souls, as he lay awake in a canvas tent far from 'home.'

Understanding he may never sleep soundly again, Eddie wonders about Errington's soul. Does it cling to the life she waited so long to live; to the baby, strong and contented; to the man so deserving of her love?

Or does it soar; toward the baby who lacked fire, unable to draw on the strength of his name?

47

Mary Keyes watches as Doctor Barlowe retraces his steps down Lowther Street. Perhaps, it was wrong of her to let the doctor in; declaring her 'belief' that Doctor Barlowe had been summoned to relieve Doctor Vardon.

When Mary had first joined the modest home, there'd been laughter and music. The rustle of Mrs Moss's skirts; the sweet smell of pipe tobacco interspersed with the aroma of baking – Mrs Moss, frequently, insisting upon taking charge in the kitchen.

At once, welcoming – lacking the air of consequence one might expect from the daughter of a parliamentarian and woollen mill owner – Mrs Moss carried herself, gracefully, joyously; the picture of happiness. Her *bright eyes* and dimpled smile, her warmth, projected itself onto all who looked upon her. In those early days, Mary could not have imagined Mrs Moss falling victim to fainting episodes, requiring the use of smelling salts and extended periods of bed rest. It seemed then that nothing would break Mrs Moss's strong and happy spirit.

Even when Mary had done something displeasing, accidental or foolish, Mrs Moss would gently, but firmly, make the situation known before laying the matter to rest; returning to her love of literature; geography; astronomy. And she was none too scared of a little scrubbing – though Mr Moss didn't take too kindly to hearing of her efforts.

Indeed, Mrs Moss had been a kind, articulate lady of the house, whom Mary was glad to serve. Not more than six weeks into her employ, Mary had experienced a great kindness at the lady's hand; Mrs Moss insisting Mary return 'home' when Mary's sister had fallen ill.

Believing she witnessed in Mrs Moss similar symptoms to that of her late sister – the whites of her eyes turning yellow; skin too, the colour of oil, stretched tight against the bone – Mary looked upon Doctor Barlowe as their saviour.

Standing at the top of the banister, by the frothy white vine – the cat swishing about her feet – Mary shivers at the dwindling sight of Doctor Barlowe. An emptiness forming in the pit of her stomach, she notices a figure, standing in line with a nearby oak; the tip of a bowler hat, the ivory handle of a brolly sticking out past the textured bark.

Mary cries out, waving him over. 'Yes, hello!'

KNOWING IT SHOULD BE AUSTIN WITH HER NOW, while a warm breath still passes between her lips, Eddie hurries over the still wet ground, passing between a phaeton and a bicycle before crossing over King Street.

Outside the church, his movement is slowed by the influx of people flooding through the double doors in time for mass. His heart sank; hopes of finding Austin all but dashed.

'Doctor Barlowe,' Mrs O'Hare says, breathlessly, catching up to him, apron in hand. 'Have you news...?'

'It's…' Eddie shakes his head.

Mrs O'Hare's lips part in the absence of words.

Eddie scans the crowd.

'I saw Mr Moss… Just now, on a phaeton, heading…' Mrs O'Hare signals the direction in which the carriage fled.

Eddie looks back toward Lowther Street; Austin must already be returning home. Looking back wistfully, Eddie's gaze becomes stuck; trapped within the sight of eyes so dark they are almost black. Startlingly beautiful in their darkness and their depth, dreamt of daily since that first visit to the Hotel Kress and thereafter.

It takes everything for Eddie to pull away from *his* gaze as he returns to Mrs O'Hare; understanding now that he need not have struck a deal with God.

Eddie makes a show of pressing open his pocket watch, then replacing the lid. 'Sorry… I really must –'

'Yes,' Mrs O'Hare agrees.

Stumbling through the crowd, Eddie rushes. *Is it so wrong?*

Already, he can feel *his* hand rising to meet his cheek, the warmth of *his* touch sending a shiver down his spine. Almost losing his footing – the gravel, turned to slosh from the rain – Eddie calls out. 'I couldn't go without –'

But the dark eyes reach past Eddie.

Eddie follows the line of vision to find Mrs O'Hare, holding up a parcel. 'Doctor Barlowe; your cookies.'

Eddie shrugs, apologetically. His body, propelling him toward the touch it longs to feel, holding the gaze of those dark, wondrous eyes until –

His eyes press shut.

The absence of sight only serves to amplify the rattling and screeching; the sound of his own breath; the desperate beating of his heart as the railcar keeps coming.

SERGEANT O'HARE – NEWLY APPOINTED INSPECTOR O'Hare – slices the top off a hardboiled egg, yellow yoke escaping as he scoops out the shell, smoothing the egg onto his toast. Though usually attentive to his wife's needs, O'Hare finds himself out of sorts. Focused on the work of preparing his toast, heavy-handed with the salt showering over his eggs, O'Hare takes up *The Galt Daily Reporter* deposited at the edge of the table by their eldest son.

'That the story then?' the son asks, though such an incident was always going to make front page.

O'Hare draws the newspaper close. 'Take a seat, lad,' he says with a furrowed brow, not yet lifting his gaze. 'Hmmm, doesn't comment on how the police are managing things.'

'What are you going to do, Pa...? Now that you're an inspector, I mean? Is someone going to get in trouble? You going to lock someone up? Or is that someone else's job now?'

The previous day, O'Hare had come home early to share the news he'd been promoted, to find Mrs O'Hare sitting at their bedroom window, clutching her locket and biting her nails down to the quick.

'Fool should have been looking where he was going,' O'Hare says, placing the newspaper down to return to his eggs. 'Even the boy knows to look both ways.'

O'Hare looks to his wife's stricken face, worry lines about her eyes, the brightness faded from her cheeks.

'You're not wearing your mother's locket,' O'Hare says between mouthfuls, yoke at the corner of his mouth.

'Hmm?'

'Your locket. You're not wearing it.'

Mrs O'Hare reaches for the space where the locket normally rests.

Softening, O'Hare reaches his hand across the table, closing the distance between them.

'Heeey,' he says, in the gentle voice you might use to gain a horse's trust. 'He'll pull through.'

Mrs O'Hare crosses herself as if concluding her prayer, before bringing her gaze to meet her husband's.

'Who's his doctor?' O'Hare asks, with genuine interest. 'Doctor Vardon, I suppose?'

'Yes,' Mrs O'Hare nods. 'Yes, I believe so.'

'Well, that's something,' O'Hare says, wiping away the caked-on yoke. 'If he doesn't survive; it won't be from a lack of expert medical care.'

48

Beneath the underbelly of wooden arches, Austin kneels before God, consumed in silent prayer. *'Awake thou that sleepest, and arise from the dead, and Christ shall give thee light;'* the words of Ephesians 5:14 coming to him as he opens his eyes, recognising the divinity of the cross. The breaking of light through stained glass edged with lead; a depiction of Mary and child, surrounded by a halo of white light. The Almighty Lord revealing Himself to Austin in glorious bands of light.

Here, in this church, enveloped in His love and protection, Austin is renewed with a transformative courage. Not like that felt when in uniform, trooping around Wellington Showgrounds prior to setting sail for Cape Town in a nervy rush of excitement. An upturned slouch hat, held in place with Lion's head clip, a bandolier slung across his shoulder; all accoutrements to a war that would become anything but show. No, *this* strength is beyond man's design, greater than man itself, for *'Who shall separate us from the love of Christ.'* – *Romans 8:35*

With a final blessing from Reverend Herbert, Austin

rushes away from church; avoiding the incoming masses with the help of a waiting carriage. Dismissive even of Hobson, the Pattinson family butler; who's already passed on Mr Pattinson's intention to fund 'the boy's' education. Perhaps, baby George, will attend the most prestigious school in Ontario – if not, then in South Africa – but with Errington the way she is, Austin can scarcely plan a day ahead. Anything beyond the immediate future is almost unthinkable. But as Austin rests back against the leather upholstery of the carriage – the clip-clop of the horses' hooves a backdrop to his thoughts – he dares hope for a future they are yet to plan.

Though her eyes remain closed, Errington responds to the doctor's touch with a warmth in her cheeks. It is a happy, *settling* feeling: a momentary respite from the pain before a rush of cool air burns her throat. And even as the coughing subsides, there is a continuous weight pressing down on her chest, making it difficult to breath. As the hand touching hers leaves with a final squeeze, there is a clatter and a thud. The sound of gushing liquid, followed by a shuffling of books. A scratching against paper as Errington imagines the nib of a fountain pen depositing its ink on a newly laid page.

The doctor seems to be narrating the words as he writes. *Dear Austin.* But soon, the words fade; like a cylinder on a phonograph commanding the eardrums, playing and crackling, before dropping out into a space void of music.

Errington listens intently – waiting for the replacement of another cylinder, for the music of his voice to begin again – but there is nothing. Nothing, but a distant cry, sounding more feline than human. Curious of the sound, Errington draws closer, out of curiosity, then necessity. There is a tingling at her breast, as though it is newly engorged with mother's milk.

Errington opens her eyes with a start. Her body feels damp all over and her nightgown sticks to her chest. The room is quiet and still, which causes her a faint sense of alarm, then settling as she registers the baby, sleeping soundly in his cradle, tucked beneath knitted blankets – a closely held reminder of everything to live for, a reason to go on fighting; a product of *their* love.

Comforted by the sight, yet no more capable of keeping her eyes open than she is of reaching forward to hold the sleeping babe, Errington's eyes fall shut; and immediately senses the bright sun warming her face. Leaning back in the stern of the boat, drifting –finding herself in that place where they always imagined themselves to be. On or by the water, his head resting at her shoulder or, sitting opposite, perhaps, Austin gently guiding the oars.

In this imagined moment – *how real her imaginings have become* – Austin rests the oars, letting the boat drift through the bulrushes. Smiling up at him, Errington dips her fingers through the silk of the water. Alone together, and yet the feel of the water, the warmth of the sun, reminds Errington of their existence within the universe, a small part of something greater. Comforted by his presence, by Austin's familiar touch – they are not holding hands and yet she can *feel* his touch – Errington drifts, happily. The sun is warm. The water, smooth. The feeling is delicious; light, freeing. It is a place she can linger. A place she might go on living, were it not for the cries, growing louder, felt deep within her bosom.

Sinking deeper, floating further, Errington moves toward the sound. There is a lightness to her body, a weightlessness as she soars toward her baby. She is surprised by the way the warmth of the sun follows her, the way its light guides her to the infant. There is relief, a kind of welcome surrender, in the joining of mother and child. The baby coos as his mother draws him near; the fire he'd lacked on earth settling as Errington rests her soul beside his.

WITH A SHAKY HAND, GEORGE RECORDS HER NAME beneath the names and dates pertaining to his wife and first-born child, held within the front page of the family Bible.

Ellen Errington Pattinson, 1881 – 1911.

Buried in the family plot, her name shall be written exactly as it is written here, a 'P' for Pattinson marking the top of the headstone, the family name at its base. Below Errington's name, the headstone shall read:

Infant son, Richard Austin – 1911 –

George remembers how Maisie's heart would break for the lives barely begun – their strolls around the cemetery, full of mourning for the infants lost via the perils of childbirth, or the children who drifted out to sea and never returned. Sad though they were, George understood these deaths to be a matter of course; part of the random mystery of who lives and dies.

Errington was twenty days away from her thirtieth birthday. Though cut short, hers was a life that would leave its mark; she would be remembered and missed. In this way, she'd been blessed.

Hobson hovers at the doorway, catching George's gaze in shared sorrow. George pressing his lips together, preparing – somehow – to go on; no longer accepting life and death as 'a matter of course.'

Already, George has made arrangements to offer the surviving child – his namesake – love and protection. He is adamant that Austin remains in Preston, so that George may have some sway over the child's upbringing; ensuring every opportunity for the boy to become a man befitting the name of his good mother. *'Here where shadows flit.'*

George lowers his reading glasses, breathing out a sigh.

'Perhaps,' George begins, considering the time Errington had on earth, her mark left on the world, the pain she's left behind. 'Perhaps, she's better off,' he says – though it hadn't seemed quite so cold until it reached his lips.

CERTIFICATE OF DEATH

At Preston, on May 27th, 1911,
E. Errington Moss
*Cause of death Liver Abscess and Heart Failure. In her thirtieth
year.*

*Wife of Austin Moss, daughter of George Pattinson, Preston,
Physician: T.W. Vardon M.D.*

49

E. Mary Moss,
12, The Waldrons,
Croydon, England

29 May 1911

Mr Austin Moss,
   PRESTON.

Oh! My dear, dear Austin how can I speak to you, so far away and in such overwhelming trouble? I know not what to say except; God help you to bear it and to acknowledge Him as Lord over all. He gave and hath taken away. When you open this, you will have realized in some measure that she has gone, and you are left to mourn alone! Oh! My dear, dear boy, my heart bleeds for you, and I can find no words, except to write once again: <u>God help you</u> – He can, <u>that</u> I know.

Your dear Father would have been able to sympathise with you better than I, for he lost his young wife when you were born and often talked to me of his feelings when she was so suddenly taken away, but it was a blessing to him in the end and now they are both with the Lord, saved in the Lord Jesus Christ; blessed forever – My dear, dear boy, I mourn with you – indeed I do and I can only pray you may be helped to brave this unlooked for desolating trial – You have my heartfelt deepest sympathy, though my words are few and poor.

    Ever,

    Your loving mother.

Bert Moss,
Hastings, Hawke's Bay,
New Zealand

11 July 1911

Mr Austin Moss,
    PRESTON.

My dear old Austin,

    We have been greatly shocked to hear of your painful loss, and when the news came today I found myself wishing I could be with you to help you, for though on such occasion words may not be spoken, there is a lessening of the sting when the sorrow is shared, and one may feel the pain as acutely, but the relief in being assured of a sympathetic listener and moreover the grieving with you of a great friend, or relative all tend to the bearing of a sorrow – I was glad to hear dear old Ella was off to Canada to be with you, you are old chums, and you would have to go a long way to find her equal for love and sympathy. She both knows how to talk and how to be silent, and one feels the bond whichever she does.

    I can picture you preparing for harder work than ever,

and, perhaps, throwing even more of your energy into business if that can be – It means a tonic which those who have to bear much, gladly avail themselves of. A strong man has some strange fights the world knows little of, and mostly the battle is raging in the mind and conscience, when others do not realise that much is happening, but work and Ella for a companion should help to soothe the bitterness of loss.

You will have the privilege, for it is a privilege, of guiding your child and responsibility also, and as it grows it will become a greater and priceless blessing. Your pleasure will be teaching all that Errington would have liked it taught and in striving to attain the standard Errington would have set, and in after years the honour shown to the father will be shared with the honour and love it will have been taught to show to the name of the good mother it lost.

Best love to you,
Your affectionate brother,
Bert, Hastings, Hawke's Bay, N.Z.

There is an eerie stillness about the room. The curtains, shut. The lingering orange blossom scent, destined to fade. Austin can feel Errington slipping away; his eyes, stuck on the unfinished needlework abandoned on her dresser, her incomplete initials embroidered on a handkerchief, the needle held in place.

When Austin closes his eyes, he can still see her there in his mind's eye, leaning back in the stern of the boat. A place his imagination knows well.

'Best Beloved,
Are you up in your room this afternoon, I wonder? Or are
you sitting here beside me, looking out over the water – with
your head resting on my shoulder...?'

Austin inhales deeply, *her* scent intensifying as he rests his head against the welcome pillow of her blouse.

Little Nell, eh? Errington muses, bringing Austin's awareness back inside the boat; a smile emerging, a dimple at her cheek, a warm, inviting glow *'like apple blossom white and red.'* The glimmering sunlight giving Errington a hazy brilliance like the glare of a dream. Playfully, she dips her fingers through the silk of the water, then smiles up at Austin. There is laughter in her voice as she speaks of Dickens' Little Nell – and of herself;

Without the tragic end, I hope?

Like the bullet bouncing off the bandolier strung across Austin's shoulder – the bullet meant to kill – this recalling of memory takes Austin's breath away. Gone is the gentle hush of the river as they glide through the water, the brush of reeds against the boat, the sound of oars dipping in and out.

Yes, Austin breathes. *Without the tragic end.*

Beyond the unfinished needlework, rests Errington's locket. Austin holds it in the palm of his hand; a keepsake once laid close to Errington's heart. Pressing it open, Austin lays eyes upon the two men central to Errington's life; Austin, donning his flat cap and pipe, pulling an oar through the water; and a young George Pattinson.

Looking between the two men – a space Errington had always occupied – Austin contemplates. Though his instincts tell him to flee, no longer does his heart beat for the *'great lure of the wild.'* Kipling's words, no longer holding the meaning they once did. *'He must go – go – go away from here! On the other side of the world he's overdue.'* Poetry, referring to 'The Feet of the Young Men.'

As Austin presses the locket shut, as if making peace with settling in Preston, closing the chapter on another life, Austin thinks of Mother's letter – *'acknowledge Him as Lord over all.'* Of Bert's words too – *'your pleasure will be teaching all that Errington would have liked it taught and in striving to attain the standard Errington would have set...'* Austin, stumbling upon these thoughts as if his own.

Though Austin's hair has turned white overnight, his body consumed by something deeper than pain; Austin reaches for some *'small hope,'* latching onto it as a newborn might grasp onto a finger. Clinging so tightly; the waking of the child, the sounding of its cry startles him. Austin, dropping the locket to the floor. Its chain landing splayed out across the edge of a piece of paper protruding out from beneath the dust ruffle. Reaching down, Austin draws the paper near, noticing his own letterhead, *Crown Furniture Co.* in the top right corner; then the author's signature, *'Yours in good faith, Eddie.'* Turning the note over in his hands, Austin scans its contents. *'Dear Austin,'* it reads.

But as Austin begins to read the instructions left by his doctor friend something happens; sucking moisture from his mouth and calling it to his eyes. Something landing as a weight at his chest, threatening the beating of his heart. He cannot read on. It is too painful; the light upon which he relies, too dim. The baby cries.

Though there is movement just outside, the door remains shut. Austin forms a half-clenched fist, screwing up the note, letting it fall to the floor. The baby's cries grow. Its strong set of lungs; life in its immediate existence. Austin moves toward the sound.

The baby coos as his father draws him near.

EPILOGUE

'That'll be all,' Mrs Merriweather says, dismissing the young maid whose face is yet to wear the look of hard work.

Sarah stands at the top of the stairs, seemingly immovable. News of the accident, still so fresh.

'Away with you,' Mrs Merriweather says, struggling to stand within the girl's sympathetic gaze. 'See the cook. You may report to me before you leave.'

As the young maid disappears behind the door to the dining room and through to the kitchen, Mrs Merriweather lets her shoulders drop. Steadying herself against the railing, letting it support her weight, her cheeks flushed with colour. Her face, hot and heavy as she slips back beneath the undertow of impossible thoughts plaguing her all night and into the morning too; thoughts of the young doctor's improbable survival.

Halting at the base of the stairs, she takes in the room, now cleared of Doctor Barlowe's belongings – a neat boarder, as he was – the room appears devoid of remnants of the young doctor's stay. And yet, she can still see his boyish smile beneath a pencil-thin moustache, his soft, golden locks parted to one side. She can hear his gentle, well-considered turn of phrase, well-mannered and overly polite. The kind of man she'd hoped her son might be had he lived to become a man.

Certainly, Doctor Barlowe's looks, his soft, golden locks, had recalled the image of her own son – who, at the age of three was found face-down, floating beside the lily-pads of the Maplecroft pond, his skin turned blue. Though she experienced a great many kindnesses at the hand of Mr Pattinson; nothing would bring Tommie back.

From the first, Mrs Merriweather had been drawn to Doctor Barlowe, not only because she believed this is how her boy might have looked – he would have been in his twenty-third year upon Doctor Barlowe's arrival – but for the doctor's goodness. The way he lived in search of truth. Not just *his* truth, but a truth one could hang their hat on.

That's why she was always doing Doctor Barlowe's bidding. Why she made sure he was well fed, contented, and why she made it her business to set anyone straight – anyone within her station – who dared speak ill of the man. For, Mrs Merriweather believes; we are not all built the same.

Bracing herself to prepare the room, she peels back the sheets. An uncomfortable feeling sets in; there is too much of him gone. Turning about the room, slowly, as if donning a gown she would never have the good fortune to wear, Mrs Merriweather catches sight of the mirror sitting atop the dresser. Beneath the mirror are a set of drawers.

Slowly, she pulls open one drawer at a time. Seeking some small token of the young doctor, of the man who had stirred in her such vivid, painfully perfect memories of her son. A stray coin. A handkerchief embroidered by his mother's hand. Cufflinks. Something small to slide into her apron pocket – like the curl of Tommie's golden hair she keeps in memory. But there is nothing.

As she recalls the space by the attic window, how her hand had pressed against the glass – forever, would she regret her decision to remain there, failing to bid the doctor farewell – she is tormented by the vision that follows. When she had come to her senses, too late, and thought to pray for him; only to discover the young man in the way of an oncoming car, much too close, much too fast to come to a halt.

Throwing open the doors to the clunky, freestanding wardrobe with the clattering of coat hangers, she sinks down to her knees, desperate and defeated, her face and hands at the mercy of an empty wardrobe as she breathes in its musty, cedar scent.

Had the young maid returned moments earlier, this is how she would have found the head parlour maid. But it is here, at this lowest point, that Mrs Merriweather finds her feet. By the grace of God, she finds a strength, both maternal and divine, and by the time Sarah appears, Mrs Merriweather is standing over the bed, her body, supporting the lumpy, spring mattress as she exposes what lies beneath.

Though the letters are gone – a hiding spot discovered one morning upon turning the doctor's mattress after he'd declared a less than perfect sleep – a single envelope remains.

Taking up the weighty envelope in her hands, she pushes two fingers against its opening to peer inside. Satisfied, as if only to confirm the leather-bound book remains, she turns the envelope in her hands, noting the intended recipient, the stamp already pasted in the top righthand corner. Licking the edge of the envelope, transferring the sickly-sweet taste of tree sap onto her tongue, she presses her fingers over the seal, smoothing it over.

The envelope, its contents, become heavy in her hands; perhaps, she is guilty of meddling.

'Mrs Merriweather?' Sarah says, finally gaining her superior's attention as she stands at the base of the stairs, donning her coat and hat, and clutching a wicker basket. 'Cook's given me quite the list, so if there's nothing else...'

Shaking her head, she dismisses the young maid, before calling her back.

'Sarah?'

The young maid's face is marked with surprise.

Already, the envelope feels lighter; her spirits lighter too, as she sees to the last of Doctor Barlowe's affairs.

'Doctor Barlowe left this...,' she says, sliding the envelope into the young maid's basket. 'Post it, will you?'

APPENDIX

THE GALT DAILY REPORTER,
Monday, May 29, 1911

DEATH OF MRS A. MOSS, NEE PATTINSON

DEEP REGRET FELT IN THE TOWN OVER SAD EVENT.

After a serious illness of three weeks duration, Mrs Austin Moss quietly passed away at her home on Saturday evening at 9 o'clock.

Mrs Moss (nee Ellen Errington Pattinson), was the eldest daughter of Mr George Pattinson, M.P.P. In her thirtieth year, she was born in Preston and lived here all her life. Blessed with a pleasant, cheerful disposition and a sweet, womanly nature, the deceased was a true friend to many and beloved by all who knew her. Her death will engender personal grief in the many citizens whose respect and esteem she had deservedly won, and her memory retained in the thoughts of many kindnesses received at her hands.

Since news of her serious illness was reported, her condition has been the subject of much anxiety among the people of the town. The saddest aspect of her untimely death is the brevity of her marriage. On April 27, 1910, she became the wife of Mr Austin Moss, and a brief few months later, her health deteriorated, despite expert medical treatment.

Besides her husband and baby son George Francis, she is survived by two brothers and two sisters, Lynn, Frank, Ruth and Elizabeth Pattinson, all at home.

The funeral will take place at 2.30 o'clock this afternoon to the Preston cemetery.

– The Galt Daily Reporter, Monday May 29, 1911

AUTHOR'S NOTE

Upon clearing out her parents' home in the 1980's, my mother discovered the love letters of Austin and Errington. Brought back from Canada to my parents' home in Australia, resting in an archival goldmine of letters, documents, photographs, journals, it wasn't until years later the letters became known to me as my mother shared her enthusiasm for their words and their story. Together, we read and transcribed the letters, piecing together the details of their past.

Austin and Errington's story has consumed me for years. I first began this work, pregnant with my first child, who turned eleven at the time of *Maplecroft's* publication. It is a story I have been unwilling to let go of. For me, the great tragedy of their story now would be for it to remain untold.

As their descendant, a writer and teacher of History, I have endeavoured to honour Austin and Errington by telling their story in the most complete way. But as any lover of history knows, our picture of the past is incomplete. It's why we yearn to know more.

There is so much of Austin and Errington's story, the interesting and the mundane, that I cannot know for sure. It is because of this unknown, and the desire to tell a compelling story, that I have written Austin and Errington as historical fiction.

I cannot not know for sure why Errington suffered so many long enduring absences from her great love, or what ailed her. I may only rely on research of the era and family folklore. Thus, *Maplecroft* expresses just one theory about why the lovers were kept apart. The character of Eddie, wholly fictional, is used to support this theory. The role played by Doctor Vardon in this narrative is entirely fictional. So too, is the modern story, save for the cottage, though the passion for Austin and Errington's story and the desire to know more is my own. Slight adjustments to dates have been made to support the flow of the story, such as the date Errington was at St. John's Hospital. Austin and Errington's letters included within *Maplecroft* are largely unchanged.

ACKNOWLEDGMENTS

There is a tapestry of people and places to whom I am indebted in shaping Austin and Errington's story. Those insisting love *is* enough when I spoke of my anxieties as to whether this story might find readers: could Austin and Errington mean as much to someone else? Those who allowed me into their home when I knocked on their door declaring myself a 'writer': there to witness the same architecturally-designed house as *Maplecroft,* or the inside of Austin and Errington's marital home. The good people at the Cambridge Archives and The Region of Waterloo Museums. The very streets where Austin and Errington once stood. Leafy Major Street, Toronto. The space where *Maplecroft* once sat high on the hill of Eagle Street, Preston, Ontario; now a carpark. Austin and Errington's marital home; there, a new baby being soothed by its mother. The engraving 'Geo. Pattinson & Co.' above the entrance of the old woollen mills, turned into office space. A precious surviving feature of the past.

To friends and family who cheered me on long before I had the confidence to call myself a 'writer'. To my father, Dom, and his indulgence in long, literary discussion. To my mother, Liz, for lovingly preserving Austin and Errington's letters; and to my grandfather, George Moss, who first sought them out and kept them safe. To my husband Joe, for lifting me up when my dreams of becoming a writer seemed hopeless. It is his great imagination to which I owe the existence of many of the fictional characters and plotlines. To my children, for recognising my writing as 'work'. To my first readers, particularly Brigitta whose feedback was exactly what I needed. To my proofreader, Liz. Your wonderful, suggested edits added to the richness of the work. To my cover designer, Ally. Your commitment to this project exceeded all expectation. To my old writing group and the writing community who continue to inspire me. To Austin and Errington, for expressing their loving and longing in the most beautiful way. And finally, to my readers for keeping their story alive. Thank you.

ABOUT THE AUTHOR

Mary-Clare Terrill is an Australian-Canadian writer. Her debut historical romance novel, *Maplecroft,* is based on the true story of her great-grandparents and their lovingly preserved love letters. It is the first book in the *Maplecroft* family saga.